EXES and EXCESS

EXES and EXCESS

Kendra Martin

ARCHWAY PUBLISHING

Copyright © 2016 Kendra Martin.

All rights reserved. No part of this book may be used or reproduced by any means, graphic, electronic, or mechanical, including photocopying, recording, taping or by any information storage retrieval system without the written permission of the author except in the case of brief quotations embodied in critical articles and reviews.

This is a work of fiction. All of the characters, names, incidents, organizations, and dialogue in this novel are either the products of the author's imagination or are used fictitiously.

Archway Publishing books may be ordered through booksellers or by contacting:

Archway Publishing
1663 Liberty Drive
Bloomington, IN 47403
www.archwaypublishing.com
1 (888) 242-5904

Because of the dynamic nature of the Internet, any web addresses or links contained in this book may have changed since publication and may no longer be valid. The views expressed in this work are solely those of the author and do not necessarily reflect the views of the publisher, and the publisher hereby disclaims any responsibility for them.

Any people depicted in stock imagery provided by Thinkstock are models, and such images are being used for illustrative purposes only. Certain stock imagery © Thinkstock.

ISBN: 978-1-4808-3187-2 (sc)
ISBN: 978-1-4808-3188-9 (hc)
ISBN: 978-1-4808-3189-6 (e)

Library of Congress Control Number: 2016943574

Print information available on the last page.

Archway Publishing rev. date: 6/30/2016

This book is dedicated in loving memory to the 'Carla' I had in my life…

Cathy

*She was a beautiful, loving woman who gave generously
and had a smile and heart the size of New York….
She always had my back. She rescued me repeatedly during our puberty
(wonder) years, adult situations and oftentimes from myself….
Cousins born four months apart, Cathy and I were placed
in the same crib, graduated high school together and were
like twins because we looked alike and dressed alike…*

…I miss you…

'when everyone else saw caterpillars, Cathy saw butterflies'

Acknowledgments

To my husband: Thank you Ed for believing in me and this work. And for over 30 years of love that was first and foremost my inspiration. It meant so much to me that you took the time to read every word, and you gave me so much help and feedback. And thank you for being a husband that allowed me to spread my wings, and for continuing to love the crazy that is me. I love you dearly…

To my children: Thank you Billy, Morgann and Jeremy for being the loves of my life and allowing me the time and space to do this and to be me. Mommy loves you so much…

To my mother: Thank you Mommy for being a woman so open-minded and who always spoke your mind. And thank you for raising me to be so much like you. You've always believed in me and gave me more credit than I probably deserved. I love you more each day…

To my mother-in-law: Thank you Mom for encouraging me and critiquing my work as only a great teacher could. I love you and appreciate all you've done…

To my big/little sister Claudia Elaine: You've always been my cheerleader. But more than anything you were the wind beneath my wings. Being in your presence continues to be my strength in *so* many ways. Thank you for continuing to push me. I love you…

To my brother William: Thank you for keeping me grounded. At least you tried. (smile) You were always the 'common sense' in my life and you gave me the confidence to believe I could do anything. Thanks to you and my sister-in-law Regina for all of your support. I love you both…

To Natalie: Thank you Sister for friendship unparalleled. Your unwavering loyalty, unconditional love and never ending support continue to be my measuring stick for true friendship. Together with Cathy, we did the damn thing! We made no excuses for our absolute love for one another. And because of that, the devotion between Felicia, Carla and Annette easily comes to life in this work. I love you…

To Lenora: Thank you little sister for more things than I can mention. Your encouragement and time spent reading meant so much to me. Thanks to you and 'Big Will' for all you do. I love you…

To Linda: Thank you Sis for always…always being there. No matter what I ask, you dig deep and go above and beyond for me. I love you…

To San: Thank you for always making me laugh and encouraging me in ways that I can't mention. I sometimes think we wrote this book together. Every woman needs a 'San' in her life, and I'm blessed to have the original as my BFF. I love you Sis…

To Beth: Thank you Sis for unconditional love and friendship. Your drive drove me more than you will ever know. Always willing to listen, and always a light when my patience wore thin and I found myself in a dark place. I love you my friend. Here's to you…

To my brother Godfrey: Thank you for indulging me with my endless questions. I appreciate your honesty when I needed the unadulterated thoughts of another man. You have been a great brother and friend. Love to you always...

To Alice: Although you're no longer with us, I cannot and will not ever forget what you meant to me. You were my safe place during the storms in my life. You're sprinkled throughout this book in places only you and I know. Thank you for love and friendship most people never get to experience. I love you and miss you so....

To Ruthie: Thank you for more than you'll ever know. I drew from your wisdom many times during the creation of this work. Our friendship has meant the world to me. I love you dearly....

To Cheryl: For literally screaming your support of my work and offering such positive feedback. I love you my dear sister...

To Stacy: Thank you for taking so much time with me. I so appreciate your help with editing and your honest critique. I love you Cousin for that and so much more...

To Karen: Thank you for reading every word, your feedback and for encouraging me so much. While completing your Masters! You've been my sister/friend from day one. I love you for always being so genuine....

To my Wonderful Wilson/Woody/Johnson Family: For acknowledging my work at our family reunion. That meant the world to me. Thank you for your 'special' and continued support. I will love you always and I will never forget your sacrifice...

A special mention to my nieces and nephews, Godchildren and those who call me Auntie or Mom: You all are so precious to me. It's so heartwarming to watch our next generation follow in our footsteps, loving and supporting one another. And the loving way you've supported me in this work, please know I will never forget it. I love you all to pieces....

To those who allowed me a peek into your private lives and answered my questions about places I'd never been: Figuratively and literally. You know who you are. Thank you…

Special thanks to my 'other moms' Aunt Dorothy and Aunt Jacquie; my dear friend Silena for supporting me at every turn; to Alisa for pointing me in the right direction; to Whitney for encouraging me to finish this work; Remembering my 'village moms', who poured into my life like liquid gold from Heaven..Ruby Turner, Rosa Payne, Helen Matthews, Carol Gomez and Mary Alyce James; Thanks to 'Something Special' (you know who you are). And to all of my friends and family, who indulged me, supported me and sacrificed so much. I love you and appreciate you so much…

And then there's Glaaaam. My precious and forever Sisters who together, we've fed the hungry and homeless, clothed and helped those who had nothing and received such joy simply paying it forward. And your support of me and this work has been priceless. Morgann, Beth, Natalie, Valerie, Shirley, Lisa, Golena, Jeannine, Margie and Shell….You are my Sisters Always! I love you so much…

More than anything, I Thank God for giving me this opportunity to indulge in my love and desire to write. You gave me an avenue to share this work and the ability to express it. So for this and so much more…I give You Love and Praise. Father, I Thank you…

Prologue

Summer 1999

"Felicia, will you please stop fidgeting. I'm not done with your hair and we still have to get your make-up on."

My soon to be sister-in-law and many others were all over me that day. I suppose that's normal on one's wedding day. At eighteen, the consensus was I was too young to get married.

But this had been my dream for as long as I could remember. I was becoming Mrs. Todd Wilson. We loved each other and our parents were hesitant, but gave us their blessing. Todd and I dated for a couple of years, and when he asked me to marry him, I was more than happy to become his wife.

At twenty years old, Todd was a handsome, hard working man who loved his family. We remained chaste while dating because I refused to give myself to anyone except the man I married.

Chapter One

Spring 2006

"**Are you sure the phone is hung up properly Todd?**"

"Yes, Mom. I'm sure."

I haven't heard from Big Todd since yesterday. That was so unlike him. I asked, "Did your father say anything else when he called yesterday?"

"No, Mom. Just that he was gonna stay at Uncle Kenny's house because they were still playing cards."

I decided to call Uncle Kenny's house, even though his girlfriend wasn't very friendly. Normally I wouldn't check up on Todd, but nothing about that weekend was normal. When Faye finally answered the phone, she was clearly out of breath. I said, "Hi Faye, this is Felicia. How are you?"

"I'm okay."

"Would you mind asking Todd to come to the phone for a minute?"

"Felicia, Todd isn't here. He and Kenny went out for drinks last night, but he hasn't been here today."

"Oh, okay. I'm sorry for bothering you. Thanks Faye."

"No problem. Talk to you later."

I was at a loss for words. I began to worry about my husband because he didn't have a habit of staying out all night unless he was with his uncle playing cards. *Why did he lie?*

By early evening, I'd fed the kids and talked to Todd's sister and cousin, Carla and Annette. We all grew up together and were very close. No one had seen Todd.

When I finished the dishes, I heard the car pull in the driveway. I stepped out of the side door, still drying my hands. I said, "You all sure played cards a long time. Did you win?"

"Yep, we just finished about a half hour ago. Whatcha cook? I'm so hungry, I could eat a bear!"

As he followed me into the kitchen, I was fuming! But I fixed his dinner and sat down at the table while he ate. He asked, "What are the rug rats up to?"

"They're *supposed* to be upstairs reading. I told them if they read for an hour, they could have an hour on the PlayStation."

"Good. I'll go up and play with them."

When he finished eating, he went upstairs and hung out with his sons. Although I was beside myself, I continued to act as though nothing was wrong. I couldn't understand the lies.

While I was watching TV, he came down about ten thirty and announced, "I'm gonna go and play cards. I just talked to Uncle Kenny, and the guys wanna play again."

"Okay, tell Faye I said hello."

As I watched him walk out, he'd obviously showered and shaved and was smelling *way* too good to be playing cards with a bunch of guys. I went upstairs and found both boys asleep. I looked around our room and decided to look for any evidence of where he'd been or where he was going. After finding nothing, I decided the evidence would eventually find me.

I never thought my husband would cheat on me. I just couldn't make that make sense in my head. He and I had great sex, so why would he? Aren't the men who cheat the ones whose wives deny them? I never did. I mean, our marriage wasn't perfect, but whose was? Todd and I never had sexual problems. There had to be something else going on.

It was a chilly April night in Rochester, but I felt the need for fresh air. I went outside on the back deck wondering where my husband went. I couldn't concentrate on anything. That's when I realized I'd never rest until I knew.

I got in my car and went the three blocks to Uncle Kenny's. I had to know if he was there. He wasn't. There were no cars in the driveway except Uncle Kenny's. Faye didn't have a car. There were no lights on. It was about ten minutes to twelve and they'd gone to bed, I'm sure.

The next day I told Todd I had errands to run, and would be stopping by Carla's. He said he'd be there with the boys. I'd already called Carla and Annette and told them I needed to see them as soon as possible. Carla said her husband, Earl, was taking their kids to Chuck E. Cheese's for a birthday party, so Annette and I agreed to meet at Carla's.

When I arrived, Annette already had a glass of wine and Carla said, "Before I had a drink, I wanted to know what the hell is wrong!"

Annette said, "Well, I knew I would need one, no matter what the hell you had to say!"

After briefing them on the events of the weekend, Carla said, "Well, you know Earl has cheated on me repeatedly. It sounds to me like Todd has now joined the club!"

"But Why?! Why the hell is he doing this?!"

I was so upset, I began to cry. Annette walked over to me and said, "Felicia, stop it! Stop that damn whining right now! Todd is a man, and that's what most of them do! They can't help it."

With that, she laughed and said, "Licia, not that it's funny, but I'm still amazed at how naïve you are."

She put her arms around me and said, "Okay, just this once you're allowed to cry. But get that shit out and let's move on!"

Carla said, "I swear Nette. At times you are so damned insensitive!"

My girls comforted me while I had a good cry. I said, "Annette, there's no good reason for him to cheat. I give him all the sex he wants. It doesn't make sense."

"Felicia. When it comes to sex, it doesn't have to make sense. That's why I do my thing. 'Cause I know if Tony gets it served to him on a platter, he's gonna take it!"

I never understood Carla or Annette's position when it came to infidelity. Annette believed all men cheated. So she did it, although she'd never caught Tony doing anything. Whereas Carla knew Earl cheated, but she said it was just sex, and she wasn't giving *any* woman her husband over a piece of ass!

Carla poured herself and me a glass of wine. She handed it to me and said, "Listen, you've been married for almost seven years. My momma always said men usually start that shit at seven years, although Earl started at five, as far as I know. Believe me, you'll get over it!"

The following weekend when Todd announced he was going to play cards, I said, "Great! I'm going too!"

"What? Why?"

"Well, I thought it would be nice if we started doing more things together again. Is there a problem?"

"What about the boys? We can't take them with us."

"I know that. They're spending the night at Carla's. Are you ready?"

I could tell he was furious, but he tried his best not to show it. He said, "Licia, I have a better idea! Let's you and me go out on the town tonight. You're right. We need to spend more quality time together."

"Oh Todd. That is *so* sweet! And I'd love to go out, just you and me. But not tonight. I want to play cards, so let's go!"

"Felicia. Listen. I wasn't going to Uncle Kenny's tonight. I been playing with another group of guys I work with. I didn't tell you, 'cause I know how you get."

"You know how I get? How do I get Todd?"

"See, look at you! You get all argumentative! That's why I don't tell you shit!"

I got *very* quiet. I said, "Todd, I'm not arguing. I asked you a simple question. What's wrong with you?"

"I'm a grown ass man Licia! And I shouldn't have to explain…"

He threw his hands up, headed toward the door and said, "I'm out!"

He performed exactly as I expected, although I *hoped* he wouldn't. I also hoped the evidence would find me. If I was a patient woman, it probably would have. But since I'm not, I had to plan.

I rented a car and a co-worker agreed to pick me up and take me to get it. I told her my car was in the shop. I parked it around the corner, so no one would know I had it. So when Todd stormed out, I would simply walk around the corner, get the car and follow him.

My first problem occurred when he went in the opposite direction of the parked car. So instead of walking, I had to *run* around the corner and hope I catch up with him. Hence, my second problem. I lost him. So me and this full tank of gas made an attempt to locate this cheating bastard. I had no idea how I found him, but after about forty five minutes and an entire 'Best of Prince' CD, I actually saw his car.

I pulled up close to confirm the plate number and I also checked to make sure he wasn't in the car. That's when my third problem surfaced. Do I sit and wait, or knock on every door until I find him? I opted to wait and see. So I pulled across the street and turned the engine and lights off.

After a while I was hungry *and* thirsty. There was a gas station/corner store within walking distance, but I didn't want him to come out and see me. So I started the car and pulled off, just in time to see him and some chick walking to his car. He was oblivious to me, so I backed up and got back into the parking space. I didn't turn the car off, in case I needed to follow him.

My vision was blurred because the tears and heartache came all at once. I so needed to cry, but felt I couldn't afford to take the time to do it. He finally pulled off, and luckily I was able to follow them without him having a clue.

We eventually ended up at Red Lobster. So, he's taking her to dinner and the last time he took me to dinner was...hell, I can't even remember! And at Red Lobster of all places, where he could be seen and further humiliate me. I didn't know what I'd do if I caught Todd. I caught him, and didn't know what to do. I didn't believe in public confrontation, so I turned the car around and went home.

When Todd and I were first married, I was a virgin. We were both born and bred here in Rochester, NY. We were so young and so full of visions of the future. Seven years later with two sons, I felt as though life somehow passed me by. I felt as though my gifts of virtue and purity were wasted on a man who never had what it took to appreciate them. And my gifts of fidelity, trust, loyalty and commitment he'd flushed right down the toilet. Right along with our marriage.

I began to see how far behind and less informed I was, compared to my peers. Carla also married young. She and her husband also had two boys.

Annette on the other hand, enjoyed her youth longer than us. She dated and eventually married at twenty four years old. She had one son.

We were all in our mid-twenties, but I felt as though they were eons ahead of me. Carla was six months younger than me, and Annette was two years older. I'd never considered cheating on Todd. I never thought he'd do it in a million years. He seemed to enjoy sex with me so much. What had I done to cause him to do this?

Carla was wrong. I *never* got over it. Because to me, this wasn't *just sex*. To me, just sex was something I never should've found out about and certainly not something you took out to dinner in a public place.

I came to understand that he was a selfish man who not only cheated *on me*, but cheated me *out of* what I really deserved. I *deserved* and had earned the right to be respected and not discounted that way. He didn't even have the decency to be discreet for the sake of our family and friends, let alone for his wife and children. I meant nothing to him.

So in the span of twenty one days, I'd rented an apartment and spoke with an attorney. When he came home from work on that infamous Friday, I was waiting for him.

I said to him, "Remember a few weeks ago when I wanted to go with you to play cards?"

"Yeah, I remember. What about it?"

"Do you remember what you said to me after you got mad and just before you walked out?"

"No, not really."

"Well, let me demonstrate."

I walked to the door, turned to him and I said, "You said to me, *I'm out!* Well Todd, it's my turn to reciprocate!"

He opened his mouth to speak, but I put my hand up and stopped him. I said, "You see, I know all about your extracurricular activities. I've seen the *guys* you play cards with on Brooks Ave. I even followed you the night you took her to Red Lobster! So on your dresser, you'll find my new address and phone number. And if you're not calling regarding your sons, please don't bother! Oh, and one more thing Todd. *I'm out!*"

It took a year because he fought me, but I finally got my divorce.

Chapter Two

Winter 2007

Working for IBM has had its perks but it also proved to be a pain in the ass at times. Like the night I was at the annual Christmas party with all of the office staff and hating it. Although we got along really well, I never felt we had much in common. They're all degreed and I simply worked my way up. I never went to college. I sometimes felt they looked down on me. Or was it I looked up at them? I wonder.

Anyhow, there was a guy there that made me feel quite uncomfortable. He kept looking at me, and I assumed he was someone's husband or boyfriend, because we didn't work together.

Todd and I had been apart for over a year, and I hadn't even looked at another man. He gave me my portion of the equity in the house, and I was looking for something small for the boys and me. The only reason I was out was because it was expected of us.

And what I was dreading was ten seconds from happening, because that guy was heading my way. He said, "Hi. My name is Harold. And you're..?"

"Felicia. Felicia Wilson. Nice to meet you."

I extended my hand and he shook it. He said, "I noticed you're alone and I am too. Do you mind?"

He sat his drink down, and was pointing at the chair next to me. I said, "No, not at all."

That was a lie, because I did mind. A lot. But after about twenty minutes of small talk, I began to enjoy Mr. Harold Benson. He was quite articulate and charming. I learned he'd just started ten days earlier and worked two floors above me, which would explain why I didn't know him.

He had beautiful milk chocolate colored skin and was very handsome. He told me he was from Detroit, which is where he'd relocated from. He helped make the night bearable and we exchanged numbers and eventually called it a night.

Two days later while my parents were visiting, my phone rang. It was Harold. He asked if I would consider going out with him. Just dinner and maybe a jazz club or something. I told him I needed more notice than that, and besides, I didn't think I was ready for dating yet because I was still trying to get settled after my divorce.

He asked if I had plans for the Christmas break, only because he was all alone for the holidays, and wasn't planning to go home. Well, of course I felt bad for the guy, so I told him I'd call him back to discuss it further.

Carla and Annette made it perfectly clear that Todd and my divorce was ours and not theirs. We never missed a beat. While talking to Harold, the two of them walked in. They were covered in snow and it looked like a blizzard outside. After removing their coats and boots and speaking to my parents, they came into the kitchen where I was and I told them about Harold.

They were very interested, so I described him and they both felt I should go out with him. Annette said, "Girl, you gotta start somewhere. I know dating someone at work can be a bit awkward, but dinner's not a big deal. Besides, isn't time to get your pipes cleaned out? How long has it been since Licia?"

We all laughed but I was laughing only on the outside. I was still pining for Todd. Annette then said, "You don't have to hit *that* necessarily, but you can go out with him to get your feet wet. Then you can find somebody to kick it with."

My dad walked in and announced that he and Mom wanted to keep the boys for the night. Carla said, "Girl, you deserve a break. Go ahead and let the boys hang out."

I agreed and Mom walked in and said it was time to go because the weather was getting worse. The boys and I gathered their things and off they went with Grandma and Grandpa.

Annette couldn't wait for the door to close before she said, "Licia, get your ass on that phone and call that man. Tell him you changed your mind and would love to get something to eat. Better yet, tell him to get some take-out and bring it here, since the weather is so bad. Girl, you gotta work it!"

"Annette, I am *not screwing* that man. Are you crazy? Are you aware I've never had sex with anyone but your cousin?"

That's when Carla piped in. She asked, "Does that mean your headstone will read, *never had anyone but Todd*? Licia, you better accept the fact that at some point you will either sleep with another man or die a frustrated old maid."

I thought about that and got up and poured wine for each of us. I wanted to suggest an old fashioned slumber party, but *they* had husbands and children expecting them home. I said to Annette, "I've always wanted to ask you something. How are you able to sleep with other men and still go home and sleep with Tony?"

Annette laughed and said, "Actually, I try my best to avoid it. What I mean is, if I have a *date*, I try to avoid Tony that night. I've lied about periods more times than I care to count. Ha-ha. And believe me, most men rarely question it."

Since I'd gotten the courage to ask that question, I thought I'd try another. I asked, "Why do you do it?"

She took a sip of wine and I realized Carla was leaning forward as well. Annette looked at both of us and said, "I'll tell both of you all you want to know if you stop looking at me like I'm some sort of freak."

We all fell out laughing and began a dialogue that lasted well into the night. I learned a lot about both women that night and they learned what little there was to learn about me. But more importantly, I learned a lot about being a woman.

Annette and Carla are both tall and slender, and they both have beautiful hazel colored eyes. Annette has a funky shoulder length hair cut and has honey colored skin. Carla wears a much shorter haircut, and has lighter skin. They look more like sisters than first cousins. I'm the shortest of the trio. At five foot five, I have pecan colored skin, longer hair and I'm more curvy. Annette has always said I have a bangin body and should learn to rock it.

Annette said she cheated because she was restless and needed attention Tony didn't give her. She also said she craved things sexually that he wasn't into, like oral sex. Carla said she and Annette should switch husbands, because she hates oral sex and Earl loves it. She said that's why *he* cheats.

I sat there with no comment because Todd never brought it up. I assumed Todd wasn't interested in it and neither was I. So Annette has satisfied her cravings with other men for years, and Tony is none the wiser.

I asked her if Tony satisfied her. She said, "Yeah, I guess. But it's different because I love him. He and I make love and I love how he makes me feel, but I don't always climax with him."

Then she really threw me for a loop. She said, "That's when Bob comes in handy."

"Is Bob one of your friends?"

She and Carla laughed and Carla asked, "Licia, you don't know who Bob is?"

"What the hell is so funny? And how would I know him?"

"Bob is an acronym for Battery Operated Boyfriend, or the sisters call him a Battery Operated Brother. A vibrator."

It took me a few seconds to get a full understanding. I blushed so hard, my face almost went up in flames. I guess I'm so far behind that I appear to be a child to these women. How is it that I'm so uninformed?

That's when both women informed me that yes, they are both owners and operators of vibrators and that it's as natural as men taking too long in the shower and coming out smiling.

I asked why married women would want them. They said for the very reason Annette just explained. Husbands don't always take the time to ensure our satisfaction like they did earlier in the marriage. Carla said most men would kiss Bob if they understood that Bob has probably prevented millions of women from having affairs or just leaving their asses.

I began to wonder what else I was in the dark about. I accepted my naïvety, but to hear this from my best friends was very unsettling.

I asked them how come after all these years I'm just hearing this. They said because I think different. And that I always seemed content with the status quo. And frankly, they didn't think I could handle it. All of it true.

Poor me. Lost in a fairy tale world of marriage, white knights and all of the pathetic trimmings of unreals and *not* ever afters. What the hell could have made me this way? Well, that was about to change. If nothing else, I was going to discover the inner workings of Felicia. What it was that really made me tick.

I never called Harold back, and eventually my girls went home to their families. But as I lay in bed that night, I began to visualize Felicia in an entirely different light.

The next day was sunny and clear, but very cold. It was six days before Christmas, and I was off of work until after the New Year. I decided to take advantage of the boys being away and cleaned the apartment from top to bottom. I was wrapping the last of my gifts when the phone rang. He said, "Felicia. Hi, it's Harold. How are you?"

"Uh, I'm okay. I apologize for not getting back to you. I had company last night very late."

"Don't worry about it. I just thought I'd take a chance and call you before you got out and about today. What are your plans for the day?"

I thought about that and said, "Not much really. My kids are with my parents so I'm just finishing up with Christmas stuff and getting the house in order."

Then I surprised myself when I asked, "What are your plans?"

"Well, other than a trip to the post office, I don't have any. Would you like to do something? Maybe lunch or a mall trip? I'm done Christmas shopping, are you?"

"Yes, I am. I can't stand to Christmas shop this close to the holiday."

"Me either. But I do like to go to the mall and enjoy all of the holiday stuff. I guess it's the kid in me."

How sweet, I thought. Then I said, "Sure, why not. I suppose we could grab something to eat at the food court and enjoy the festivities at the same time."

"I'd like that. Where do you live? I can come and get you. I just need directions because I'm still trying to learn my way around Rochester."

After giving him my address, I began to tell him the general vicinity of the apartment and he asked, "Felicia, do you live in Corn Hill?"

"Yes, do you know where that is?"

He laughed and said, "I sure do. I also live in Corn Hill."

He lived around the corner from me.

Forty minutes later, Harold was ringing my door bell. I decided not to get too fabulous, so I just put on a sweater and jeans, a little make-up, and a French twist in my hair.

While I was dressing, I wondered what Todd would think if he saw me with another man. For some reason, the thought sort of appealed to me. I guess it's time for me to grow up.

What I saw when I opened the door was no longer just a co-worker. I now saw Harold as a man. When he stepped in, he handed me a bottle of my favorite wine. He remembered from our conversation at the Christmas party. I was instantly impressed.

We had a great time at the mall and discovered we were both born in November and that we both liked Philly Cheese Steaks. We rode the train and had Starbuck's coffee. My mom called me earlier asking permission for the boys to stay another night, so when he brought me home, I asked him in to have some wine.

I brought the wine and glasses in the living room, and was about to put down my load when he stood and relieved me of the wine, and asked for the corkscrew. I went back into the kitchen to get it, and when I turned around, I bumped right into him. He scared the shit out of me, sneaking up behind me like that. I let out a yelp, and he said, "Oh, I'm sorry for scaring you. I just wanted to help."

I was so aroused. I couldn't believe how a simple touch could be so exciting. I put my head down and went back into the living room without responding.

We made small talk the rest of the evening. I was certain my discomfort was obvious. About nine o'clock, Harold decided to call it a night. He stood and then I stood. He began to walk toward the coat closet and I followed.

He turned around and I stopped in my tracks, making sure to stay a safe distance away. He asked, "Did I do or say something offensive Felicia? It seems your mood changed."

"No, absolutely not. I have a tendency to drift at times. I apologize for that. I hope I didn't offend you?"

He smiled and said, "No Felicia, it's perfectly understandable. It's just that I had hopes of talking you into a late night latte at a place I found downtown that stays open late. Would you be interested?"

I looked at him and he made this stupid pouting face like he was gonna cry if I said no. I cracked up. He did too. I said, "Why not? Give me a minute to get my boots and coat on."

So we went downtown and had lattes and fresh cinnamon buns, and I had the biggest sugar high imaginable. I think I laughed at everything he said. He seemed just as silly as me.

When he brought me home, I insisted he stay in his warm car, but he wouldn't hear of it. He helped me with the key and turned me around and kissed me on my forehead. He said, "Felicia, you've made this the greatest day I've spent thus far in Rochester, N.Y."

It seemed as though all of my organs ceased to function. I thought I was melting right there in the doorway.

I decided to do something unexpected. I put my arms around his neck and kissed his cheek. He turned and kissed my lips. Passionately. Thoroughly.

We were somehow in my living room. He closed the door and I was against the wall. He became gentler. Calmer. We were still entangled by the same kiss. Changing us forever. I felt him harden. More. And more. But he was not like an animal. Instead he was controlled. But passionate.

His hands were on my bare back. Somehow. And he was killing me, from behind with his hands and from the front with his hardness.

He leaned into me. And when his hands cupped my breast, I emitted the first sound. *Ummm*

Still kissing, the longest kiss. His tongue was making love to my mind. And now my neck. *When did we end the kiss?*

I had *never* been taken in such a way. Nor had I *ever*, exploded in this manner. I opened my eyes, and saw the reason for my intense pleasure. He had my nipple in his mouth, and seeing it, I began to soar to places foreign to me.

Against the wall. In my living room. I came in the arms of a man I'd known less than a week. With all of our clothes on! *What the hell just happened?* I had never had an orgasm like that. So powerful that I began to slide down the wall. I had lost all control.

He raised me back up. I was in a daze. He whispered in my ear, "Are you okay? You're far sweeter than I imagined. I'll stop if you want me to, but I hope you don't."

I just shook my head, and he began to undo my jeans. I was hoping we would at least move to the sofa. But he kept me right there. I couldn't believe I was about to get laid up against the wall. That was funny to me.

He took off one of my pant legs and began to kiss my leg and my knee and then my thigh. I was anxious for him to get the rest of my clothes off, because the heat from his kisses was causing both of my legs to shake.

He then began to kiss me where my panties were and my eyes opened up. He was looking up at me and said, "You smell so good. Don't worry, I won't let you fall. I just want to taste you."

Well, that meant nothing to me, until he slid my panties over and buried his tongue inside of me. I let out a scream that had no sound. He began to eat me like it was the best thing he'd ever eaten ever. I thought I wouldn't survive it. It was shameful, but I never wanted him to stop. I wanted to die right there, being sexed by him that way.

He didn't let me fall. He sat on the floor and brought me down on top of his lap. He held me and kissed my neck until I calmed down. Then I felt his finger inside of me. He spoke softly. "I'm so turned on by you. I knew you would be good, but…wow."

He reached in his pocket and pulled out a condom. He asked, "Am I being presumptuous? Can we take this further?"

I didn't know what to say. I wanted to, but I worried about what he would think of me. So I shook my head yes and said nothing. He said, "I want you to sit on me. Would you do that?"

I just shook my head again. I was ashamed, but far more turned on than ever before. He held my hand and brought it down between us. For the first time I touched another man's hardness.

It pleased me to know he was so aroused by me. That gave me the courage to stroke him and experience his pleasure. He guided my hand and I began a rhythm that was taking him to those places I'd been.

I leaned forward and kissed him sweetly, parting his lips and finding his tongue. I sucked it softly and his moans and movements told me he liked it. I was afraid he was gonna come, but he pulled away and whispered in my ear, "Would you like to taste it?"

I froze. I opened my eyes and said to him, "Harold, you probably won't believe this, but I've never had oral sex before. What you did earlier was my first experience with that."

He looked at me with disbelief at first. Then he raised my head and looked in my eyes and said, "You're serious, aren't you?"

"Yes, very serious. My husband and I never even talked about it, let alone did it. I..."

He kissed me so sweetly and tenderly, I forgot what I was about to say. I still had him in my hand and massaged him again. He said, "Please sit on me Felicia. I can't wait much longer."

He put the condom on and I positioned myself over him. It was a tight fit, considering it's been over a year since I'd had sex. He was about the same size as Todd, but this was very different. It was so much better.

I found my rhythm with him and eventually began a slow sweet climb into heaven. I again lost control, as wave after wave of ecstasy swept over me. He held me close and stroked me into another powerful climax.

Then he put his hands on either side of my hips and lifted them up and down like he liked it. It was so sensual. I felt him beyond physical. It was extraordinary. He seemed so patient, and was now enjoying it himself.

I leaned over and kissed him on the neck, and when I chewed on his ear, he asked me to put my tongue in his ear. He held me so tight and came so hard. I thought it was so beautiful.

He held me that way a long time. Eventually I rose and kissed him softly on his lips. I told him to help himself to the bathroom and I used the other one in my room.

A few minutes later, he entered my bedroom. I turned and looked at him, and then quickly turned back. He came up behind me and put his arms around me and kissed me on my neck. He began to tell me how much he enjoyed our love making.

I told him how ashamed I was and that I thought it would be better if he left. He said, "Felicia let's have a glass of wine and talk. I think you'll feel better about this."

I told him no and that I would appreciate it if he would see himself out. He stood there a while and soon I heard the front door close.

I went into the living room and saw that his car was gone. I sat on the sofa and looked around my living room. My scarf was on the floor where it had fallen when I reached up to kiss him. I could still smell our passion.

Chapter Three

The boys were so excited. I guess all kids are on Christmas Eve. Todd was coming to get them to spend a few days with him. He was surprised I agreed to let them stay with him. I think he expected me to say no, and look like the bad guy.

Harold and I planned a romantic evening together. I'm still trying to figure out how I allowed this romance to go from zero to one hundred in the course of one night.

I felt like the biggest hoe in New York State. I couldn't even tell Carla and Annette. I didn't speak to Harold for two days, I was so embarrassed. He came over on the third day because I wouldn't take his calls. He was worried about me and assured me he didn't think badly of me. I didn't know how to face him.

I opened the door and he stood there with his head down looking at me with his eyeballs at the top of his head. His hands were behind his back and he asked, "May I enter?"

He poked his lips out, and began a pretentious sobbing. I smiled at his playfulness, and opened the door all the way. He slowly walked in and then backed into the living room. I asked, "What are you hiding?"

He brought his hands from behind his back and presented me with a dozen roses. He stayed a safe distance away. He was so very sweet. I looked at the roses and then at him. I took them, thanked him and began to explain my behavior.

He closed the distance between us and put his finger on my lip. He said, "Felicia, you do not owe me an explanation. I've known many women and I have five sisters, and I know you're not common. If anything, I should've had more control. I suppose I took advantage of the situation. So, I apologize to you. But, I would be lying if I said it wasn't great. Right?"

I could feel my face heating up again so I just turned and went into the kitchen to find a vase for the roses. He followed me and asked, "Felicia, don't you think we should talk about this?"

I didn't know what to say to him. Should I admit what he already knew, that I had never had an experience of that magnitude before. That I loved it, and truth be told, I could still feel his essence.

"Harold, please don't be offended but I don't want to discuss this. I acted shamefully and I'm trying to deal with it."

After putting the roses on the dining room table, I went into the living room. I sat on the sofa, and he sat opposite me in a chair. I looked at him and said, "I'm so rude. Is there something I can get you?"

He laughed and said, "You really are a tight ass when it comes to etiquette and protocol, aren't you?"

We both laughed and he asked for a soft drink. I went and got both of us some pop and sat back down.

He said, "Felicia, the last thing I want is for you to be uncomfortable around me. I'm just a normal guy with a normal life. I like you a lot. And I promise you I will not pressure you about sex, but I think it's important for your sexual health that you talk about this. If you don't, you'll forever think you did something wrong, when in fact you didn't. If I thought you did, I wouldn't be here. Granted, you don't know me that well, but I don't associate with common women."

I looked at him and began to relax a little. He continued. "What happened the other night was a natural occurrence. I admit that it doesn't always happen that quickly or passionately, because usually people who are attracted to one another act on it slower. But sometimes it happens like it did with us. Are you starting to feel any better about it now?"

I smiled and said, "I guess I feel better about it. I've always been so different. That was like going against the grain of everything I was taught and believed in. Sex with someone on the first date, it just seems so taboo. And...well, I can't even discuss what else we did."

I turned my head and picked up my glass. He asked, "What else did we do?"

He looked at me questioningly. He then asked, "Are you talking about oral sex? Felicia, you do realize oral sex is a part of sex, like kissing is, right? I mean, what do you use to kiss with? The word oral means with your mouth, right? And sex or foreplay involves stimulating the whole body, right? Men and women kiss breasts and insert nipples in their mouths. We kiss necks and ears and insert fingers and toes and earlobes and tongues into our mouths. If that's normal, why is it other parts wouldn't be? Are you hearing me?"

I never thought of it that way. I guess it was easy to assume it was wrong or nasty because I'd never done it before. I was starting to feel much better. At least about him and about the fact that he didn't look at me differently.

He reached across the coffee table and touched my hand. He repeated himself and asked, "Felicia do you hear me?"

"Yes I do, and I appreciate you for explaining it that way. But, are you sure? I mean, you're not just saying it, right?"

He got up and came around the table and sat next to me. He said, "I'm very sure. As much as I enjoy your company and want to hang out with the only friend I have here, I would drop you like a hot potato if I thought you were loose. That has never appealed to me."

I smiled and sat back and said, "So, what now? We aren't even friends officially, and now we find ourselves here. What do we do?"

"I say we do nothing except enjoy each other's company. If you don't want sex, we won't have sex. Is that what you're worried about?"

"Yeah, I guess."

"Well, don't worry about that anymore. Okay?"

I smiled and nodded my head. He said, "Now that I have you talking, would you share with me what you thought of our experience? It was wonderful for me and I'd like to think you also enjoyed it."

Damn, I thought I'd successfully avoided that question. I said, "You just won't give it a rest, will you Harold?"

He laughed and said, "I'll be honest with you. I've never had anyone respond that way with me before. It was one of the greatest sexual experiences I've ever had. And I guess my male ego wants to hear you say that it was special for you as well."

After a moment I was able to look at him. I was so bashful about such things. But finally I said, "Yes, it was very special. It was also very scary. I felt like somebody trying crack for the first time. You've heard the stories. They say it's the best feeling they've ever had, and for the rest of their days, they're chasing that same high, never to achieve it again."

He laughed at me and he also seemed to relax more. He sat back and asked, "So are you saying that was the best you've ever had? I'll admit it if you will."

We looked at each other and fell out laughing. And for the rest of the day we enjoyed each other's company, and he never touched me.

Marcus came running into the kitchen saying, "Mommy, Daddy's here. Can I open the door?"

I told him to open the door and to get his brother so they don't hold Todd up. I walked into the living room as Todd was walking in. For the sake of the boys, we found a way to settle into a civil and workable relationship. We were both very happy about that.

He wished me a Merry Christmas and I wished him the same. He asked what my plans were for tomorrow. I said I planned to stop by his mom's to see the boys, but would be spending the day with my family. I planned to take full advantage of my time alone.

Harold invited me to his apartment for Christmas Eve dinner. I arrived exactly at six o'clock. He opened the door with mistletoe over his head and was blocking the doorway. I couldn't get in until I kissed him. I rolled my eyes at him and kissed him quickly and backed up. He smiled at me and allowed me in.

His apartment smelled of wonderful holiday scents. I would swear I smelled sweet potato pie and cornbread dressing. I was sure those smells were coming from some other apartment. We made small talk while he took my coat and I removed my boots. I brought wine like he did. He said, "Good, now we have more than we need."

He grabbed my hand and escorted me to the sofa where he had hors d'oeuvres on the coffee table. Everything looked wonderful, but I went right for the shrimp. I asked where he got it prepared.

He said, "I prepared it. I cooked everything for tonight. My dad is a chef, and taught all of us to cook. I'm the best cook of all my siblings, and they're all women."

I could see his chest filling up and I laughed at him in spite of his arrogance. He said, "We're having a simple meal of Cornish hen, cornbread dressing, greens, seafood salad and sweet potato pie for dessert with French Vanilla ice cream. The ice cream is store bought. I didn't have time to make it this time, but this summer I'll make you some."

I sat there with my mouth opened trying to decide if this guy was for real. I looked at Harold Benson and was starting to believe he was a keeper. But can anyone be that perfect? I doubt it.

After dinner, which was absolutely delicious, we went into the living room and had Amaretto flavored coffee. He took out his Scrabble game and looked at me questioningly. I sat up and said, "Yes, I'd love to play!"

We had a ball. He won two out of three games and asked if I wanted some wine before he presented me with my gift. I wasn't expecting that especially since I didn't bring a gift for him. I told him I didn't realize we were exchanging gifts.

He said, "We're not. I said *gift*, not Christmas gift. It's something I picked up for you shortly after we met. Because you're an intelligent woman, I thought you would appreciate having something like this. Now, it's not meant to offend you but to help you become more informed about the world of sex. And it certainly is not my way of trying to get in your pants. Okay?"

Well, I was so afraid it was a Bob I didn't know what to do. He saw my fear, sat next to me and said, "Felicia, you're the sweetest breath of fresh air I've encountered in ages. Your innocence has enchanted me. But your naivety frightens me. So, I've taken it upon myself to introduce you to some basic things. Will you let me?"

Before I could answer, he went behind the sofa and handed me a book. It was titled, 'An In-Depth Look at Sexual Positions and Oral Sex'.

I felt like a ten-year old. He said, "Don't feel bad, please. Look, I bought two."

He went under the coffee table and showed me another one. His was obviously well read. He said, "I'm sure your mind is going a thousand miles a minute, but I found of all the books I researched, this one is probably perfect for you. It describes in detail various positions and the most likely pleasure to be experienced from each. Additionally, it teaches you how to receive and give oral stimulation. I learned a few things myself."

Without saying a word, I perused the pages and finally looked up at him. I asked, "So what is the method to your madness here? How do you plan to introduce me to whatever, without touching me? And although I'm choosing to believe your intentions are good, what do you hope to get out of it? A better sex partner?"

"I knew I was taking a big chance giving this to you. But I was so afraid someone would take advantage of you at some point, because of your vulnerability. So I'm willing to risk losing your friendship and protect you, than to sit back and watch some guy use you. You gonna be mad at me long? Cause I can't stand that. I cry myself to sleep when you're mad at me."

I looked at that Negro and laughed. And he laughed. I finally said, "Damn Harold. Am I that stupid?"

"Okay Felicia, this is your first lesson. You are not stupid at all. What you are is extremely passionate and inexperienced about taming that fire inside of you. If I was a different kind of man, I could've turned you out. That night. You are highly sexual when the right buttons are pushed. I learned in thirty seconds what some of those buttons are. I realized later what some of the others are. You must learn how to suppress some of that or the next person who kisses you might use you. You understand?"

"What are the buttons, Mr. Benson?"

"I knew you were gonna ask me that. First of all, being with someone that is fun and interesting. I'm not beating my own drum, but we clearly had a good time that day. It was evident we had a few things in common. But what we did that day, anyone could have done. That doesn't make him a good guy. Just a smart one. Secondly, you'd been without sex for a long time. That was just luck for me, not so much for you."

"What do you mean? I enjoyed it too. And honestly, if I'd had that in my marriage, maybe my ex wouldn't have cheated."

"That's why it's really important you maintain your power over sex. Do you understand what that means?"

"I'm not sure."

"Some people allow sex to play too big of a role in their lives. For instance, marriages and families have been devastated by infidelity, like you experienced. You allowed sex to have the power to do that."

"So you're blaming me?"

"Not at all. I've had enough sex to know that it's usually loveless. It's usually two people willing to give one another pleasure. But you made a decision to be heartbroken by it. I'm not saying you were wrong, just that you had other options."

I stared at him. I finally said, "You're right. Because of how I was raised and my humiliation, it never dawned on me to stay."

"Exactly. Another way we give sex too much power is assuming it means more than it does. Just because a guy lies down with a woman doesn't mean he loves her. Or even likes her. It's just sex. Remember that Felicia."

"Are you trying to tell me something?"

He smiled and blew me a kiss. He said, "Absolutely not Felicia. I just don't want you to get used. Okay?"

I smiled at him. He sat up and touched my face. He asked, "Felicia. What am I gonna do with you?"

He leaned forward and kissed me. I got up and asked where the rest room was located. He pointed to the left and off I went. When I returned, he was in the kitchen putting dishes in the dishwasher. I walked in, rolled up my sleeves and helped. We chatted, put food away and had fun cleaning up.

Before I covered the pie, I got a knife and sliced the smallest sliver. I had my back to Harold and tried to sneak the pie in my mouth. I almost had it in, but half of it fell on the counter. I looked to see if he noticed but he was busy wiping his hands.

So I turned back to pick it up and he came up behind me, picked it up and put it toward my mouth. But as I was closing my mouth around it, he pulled it out. I turned to look at his silly ass, and he leaned closer and that familiar hardness was against me. His other hand was around my waist, allowing him to press firmly into me. He kissed my neck and whispered in my ear, "Eat your pie Felicia. I want to show you something."

I was so turned on that I opened my mouth and he put his finger in slowly. In and out. I ate the pie but I also understood what else he was doing. This time I wasn't embarrassed. Well, not too embarrassed.

He was so aroused. I could feel him pulsating behind me. He moaned in my ear, and all of that had me so hot for him. I was about to turn around, but he stopped me. He said, "Let's not rush this. Let's enjoy it for a moment."

Still up against me, he trailed his other hand up the front of my chest where he massaged and rubbed my nipples. They were as hard as he was and I could barely stand it. I continued to suck the finger in my mouth and he said to me, "Sweetheart, use your tongue on it. Keep it moist and gently suck it, in and out, in and out."

I obeyed. And I liked it. It was strange, but it was so sexy to me. His other hand was now invading my lower body. He was rubbing me between my thighs, and he said, "Damn, I need your help. Please unbutton those damn pants for me. I'm not as good as I used to be."

I giggled and unbuttoned them. He began to massage my private parts in unison with everything else he was doing to me. I was beside myself. He inserted a finger inside of me, and my body instinctively began to move. I knew I was gonna melt all over him. And when he put his tongue in my ear, I exploded within seconds.

I knew I was loud, because he bit me on my neck gently to bring me back. He kept touching me until it was over and then he finally turned me around. He put his finger in his mouth and closed his eyes saying, "Ummm, you're like butter Baby."

He leaned forward and kissed me a long time. I could still feel his hardness and he removed my pants. I thought, *he must love doing this outside of the bedroom.*

He kissed me again and sat me up onto the counter. He slowly removed my panties and looked at me. He rubbed my thighs and began to kiss my tummy. He opened my thighs and put his head between them. My head went back and I held on to his shoulders. I lost all control. I actually begged him to stop.

It was like a fire was let loose inside of me, and I was fighting to contain it. I lost the fight. I came again. I was dizzy and struggling because my legs were shaking. He picked me up and carried me to his bedroom. As I was leaving the kitchen, for some reason, I was wishing Annette was a fly on the wall, witnessing her girl gettin' her freak on.

Harold was amazing. He removed his clothes and got on the bed next to me. He kissed me and asked me if I was okay. I shook my head yes. He held me and whispered in my ear, asking if I would like more. I again shook my head.

He got a condom out of his nightstand. He asked if I knew how to put one on. I admitted I'd never done it before, and he said I needed to learn. So he directed my hand toward his penis and he opened the package.

I began to massage it and he let me know he liked it. I actually looked at it this time and he was watching me. He handed me the condom and said, "I need to be a little harder. Do you think you can help me out?"

Then he chuckled and said, "I can get a piece of pie?"

I was nervous all of a sudden. He smiled and said, "It's okay if you'd rather not. I'll never pressure you."

I relaxed a little. I didn't think I was ready. I asked, "Is that something you like?"

"Honestly, yes I do. But I also like this."

He removed my blouse and bra and began sucking one nipple while touching the other. I closed my eyes and leaned back onto the pillow. He crawled up over me and continued making love to my breasts. It was *so* good! I couldn't believe how wonderful he made me feel. When he stopped, I sat up and he said, "Lay back down."

"Aren't I supposed to put the condom on?"

He smiled and said, "Yes you are."

I retrieved it off the bed and put my hand on his penis again. Surprisingly, I decided I wanted to taste him. So I leaned forward and put the head of it in my mouth. He responded immediately. I remembered his instructions and used my tongue and saliva to make it wet. Then I moved up and down it's length and realized it wasn't bad.

I felt his hand on my face and I looked up at him. He was enjoying it immensely. So I did it again. All of a sudden, he stopped me. I thought I'd hurt him or something. In a very husky voice he said, "Felicia, put the condom on Baby".

"What's wrong? Did I hurt you or mess up or something?"

"No Baby, you were great. Please...put it on."

So I fumbled with it and he asked me to turn over. Once he was inside of me, he wasn't the same as before. The patient, gentle man became a passion driven man, and I loved that too. He wasn't brutal but he was deliberate, and he told me how good it was and how I was the sexiest woman he'd ever had.

And when I came, he came with me, and it was an explosion so powerful, that if Santa had been on the roof, he would have thought it was an atomic bomb.

I passed the hell out. I'm sure of it. I must have because I didn't wake up until I smelled bacon cooking. I attempted to rise, but my head was spinning. A sex hangover? What's that about?

I got up and went into the master bathroom. He'd set a new toothbrush on the counter with toothpaste and mouth wash. There was a wash cloth, a hand towel and a bath towel lying across the rim of the tub. There were two different kinds of soap, unopened lying there also.

What kind of man was this? I must have had a nervous breakdown, and was dreaming this, right? 'Cause there was no way in hell this man was real.

I entered the living room wearing his bathrobe. He looked at me and smiled. I smiled back. He said, "Merry Christmas Felicia!"

I looked at him and said, "Wow, I forgot that it's Christmas. Merry Christmas to you too Harold."

We both laughed. I couldn't believe I was in a man's apartment on Christmas morning after sexing him all night on Christmas Eve. I should've been with my children. I'd lost it for real. He came over and kissed me and asked, "How did you sleep? Did you find everything okay in the bathroom?"

"Yes, everything was great. And you're great Harold. I've never met anyone like you before. We seem to get along so well together. Why me? I mean, why are you being so kind to me?"

He raised my head and said, "I could ask you the same question Felicia. Look at us. Together on Christmas morning. I was so depressed because I thought I would spend the holidays alone. Yet somehow, I ended up with you. Much more than I could have asked for."

I looked at this man who had changed my life. Did he realize that? I said, "Harold, don't you think we're moving a bit too fast? As I stand here looking at you, I can't imagine you not being in my life. That can't be good."

He smiled and said, "Then don't."

I finally made it over Todd's mom's house. After a morning of love making, Harold released me to be with my family, only with the promise that I'd come back and spend the night with him. When I walked in, I was greeted just like I was still in the family.

I was loaded down with gifts, so Carla came over and helped me out. She asked, "Girl, where've you been? Me and Annette went over your house this morning, and you weren't there. We called your parents, thinking maybe you stayed with them overnight and I think we upset them, because they said you told them you were gonna spend a quiet evening at home. What's up?"

"I just left my parents. They're fine. I explained to them that a friend invited me over, and we hung out late. I guess I didn't hear you knocking."

"Licia, why are you lying? We called and knocked. And the next time you decide to lie, remember to leave your car at home."

She turned to walk away, and I grabbed her arm. I said, "Carla, I'm sorry. I was wrong to lie to you. But I need time to sort this mess out. I'll say this. Remember the guy I met at the Christmas party? I was with him. I just didn't want you to think I was a slut or something."

Carla smiled the biggest smile I'd ever seen. She grabbed my arm, and pulled me into the hall. Annette was looking for us and saw us go out there. She asked, "What are you two doing out here? And where were you this morning?"

Carla said, "I already told her, Nette. She 'bout to tell us who she was under last night *and* this morning."

Annette said, "Well I'll be damned!"

I was half embarrassed and half excited. I said, "First of all, it was Harold. You won't believe what I've been up to. I'm no longer the prude I was a week ago, that's for sure. But I want to tell you later, not here. Can we get together tomorrow?"

They both agreed they would come over tomorrow about three o'clock. We went back with the family and Marcus and Todd Jr. came over to greet me. I reached down and hugged the two of them at the same time. I said, "Merry Christmas Guys!"

"Merry Christmas Mommy!" they both replied back to me in unison. I hugged them so hard that Todd Jr. said, "Mom, you're choking me."

I released them and they told me, at the same time, everything Santa brought them. I told them I had a few more things for them and that Grandma and Grandpa also sent them something. They ran for the packages.

Then Todd's mom said, "Hey Licia! Girl, you better get over here and give me a hug."

I went over and said, "Merry Christmas Momma!"

I gave her the biggest hug and kiss. I hadn't seen her in so long. Then I kissed Aunt Pat, her sister who is Annette's mom, and wished her a Merry Christmas also. I went around the room, speaking to all of Todd's family, who had been my family forever.

Although it seemed a little odd, no one treated me any different. I sat down next to Momma and she said, "Girl, you look like a million dollars. What's going on?"

If I was lighter, I'm sure I would be as red as a beet. I said, "Just working and trying to keep up with those boys, Momma."

"Hmm, if you ask me, I would swear you been up to more than that. You look like you're glowing. You ain't pregnant, are you?"

Todd sat straight up in his seat, considering he'd been eavesdropping the whole time. Annette started laughing and Carla said, "Ma, why would you ask her something like that?"

Aunt Pat said, "Well if she is, it ain't nobody's business. Debra you so nosey."

We all laughed and I got away without having to respond. Todd was staring at me the whole time I was there. He never said much, but I guess he saw the change in me too.

Before leaving, I asked him when he planned to bring the boys home. He said in a couple of days. I asked him to just let me know and I'd pick them up. I didn't want any surprises. He insisted he would bring them since they had so much stuff to bring home. I let it go at that, and kissed my boys goodbye.

I went home and relaxed. It had been a long day, and night, and I'm sure that's why I fell asleep in the chair. The next thing I knew, I heard what sounded like a jack hammer. When I gained control of my senses, I realized someone was knocking on my door.

I looked at the clock, and realized I was late going to Harold's and now he was here looking for me. I took a deep breath and opened the door. I began to say how sorry I was when I looked into the faces of Carla and Annette. I was so surprised to see them that I just looked at them. Annette asked, "Damn, can we come in? Are you alone?"

"Yeah, come on in."

I rubbed the sleep out of my eyes and said, "I'm late for my date with Harold. I promised him I would come over by eight o'clock and it's almost eight thirty. I need to call him. Help yourselves to something to drink and pour me some wine please."

I picked up my home phone and realized I didn't know his number by heart. Luckily, my cell phone was next to it. Annette saw me and cracked up. She said, "You act like a crack head. Ha-ha. But I know the feeling!"

I turned around and gave Annette the bird. Then I said, "Trick, I'm sure you do know!"

She laid back in the chair and cracked up again. I dialed Harold's number and he answered on the first ring. I told him I'd fallen asleep and was so sorry. He asked, "You want me to come over there? I really don't want you out now. It's getting late."

"Well, my cousins just dropped by and I don't want to rush them. Would you mind coming later?"

"No, I don't mind Felicia. Just call me when they've left."

I said okay and we hung up. When I turned around, the two of them were looking at me and shaking their heads. Carla said, "This is unbelievable. Licia got herself a man."

"I do not. You need to stop trippin'. We're just enjoying each other. You know how it is when you meet someone new. It's very exciting at first. I'm sure after a while, we'll just be friends."

Annette said, "Yeah, yeah whatever. We want to know what the hell happened that you gave it up so fast. He didn't rape yo' ass did he? 'Cause I'll put a cap in his ass. I don't play that shit!"

Carla and I both laughed at Annette trying to act like a gangsta. I sat down, took a long sip of my wine and told them, start to finish, what I'd been up to over the last week.

When I was done, they both had their mouths opened and were dumbfounded. Annette finally asked, "Does he have a damn brother? Cause he need to be one of many, for real."

Then she shook her head and said, "To hell with the brother, where is his daddy? That's who I need to meet *first!* Then the brothers! Ha-ha!"

"Sorry Nette, all he has are sisters. Five of em!"

Carla, who had been silent finally said, "Girl, what are you gonna do with him? I mean, it sounds like he really likes you. Do you think it'll get serious?"

Annette piped in and said, "Carla, what the hell kind of question is that? He's not a stray dog! He's a man! She's gonna *fuck him!* Damn, why you have to make more out of it than that? It's just sex!"

Annette looked at me and said, "Felicia, don't get hooked on this man. He is one of many, believe me. You'll find yourself married and going through the same shit you went through a year ago, cause ain't none of them faithful. That's why my ass ain't."

I asked, "Nette, has Tony ever cheated on you?"

She opened her mouth to answer, then got up and went into the kitchen. Carla looked at me and we followed her.

"Nette, has he?"

She slowly turned and said, "I think so. Early in our marriage I overheard him on the phone. He was talking real sweet to someone, and a few days later I saw him with her. Yes, I watched him leave his office and pick her up. But I didn't follow them. And I've never confronted him with it. It's funny because I always cheated so I wouldn't be hurt by him first. But it doesn't matter. When you love someone, it always hurts to see something like that. Even when you're low down like me."

She sort of laughed, but not because she thought it was funny. I felt sorry for Annette. She apparently had all of those men to fill some endless void. And not just a sexual one. But she pepped back up and said, "I mean it Felicia. Don't get all wrapped up in this guy. There's so much more you can do besides wash some man's drawers!"

Carla said, "Annette, if you don't like being married, why don't you get out of it? You're still young and attractive."

"See Carla, what you just said proves you still don't get it. I'm not staying in my marriage because I can't find *another* husband! I'm staying because I love my husband and I want my son, his father and me to be a family. It may sound arrogant, but I've never had a problem finding a man."

"But you're always so anti-marriage. Why is that?"

"Because some people are better off not married. Like me. I should've never gotten married. I don't regret my baby Tony one bit, but if I could've done things differently, I would have. The thing is, Tony was the kindest man I'd ever met. He was giving and he loved and adored me. And I know no matter what goes down, Tony will always take care of his son."

I was watching this tennis match of sorts between cousins and realized they were so different. Funny how circumstances brought stuff to the surface. I wondered if they remembered I was even there.

I said, "Hey guys, remember me? I was hoping someone would say something about the fact that I just had a penis in my mouth for the first time! Hello!"

Both women looked at me and laughed their asses off. Annette said, "I told you before it wasn't a big deal. You just have to make a decision not to be grossed out by it. But if you're determined not to like it, you'll hate it, like Miss Carla here. If she would settle down and have a drink or two, she would be able to satisfy her husband and he wouldn't be out in the streets trying to get his wax job elsewhere with who knows what. I told her when she allows him to put his tongue in her mouth, that's worse than a penis any day. If she makes it perfectly clear she wants him to shower before engaging in oral sex, he'll take four or five showers a day for her."

Carla looked at Annette and said, "I hear ya. But I still don't see how *you* enjoy it."

I said, "I think I understand. What I discovered was how much *he* enjoyed it. That seemed to turn me on and made me eager to experience his pleasure. Doesn't it make you feel good to make Earl feel good?"

Carla thought about it and said, "Actually it does. I never thought of it that way before."

Annette said, "How many times have you heard a man say he enjoys pleasing you?"

Carla and I looked at each other and then back at Annette. I said, "To tell you the truth Nette, Todd never said that to me. Harold on the other hand, made it clear from the beginning that he enjoyed giving me pleasure. I think Todd assumed because he was enjoying it, I was too. Being with Harold has caused me to reexamine so many things. I guess when everybody was saying we were too young to get married, they were right. We had no idea about sex or much else."

I turned to Carla and said, "Carla, Annette was smarter than us because she waited and dated before getting married."

"Yep, you're right. And now that I think of it, I wonder if Earl even cares if I enjoy it."

Annette asked Carla, "Have you communicated any of this to your husband? Is Earl aware you feel this way?"

She laughed and said, "Shit Nette, I just realized it myself! Although I wasn't a virgin when I got married, I was with a young knucklehead who didn't know what he was doing either."

We all laughed and drank more wine. I realized it was getting late, so I said, "I hate to break this party up, but I got business to handle!"

We all laughed and soon I kissed my sisters goodbye. I called Harold and then I took a quick shower. I was anxious to learn more from this man who just floated into my life like a dream.

When he got there, he was laden with bags. He said, "I thought I'd fix us an exotic brunch in the morning, so I shopped in my kitchen. Am I being too presumptuous?"

I smiled a coy smile and said, "Of course you are. But you were right in your assumption."

I couldn't help but put my arms around him and tell him that I'd missed him. He kissed me tenderly and echoed my sentiments. He said, "Umm, you smell so good. Are you hungry?"

I said no, so we put the food away and grabbed a bottle of wine and went into the living room. He said, "I realize it's early in our romance, but I would love to meet your boys. I'm not sure what the protocol is, but I wanted you to know I'm ready for that whenever you are."

"I'm not sure either, but let's wait a while until things are back to normal. We're both off of work and they're with their dad, so our lives are sort of on hold right now."

He agreed and we began a dialogue of our personal lives and families. I told him I'm an only child, and I've lived in Rochester all of my life. I married at eighteen and it ended after seven years.

And he told me his five sisters all reside in Detroit as well as both of his parents. Two sisters are older, and both are married and each has one child. The other three are younger and still in school or college. Harold is twenty eight years old and the third child. He's never been married and has no children.

He attended Temple University where he graduated with an Engineering Degree, which also explains his love of Philly Cheese Steaks. Of course, I was impressed and a little bit intimidated as well. With no degree, I wonder what he really thinks of me. But like Annette said, just enjoy the ride.

He slid over next to me and said, "I brought your book. This time we'll actually look in it, that is, if you want to."

I leaned over and kissed him on the lips. I said, "I'll make a deal with you. I'll study the book in my private time, and you and I can do what comes naturally. How's that?"

He got up and pulled me into his arms. He said, "That sounds *very* good to me. But will you promise me you'll read it?"

I shook my head yes. We turned the lights off and locked up, and proceeded into my room where I took another flight to that place where only lovers go. I'm pretty sure he went there too.

Chapter Four

The phone was ringing as I was walking in the door. I asked Marcus to grab it since I had both hands full. He said, "Mommy, its Aunt Annette."

I picked the phone up and said, "Hey Girl, what's up?"

"Hey Licia. Not too much. Tony is trying to be romantic and is planning an intimate dinner party for eight for Valentine's Day. Girl, you know that ain't my type of party at all! Anyhow, isn't it time you brought Harold out of the damn closet? I can't believe you're still hiding that man."

I laughed and said, "Nette, you know you're wrong for that! I am *not* hiding Harold in the closet. I just haven't introduced him to *your* family. My family has met him."

"Well, Carla and I are highly offended we haven't met him. I thought we were dogs! What's up with that!?"

"The truth is, I really like him and I know how adamant you were that I shouldn't fall for him, but I have. I didn't want you to look at me like I'm a fool or something."

"Girl, please. Ain't nothing wrong with that as long as he feels the same way. Besides, I said that because you were so vulnerable then, and I didn't want you getting hurt or used. Understand?"

"Yes, and I appreciate that. So, are you inviting us to your party? Are Carla and Earl coming?"

"Yes to both questions. But there is one other couple coming. Todd is coming with a date."

My mouth was suddenly dry and my mind was spinning. I heard her call my name.

She laughed and said, "You knew it had to happen eventually, right?"

"Nette, I don't think I'm ready for that. I mean, if Todd wasn't coming, I would come. But I'm not feeling an intimate dinner with him and some chick all up in my face."

"Licia, calm down. The last thing I want is to cause WW3 up in here. You know Tony and Todd are close, and Tony wants him here. He also knows that you and I are like sisters and that I want you here. It's not like you and Todd are enemies. You get along great. And besides, you need to meet Miss Thang if she's his woman, because she'll be around your boys."

Of course, she's right. But I also don't want to put Harold in that situation. He'll be so uncomfortable. So I said, "Annette, let me get back to you. I need to talk this over with Harold."

She said okay and we hung up. I told Marcus to put the food away and I went into my room to undress and unwind. Todd Jr. was at his basketball game and his dad was there and would bring him home, so I was taking this time to relax, or so I thought.

Marcus came running into my room five minutes later saying, "Mommy, there's somebody at the door. Can I open it?"

"No, Marcus. I told you not to ever answer the door unless I ask you to. Just wait for Mommy to get some clothes on and I'll get it."

I threw my robe on and looked out. No one was there. I asked, "Did someone knock or ring the bell?"

"No, but I saw the man in the brown truck and the brown clothes come up when I was looking out the window, and he put a box in front of the door."

I opened the door and got the box. He said, "Wow Mom, what is it? Is it for me or for you?"

I laughed at his excitement. It was addressed to me and from some lingerie company. I told Marcus it was for work. I didn't want to open it in front of my son because I assumed it was from Harold and was something sexy. I told him to watch TV while I went in my room to rest.

I closed the door and opened the box. And just as I suspected, it was a beautiful cream colored nightie with a pair of crotch-less panties to match. I thought the color was a little boring, but the nightie itself was very pretty.

I reached for the phone to call Harold to thank him, but I decided to wait until I saw him tomorrow and wear it for him. Valentine's Day was a week away, and I decided I'd find something special I'd wear then. I tried it on and it fit perfectly. I put it away and lay back down to rest. I had a lot to think about after that conversation with Annette.

The sound of the doorbell woke me. I was scrambling trying to get my shirt on when Marcus said, "Mommy, its Daddy and Todd at the door. Can I open it?"

"Marcus are you sure it's them?"

"Yes 'cause I can see them in the window."

"Go ahead and open it then."

A few minutes later I came out, and Todd and his father were in the kitchen getting something to drink. I asked, "How was the game?"

They both spoke at the same time. I laughed and said, "One at a time."

Todd Jr. said, "Mom, it was great! The game was tied and I saw where Billy was wide open. So when I got the ball, I passed it to him and he laid it up with four seconds left in the game. We beat the first place team!"

His father nodded and said, "Licia, it was just like he said. Todd made the pass of the century! It was great!"

I congratulated him and patted him on the back. I then asked Todd if he had a minute to speak with me. We went into my room for privacy. I said, "Todd, I got a call today from Annette and, well, it's a little embarrassing but I need to ask you a personal question. Is that okay?"

"Yeah, what's wrong?"

He came toward me and I backed up. He asked, "What's the matter Licia? Is something wrong?"

"Todd, nothing's wrong. It's just that Annette said you're planning to attend their dinner party next weekend, and I was also invited."

I watched him for some sort of reaction, but there was none. I waited a while longer and he asked, "What about it Licia? What, you wanna know about Gina? I mean, I assumed my nosey ass sister and cousin already told you about Gina, right?"

"Actually no, they didn't. I guess they figured I was too busy with my own shit to be concerned with your flavor of the month."

He laughed and said, "Okay Licia, let's get something straight. Gina and I have been dating for months now. It's not what you think, okay?"

"Todd, what I think really isn't important. The reason I'm mentioning this is because I didn't want either of us put in an uncomfortable situation unless we were both aware of what we were getting into. Understand?"

"Yeah I understand. And I appreciate the heads up, 'cause they sure didn't tell me you would be there and…."

It finally dawned on him what I was saying.

"Ain't this party for couples?"

"Yes it is. And yes, I'm bringing a date. That's what I've been trying to tell you."

He smiled and said, "Oh, okay. I didn't know you were dating, but yeah, I understand. That's good Licia. I mean, I'm happy for you."

"Thanks, but now you see why I wanted to tell you now instead of us acting like this and being uncomfortable all night at the party. Are we ready for this? And will uh, Gina be okay knowing your ex-wife will be there? By the way, my date's name is Harold, okay?"

"Yeah, okay. And Gina, she cool. He know I'ma be there, right?"

"No, not yet. Annette just told me and I haven't even told Harold about the party yet. But I want to go, and I think it's time for me to grow up and, as Annette says, take Harold out of the closet."

"How long you been seeing him?"

"About six weeks."

"Have the boys met him yet?"

"No they haven't. No one has except my parents. But I plan to introduce him to the boys Friday. We're all going bowling and to dinner."

We both stood there looking at one another, I'm sure wondering how our lives had come to this. Eventually he said, "Well I guess I better get going. And I'll see you next week at Annette's."

"Yep, sounds like a plan."

As he left my room, he looked at me as if he knew I wasn't sleeping with this guy. I asked, "Why you looking at me like that?"

As he entered the living room he looked again and chuckled. He said,

"I ain't looking at you no kind a way Licia. Just surprised, that's all. I didn't think you'd start dating so soon."

Todd Jr. heard him and said, "Daddy, Mommy's not dating nobody. Why you say that?"

Our son stood up with his chest out like he was the man, and wanted his father to be clear that ain't no man been up in here.

When Todd left out, I went behind him, following him to his car. I asked, "Todd did you think I would sit around and be an old maid?"

"No Licia. I guess it just didn't dawn on me one way or the other. I guess no matter when it happened it would have surprised me. Although at Christmas, when my mother asked you why you looked so good, that was the reason."

"Todd, I thought you and I would be together forever. But when you preferred other women over me, it destroyed us."

"Licia that was never the case. It was just sex and I guess I wasn't mature enough to handle it. I'll always love you and I appreciate how well you're raising our sons. I just hope we both find the best life has to offer."

I instinctively put my arms around him and said, "Todd, it means the world to me to hear you say that, and I'll always love you too. And I also hope that life is kind to you."

We parted and I walked away holding back tears. He got in his car and I went back inside. I asked the boys to give me some quiet time and I went into my room. Once again, I grieved my failed marriage.

Friday was a busy, busy day. After work I had to get home, get the boys situated and sit them down to drop this bomb on them that Mommy and a friend would be taking them out for bowling and dinner. And then they'd be spending the night with Aunt Carla and their cousins.

So we had to pack their things, get them cleaned up and I also had to get myself prepared for my intimate evening with Harold and the new nightie. I intended to show him my complete appreciation for the gift.

Sex with Harold continued to get better. I was sure I'd fallen in love with him. We had so much in common and loved to do new and different things together.

I spoke to Annette the next day, and I told her that Harold and I would be attending the dinner party. Harold agreed to go but I still hadn't told him that Todd would be there. I planned to tell him face to face.

When the boys and I were leaving to meet Harold, we noticed another package at the door. I didn't have time to open it, but it was addressed the same as the other one, so I put it inside the living room, and we left. Harold's thoughtfulness was touching, but I needed to insist that he cool it with the gifts.

We'd successfully avoided drawing attention to ourselves at work and as far as we knew, no one suspected we were dating. I felt we were going too fast but I loved the attention he gave me and I was enjoying this different way of having a man.

It's not at all like my marriage was. Todd rarely took me anywhere unless it was some family thing. He had no interest in the arts or cultural things. He was not politically minded nor was he at all interested in things to do with enhancing our sex life. *His* yes, but not ours. Yet Harold was all of that.

When we finished our meal, Marcus asked the question I'd been dreading. He asked, "Mr. Benson, are you my mommy's boyfriend?"

He giggled behind his hand and poked Todd Jr. in the ribs. Todd was not at all amused by any of it. In fact, although always polite, he did not appear to be having a good time at all. Todd spoke up and said, "Marcus, stop asking stupid questions! Mommy doesn't have a boyfriend. She already told us that Mr. Benson is her friend from work, just like Miss Trina is her friend from work, understand?"

Harold said, "Todd, you're right. I'm not your mom's boyfriend. But we're very good friends and we'll be seeing a lot of each other. And if it's okay with your mother, I would like for you guys to call me Harold."

He looked at me and asked, "Is that okay with you Felicia?"

I thought about that and said, "Actually, I think Mr. Harold would be more appropriate. They're too young to address adults by their first name."

Harold asked, "So, how old are you Todd?"

Todd sat up and said, "I'll be seven this year and Marcus…"

Marcus cut him off and said, "Mr. Benson, I'll be five in June! I go to preschool and my mom said I'm very smart!"

Harold smiled and said, "Yes Marcus, I can see how smart both you and Todd are."

I was enjoying this little conversation and Todd seemed to be warming up to Harold, slowly but surely.

After dropping the boys off at Carla's, I thought about a lot of things on the way over to Harold's. I realized how much I'd changed in these weeks after meeting him. A lot. There I was, totally prepared for a night of unbridled sex with him. I *never* went through this with Todd. A shower and something sweet smelling was about the extent of it.

But for Harold, it was a bubble bath and total exfoliation. Hair removal and products that both smell and taste good, because he was capable of inserting any part of my body in his mouth. We were capable of using three condoms on any given night. I never knew one could enjoy the human body so much. What was I going to do with him, like Carla asked me?

After having a couple of margaritas, and discussing the impending dinner party next weekend, I told Harold I had a surprise for him. I went into his room and lit eight candles and put on the new nightie. When I went back into the living room, he was very pleased. He was all over me and said, "You look so sexy Babe. Did you buy it just for me?"

"Stop playing Harold. You know you sent this to me."

He looked puzzled and said, "I assure you it wasn't from me. I wish I could take credit for it, but I can't."

I stepped back and looked him square in his face. He was very serious. He also stepped back. I said, "Honey, if you didn't send this nightie to me, then who did? There was no card or anything identifying who sent it."

Then I remembered the other box. I said, "Oh my God Harold. On our way out earlier, the kids and I noticed another box and put it in the house. I never opened it but noticed it was from the same lingerie company. It must be some computer glitch and I'm getting someone else's packages. I'll have to call them tomorrow and find out."

"They'll probably expect you to send the other one back. But this one is going to get plenty of use tonight."

He embraced me, but something in his touch was tentative. I stepped out of his arms and said, "You don't believe me, do you?"

"Yes Felicia, I believe you. I don't usually believe in coincidences, but I'm sure you're right and this is just an error. Was the package addressed to you?"

"As a matter of fact it was. Which is strange, I admit that. But if you didn't send it, I can't imagine who did. I assure you I'm not seeing anyone else, nor do I even have the time, energy or desire to. It's important to me that you believe that."

He embraced me again and said in my ear, "I told you I believe you"

He gently removed the straps of the nightie and exposed my breasts. He held my hands and guided me over to the sofa where he sat me onto his lap. As he began to taste and nibble on my nipples, that old familiar stirring began in that place that makes me a woman.

I raised my breasts up to him, begging for more. He liked it and asked me to rub and pinch one nipple while he sucked on the other. It was very exciting as he watched me, and I felt him harden underneath me.

He put his finger in my mouth, and I licked and sucked it the way he likes it. He removed his finger and replaced his hand with mine on my breast. He raised my breast up and asked me to lick it. I was leery at first, but wanted nothing more than to make him happy.

So I bent my head down and for the first time, tasted my own nipple. It was like a bolt of electricity went through me. He said, "Suck it baby. It's extremely exciting for a man to see a woman pleasure herself."

As I began to suck my breast, he reached for my other hand and put it between my legs. He began to stroke me with my own hand and then said, "Go ahead, you do it."

It was weird and shameful, but it felt good, so I did as instructed. He laid back and watched me. Eventually, my shame overwhelmed me and I stopped. He kissed me on my neck and asked, "What's wrong Babe? It's supposed to feel good, don't be ashamed about that. Or are you uncomfortable with me watching you?"

I didn't respond, so he said, "I guess that's something else you've never done. Am I right?"

I just shook my head the way I do when he embarrasses me. He said, "It's natural for most people and now you know that it feels good, right?"

"Yes, but I did it to please you. I wouldn't do that without you."

"Okay Babe. I won't embarrass you anymore."

He leaned forward and kissed my neck again, and I cradled his head in my arms and enjoyed every minute of it. I was so hot for him that I reached down between us and tried to pry his hardness out of his pants. Instead of making me wait like he usually does, he released himself and positioned me right over him.

As I welcomed him inside of me, I contracted around his hardness and knew I'd be quick. It was so explosive and so powerful, that my eyes watered. He had to hold me up because I thought I was going to fall over backwards.

I came for what seemed an eternity. The tears escaped and fell down my cheeks. Neither he nor I knew what to do with me. I let out a sob and said softly, "I can't believe I've missed out on this all of my life."

He held me so tight. He said, "I can't either. I've never experienced anything like what you and I have."

We finally made it to the bedroom, where the candles were going strong. I said, "I forgot about the candles. But it smells so good in here."

"Yes it does. Thanks Babe."

"You're welcome Hun. How do you like this?"

I removed the nightie and panties and stood before him naked. I'd never done that before. I turned around and let him see all of me. He sat on the bed and appeared to be mesmerized. I asked, "You like?"

With his index finger, he motioned for me to come to him. I said, "Not until you answer me."

"Oh, I like it! But I can show you better than I can tell you."

When I reached him, he put his hands around my face and said, "Felicia, I have to admit something to you. I've been in love with you ever since I stood in your bedroom, and you asked me to leave. Although you have children and were married for years, I feel as though I've been handed a virgin. And never have I known a woman with your sweetness and loving kindness."

My eyes watered again and I said, "Oh Honey, I don't know what to say. I'm certain that I love you too, but I kept thinking it was too soon and I was just imagining it."

He pulled me on top of him and kissed me so deep and so passionately,

I could literally feel the love in his kiss. He eventually rolled me over and said, "Please don't move."

He got up, undressed and watched me watch him. He said, "Don't turn away. Please don't turn away from me. I want you to look at me like I looked at you."

I continued to watch him until he was completely nude and then I motioned for him to come to me like he did. He said, "Oh no, not until you tell me if you like it. Ha-ha."

"Yes, my dear. I like it a lot. Now come over here and I'll show you."

When he got on the bed, he laid me down and introduced me to sixty nine. I didn't think it was a real thing. He lay on his side and I did too. I didn't like it as much as other things Harold taught me, but he seemed to like it. Soon, he turned me over and entered me from behind.

He seemed different. We were both enjoying it so much more than usual. His intense passion caused me to scream like I've done since the first time we made love. I was never a screamer before. He slowed and ground into me sweetly, bringing me down, but not taking away even one ounce of pleasure.

He asked if I was okay, and I said yes. He turned me on my back and wasted no time in reentering me and was soon on his way to his own release. I love when he comes.

It seems he's pouring his everything into me, and with his declaration of love earlier, it seemed more thrilling for him than ever before. We laid there a long time. I was cradled in his arms and laying with my head on his heart. And as it slowed to a normal beat, I began to drift to sleep.

When I woke up, I was still in his arms. I had to go potty, so I eased myself out of his embrace and hurried to the bathroom. That's when I realized what we'd done, or should I say, failed to do. We forgot to use a condom.

How did we manage to forget such a thing? I went back into the bedroom and he was looking at me. I realized I was naked, and began to feel self-conscious. I quickly crawled under the covers and said, "Harold, we forgot to use a condom."

He hesitated a moment and said, "Damn. That's why it was better than ever. Umm-umm, I thought you'd put some kind of spell on me Woman! Wow, so that's what I have to look forward to the rest of my life?"

"Harold this is serious! What if I'm pregnant? How can you be so casual about this? I have no intention of having any more children."

He didn't respond. I asked, "Harold, did you hear me?"

He got up and went into the bathroom. I sat there wondering what the hell was wrong with him.

When he came back, I opened my mouth to speak, but he held up his hand and said, "Listen Felicia. I realize you have two children and you're probably not interested in, or have even considered having any more children. But if we get married, do you mean to tell me you won't bless me with just one child? Just one and I assure you I have no preference of a male or a female. Before I met you, having children wasn't important to me. But… since falling in love with you, well…it's important now because *you* would be their mother."

I was so stunned and dumbfounded, my ears were ringing. *Married! Children! Was he crazy? Oh hell no! No more babies for me!*

I sat up and said, "Please Hun, let's just go to sleep and talk about this in the morning! Please Harold, I don't want to fight with you. In all this time, we've always been reasonable with each other so please, let's not fight. Okay?"

He seemed reluctant, but got in bed and laid there looking at the ceiling. I laid my head on his chest, yet he made no move to even touch me. After a long silence he said quietly, "I assumed we were so perfect for each other. It was unimaginable that Heaven had opened up and gave you to me. It never dawned on me that you would deny me children."

I began to rub his chest and I tried to comfort him, but to no avail. He removed my hand and turned over and looked at me. He asked, "Felicia, don't you love me? Have I been so delusional that I've totally misread you?"

"Of course I love you! How could I not! I've never known anyone as special and loving as you in my entire life! And no, you're not delusional at all. It's just that I'm so shocked you were thinking marriage and children. I'm extremely flattered, but it scares me because I've been married. I've had children. And selfishly, I could exist just like this forever with you. But realistically you deserve far better, and I realize that now."

I looked at him and tears began to form in my eyes. I said softly, "Oh my God. I'm about to lose you. I can't believe that the night we confess love for each other has become the night that I lose you."

I tried to get up, but he grabbed me. I was falling apart. He held me while I cried and I begged him to let me go. He kept saying we would work it out and for me not to upset myself further.

But the reality was right there in black and white. So even though I calmed down and relaxed in his arms, I began that lonely discussion with myself again, about what I would do without the man I loved.

Although I'd resigned myself to the fact that Harold and I were old news, the following morning we made love passionately. We said very little to each other, probably because we were trying to medicate ourselves on sex.

As I prepared to go and get my sons, he asked about visiting the next day and maybe taking us out for an early dinner. I told him I'd let him know and then I left. I later told him the boys had chores and that Sunday would be spent preparing for the school week. He said he understood, and would call me tomorrow.

Interestingly, when the boys and I got home that Saturday afternoon, there were two more boxes at my door. Both from the same lingerie company and both addressed to me. I took all three into my room and just looked at them. Then I grabbed the phone, got the number from the operator, and called the Pretty Sensations Lingerie Co.

The items were purchased by a James Saunders. They were hesitant to give me any other information, but the rep did say his billing address was in Rochester, NY.

I looked his name up in the phone book and found three of them and four J. Saunders. I considered calling them all, but then decided against it. I eventually went and fixed dinner.

Sunday evening the boys and I were watching TV when Harold called checking on me. He said he needed to talk to me, and would really like to see me tomorrow. I didn't usually hang out during the week, which he was aware of, but he was insistent and said it was extremely important. And really, the only reason I made an exception was to get the break up over with. No sense in hanging on.

While the boys were getting ready for bed, the doorbell rang. I couldn't believe he was unable to wait until tomorrow and frankly, I thought him insensitive coming this time of night, knowing I'd be busy with the boys. When I went to the door, I barely looked out the peep hole when I saw that it wasn't Harold. So I looked again and it was a strange man. I asked, "May I help you?"

"I'm your neighbor from downstairs, and I have a sick little girl. I apologize for the time, but since you also have children, I thought maybe you would have something for chest congestion, like Vicks to rub on her chest or something."

My hesitation was very brief. I opened the door, and there standing in front of me had to be the finest man I'd ever seen. Pecan complexion, short brush cut, at least six feet tall, the sweetest mustache and dimples everywhere it seemed! He said, "I swear, if Aysia wasn't so sick, I wouldn't bother you. I was afraid to take her out in this weather, and wouldn't dare leave her. Even now, I'm not comfortable. She dosed off...."

"Don't worry about it. I do have Vicks. Let me grab it. Come on in."

"You shouldn't just invite people in you don't know. I'll wait right here, but thank you just the same."

I ran into the bathroom and got the Vicks. Then I stopped to look in the mirror to see just how bad I looked. Not as bad as it could have been, that's for sure. I ran back to the door and gave him the Vicks. He said, "Thank you so, so much! I forgot to ask you your name."

"Felicia Wilson."

"My name is Sam McElroy. It's nice to meet you Ms. Wilson. I live right under you, Aysia and me. And since I'd seen your boys around, I thought of you. She had a touch of asthma when she was younger, so I get nervous when she catches a cold."

"No need for explanations. And please, call me Felicia. Go and take care of her, and if I can do anything to help, please don't hesitate to ask, uh, Sam, right?"

He smiled that brilliant smile and said, "Right! And if you ever need anything, a cup of sugar or whatever, I hope you won't hesitate either."

"I appreciate that Sam. Take care and I hope Aysia is better soon."

He was walking away and said, "Thank you so much. I hope so too."

And just like that, Mr. Fine Ass Sam was down the stairs and gone.

Chapter five

When I knocked on Harold's door the next day, I was so sad. I tried all day willing myself not to cry. I really loved Harold, and losing him so soon didn't seem fair. He opened the door and said, "Come on in. I'm cooking shrimp and pasta, and I don't want to ruin it. I'll be right with you."

I walked into his apartment as he ran into the kitchen. He removed the angel hair pasta from the stove and took it over to the sink. He began draining it, while smiling at me lovingly, indicating that it was perfect.

I began to feel bad for disappointing him. He always catered to me and I believed he really loved me. I hadn't given it much thought since he brought it up the other night, but he deserved at least that much.

So as he was preparing the veggies, I began to think about being his wife and trying to see another child in my arms. All I could see was diapers, breast pumps, loads of laundry, nine months of pure hell, labor pains, terrible twos, and on and on and on.

I could not for the life of me imagine doing that again. No way in hell! I got up and said, "Harold, I think my coming here has been a mistake. Let's talk tomorrow on the phone, and we can bring closure that way. This is too painful for me."

I ran for the door and so did he, almost colliding into me. He said, "Felicia, I was wrong and I'm sorry. Please don't punish me for being so eager! I moved too fast and…"

He grabbed me and held me with all of his might. He was heartbroken! Absolutely heartbroken, and I'd managed to do this to him in the course of one night! I said, "Harold, you must admit that you deserve better than me. You should have someone willing to give you all of the children you want and I'm just not her. I love you more than I've ever loved any man, including the one I married, and it's for that reason that I want to see you happy. I'll never forgive myself for hurting you like this."

"Felicia it's my fault for coming on too strong and too fast. I scared the hell out of you, I realize that now."

We went back into the living room and sat down. He said, "Felicia, can we just talk about something else and enjoy our dinner? How much time do we have?"

"Todd agreed to get the boys and keep them overnight."

He reached over and held both of my hands. He looked down at them and said, "I don't want to lose you over this. I feel confident we can work through it, I really do."

"Harold. I'm afraid that two or three years from now, I'll look into your eyes and know you're yearning for a child and possibly even bitter over it. That would kill me."

"Felicia. Let's not talk about it for a while. Can we agree to do that?"

He looked at me with those puppy dog eyes and I was sad for him. I knew we were putting off the inevitable, but I agreed. We enjoyed our meal, and had light, but strained small talk.

When it was time to leave, I knew there would be drama but I also knew the sooner I made my exit, the sooner it would be over. So I said, "Harold, I really should get home. I've got tons of laundry I neglected this weekend and I have the perfect opportunity to knock it out. Let's talk tomorrow and maybe plan to meet for lunch. Are you free tomorrow?"

"Sure, I'd like that. Let me walk you out."

I was surprised but relieved. He was helping me put my coat on and pressed his body against mine. His breath on my neck and his tongue on my ear lobe made my head spin. He was so hard that my immediate response was to reach behind me and touch it. But somehow I gathered my wits about me and said, "I really should go. I'm sorry, but I can't...."

His tongue was now in my ear and his free hand was rubbing my sweet spot and I was losing control. But I managed to step away from him. He said, "I hoped you'd at least be responsive to that. What's happened Felicia?"

"You know I love it when you touch me. I just need to get home."

He put his hands up and walked into his bedroom. I stood there trying to figure out what to do for him. After a few minutes, I laid my coat down and walked into his room. He was walking out of his master bathroom with nothing but his shorts on.

I sat on his bed and motioned for him to come over to me. He ignored me and began lighting the candles that were still in his room. I said, "Honey, please come over here. I have something for you."

After lighting all of the candles and still not saying anything, he walked toward me. I said, "Come closer. My goodness, I've never had to deal with you mad at me."

"I'm not mad at you. I'm mad at myself for being so stupid."

"If it's any consolation, I would be your wife in a NY minute! I'd marry you tomorrow if that was all you wanted or needed from me. So bring your ass over here and see what I have for you!"

He smiled and walked over to me, and without warning jumped on the bed and began to tickle me. I screamed and begged him to stop. We laughed lovingly with each other. He touched my face and seemed better.

I sat up and he got off of the bed. I stopped him before he could walk away. I began to massage his thighs and then I grabbed those cheeks. I leaned forward and kissed him through his shorts. I reached inside and got what I was looking for.

He moaned in anticipation, and I rubbed it against my face and kissed it. I looked up at him and asked, "What would you like me to do with this thing? Should I put it back or should I, should I…?"

He reached down and cupped my face and asked, "Are you trying to kill me Felicia? How much do you think I can take in one day?"

I leaned forward and put it in my mouth and began to love him just the way he liked it. I reached for those butt cheeks again and brought him closer and deeper. He made love to my mouth so good. And then he stopped. As usual. I asked, "Why do you do that?"

He began disrobing me but kept my bra and panties on. He said, "You're so sexy in your undies."

"You never answer me when I ask you that question. I think you're enjoying it, and then you stop me as if I've done something wrong. Why?"

"I love your naiveté. It's warmed my heart since the day I met you. Do you know the difference between giving head and a blow job?"

"No, is there a difference?"

"Yes, there is. What you do is give me head. A blow job completes the task. Meaning, you would continue until I climax. Some people prefer head and some prefer bj's. Do you understand?"

"I think so. Which do you prefer?"

He laughed and said, "Babe it doesn't matter to me. Whatever you're comfortable with, okay?"

"I've never experienced a bj, so how can I have a preference? You never let it happen. And I read in the book you gave me that some women enjoy it as much as their partner."

"I can't believe it! You've actually read the book?"

"Most of it, yes."

He caressed my breasts through my bra and said, "You have the loveliest body I've ever seen."

He buried his face between my breasts. He removed my bra and began to feast on me. I began to wonder how many women this man has had because he was an expert at love making. Or was it because I had so little to compare him to? My whole body was on fire.

When he finally removed himself from my chest and moved further south, I thought that would certainly take me outta here. He began kissing me with my panties still on. It drove me nuts! I squirmed away and said, "Harold, I can't take that."

He smiled and removed his shorts. He was so hard. He removed my panties and crawled between my legs, and was just about to put it in when I stopped him. I knew it would be a downer, but I said, "Honey…we can't forget the condom."

He stiffened and collapsed right on top of me. I said, "Honey I'm sorry. But…"

He put his hand up, got the condom and put it on. He got on top of me, kissed my neck and whispered in my ear, "I love you so much. Get up and let me watch you."

He pulled me up and sat me in a straddling position facing him. He said, "Come on Babe. Sit up here and show me how good it is."

I sat on his hardness and slowly took each inch. It was so good. The more I took, the more I realized he was gonna get his wish quickly. As I began my love dance on top of him, he again went to my breasts. He pulled me closer and whispered, "I can feel you throbbing all around me. I know you're gonna give me what I want soon."

As the stars in my mind began to burst and explode, body and mind separated, and I only knew that his arms around me were all that kept me from falling yet again.

At ten thirty he woke me up. He likes to wake me up by snuggling up against my neck. He said, "As much as I would love to have you all night, I know you'll be upset in the morning without clothes and stuff to prepare for work."

"Have you used any vacation or sick time this year yet?"

"No I haven't, have you?"

"No, I haven't either."

He looked at me and I looked at him and we both relaxed and slept the rest of the night.

I made it home around one o'clock the next afternoon. I was greeted with another box. This one was bigger than the others. I tried to remember what day I called them because I shouldn't be receiving any more.

By the time I put a load of clothes in the washer and poured myself a glass of wine, my doorbell rang. I couldn't imagine who it could be. I peeked out of the window and saw Sam.

I opened the door and he was standing there with a container of Vicks and that notorious smile. Damn, this brother is fine. I said, "Hi Sam. How is Aysia?"

"She's much better, thank you! I saw you come in and wanted to bring you this Vicks I picked up for you. I used all of yours and it was a God send. I really appreciate your kindness the other night."

"Don't mention it. It was my pleasure to help a neighbor."

We both seemed at a loss for words, but neither of us seemed ready to end the exchange. So I said, "I just poured myself a glass of wine. Do you care to join me?"

I couldn't believe I did that. *Little ole Licia, inviting a virtual stranger into her home, just cause he so fine! Ha-ha.* He smiled and said, "I would love to Felicia, but only if you let me bring the wine. I have a friend stationed in France, and he sends me a wonderful selection and lots of it. Would you like to try some?"

"Do you have any white wine?"

"Absolutely! I'll bring you a few different ones to try. How's that?"

"Sure, that sounds great! When you get back, just come on in. I'll leave the door unlocked for you."

He said okay and went running down the stairs. I turned and checked my apartment, making sure everything was in place. Then I checked to make sure *I* was in place.

After about ten minutes, he knocked and walked in. I was standing in the kitchen trying to figure out which glasses to use for authentic French wine. I told him to make himself at home. He said, "Nice place. How many bedrooms?"

"Just two. I'm hoping to buy something small within a year or so. What about you?"

"We also have a two bedroom. After Antoinette died, that's my late wife, Aysia and I decided we didn't want to live in the house anymore. So, I'm renting it with the hopes of selling it soon. Then I'll probably buy something else or relocate."

I walked into the living room and he was sitting comfortably on the sofa. On the coffee table, there was four bottles of wine. Three white and one red. I said, "Sam, I'm awfully sorry to hear about your loss. It must have been devastating."

He sat up and said, "Felicia, I didn't think I would survive it. And to have a then five year old daughter looking at me for everything, it was more than any person should have to endure. But here I am, eighteen months later, and although not completely back together, life has finally settled into some type of normalcy. Aysia now seven continues to miss and need her mother, but I'm blessed to have a couple of sisters and with Antoinette's sister, Aysia's aunts really are there for her."

He picked up the corkscrew and a bottle of wine and said, "This is one of my favorite white wines. If you don't like it, we can try another."

I looked at his hands and saw how large and masculine they were. I watched them as he opened the bottle with ease. I was impressed at how well groomed they were, and almost became hypnotized watching the man. I wanted to ask more about his wife, but decided I'd wait for another opportunity.

After pouring the wine, he handed me a glass and said, "Here's to children, and how they sometimes cause us to meet the nicest people!"

We tapped our glasses together and drank with our eyes glued to each other. He asked, "Well?"

I swirled the wine around in my mouth and swallowed it. It was fabulous! I said, "Oh my God! Sam, this wine is wonderful! I'm sure it's very expensive."

"Yeah, it is. But as long as Gary's in France, we're good."

We both laughed and took another sip. I shared with him that I'd been divorced for over a year now. I asked if he thought he'd ever marry again. He said, "Probably not anytime soon. I think as long as Aysia has her aunts, I'll keep her life as simple as I can."

We chatted a little longer and he said, "Well, I guess I better get back downstairs. I have to be at work at four o'clock."

"Where do you work?"

"At Bausch & Lomb. I've been there twelve years now. Where do you work?"

"I've been at IBM for almost six years."

He smiled and said, "I've really enjoyed getting to know you Felicia. I hope we can do this again sometime."

"I enjoyed it too. And thanks for the wine. Maybe on weekends, the kids can do something together."

"I'd really like that because Aysia and I have run out of things to do and places to go. You want to exchange phone numbers?"

"Yes, I guess we should."

I went over to my desk and got a pad and pen and we both wrote down our numbers. We said our goodbyes and he was gone. I knew it was wrong, but I couldn't help wondering what he was like in bed.

Harold was very attentive the next couple of days. Even though we agreed we wouldn't see each other during the week and would remain aloof at work, he was sending flowers and coming by my desk.

Thursday evening during a phone conversation, I reminded him of the dinner party on Saturday. He said, "I'm looking forward to meeting your friends. But I would like to see you earlier to give you your gift. Is that possible?"

"I don't think we should exchange gifts Harold. I think we should be more realistic about this and just exchanged cards."

"First of all, I already have your gift and I want you to have it. Secondly, Valentine's Day is for lovers, and you are the only person in my life that qualifies. Why are you so pessimistic? I remember you saying you'd marry me in a heartbeat. Was that just talk or do you really love me?"

"I love you with all my heart. But the reality is I've accepted the fact that we want different things."

He was quiet for a while and asked, "Do you actually believe I would let you go because of that? I admit I was disappointed, but I'm not willing to forfeit our relationship over it. Are you?"

I didn't answer his question.

I asked, "What time do you want to come over Saturday? The party starts at six o'clock."

"How about five fifteen? Is that okay?"

"Yep, that sounds good."

The doorbell rang. Todd Jr. went toward the door and Harold asked, "Was that your doorbell?"

"Yeah, can you hold on a second? Todd, do not touch that door!"

I heard Harold saying something on the phone. I picked it back up and he was saying "Felicia be careful. It's late!"

I said, "Let me call you back Harold. I need to see who this is."

"Felicia, call me back or I'll be over there."

"Okay, I promise."

I hung up and went to the door. By then whoever it was rang the doorbell again. I looked out and saw Carla. I opened the door and Annette was coming behind her. I asked, "What are you doing out this time of night? Is something wrong?"

Carla said, "Dang, it's only eight thirty. You call this late?"

She and Annette came in and I told the boys to get ready for bed. They said their hellos to their aunts and left. I asked if they wanted something to drink and they both declined. I asked, "Okay, what's up? You both know you're not out like this normally. And now neither of you wants a drink. I know something's up."

Annette fell out laughing and Carla had that *I'm clueless* look on her face. Finally Annette said, "Girl, guess what?"

I looked at Carla and she was now looking at the ceiling. I turned back to Annette and she said, "Guess who's having an affair?"

My eyes got big and I looked harder at Annette. Carla hadn't changed her stance. I asked, "Are you gonna tell me or what?"

When I looked at Annette again, she moved her head toward Carla. I looked at Annette with my eyes popping out of my head trying to get the correct understanding. Again, she motioned toward Carla. I said, "Uh-uh. No way. Carla, would you please tell me that Annette is crazy? And if not, you better tell me every freakin detail, you tramp!"

They both fell out laughing and I stood there with hands on hips, waiting to hear what the hell had gotten into Carla, besides some man's penis, obviously. Carla finally said, "Come over here because I don't want the boys to hear me."

I raised my finger at them, motioning for them to wait a minute, and I went into the boys' room. One was knocked out and the other one was sitting up with the TV on. I told Marcus to turn that TV off and to go to sleep. I closed their door and went back into the living room.

The girls were in the kitchen pouring wine and there was another knock at the door. I said, "Oh shit, I forgot to call Harold back and he probably thinks someone has murdered us!"

I ran to the door and he stepped in looking like a worried parent. Annette and Carla stood there looking at him while he berated me for not calling him back. I said, "Harold, I'd like you to meet my sisters Carla and Annette. Guys, this is Harold. My new Daddy."

They laughed and walked over to him and shook his hand. He was also laughing and said, "I'm pleased to finally meet both you. I've heard a lot about you. I do wish it could've been under better circumstances."

Annette said, "We were anxious about meeting you on Saturday, but today is good too."

Carla laughed and said, "We've also heard a lot about you, and the pleasure is all ours."

I said, "Hun, would you like a glass of wine?"

"No thanks Babe. I'm gonna go on home. Call me tomorrow."

I walked him to the door. He turned and kissed me on the cheek and whispered, "I like them. They're funny."

I kissed him back and said, "They're my girls!"

I turned and they were looking at me. Carla said, "Girl that man is fine. You didn't tell us he looked like that."

Annette said, "Um-hum. That's why her ass was hiding him. Didn't want nobody to know she was rockin' like *that*! Damn Licia, I ain't mad atcha!"

I smiled and waved them off. His looks had nothing to do with how I felt about him. I said, "Let's not get off track. Dish Carla!"

She said, "Girl, you won't believe what happened to me! The father of one of my students hit on me."

I crossed my arms and said, "And?"

She threw her hands up and said, "I don't know how it happened. One minute he was pissed as hell, and the next he was sending me flowers and asking me out for coffee. I met him and he asked if he could spend some time with me."

I looked at Annette and then at Carla.

I asked, "Why would you do something like that?"

"I was so excited that another man showed that much interest in me. He told me I was pretty and sexy, and…well, Earl never does. Then he invited me to a hotel room. I wasn't gonna go, but I was intrigued Licia."

I put my hand over my mouth and she continued.

"I walked in the hotel room fully intending to tell him this is wrong and definitely not something I've ever done. But he kissed me. It was so intense that I began to kiss him back. And that man was so passionate and was so into me that I just about lost my mind that day. His first name is Carlton, do you believe that? We almost have the same damn name! I've met him two more times and each time he gave me a piece of diamond jewelry."

On her wrist was a simple but pretty bracelet and on her neck was a charm. Annette hollered and I was speechless. Annette said, "Damn. Ya'll gettin' more play than me!"

I said, "I can't believe this. You better be careful Carla."

"I can't believe it either. He's so sweet and I really like him. What am I gonna do?"

Annette said, "Like I told Licia. Fuck him!"

Friday was a busy day. I got out of work at one o'clock so I could pick up my dress and shoes, get a manicure and pedicure, and get the boys home and settled.

When we got home, again there was another box. I had completely forgotten about those damn boxes. There must be six of them now. I *must* send them back on Monday, I thought.

I ran in the kitchen and threw together a big pot of spaghetti. I wanted it to last all weekend. Then I went and got the boy's clothes together for the entire weekend.

It was a mild day, so the boys went out to play. They soon came back in and Sam and Aysia followed them in. Todd said, "Mom, someone is here to see you."

I came out of the kitchen and saw them. Aysia was absolutely beautiful, and truly delightful. I said, "Hello Aysia, how are you?"

"I'm fine, thank you! How are you Mrs. Wilson?"

I leaned back and looked at this seven year old and said, "I'm very well, thank you!"

I looked at her father and said, "Hi Sam! Come on in and have a seat."

"I think the kids want to go back outside. Is that right Guys?"

They all said yes. He said, "Aysia. Stay with the boys, okay?"

"Yes Daddy, I will!"

And I said, "Guys, you all stay together, you understand?"

They said, "Yes Mom. Come on Aysia!"

And out they ran. Sam sat and said, "I hope I haven't interrupted you Felicia. And whatchu cooking in there Girl? It's smelling good up in here!"

"A big pot of spaghetti so I won't have to cook this weekend."

"Sounds like you have a big date for Valentine's Day. You have plans?"

I laughed and said, "I'm going to a dinner party tomorrow evening. What are your plans?"

He sat back and said, "No plans. I haven't dated since being single again. It's not easy for me. I'm very shy with women."

I sat down and said, "Sam, I would've never thought that. You seem so outgoing and frankly…"

"What?"

I got up and said, "Nothing. I'm sorry. You want some wine? I haven't opened either of the other two bottles you brought me."

He came into the kitchen and asked, "What were you gonna say?"

I handed him the corkscrew and said, "I can't believe you aren't being trampled by women. You're so handsome and nice."

He laughed and seemed to actually blush. He said, "I do get my share of offers, but none I've been interested in. I still feel married, I guess."

We went back into the living room and he poured the wine. The kids came running in and started asking about going to McDonalds. Sam said, "I'm sorry. I promised Aysia I'd take her. Let me take your boys and that will give you a little time to do what you need to do. My treat."

"Sam, I can't let you do that. My boys are a handful."

He got up and said, "They're boys Felicia. I can handle them, believe me. We'll be back in an hour or so. I'll make a deal with you. We'll eat the spaghetti Sunday, how's that?"

"All right, it's a deal. But let me give you money for them."

I went for my purse and he and the kids were halfway out of the door. He turned and said, "We'll be back. Lock the door."

I locked the door and went into the kitchen. I saw the opened bottle of wine and quickly put a top on it and I put it in the fridge. Then I went back to the boys' room and finished packing their clothes for tomorrow night. I also packed an overnight bag for myself, assuming I would be going to Harold's after the party.

I laid across my bed and relaxed. I turned my head, looking for the remote and the six boxes caught my eye. I began thinking I should just keep them. I can't believe I'll have to haul that mess to the post office Monday. This is insane. I found the remote, turned on the TV and fell asleep.

I woke up thirty minutes later, after dreaming about Sam. I got up and went to the bathroom, unable to believe what was going through my head. In my dream, I was having sex with Sam. I kept telling myself as I entered the kitchen that it was normal because he's so handsome and people can't help who they dream about.

I put the food in the fridge and finished cleaning the kitchen. But I couldn't seem to get the visual out of my head. I picked up the phone and called Harold.

We confirmed our pick up time for tomorrow, and that's when the boys began knocking at the door. I said, "Honey, the boys are at the door. Let's talk tomorrow."

He was still on the phone when I opened the door and Aysia came in saying, "Mrs. Wilson, we had so much fun!"

"That's great Aysia! Come on in."

Harold asked, "Who's that?"

"Our little neighbor from downstairs. She and the boys were out playing. I'll talk to you later, okay?"

He said, "Okay..." And before he could say anything else, I said goodbye and hung up. Sam was approaching the door and I was afraid if he heard a man's voice, he'd hit the ceiling. I felt bad lying to him, but he would not understand some man taking the boys out.

When Sam walked in, I felt a familiar stirring in me. I couldn't believe I was having those feelings for this man when my heart was around the corner with Harold.

Even though he and I are having troubles and it seems like things won't be permanent, I still love him. Sam asked, "Felicia, did you knock out that whole bottle Girl?"

I laughed and said, "No, I'll get it. And why do you call me Girl?"

He laughed and said, "Because you keep it real and I feel like I'm with my sister or something when I'm with you."

Marcus asked, "Mom can we go in our room and play?"

"It's okay with me. Are you okay with it Sam?"

"Sure."

We finished the wine and talked about them for the most part. Then Sam reclined on the sofa and asked, "So how did you get the courage to get back in the dating game?"

I thought about how to answer that. Then I said, "Actually, I met this guy who refused to take no for an answer, and I went out with him during the holidays. We've been dating ever since."

"How personal can I get?"

I felt all the heat in my body rush to my head.

I laughed and said, "That depends."

"How long before you became intimate? I realize I'm making assumptions, so please don't be offended if that hasn't happened."

I reached for my glass and felt silly because it had been empty for five minutes. He asked, "You want me to get another bottle?"

"I have the last one in the fridge. Let me grab it."

I jumped up and almost ran into the kitchen. When I came back he said, "I think I embarrassed you and I apologize. Please don't answer that."

"Yes, you did embarrass me. But it's okay, really. I'm shy about things of the sexual nature, but I'm trying to do better."

He poured the wine and handed me my glass. Before drinking, I said, "Here's to friends!"

He nodded and we both drank and I loved it. I said, "Sam, Harold and I are intimate. It was odd for me because my husband had been my only lover. I think the anticipation is worse than the actual act."

"You know what? That's my problem too. The anticipation. How long before it happened?"

I didn't dare tell this man that he hit it on the first date, so I said, "After a few weeks and a lot of talking and going out. Is there someone in particular you're interested in?"

"Yeah, there is someone I've had my eye on for a while now. I've never approached her, so she doesn't have a clue."

I sat up and said, "That's great Sam! Where did you meet her?"

"I met her a few months ago at my sister's. Her name is Cathy and she's pretty and quiet, but personable. I think my sister is trying to set us up because now every time Cathy is there, Cynthia calls me to help her with something or asks me to bring Aysia over."

"Do you think she likes you too?"

He smiled and said, "Maybe, but she's not obvious. Just a kind smile here or a subtle look there."

"Ask your sister for her number. You'll know by her reaction if she's playing matchmaker and if Cathy likes you or not."

"I should have known to ask another woman how to do this."

"What is that supposed to mean?"

He laughed and said, "No offense Felicia. I was just remarking about how brilliant you sisters are. Either that or the brothers are just clueless!"

We both laughed and enjoyed the rest of the evening while the kids played and we talked.

By five o'clock the next evening, I was ready. I had to admit, a sister was looking good! Completely in red, with silver and diamond accessories. Well, pretend diamonds. But I was fabulous anyhow.

My doorbell rang at five-twenty and I opened the door for my man. He was quite handsome in his chocolate colored suit. He stepped in and looked at me and said, "Damn Babe! You look good enough to eat!"

He turned me around and said, "I'm not sure I want to share you tonight. You're absolutely stunning!"

"Thank you kind sir. You're quite dashing yourself! Let's have a glass of wine. The wine is cold and the glasses are chilled."

After pouring the wine he went into his breast pocket and pulled out a long box with a red ribbon on it. He said, "Happy Valentine's Day Babe."

He kissed me and I sat my glass down and took the box. I asked, "Harold, what is this?"

"We'll both know when you open it."

I unraveled the ribbon and opened the box. Inside, there was a beautiful diamond tennis bracelet, a pair of diamond studs and a diamond solitaire on a silver chain. All I thought was *he spent a month's salary on this.* I looked at him and said, "Honeee....it's beautiful! No one has ever given me anything like this before."

"This is just a sample of my love for you Felicia. When you become my wife, I'll shower you with love like this every chance I get. Nothing is too good for my baby."

He embraced me and I knew how much he really loved me. The tears came down my face and at that moment I knew there wasn't anything I wouldn't do for him.

Not because of the diamonds. But because the man in my arms would always have my best interest at heart, and would do anything for me. When he saw my tears he said, "Felicia, you're gonna ruin your make-up."

He kissed me and I began to again melt in his arms. I pulled away and said, "Excuse me while I go and freshen up."

I ran into my room, repaired my make-up and grabbed his gift. When I came out he was sitting on the sofa and motioned for me to join him. He poured the wine and was delighted to see the gift in my hand. He asked, "Is that for me?"

"Yes, but it's not as extravagant as what you gave me. Although it beats the book you gave me for Christmas!"

He laughed and opened the gift. Inside he found silk pajamas. He said, "I think we should stay here and wear only our gifts?"

"You're naughty Mr. Benson. But there's more. Look under the tissue paper."

He removed the paper and found a matching nightie for me. He took it out and said, "Um-um-um! Again I say we should stay here!"

"I'm glad you like it but it's time for us to get out of here. We don't want to be late and I certainly don't want to make a grand entrance."

At six o'clock we were walking into Annette's foyer. Tony greeted us and was exquisite in his tuxedo and tails. I kissed him and introduced Harold. Thank goodness we were the first to arrive.

He took Harold to the bar and Annette came out and she and I joined them. We were finishing our drink when the doorbell rang. I held my breath while Tony went to the door. I said to Annette, "Girl, you are wearin' that dress! Where did you get it?"

"Thanks Licia, but yours is really hot!"

She turned to Harold and said, "I'm surprised you let her out in that damn thing! She looks like a movie star up in here!"

He smiled and said, "You're right about that! She already fine, and in that dress I wanna…"

I said, "Harold!"

He laughed and embraced me just as Todd, Gina, Carla and Earl walked in. I was so embarrassed I couldn't even turn around to face them. Tony made the introductions so I composed myself, turned around and looked into the eyes of my ex-husband and Gina.

I extended my hand to her and Harold extended his. She did the same and so did Todd. Annette asked what they wanted to drink and so the evening began.

I couldn't help stealing glances in the direction of Todd and Gina. They actually made a nice couple. She is shorter than me and pretty in a natural kind of way. Curvaceous like me, but light skinned. She wore very little make-up and seemed to be vegetarian. Yes, I admit I observed everything about her. We drank and laughed and ate and drank some more.

I never noticed Todd being affectionate toward her, although I never got affection from him publicly either. Harold, on the other hand was very attentive and protective, and kept his hand on me on and off all evening.

Eventually, the girls went into the kitchen and made small talk. It had to be small because Gina was there. Annette asked Gina, "Do you have children?"

"No, I've never been married."

Carla said, "You're smart not to start a family without a husband."

She just smiled and asked, "Where is the restroom?"

Annette pointed her in the direction of the powder room and off she went. I have to admit she's very nice, a bit quiet and reserved, but I think I like her. Carla asked, "So what do you think of my next sister-in-law Licia?"

I almost screamed, "What!? Are they getting married?"

She and Annette fell out laughing and she said, "No Silly. I told Nette I was gonna drop that on you just to see your reaction."

I saw some leftover broccoli on the island and threw it at her. I decided to show off my presents. They were all ooing and ahhing over my diamonds and I was too.

Mimicking Gina, Carla whispered, "No, I've never been married. Like you can't have kids without a husband!"

We were bent over laughing. Then Carla added, "Aint nobody ask if you was ever married Heffa!"

By then we were hollering. Tony asked, "Has the party moved into the kitchen Ladies?"

Annette said, "Sorry Dear. I was showing off my newest acquisition."

"Oh yeah. The tattoo."

Taking advantage of the moment, Carla told us quickly of her latest adventure and Annette showed us hers. She unzipped her dress and there it was. A tattoo of a black butterfly on her hip. Carla and I were floored! We couldn't believe that crazy ass girl did that.

We eventually rejoined the others. Gina had already rejoined them. Todd and I, although not completely comfortable, got through the night much better than I thought we would. We laughed and shared with the rest in telling some of the funny stories of our past.

Gina smiled and seemed quite comfortable, while Harold laughed and kept his arm around me. He kissed me twice during the evening which sort of bothered me, but I played it off as best I could.

At the end of the evening, watching the other four walk out, we said our goodbyes to them and turned to our hosts. Annette, with her arm around her husband's waist said, "We really enjoyed you all. And as you clearly see, we're all adult enough to be in the same room with exes without tearing shit up."

The three of us couldn't help cracking up at crazy ass Annette. Tony said, "Harold, if you will excuse my wife, we would love to have you guys over again and possibly hang out and do other things together. And I definitely want to see this golf game you claim."

We all promised to get together soon and we left.

As February was coming to a close, we got a monster snow storm that dumped thirty four inches of snow on us over a day and a half. School was closed along with almost everything else on that cold Thursday morning.

Todd Jr. and Marcus stayed with Todd the night before, so I couldn't get my kids home and Harold was on a business trip in Houston and unable to get a flight in.

About nine thirty that morning, Sam called me to see if I needed anything. He said Aysia was with his sister and he wanted to know if the boys wanted to make a snow man.

I told him I was also alone, and we were both quiet until he said, "Well, we could polish off a bottle of wine with some breakfast."

I hesitated at first but then I said, "Why the hell not! You bring the wine and I'll fix the breakfast."

"That sounds great! I'll be there in about a half hour."

By the time I took the last salmon croquette out of the pan, the doorbell was ringing. Sam walked in bringing lots of cold air, two bottles of wine and that infamous smile. He said, "Lord, something smells good!"

"I hope you like salmon croquettes and grits. I was just about to scramble some eggs and cheese."

"I love it! My mom makes that."

After breakfast and a bottle and a half of wine, we were both lounging on the sofa watching TV and talking. I asked Sam about Cathy. He said, "She's very nice, but very religious and appears to be looking for a husband. Not that there's anything wrong with that, but it's not for me at this time."

Without thinking I said, "I know the feeling."

"What do you mean?"

"Oh nothing. Just thinking out loud."

"I'm not buying that. Come on, fess up!"

"Harold is hoping we'll get married. I would love to be his wife at some point, but he is also expecting me to give him a child and that is such a hard pill for me to swallow. I have no interest in having more children. What do I do?"

All of a sudden I became so full that I excused myself and went into my room. I stood at the dresser looking at my reflection and the tears that I could no longer contain.

After about five minutes, I realized Sam was standing behind me. He said, "Felicia, please don't cry. I'm sure you'll figure this out."

I turned around and began sobbing in his arms. He held me there a long time, assuring me these things always worked out in the end. I became intoxicated by his cologne and the tautness of his body. His hands were doing strange things to my back.

He eventually released me but then his hands moved to my face. He wiped my tears away and held my face in his hands.

The kiss was something out of a 1950's movie. Very slow, but inevitable. The taste of the wine and his essence sent my mind spiraling. But when I felt him harden, I knew I was in trouble. At that moment, he was the sexiest man in the world to me.

His breathing became so erratic that I became lost in the feel of him. His massive chest was against my breasts and his hands were on my behind and when he ground into me, I felt what had to be the biggest penis in all of creation.

Finally in a voice so low I could barely hear him, he said, "Felicia, let me make you feel better and take your distress away. I've wanted this opportunity since the first day I saw you."

I couldn't believe my ears nor could I believe how badly I wanted him. He kissed me again and began to unzip my pants. He reached inside and touched me.

He fondled me until my legs forgot how to work. He closed his eyes and his hardness grew even more. He put his forehead on my head and said, "Just let me taste you. I've dreamed of devouring you for so long."

He kissed and sucked my neck. He picked me up, laid me on the bed and removed my pants and panties. He lowered himself onto the bed, fully clothed. And without any shame, I spread my legs for him.

He slowly kissed the inside of my thighs and my body became a flaming mass. And when he finally inserted his tongue inside of me, I came. The only way I could describe it was incredible.

He removed my blouse and bra and began to suckle on my breasts. Then he went back to the spot of his and my desire, feasting and moaning and making me scream more than ever in my life.

When he finally seemed to have his fill, He asked, "Now that you've given me what I've wanted, what can I give you?"

Was he crazy? He was lying beside me and I looked at him. I still couldn't believe how fine this man was. I said, "Sam you can't be serious. That was amazing."

He took my hand and put it on his hardness. He asked, "Are you sure you don't want more? I wouldn't want to leave you frustrated."

I was so intrigued that without thinking, I moved my hand along the length of it and gauged that it had to be at least ten inches. At least!! Hell no! I didn't want any parts of it!

But what I was feeling, both in that place and in my hand, were *both* very hard to deny. And his passion for me was unmistakable.

Finally I said, "Sam you're huge! I mean, I'm sure I've never had that much before. I'm afraid you'll hurt me."

"Felicia, I promise to be gentle. I've learned to take my time because of that. Don't you trust me?"

"Of course, but I would hate to try and not be able to finish or something stupid like that."

He got on top of me and began to kiss my neck and proceeded to hit all the places that he'd hit only moments before. He finally undressed and before me was indeed the largest penis I'd ever seen.

He laughed and told me to stop staring at him like he was a freak or something. That sort of relaxed me. He asked about a condom and I reached into my night stand and gave him one.

He parted my thighs and placed his head there again and reignited my fire. He leaned over me and inserted one of my nipples in his mouth and sucked it so hard and so sweet that I thought I would die from it. And when he began to put it thing inside of me, it was the beginning of the end.

That night as I lay in my bed, I couldn't believe what I'd done. I couldn't even bring myself to look into the mirror. I couldn't sleep a wink. My boys were still with Todd and Gina. Harold was still in Houston. Sam was downstairs, I assumed, sleeping like a baby.

Never in my wildest dreams would I have thought I could behave so shamelessly. We made love all day and true to his word, he was gentle with me and we both loved it.

The next morning, Sam was at my door before eight o'clock. He came in, picked me up and sat me on the sofa. He said, "I'm here to prepare you breakfast."

He returned to the door and grabbed a bag containing eggs and bread. He said, "Sorry, but that was all I had."

I laughed and said, "Don't worry about it. I have bacon in the fridge."

"That's perfect because that's about all I know how to cook."

After breakfast, the boys called saying their dad would be bringing them home later that afternoon. Sam left to get Aysia. I sat there with my thoughts. I've never cheated before in my life. *Who is this woman I've become?*

I spoke to Harold and he told me he'd be back on Sunday. That evening Sam and I talked on the phone and I told him I could not do that again. He said, "I'm sorry Felicia. I would never want to do anything that would jeopardize our friendship. It was just sex. I'm sure we can get past this."

I was so tired of people saying that to me. I asked, "When did sex become so casual? I admit what happened was as much my fault as yours, but it seems to mean a lot more to me than to anyone else. So it's gonna take a while for me to *get past this.*"

While preparing dinner for the boys and me, I realized Harold was so right. He told me early on that I was easy prey and I needed to practice self-control. How ironic.

Again, sleep did not come easy for me. I continued to fret over my love for Harold and how he deserves a better woman than me. I still don't understand how I've changed so much in such a short period of time. While married to Todd, I never even *looked* at other men. What could be the reason I'm so out of control?

While lying there pondering life's questions, I couldn't help remembering how awesome Sam was. Damn.

Chapter Six

As spring began to thaw out old Rochester, Harold and I continued to get closer in some ways, but it seemed we still had a cloud of uncertainty looming overhead.

Carla and her beau faded after a short steamy affair. On the other hand, Annette and Tony appear to be inseparable and very much in love. During a recent conversation with Annette, she told me she had not had a *date* all year. Something was definitely wrong in the atmosphere.

Sam was the perfect gentleman. He began dating a woman he met while volunteering at Aysia's school, but it didn't last because he said she couldn't kiss and her libido was at zero. He said he never even got to second base with her and she was a bit uppity for his taste.

That was too funny to me because *that man* could send any woman's libido from zero to eighty in three seconds. Plus, he was downright gorgeous and truthfully could cause several orgasms in several women by simply entering the room.

Harold met Sam briefly one day we were headed out to dinner. Thankfully, Harold never had any reason to suspect anything happened between Sam and me.

The strangest thing of all was that crazy lingerie company. I returned the six back in February, and about three weeks later they were sent back to me. But during that time I got two more and they refused to accept them back because supposedly the account was closed and the customer left no forwarding address.

I went ahead and opened them, and each was a beautiful ensemble of lace and silk, and they were all soft pastel colors. I put them together in one box and tucked them away in my closet.

My parents usually take the kids to church with them and have been on my case about attending. I decided to surprise them by showing up on Palm Sunday. Harold and I were lounging at my apartment on the Saturday before when I told him my plans. He said, "I'd like to go with you."

So the next morning, Harold and I attended church together for the first time. My family was so happy and we all went to an early dinner afterwards. I noticed my dad and Harold speaking quietly in the parking lot, so I approached them and asked what they were talking about.

"Miss Nosey if you must know, I was telling your dad of my intentions. Are you okay with that?"

I turned to my father and said, "Daddy, don't pay attention to him. He's a crack head!"

The following week was very busy because Annette and Carla planned a trip to Disney World with their children for Spring break, and Todd Jr. and Marcus were going with them. They'd be gone for eight days and I planned to make the most of it.

Harold and I planned a long weekend getaway at Geneva on the Lake, a cozy little bed and breakfast about an hour outside of Rochester.

After settling in our room, we embraced for what seemed an eternity. He guided me to the sofa and announced we were celebrating our four month anniversary. I laughed and said, "Only you would remember that."

"Babe, today is the seventeenth day of April. And I am praying that the last four months have been as sweet and wonderful and as life changing for you as they've been for me. Because Felicia…"

And as he went down on his knee and reached into his pocket, I felt my heart literally stop.

"…I love you more than I ever thought I could love. There is nothing and no one that has given me more joy, pleasure or completed me like you."

He opened the little box, looked to Heaven and removed the ring. He looked in my eyes and asked, "Please Felicia. Will you be my wife?"

Before I answered, a single tear rolled down his face. That caused the ones welling up in my eyes to escape and flood my face. For a fleeting moment, I thought of the night I thought our love was over because he wanted a baby. He's never mentioned it again. I opened my mouth and he put his finger on my lip as if he, too, had returned there. He said, "No words."

He raised the ring and looked in my eyes. Without words, I gave him my left hand and he placed the ring on my finger. He stood and brought me up with him. He embraced me and I embraced him and it was as if we were both holding on for dear life.

When we entered the dining room that evening, I felt like a virginal bride the morning after her wedding. It seemed anyone could see I'd been making love for the last four hours. There was no one else in the dining room, so apparently we were the first to come down. After we were seated, Harold excused himself and went to the restroom.

Minutes later, a very graceful and beautiful middle aged woman approached me. An equally handsome man was behind her. Without asking, she sat at our table, smiled and said, "Felicia?"

"Yes. I'm sorry but, do I know you?"

She smiled again and looked back at her escort. He said, "Pardon us Felicia. But we wanted to be here the day you accepted our son's proposal of marriage. He's told us so much about you and we wanted to thank you personally for making him so happy."

His mom said, "With tomorrow being Easter, we thought it lovely that he chose such a special time of year to ask you to be his bride."

Both of my hands were on my face and I was sure every bit of make-up was in the wrong place. I couldn't stop crying. Suddenly, five women came over and began to kiss me and welcome me into the family. My soon to be sisters-in-law were all there as well.

When I finally looked up, I saw my future husband standing with my parents. Harold had reserved the inn exclusively for us. Now I knew what Harold and my dad were talking about in the parking lot after church.

Seafood and champagne flowed all night. Even my parents indulged and I would swear my mom was a bit tipsy by night's end. I was very concerned about the cost of such a celebration.

After an emotional and heart-warming dinner and celebration of our engagement, Harold and I retired to our room about one in the morning.

Although I told my parents I was going away for the weekend with Harold, and they had to know we would be sleeping together, I was very uncomfortable when Harold and I said our goodnights and left together. Even though we're engaged, it still seemed inappropriate and a bit blatant right in front of both of our parents.

As I was putting my hair up I asked Harold two questions. I said sarcastically, "You're quite sure of yourself Mr. Benson. How did you know I wouldn't say no?"

"I knew when I got that tear to fall, you'd be putty in my hands."

"Um-hum. I hear ya."

He came over to me dressed in beautiful navy silk pajamas and began to massage my shoulders and neck. I said, "Honey, you made me feel like a princess tonight. I'll never forget it. But I'm concerned about the cost of such a celebration. Can you really afford this?"

"Well, as much as I would like to take credit for it, I must admit my parents insisted on paying for all of it."

I stood immediately and turned to him. I said, "Harold!! How could you allow your parents to do such a thing?! They've got Melissa and Karen still in college and Tammy is starting in the fall. Oh my, I feel just awful. We need to find a way to pay them back for this!"

Harold had the oddest smirk on his face, which caused me to stop ranting and ask him, "What's so funny?"

Laughing he said, "First of all, Karen is a professional student. She's been in school almost ten years and she's so smart, she's been on scholarship most of that time. And Sweetie, my parents will never miss that money. Last year, their gross income was over 3.6 million dollars. Not to mention the millions they've made in investments. Dad's not just a chef. He and Mom own twelve five star restaurants in the Michigan and Illinois areas, and my mom is a professor at Michigan State University. She's also a published author. Dad flew in his own cooks. Feel better?"

I was stunned. I asked, "Harold, are you serious?"

He laughed and took me in his arms and said, "Babe, I guess you could say you're marrying a rich man. Sort of. And since I'm spilling, I might as well tell you that Dad has been trying to get me in the business for the last five years, and now you will be their next target. His argument now is that with a family, I need to get groomed to take over. By the way, they can't wait to meet Todd and Marcus."

All of a sudden, I felt like I was meeting this man all over again. I felt as though I didn't measure up at all. I was starting to think I'd made a *huge* mistake accepting his proposal. I said, "Harold, why on earth did you keep all of this from me? I find it hard to believe your family could look at me and be happy with your choice. Did you lie to them about me?"

"Felicia, I wish you could've been a fly on the wall listening to them rant and rave about you. I overheard my dad telling the kitchen staff that he couldn't have chosen a better woman for me himself. He spoke of your beauty and how he watched you pour so much love on your parents. And excuse me, *did I lie?* How could you ask such a question? Lie about what?"

I opened my mouth but nothing came out. I walked away and turned around. I looked at my fiancé and asked, "So…..they like me?"

Over the next two weeks, it took all I had not to let the cat out of the bag. I swore Harold, Mom and Dad to secrecy until I was ready to tell the Wilsons, and more importantly my sons, the big news.

How I kept it from Carla and Annette, I'll never know. What I did know was that they were going to be super mad when they found out I'd been engaged for two weeks and didn't tell them.

Relaxing in a hot bubble bath is a rare treat, but today I have the privilege. With my head back and eyes closed, I spent the last hour listening to Memory Lane as Tony reminded us all of better times through the music of the sixties, seventies and eighties. I try to listen to it every Saturday morning on Rochester's only African American radio station, 104 WDKX. The call letters stand for Douglass, King and Malcolm X.

Upon their return from Orlando, the boys drove me nuts with their stories of Disney World. So I asked Todd to relieve me this weekend and that I would make it up to him.

Since the divorce, he'd really stepped up and shared in the responsibility of the boys. I made a mental note to mention that to him. So much to remember.

Harold surprised me with a laptop. My life had suddenly become so busy and overwhelming. His mom called me anxious about how soon we would set a date. When I told Harold maybe next spring, he had a fit. He wants it this year, preferably this month.

He said since I'd already been married, he assumed I wouldn't want anything too extravagant. He was right of course, so why the delay? I couldn't answer him. But I did tell him that I would answer all questions by the end of my weekend of solitude, which disturbed him as well. Why would I want a vacation from him, he asked? Questions, questions, questions. I'm tired of all the damn questions.

I prepared myself a scrambled egg sandwich and sat to watch TV when the doorbell rang. I was tempted not to answer, but decided I would. I looked out and saw my sexy neighbor Sam. He and I talk a lot on the phone these days.

For some reason, he's the only one I told of our engagement. Smiling, I opened the door and Sam reached down and picked up a box he'd brought with him. I asked, "What is that?"

"In celebration of your news, I thought you'd want some nice wine to have around."

As he carried the box into the kitchen, I couldn't help but notice again how fine and muscular he is. Damn, this man must truly be my test, I thought. But true to his word, he had not done anything or said anything that even remotely resembled romance.

He finally started dating regularly, and had a couple of female friends that he really liked. I said, "Wow Sam, this is really great! Thank you so much!"

"This wine was piling up in my apartment and I figured you would gladly help me dispose of it."

"You got that right. Gee, I could use a glass now."

Sam reached into the crate and handed me a cold bottle. He said, "Three are already cold. Set it on the counter and I'll open it for you. By the way, do you know you have a flat tire?"

"Well, it's not flat. I have a slow leak. I need to get it fixed."

"Give me your keys. I'll take it around the corner and take care of it for you. There's probably a nail or something in it."

"No, I don't want to put you through that."

"Girl, give me the damn keys. I'll be right back."

When he returned, I fixed him an egg sandwich and we ate and drank a bottle of wine. It was only eleven o'clock on that Saturday morning. He and I settled in after popping a movie in, and eventually we both dozed off.

What woke me up was both disturbing and exciting. Sam was lying on my chest with his hand between my legs. He had unbuttoned my shirt, and was nursing on my breast. Both sensations were driving me crazy and I sighed, *"Oh Sam"*.

He looked up at me and said, "Felicia, I'm so sorry. I couldn't resist you. I don't think anyone has turned me on like you do. Please don't hate me."

He sat up and revealed the biggest hard-on. I was trembling both from fear and desire. I said, "I admit I'm just as turned on by you. But…"

Suddenly, the doorbell rang and both of us froze. I ran to the window and there was Harold standing on my stoop. I didn't know what to do. I thought of not answering for real this time, but he waved at me. Damn! He saw me. Why the hell didn't I look out the peep hole? Shit!

I turned to Sam and said quietly, "It's Harold!"

He pointed at my shirt and I panicked. I tried to button it quickly but my fine motor skills left me. Finally intact, I opened the door. Harold stepped in and was about to open his mouth when he saw Sam coming out of the kitchen.

Sam had gone in there so Harold wouldn't see him on the couch and think he'd been there long.

Sam said, "Hey Man, how you doing? I just brought you guys a box of wine. I hope I'm not out of line, but I must congratulate you on your engagement."

He extended his hand and Harold gave him a tentative hand shake while looking at me. Sam said, "Sorry, but I gotta run. Aysia is waiting for me to pick her up. Take care."

As Harold raised his glass to his lips, his gaze never left me. I couldn't keep still, so I fussed in the kitchen while he watched TV and drank his juice.

He never said a word about Sam being here except he thought I wanted it kept quiet. His silence was unnerving, so I went in and asked, "What are you watching?"

"Felicia, have you set up your laptop yet?"

"No, not yet. I'm planning to do it this weekend."

"Are we getting married this year Felicia?"

"Why so serious Harold? Is something wrong?"

"I just think we need to be together sooner than later. I think we need to find a house and live together, and then you can take all the time you need to plan the wedding. I'm not comfortable with the idea of us residing separately for another year."

And there it was.

He called for take-out and went around the corner to pick up the Chinese food. While he was gone, I quickly called Sam and he quickly answered. He said, "I've been worried to death about you. Are you all right? When did he leave?"

"He just went to grab dinner. Thanks for covering for me like that. I would never have handled it that well."

"I sat in the window all afternoon waiting for his car to leave. I finally accepted the fact that he wasn't leaving. And Felicia, I'm so sorry I put you in that position. I promise to make it up to you. I mean, I…"

"Sam, this has to end. I don't wanna lose my buddy, but our attraction to one another is too dangerous. I'll call you tomorrow when the coast is clear and hopefully we'll find a solution to our problem. Okay?"

"Okay. I'll talk to you then."

After hanging up with Sam, I went into my room, freshened up and slipped into a lounging gown.

"Harold, you're hurting me Honey. Why are you so rough?"

He didn't answer me. He just rolled off and turned his back to me. I asked, "Harold, what on earth is wrong? Harold?!…"

Finally, he turned over and looked up at the ceiling. He said, "Babe, I'm sorry for my behavior. When I walked in and saw Sam today, I thought my worst fear had come true. I couldn't for the life of me understand why you wanted a weekend of solitude. As rare as it is that we get a chance to be alone for an entire weekend, I assumed you'd jump at the chance to be with me. And you not wanting to get married right away has me puzzled as well. So instead of fretting the entire weekend, I thought I'd come over and surprise you with dinner and a movie or something. I guess my jealousy got the best of me. So again, I apologize."

"Oh Honey. First of all, I did have time earlier to ponder some things and I've decided that a fall wedding, *this year*, would be just beautiful. How does that sound to you?"

He turned toward me and said, "Babe that sounds great! And...."

"Wait, let me finish. Secondly, you must admit that with all that's occurred recently, my life is about to change drastically! So yes, I really did need, still need, some very quiet time to put some things in order in my mind. Okay?"

"Okay Felicia."

"You know you dropped some heavy shit on me last month about your family. It took me long enough not to feel inferior with you, and now there's an entire clan just like you. I'm just a simple girl, from a simple family with very simple means. For instance, I'm worried that my dad is gonna try to pay for our wedding and try to make it as nice as our engagement party was. That would bankrupt my parents. They barely make it on their measly fixed income as it is."

Harold gently stroked my thigh and said, "Felicia, Baby, I already spoke to your dad about it."

"You what! Oh no Harold! My dad is a very proud man! What did you say?!"

Very quietly he said, "I told him that I'd been saving for my wedding for a long time and that my gift to *you, my bride*, would be to pay for her wedding. I told him that it's been a tradition since my grandfather and father both gave their brides the same gift. My dad began saving when I was born and gave it over to me when I turned twenty-one. Felicia, I admit I made it up because I didn't want them burdened with it either."

"What did he say?"

Harold smiled and said, "He told me he was gonna be proud to call me his son. Anything else?"

I smiled too. What a thoughtful man this Harold Benson was. I said, "Thank you for that. It's important to me they understand that I need them as much as I ever have. I'll always cherish your sensitive way of handling delicate situations."

He took me in his arms and we took another flight to that place reserved just for us.

I don't think he noticed I never addressed his concern about Sam.

I arranged three important meetings. Tuesday at lunch time with Annette and Carla, announcing my engagement and resolving my dilemma around bridesmaids and a matron of honor. Tuesday evening, Harold and I will meet with Todd and the boys to tell them our plans. Tonight with Sam.

Usually Mondays zoomed by, but that Monday seemed to drag on forever. I was dreading this meeting because unfortunately, I was losing my friend. He claimed he had the perfect solution. I doubted that.

We agreed to meet at his place while the boys were at T-Ball practice with their dad, and Aysia was with Sam's sister. When I got there I noticed he had a fireplace, which I didn't have. On the mantel was a picture of his late wife. I looked at it. I was shocked that she and I had similar features. I asked, "Why are you attracted to me?"

"What?"

"She and I look alike."

"Felicia. You don't think I'm some nut case that thinks she returned to me through you, do you?"

I didn't answer him. I didn't know what to think. I was more concerned with getting this resolved. I finally asked, "Sam, what is your perfect solution to our problem"

"I think there are only two ways to handle this. One of us moves, and I mean far away. Or we continue seeing each other."

I was speechless. He began to pace back and forth. Then he said, "Felicia, I've had sex one time since my wife died. I've tried with other women, but something continues to get in my way. *You!* I find something wrong with everyone. And I don't mean to embarrass you, but when I need to relieve myself, its visions of *you* that I fantasize about."

I was still speechless, but now my mouth was wide open. I couldn't believe what I'd just heard. He came over to me and said, "I've thought it through, and I think it can work."

"Has it dawned on you that I have a fiancée?!"

"Yes, I realize you have a fiancée, and I will never do anything to interfere with that. I'm just saying that we're both hungry for each other and what really is so wrong with us feeding that hunger?"

He came closer and began kissing my neck. I said, "Sam, this is insane. I think I should leave."

I started to pull away, but he gently held me there. He said, "Please Felicia."

As I pulled into the parking lot of Red Lobster, I saw my two best friends waiting for me. They were talking while sitting on a bench near the entrance. Annette threw her head back and laughed and Carla laughed as well. I loved those two so much, which was why I decided not to choose either one of them. As I joined my girlfriends, I asked, "So, what are you all laughing at?"

Annette said, "That damn Carla always talking about people."

Carla said, "I'll never understand why some women think wearing five different hairdos at one time looks good. It aint nothin' but a hot mess! Ha-ha!"

Once we were seated and chatting, I reached into my pocket and slipped my ring on. I kept my hands under the table and announced, "I really need your help with an urgent matter. Could I please have your attention?"

They stopped talking and Carla asked, "Licia, nothing's wrong is it?"

"Actually no, but...."

Carla said, "Hello Harold!"

I turned around and there he was. He kissed me on the cheek and slid into the booth next to Carla. He said, "I apologize for interrupting your lunch ladies, but I was missing my baby so much that I decided you guys wouldn't be too mad if I joined you. Is it okay?"

I frowned at him and Annette's lip went up. But Carla said, "Of course it's okay!"

He smiled and turned to me and said, "Babe, I noticed you were about to tell your friends something. Please, don't let me stop you."

He smiled and put a menu up to hide his face. I laughed and said, "He's just nosey and wanted to be here when I....uh... Listen guys. Harold asked me to marry him and I accepted. We've decided on a fall wedding."

I took my hands from under the table and showed them my ring. Both screamed quietly and jumped up. Annette hugged Harold and Carla hugged me. Then Annette hugged me. She said, "Felicia, I'm so happy for you!"

Carla said, "Oh, me too! This is so exciting!"

Then they both said, "Congratulations Harold!"

Harold and I confessed that we'd been engaged for almost three weeks now, but that I needed time to sort things out before announcing it. I asked Harold, "Did you talk to your sisters yet?"

"Yes, and they are both planning to attend. I told you they'd be here. Why did you want me to call them?"

I turned and reached for Annette and Carla's hands. I said, "I've been pulling my hair out because I didn't want to choose between you two. I love you both the same and I refused to allow tradition to dictate that I could only have one matron of honor. So if you both agree, I would love for both of you to honor me with the distinction of being my matrons of honor."

They looked at each other and both agreed gladly. The waitress soon took our orders and we began to talk of our fall wedding. Harold said, "I still don't understand why you had me call my sisters?"

"Because I'm going to ask them to be my bridesmaids, and I didn't want to ask anyone not planning to attend. Also, it's only right that I ask them and not you. Okay Mr. Nosey?"

As we were leaving the restaurant, I told the girls not to mention this to anyone yet because we were planning to tell the boys and Todd this evening, and I didn't want them to hear it from anyone before I told them. They said okay and were off. I looked at Harold and asked, "Why did you really come here today?"

"Cause I'm just like a kid and wanted to see the expression on their faces. Are you mad?"

"No, not really mad, but I don't want you to think you can just show up when I'm having time with my girls. Agreed?"

He saluted me and said, "Yes Ma'am. I promise not to infringe on your girl time ever again."

We both laughed and he walked me to my car. He kissed me and said, "This is the most exciting time of my life. Here, this is for you."

He handed me an envelope and inside was a cashier's check for five thousand dollars. He said, "I'm sure you will need to put down deposits and make purchases soon. I don't want anything to stop you from having everything you want. I'll give you more next month, but if you need it sooner, just let me know. See you at your place about six?"

I didn't know what to say. I nodded yes and he kissed me on the forehead. He said, "Gotta run. I'll call you later."

And he was off. I yelled at him, "Thank you Honey!"

He raised his hand and waved goodbye.

Sitting at my desk, I was trying to decide if I even knew myself anymore. I had a fiancée who was a dream come true, yet I'd just agreed to continue an affair with a man because he had a large penis. *Was I insane?*

After he pleaded with me last night, I slept with him again. My attraction to Sam was so strong, that I began to have reservations about marrying Harold.

I wondered if just being single and enjoying my freedom would be more ideal for me. I wanted to blame Harold for taking away my innocence, but the truth was no one was to blame but me. I only had to say no.

When I thought about it, I never said no. I said yes to Harold *and* to Sam. Everytime!! It seemed I truly was out of control.

I was torn about telling Carla and Annette about Sam today, but Harold's surprise visit made that decision easy. I was also thrown when Harold, again, showed up unexpectedly. I had to *really* be careful with Sam, knowing Harold had a habit of doing that.

After Todd came into the apartment and he and Harold shook hands and exchanged pleasantries, I asked him to have a seat and I went and got the boys. They ran in and spoke to Harold, but leaped and jumped all over their dad. Marcus said, "Daddy, my birthday is in eight days! Did you remember?"

"Marcus, how could I forget my little man's birthday?"

I noticed Harold watching the exchange between father and sons and I swear I saw desire in his eyes. Poor Harold. That was something else I had to figure out. Todd asked, "Felicia, what is it you need to talk about?"

I looked at the three of them and said, "Harold and I have decided to get married. We wanted to tell everyone all together so if you guys have any questions or concerns, we're all here to answer them for you. We're planning a fall wedding, and would like for both of you to be a part of the ceremony. Okay?"

All three looked stunned, which is what I expected, so I asked, "TJ, what do you think of us getting married?"

"Mommy, does that mean Daddy won't be our dad anymore?"

Todd said, "Of course not Champ! No matter what happens, I'll always be your dad. Always remember that. Okay Guys?"

"Okay Daddy!"

Todd stood and turned to us and said, "Congratulations! I couldn't ask for a nicer stepdad for my boys. I'm truly happy for both of you."

He nudged the boys and they said in unison, "Congratulations Mom! And Mr. Harold."

Neither seemed sure or sincere, but it was a start.

Chapter Seven

I so enjoy going to the salon with my girls. We all took the day off from work for a Girl's Day. Annette and Carla were getting manicures while I was enjoying a pedicure. Head back and eyes closed, I couldn't believe the events of the last couple of days.

First, while taking the trash out, I would've sworn I smelled Harold's cologne. I looked around and dismissed it when I saw no evidence of him. When I was back inside, I went into the boys' room and glanced out the window.

Harold in sweats and a baseball cap, was jogging across the back of the apartment complex heading toward his apartment. I was floored! I also knew that if I spoke to him about it, he would deny it.

Secondly, when I got home from work yesterday, another package was at my door. But this time, it was from Tiffany's. *Tiffany's!* Who the hell does that?

I sent the others back, and again, they returned them to me. I hate to throw them away, so maybe I'll just donate them. At this point, they give me the creeps. I took the Tiffany's box to the post office this morning and returned it.

Harold left yesterday for a conference in Atlanta, and will be gone for seven days if he told the truth. After a long conversation with myself, I decided it was time to change my strategy.

Since its Friday, that evening Todd and Gina picked the boys up for the weekend. Todd finally told me that he and Gina are living together. Gina has no children and is content with being a part time mom to Todd Jr. and Marcus. She's great with them and they really like her.

Thirty minutes after the boys left, Sam called. I asked, "What's up with you? No hot date tonight?"

"Felicia, why do you ask me about other women? I told you that's not working for me. It's you or nothing for me right now. And right now, I'm missing you *real* bad, Girl. Can I see you?"

I swear, every time that man calls me Girl, it does something to me. I said, "Sam, you know I told you about Harold spying on me. I really need to lay low for a while. Besides, Annette and Carla are coming over."

"Do you still have wine?"

"Yes, tons of it."

I realized Sam was grasping at any reason to come up here. So I said, "I'll tell you what. When the girls get here, come on up and meet them. Have a glass of wine and then go back home."

Before I could pour each of us a glass of wine, my doorbell rang. Annette got up to answer it and I said, "Please don't faint when you see the gorgeous man on the other side. He's a good friend of mine and off limits to your hot ass!"

"Why would you invite some man over here? We don't have all night and we're supposed to be having a quiet night just for us."

Before I could answer, Carla came from the bathroom and Annette opened the door. As Sam entered, they both froze. I laughed so hard, I had to sit my glass down.

He was freshly shaven, dressed in a grey silk shirt and black slacks. Annette's hazel eyes began to twirl and Carla just sat down without taking her eyes off of him. Finally I said, "Ladies, this is Sam. He's my neighbor and his daughter and my sons are playmates. He's kind enough to keep me stocked with some of the best wine in the world, so I asked him to join us for a glass this evening."

Then I turned to Sam and said, "Sam, these are my BFF's. Annette opened the door for you and this is Carla."

Sam graciously took Annette's hand and kissed it. He said, "Ladies, it's a pleasure meeting you."

Then he walked over to Carla, raised her hand and kissed it too. He motioned for Annette and me to sit, and then he sat next to me. For the next ninety minutes we drank wine and he charmed and amused them with his anecdotes. They were upset with me when I said, "It's time for Sam to leave ladies. He has an early morning."

He looked at me with disappointment, but finally left after one last round of hand kisses and dimpled smiles.

Once the door was closed, Annette said, "If I wasn't absolutely sure you're fucking him, I would've followed him home. What the fuck Girl!"

I attempted to speak, but nothing came out. Carla said, "Annette, Licia ain't messing with that man. She's about to get married. Are you crazy?"

I got up with my glass and went into the kitchen. Carla followed me and asked, "Right Licia?"

I opened the fourth bottle of wine, poured a healthy glassful, and brought the glass *and* bottle back into the living room. With Carla behind me, I sat them on the coffee table and was about to sit when she grabbed me and turned me around. She asked, "Licia, is it true?"

"I've been trying to tell you about this for weeks. Every time I was gonna tell you, something stopped me."

Annette said, "Licia, he acts like he's in love with you."

"I know he's in *something* with me. But I don't think its love. I think its lust."

I told them everything. Poor Carla was like a mad woman, shaking her head and calling on the Lord. She asked, "Nette, how did you know?"

I asked, "Yeah Annette, how *did* you know?"

She turned to me and said, "The way the two of you looked at one another. And the way he would drape his arm over the back of the sofa and touch your shoulder. He had that male *this is mine* thing going on. I sure hope Harold hasn't seen it. Has he met him?"

"Yes, twice. Oh shit, you don't think he saw it too, do you?"

By the time they left, it was one thirty and I was too drunk to walk to my bedroom. Carla had us praying and Annette was trying to make me understand how dangerous my situation really was.

There was a tap on my window. I knew it was Sam. I wanted it to be Sam. I crawled off the sofa and found my legs. He was standing with his back to me, but I knew it was him.

I opened the door, and he walked in. He took me in his arms and kissed me slowly. He picked me up and carried me to the bedroom. *I am so out of control!*

While enjoying the after play of our lovemaking, Sam referred to our evening with Annette and Carla. He told me his best friend Jonathon would have loved hanging out with my friends. He said, "Jon is totally enthralled by beautiful women, and would have painted the town red with them. He loves to treat beautiful women like princesses."

"I've never heard you speak of him before. Where does he live?"

"He lives in Richmond. He owns a Popeye's franchise, and is doing very well. He has no children, never married but loves the ladies. As a matter of fact, we....never mind."

I sat up and punched him. I said, "Don't do that Sam. What were you about to say?"

He sat up and said, "Felicia, back in the day, I did some things that might freak you out. Do you *really* want to hear this?"

My first instinct was to say yes. But then I thought about it and asked, "Were you in prison or something awful like that?"

He laughed and said, "No Girl. I'm not a criminal. Do you want to know or not?"

I shook my head yes. He said, "Before I was married, Jon and I used to pick up women and have threesomes."

My hand went to my mouth and I gasped. I asked, "You were Gay?"

He hollered laughing and said, "Hell no Girl! We would indulge in a *ménage a trois* every now and then."

Although I was stunned, I tried to act as though I wasn't. He took me in his arms and said, "Jon would absolutely adore you. Gorgeous, sexy as hell, um-um-um."

My head was spinning for a whole lot of reasons now. I said, "Don't say things like that. The last thing I need is another man adoring me."

I got up and went into the kitchen. I grabbed two bottles of water and got back in bed. He said, "There's one more thing."

I looked at him and wondered why he was telling me all of this. He said, "My wife and Jon and I. We...played house every now and then."

When I finally woke up, it was twelve thirty in the afternoon. Sam was gone. I crawled into the bathroom, and before I knew it, I was throwing up. I was sick all day. I remember the phone ringing a few times, but I can't remember if I answered or not. I was dozing off and on.

About seven fifteen I heard pounding. I woke up and realized someone was knocking on my door. I tried to ignore it, but whoever it was wouldn't go away. Assuming it was Sam, I slowly got up and looked out.

It was Tony! I wondered what could be wrong. I cleared my mind, opened the door and he stormed in. I asked, "Tony, what's wrong?"

"Felicia, where is my wife? And don't hand me that bullshit about shopping! Where is she?"

I felt the blood drain from my upper body. I had no idea how to answer him. So I said, "Tony, I'm not sure. She asked me if I wanted to do something earlier, but I've been sick all day. Honestly, I don't remember much about the conversation. You see, I was asleep when she called and…."

"Stop lying for her Licia! I know you know!"

"You know I know what Tony?! And why are you accusing me of lying? Look at me! I've been throwing up all day, and right here. All day!"

We both turned toward the door as someone walked in, since the door was still opened. She had a bag of groceries to fix soup and other stuff to calm my stomach. She asked, "What the hell is going on in here? I could hear you all a mile away!"

"Annette, where have you been? I called you and texted you! What the hell is up?"

She laughed and said, "Tony, my phone died hours ago and my charger is in your car. I called Felicia, and was worried about her because she was talking gibberish. My phone died after that call, so I couldn't call you. I planned to call you from here."

Tony looked at me and then at Annette. Finally I said, "Tony, don't you owe us an apology? Annette, Tony came in here accusing me of lying for you. He was about to explain when you walked in."

Tony looked at both of us and said, "Annette, I know things haven't been the greatest with us for a while. And I admit I feared you were cheating on me. I'm sorry. And Licia, I apologize to you as well. I realize there's no way you two could have made this up, and you did not deserve to be accused of lying. I'm sorry to you too."

"Apology accepted. Now if you two will excuse me, I need to go into the other room."

Tony stopped me and hugged me and said, "Thanks Licia. I sure hope I don't catch whatever you got."

I laughed and went into the bathroom. When I came out, Annette was in the kitchen preparing my soup. I asked, "Is he gone?"

She laughed and said, "Yeah Girl. I don't know what the hell got into him. I guess I'm gonna have to be careful as hell now."

"I thought you said you weren't dating these days."

"Well, I'm not. But you never know what tomorrow will bring."

We laughed and went into the living room. Annette poured both of us a glass of ginger ale and asked, "So, what the hell happened to you between the time we left and now? Are you just hungover or are you sick?"

"It's just a bad hangover. But right after you all left, Sam was at my door. Annette, he and I are obsessed with each other and I don't know what to do about it. I can't say no to him."

"Well, I can understand that! Shit that man is fine and honestly, I would be hard pressed to deny him anything!"

"Nette, you won't believe what he told me last night. He said he and his buddy used to pick up women and have threesomes. What the hell goes on behind closed doors in this world?!"

I laughed and Annette was laughing too. Then I told her about his wife and she said, "Felicia, lots of couples are swingers or invite someone into their bed."

"But Annette, how do you have sex with your spouse after that kind of experience? Do you know people who do that?"

"Well, I know a few people who have, but *really*, most men desire to have two women. That's not odd at all. And truthfully, it's as easy as having the cash to pay for it if he can't convince the women to do it. I've been asked several times but I have no interest, mainly because he usually wants the women to have sex with each other, and frankly, I like bones in my fish."

Annette got up and laughed all the way to the kitchen. While she was in there checking on the soup, there was another knock on the door.

I was sure it was Sam. I opened the door and looked into the face of my fiancée. With my hands on my hips I asked, "What are you doing here Mr. Benson?"

"Well, future Mrs. Benson, I just couldn't bear the thought of being away from you for so long. Besides, I tried calling you earlier while I was on the road and didn't get an answer."

He kissed me just as Annette came out. She said, "Hello Harold. It's good to see you."

She dried her hands off and gave me the towel. She said, "The soup should be ready in about thirty minutes. Keep sipping that ginger ale and nibbling those crackers, and you should feel better after some soup."

Harold turned to me and asked, "What's wrong Babe? You sick?"

"Just a bad tummy. I should be fine by tomorrow."

Annette was putting on her coat and said, "I'll leave you two love birds alone. Call me tomorrow Licia. Goodnight guys."

As she was leaving, Harold insisted on walking her to her car. I waved at both of them and went into my room to freshen up. And there on the floor was the package for one of the condoms Sam and I used this morning. *Oh shit, where is the other one?!*

I ran into the bathroom and there it was in the trash can along with the condoms. I took the trash bag and put it in the cabinet. Then I ran back in the bedroom and quickly put fresh linen on the bed. Harold was knocking at the door. Thank goodness he doesn't have a key.

I ran to the door and let him in. Then I told him I needed time in the bathroom. He agreed to keep an eye on the soup and assured me he was okay. I worried while I showered if he was snooping or had found some obvious evidence that I was cheating on him.

After twenty minutes, I emerged from my room in flannel pj's, thick socks and my hair tied up. He was in the kitchen recreating the soup with what seemed every spice and seasoning I owned.

I laughed at him and he turned and saw me and said, "You look beautiful. By the way, when we get married, I'll do the grocery shopping. No fresh herbs or veggies. Not good Darling. Oh, your neighbor Sam stopped by while you were in the shower. He said he was entertaining a lady friend and needed some garlic for a late night dinner he was cooking for her."

While trying to regain my normal breathing pattern, I said, "Well, garlic is one thing I have plenty of."

I turned toward the fridge and said, "I assume you gave him some."

"Oh yeah, you definitely had plenty to spare. Does he make a habit of coming over this late?"

I was pouring ginger ale and said, "No, not really. Once when Aysia was ill, he came by frantic for some Vicks. He probably tried to call but the phone had been off the hook. I realized it when I went to take my shower. I apparently didn't completely hang it up when Annette called me earlier. That explains why I didn't get your call."

He was still fussing with the soup. He said, "I thought when a phone isn't hung up, it rings busy. Doesn't it?"

"I don't know. Did you try my cell?"

"Yes, as a matter of fact I did. I assume it's in your purse as usual."

I went into the living room and said, "Yep, I never took it out and it's probably dead."

He came into the living room with two bowls of soup with crackers. He went into the dining room and grabbed two dinner trays and we had a very nice dinner. The Sam conversation finally ended.

But my Sam problems were far from over.

The next day, Annette called me. She asked if I was alone. I told her Harold was still there, but would be leaving soon to return to Atlanta, which was a sixteen hour drive. He interrupted and said, "Actually, I'm flying back Babe."

She asked me to call her when I could talk. I said okay and hung up. I turned to Harold and asked, "Why didn't you fly here?"

"I was able to get a flight back to Atlanta, but not into Rochester at such short notice."

"Oh, okay."

After a brief pause he walked into the kitchen and said, "I flew into Buffalo and drove from there. Do you want something to drink?"

I said no and looked at the back of this man I was preparing to marry.

A little voice was saying.........something?

With May coming to a close in cold ass Rochester, spring is finally starting to feel like spring. As I pulled into the parking lot of Unkl Moe's, I was glad to see her car, because it was very crowded.

It's a soul food restaurant owned by friends of their family and we were both anxious to experience their food again. She and I decided to have lunch and talk face to face versus doing it by phone. When I went inside, our lunch was already ordered and served.

I was curious about what Annette had to tell me. I walked over to her and we both commented on how beautiful the weather was. Seventy seven degrees and sunny. We hugged and I sat down. I looked at the food and smiled because she remembered to order my double portion of cabbage.

She said, "Licia, Saturday when Harold walked me to my car, I got in and drove off, but not before I noticed him walking to the back of your complex and getting into, I assume a rental, and parking it near your apartment. Did you notice it took him a long time to come back?"

"I don't recall…oh yes, I remember now. I went into my bedroom to freshen up and realized some things were out of order. Now that you mention it, he took a long time to do what should have taken him less than two minutes."

"Well, there's more. I turned my lights off and went back in time to see him give some guy a small package and quickly walk away."

She reached into her purse and handed me a piece of paper. She said, "This is the plate number and make and model of the car the guy got in. I think he's a private detective."

I was floored, to say the least! I said, "Okay. If that's true, what could he tell Harold? That Sam and I have been seen going into each other's apartments? That we stay for long periods of time? OMG Nette! He knows! He fucking knows!"

I was on the verge of hysteria when Annette said, "Calm down Licia! I could be wrong, you know. Maybe the guy sold him drugs or something. Does he do drugs Licia?"

For the first time, I realized that I really, *really* did not know this man I planned to marry. I couldn't even answer her question. I said, "Not that I know of. But I'm so damned stupid, he could be Gay for all I know! I'm such a fool! I just trust anything and anybody!!"

"Felicia Pierce Wilson, kill the drama and listen to me!"

The sound of my maiden name stopped me in my tracks. I looked at Annette and realized I had a name to live up to. My father told me the name Pierce was one to be reckoned with, and that I must stand strong and defend its honor at all costs.

I looked again at my friend and said, "You're right Nette. Harold is just protecting his investment. My drama won't help anything."

"Licia, I hope I didn't make a mistake telling you this."

"No Nette. I need to know. I told myself recently that I needed to change my strategy. It's time for Felicia Pierce to do just that."

As we were finishing lunch, I said, "I think I'll do a little investigative work of my own. You game?"

"Of course. Whatcha got in mind?"

I had a devilish smirk on my face and said, "I'm not sure yet. I gotta tie up some loose ends first."

"Ms. Pierce, what are you up to?"

"Well, what's good for the goose...? You in?"

With a devilish smirk of her own she said, "Um-hum, I sure am."

"Just you and me. Let's not tell Carla yet."

"I agree wholeheartedly."

And so it began.

When I got in the car, I called Sam. He asked, "Girl, why you take so long calling me? I was..."

"Sam! I need to talk to you!"

"Okay, what's wrong?"

"I believe Harold has hired someone to spy on me, and if that's true, we must stop going to each other's apartments now!"

He was very quiet. I asked, "Are you still there?"

"Yeah I'm here. I guess I knew it would end someday, but I'm not ready to lose you so soon. Felicia, can't we meet somewhere else?"

"Sam, let's deal with that later. My relationship with Harold is my priority right now. You do understand that, don't you?"

Again, the silence. I said, "Sam?"

He eventually said, *"Marry me."*

Now my turn to be silent. He said, "Felicia, let's end this madness. I love you and you love me. Please, let's end the madness!"

Well, I totally lost it. I pulled over and asked him to hold on. I looked at myself in the mirror to see who would be there, because this could *not* be happening to me. I picked up the phone and said, "Sam, I can't."

I swore I could hear his heart breaking. I also heard the Pierce in me say stand strong. He said, "I gotta go."

He hung up. There I sat on the side of the road. Clearly, my new strategy needs work.

I was fifteen minutes late. I'm never late. My co-worker Trina said, "Your fiancée was looking for you."

"He's here."

"Yep. Hung around your desk for a while and left."

It became apparent that Harold and I were dating, so we announced a couple of weeks ago that we were engaged. I said, "Thanks Trina, I'm gonna go upstairs for a minute, okay?"

"Cool, I got this."

I thanked her again and went up to his department. He was on the phone. When he saw me, he quickly ended his call and motioned for me to sit. I asked, "When did you get back and why are you so mysterious about your comings and goings?"

"Not mysterious Felicia. Spontaneous. I missed you."

"Harold, if you'd let me know I could've prepared you a nice dinner, or at least sent the boys to Todd so we could be alone. I miss you too."

I stood up and he said, "Felicia, don't be angry with me. Please don't leave like this."

"You're really selfish sometimes. You need to quickly learn what it means to be a couple. I'm not angry, just disappointed. I gotta go. Call me before you leave."

I went back to my desk and wondered all afternoon if I should go and check on Sam.

I called my old high school buddy DeLisa. She works for the DMV. I left her a message asking her to call me. I also sent Annette a text about my conversation with Sam.

Then I called Todd and asked him for a huge favor. I asked him if he would get the boys from daycare today, *and* keep them for me the rest of the week, that I would keep them for his next two weekends.

He said he didn't mind keeping them and that Gina would be thrilled. I think I like her....a lot.

When I got home, I parked the car and looked around. I needed to be more aware of my surroundings, especially if someone is watching me. There was a note on my door. I grabbed it and went inside. I sat down and quickly opened it:

> Hi Felicia,
> I'm sorry about this afternoon. I hope I didn't upset you too much. Aysia is fine now. Thanks for your help. Please call me so I can give you an update. Thanks for being a nice neighbor.
>
> Sam

I picked up my phone and realized he was at work, so I sent him a text. Harold called me earlier and said he'd be working late, so I told him I'd see him tomorrow.

While in the kitchen, my phone rang. I ran to get it, and it was DeLisa. After pleasantries, I asked her if she could check that plate number for me. She agreed to help me and I offered to take her to lunch tomorrow and get the info then.

She was thrilled because we hadn't seen each other in so long. Then I called Annette and asked her to meet us. She also agreed, so now hopefully I would at least know who this guy is.

I've done very little for a person getting married in five months. Outside of securing the church and reception hall, I haven't done anything else except ask four women to be in it. Harold asked his brothers-in-law to be his best men, and planned to ask two cousins to be groomsmen.

My cell phone vibrated and it was a text from Sam. It said: Holiday Inn Express. Ridge Rd E. Room 416. 8pm. Please.

I stared at that text for at least five minutes. Although I knew the last thing I needed to do was take such a chance, in my mind I was already there and in the arms of the man I couldn't seem to get enough of.

I looked around my living room as if the answer could somehow be found there. My mind was spiraling downwards, while my G-Spot was spiraling upwards.

Marry me. Could I do that to Harold? To his parents and beautiful sisters, who all seemed to love me already? And my parents. They would be so disappointed in me. *Marry me.*

At ten minutes after eight, I was pulling into the parking lot of Holiday Inn. I was exhausted trying to live up to someone else's idea of what I should and should not do. I'd decided as I was showering twenty minutes earlier that if I lose Harold, I'll still have Sam. But I will not marry him. Simple as that.

As Sam was opening a bottle of his infamous wine, I asked if he was okay. He said, "I grabbed three bottles of wine, a change of clothes and came here and reserved this room. Then I went to work and pretended to be sick as a dog about seven o'clock. I left about seven twenty and went home because I forgot the corkscrew and laughing, he said he was too cheap to go buy another one."

I laughed but it was halfhearted. I said, "Sam, this has gotten out of hand. You do realize that, don't you?"

"I know. I know it has", he said angrily.

He was pacing and said, "I also realize I've been acting like a schoolboy after he got his first taste of pussy. Pardon my language. I've been terrible to you and feeling sorry for myself."

He turned to me from across the room and said, "Girl, you were exactly what I needed when I needed it. I've disrupted and torn into your life like a tornado, and I'm really sorry about that Felicia."

I opened my mouth to speak, but he held up his hand and said, "And about this afternoon, you know, the proposal? As much as I would be honored to have you as my wife, you deserve better. Look at me! I'm *clearly* not ready to be *anyone's* husband!"

He threw his hands up and said, "Excuse me a minute."

He walked out and left me with a heavy heart. I realized I was not in love with Sam, but I did love him. Like a friend. I felt so sorry for him and the hand that life had dealt him.

I got up and poured wine for both of us. I drank mine before he came out, and poured myself a second glass. He came out drying his hands and put the towel around my neck, pulled me into his arms and kissed me.

I looked up into those bedroom eyes and said, "No matter what happens Sam, I'm really glad we had this time together."

He took my hand and walked me over to the sofa. We both sat and he said, "Jonathon is coming for a visit. We're thinking of going into business together. Maybe you could meet him."

"Is he your best buddy you were telling me about?"

"Yep, the one and only."

"Wow, that's great news for you. When is he coming?"

"He's flying in Thursday around noon."

He was staring at me and said, "Girl, getting you outta my blood is not going to be easy. I need to make love to you one more time."

He began kissing and chewing on my neck. Although aware of the chance of a hickey, I began leaning into his kisses and wanting nothing less than all of him. And that is exactly what he gave me.

The next day was very busy for me. My boss was out of town, and she asked me to be team leader. I almost had to cancel lunch, but Trina came to my rescue. I told her I would treat her to lunch next week. She just waved me off and told me to have a good time.

I reached the DMV right at noon. DeLisa came right out and off we went. She wanted to go to Applebee's because it was only five minutes away. Annette, always on time already had a booth for us. We spent so much time catching up, I almost forgot to get the information from her. She said, "I have it right here."

She reached in her purse and handed me a piece of paper. The name on it was Julia Saunders. The address was on Mt. Hope Ave. She asked, "Do you know her?"

"I've never heard of her. What about you Nette?"

"Nope, doesn't sound familiar at all."

DeLisa asked, "What about the address? Does that look familiar?"

"Not at all. But thanks DeLisa. It might come in handy later."

"Any time Felicia. I know how I'd feel if I thought some creep was watching me!"

Again, upon my return I was informed Harold was looking for me. Being so busy, I couldn't call him right away. I was headed toward my desk around three o'clock and he was sitting on it. I walked up behind him and put my arms around him. I asked, "May I help you Handsome?"

"Be careful, my fiancée is here and might see you. Although I can't imagine anyone as charming and lovely as she is."

He laughed and turned around facing me. He said, "I was here earlier and Trina told me you took a late lunch. What's up?"

"Nothing really. Annette wanted to do lunch today, so Trina and I just switched. Did you need something?"

"As a matter of fact I do. My wife. It seems like forever since we've spent any time alone. When can I see you?"

I leaned in and asked quietly, "Sir, are you trying to get in my pants?"

He lowered his voice and said, "Ma'am, you better believe it."

After dinner, I told Harold I'd decided to hire a wedding planner. He said, "That's a great idea! Do you need more money?"

"No, Mr. Money Bags, I do not need any more money right now. By the way, I want to ask your parents about using their chefs again. I thought I'd run it by you first."

"Babe, they'll be thrilled!"

"I was hoping you'd like the idea. But your dad must promise not to do any cooking."

He laughed and said, "That'll be a first. He *is* a perfectionist."

As we continued to discuss the wedding, I noticed a different Harold. He seemed so exhilarated, like a kid in a toy store. I remember Todd not caring at all what I'd planned. By the time we cleaned the kitchen and had our third glass of wine, I said, "I'm gonna take a shower. Care to join me?"

"Absolutely! I would never deny a lady."

I laughed and went into his master bathroom, opened *my side* of the cabinet and removed my toiletries. After our engagement, he insisted on taking me on a shopping spree supplying me with everything I needed for his place.

While the water was warming, I put a drop of my Falling in Love into the shower, giving the entire bathroom a seductive scent and setting the mood.

This time last night, I was with another man and doing similar things I was about to do with Harold. If someone had told me a year ago that I would be behaving like this, I would have slapped them. Not committed, faithful, dutiful and naïve Felicia.

Harold walked into the bathroom naked as the day he was born. I looked at this man and wondered if he really is capable of spying on me. He said, "You're staring at me like you want something. And why are you still dressed?"

I was about to answer, but he said, "Never mind, I'll take care of that for you."

He began to undress me and stalled after removing my pants. He said, "Babe, you have a bruise on your thigh. What happened?"

I looked and sure enough there was not one, but two bruises on my left thigh. I said, "The other day I left my drawer open and running out of the bathroom, I ran right into it. I didn't realize I had bruises though. Wow that looks so ugly."

He kissed my thigh and said, "You gotta be careful Babe."

About four o'clock in the morning, I got up to use the bathroom. I looked at the bruises and the rest of my body. Nothing else seemed to be out of order. Then I turned around, and what I saw horrified me.

There was a hickey on my right shoulder that almost looked like a tattoo. I put my hand over my mouth, hoping Harold hadn't heard me almost scream. Had he seen it? Surely, if he had he would've said something, like with the others. Right? He didn't act like he'd seen it.

I went back into the bedroom, and gently pulled open the drawer with my night gowns. I slipped into one, and got back into bed. Luckily, Harold was laying on his right side, so I snuggled next to him with my right shoulder facing downward.

The next day I was a nervous wreck. I kept waiting for all hell to break loose. I had no idea how I would explain it. Anyhow, he was normal and had breakfast prepared before we went to work. He insisted we sit and eat. While he was pouring coffee he said, "By the way Babe...."

I started choking on my juice. I couldn't stop coughing. He got up and began patting me on my back. Hard! To keep him from asking about it, I continued to cough on purpose. I finally said, "You're killing me Harold!"

"Sorry Felicia, but you scared me."

"Well, I'm okay now. Thanks"

"Damn, I forgot what I was about to say."

I got up and said, "It's time to go."

Once at work, I couldn't seem to concentrate on anything. With Lenora back, I decided to go home early. I called Harold and told him I wasn't feeling well, and was going home. He insisted on bringing me dinner later. I was still unsure how to explain the hickey.

By ten thirty that morning, I was relaxing in a hot bubble bath. My cell phone vibrated. It was a text from Sam. It read: Hey Girl! U home? I c your car is here. Holla at me.

It was time for me to take the first step toward separation.

I emailed the wedding planner and told her she was hired. She's a friend of Trina's and came highly recommended. I was just glad to be rid of some of the work. She was adamant that I needed to get to work on my trousseau and the bridesmaids' and matrons' of honor dresses. I began perusing the internet looking for dresses, shoes, jewelry, etc.

While looking for items for my trousseau, I ran across that lingerie company, Pretty Sensations. I opened the website and low and behold, I discovered that it was owned and operated by The Saunders Holding Company. I rifled through my purse until I found it. The DMV info DeLisa had given me. The woman's name was Julia Saunders. It could've just been a coincidence, but I was sure gonna find out.

I prayed Harold and Sam would stay away. I just wanted a day to myself. And I really had to make Sam a *used to be* before he caused me to lose the best thing I'd ever had. By twelve thirty, I had a light lunch and dozed off on the couch.

After waking, I decided to do a load of laundry and I changed all of the bed linen before the boys returned on Saturday. My furnishings were very simple and plain, and I started to think about changing my décor.

Then I remembered I'd be moving soon and it dawned on me that my whole life was about to change. Harold asked me a couple of times about getting a realtor and finding a house. This was *really* happening.

I went into my closet to grab some linen, and there it was. That damn box of lingerie. Ever reminding me of…..what, exactly? There was always something spooky or incomplete about that whole thing. I went to my desk to reexamine the paperwork. Maybe there was something I could see now that I couldn't see then.

I sat down and looked at the invoice copies they'd sent me, and thank God I was sitting! No longer a coincidence, it was right there in black and white. Every item had been purchased by James Saunders!

I grabbed my phone and called Annette. She wasn't able to talk, but she said she would stop by soon because she got off early on Wednesdays.

Who the hell is James Saunders and why the hell is he sending me lingerie? And why the *hell* was Harold seen with him? The time had come for me to bring this to light. I'll be having a conversation with Harold next.

When Annette got there, I was beside myself. She brought a pizza and asked for some of Sam's wine as soon as she got in the door. She'd fallen in love with one of the red wines, so I gave her half of it and kept the other half for her to have here. She looked at me and asked, "What the hell is wrong with you?"

"Annette, I have something for you to look at."

I gave her all of the invoices, the DMV info and put my laptop in front of her to see the Pretty Sensations website. After about five minutes, she looked at me and said, "Licia, this is unbelievable! Who is this guy?"

"I know, right. But the most important question is, what the hell was Harold doing with him?"

"Oh yeah, that's right! He was the guy I saw him with. What the hell, Licia?!"

She got up and grabbed a couple of plates and handed me a slice of pizza. I said, "Annette, I'll be asking his ass tonight about this. I don't have time for this shit! If he…"

Annette put her hand up and said, "Hold on a minute Licia. You're still assuming Harold is guilty of something. I admit I saw him hand the guy something, but that doesn't prove he's guilty of anything. Just calm down and eat your pizza."

The last thing I wanted was damn pizza!

I said, "Annette…"

I put my hands over my face and cried. Annette came over and put her arms around me. As I cried in the arms of my bestie, she said very quietly, "Licia, although Harold *may be* guilty of something, I don't think it's anything more than a man so in love, that he *may have* felt the need to hire someone to keep an eye on his fiancée. One thing I know is men, and I truly believe your Mr. Benson is a keeper."

"Nette, I'm not marrying someone who wants to control me and believes it's okay to hire spies to watch me. That's insanity."

"Licia, do you still trust my instincts?"

All I could do was laugh. When we were teenagers, Annette had the most uncanny way of determining whether or not a guy was sincere, was a virgin, was a playa, and even which guys would be successful in life.

Girls would ask her to have conversations with their boyfriends, and she'd report back to them with her findings. And they paid her for that shit! It was hilarious!

After she and I finally stopped laughing, I said, "Annette, if he did hire this guy, why would someone who owns this lingerie business take a job like that?"

"I don't know the answer to that question Licia. As a matter of fact, I don't know the answer to a lot of the questions around this mystery, which is why I want you to wait so we can figure some of this shit out. Let's give Harold a week's reprieve, and totally immerse ourselves into solving this mystery. Deal?"

After dinner was over, Harold asked me if he could stay overnight. I said, "Honestly Hun, I think I'd rather curl up alone with these cramps. Are you okay with that?"

"You know, you're gonna have to get used to me lying next to you when you're on your period. You're not gonna kick me out once a month, are you?"

"No silly. Besides, I'm not on my period. It's PMS. It comes before my period."

Finally he prepared to leave, but only after insisting on tucking me into bed. He's such a sweetie, but can sometimes tear my nerves up, I swear.

As he was leaving my room, he turned around and said, "Oh, I remember what I wanted to ask you this morning just before you started choking."

I truly believed my blood stopped midstream in my veins. He said, "I got a call from Tiffany's. Why did you return your necklace? They said you never opened the package. Is that true?"

"*You* sent that?! I thought it was another computer glitch!"

"Babe, that was a lingerie company, wasn't it?"

"I didn't think of it like that. I returned anything I didn't order."

We both laughed and he finally left.

I waited ten seconds after hearing the door close, and then I ran into the living room to see him start his car and leave. I grabbed my cell phone and checked for texts from Annette. There were three.

Earlier before she left, she reminded me she used to date a guy named Benny who was a private detective. She said he'd do anything she asked. Her texts asked me to call her as soon as possible, but not after ten o'clock. It was eight-forty so I quickly dialed her number.

She said, "This shit continues to get weirder by the minute."

"What do you mean?"

"James Saunders, owner of Pretty Sensations Lingerie Company, died six years ago. His wife, Julia Saunders, took over operating the company and is still the owner. Did you know the company is right here in Rochester?"

"Nette, hold it! Too many questions! First of all, if James Saunders is dead, who was that you saw with Harold? Secondly, no I did not know the company was here. And if he's been dead for six years, why was I told the account was recently closed? I wonder if that was Julia Saunders."

Annette laughed and said, "Now you're asking too many questions. Benny said he would go there some time in the next few days and fill out an employment application. He'll try to learn as much as he can."

"I sure hope this isn't costing more than I can pay."

"Girl, I've got so much on that man that he offered to pay *me* to do this job."

"You know it's killing me to look Harold in the eye and not punch him in it. I'm glad you have faith in him, because I sure believe he's guilty as hell! Of what, I'm not exactly sure yet."

"Felicia, let's continue on until we've resolved this."

"I'm trying Nette. I would….Damn! Hold on Annette. Someone is at my door, and I *know* it's Sam!"

I peeped out and sure enough it was Sam. I didn't answer. After a few minutes, he walked away. I said, "He's gone."

Annette said, "It just dawned on me that we shouldn't dismiss Sam as a suspect here. Remember he loves you enough to propose marriage. He could be trying to sabotage your relationship with Harold. Now, where he fits in with the Saunders, I don't have a clue, but it's possible that he's not innocent in this craziness."

"I don't think so Nette. Hell, I don't know what to think anymore."

"I gotta tell you. I don't know how you can deny that fine ass man anything."

We both laughed and I said, "Annette, guess what?"

"I don't know how much more I can take. What is it?"

"Sam is the size of a horse, and gives head like a hungry animal."

She screamed and then I screamed and we both laughed and talked about sex for the next half hour.

The next morning at seven a.m. I made two calls. One to my boss, to inform her I had the flu and the second to Harold to inform him of the same thing and that I would not be back to work until Monday.

At eight fifteen, I was walking into Todd Jr.'s school and had breakfast with him. At nine-thirty, I called Annette and asked her to do something I didn't want to do, but knew I had to do, to keep my sanity.

I asked her to ask Benny to do a background check on Harold and Sam. At eleven thirty, I went to Marcus' daycare and had lunch with him.

I missed my babies.

Chapter Eight

Friday afternoon, after a visit to the salon and a little shopping, I pulled up in our parking lot in time to see Sam and a strange man coming out of his apartment. I remembered Sam telling me that his friend from Richmond was coming to visit. After introductions and pleasantries, Sam said, "Wow Felicia! You look great! Where are you headed?"

"Thanks Sam. I played hookie from work today, and decided to treat myself to a day of indulgence."

All the while Sam and I were talking, I noticed Jonathon looking at me in a way that was both flattering and unsettling. I said, "Well guys. Enjoy your night out. I'm sure the ladies of Rochester are in big trouble with you two handsome gents on the prowl."

Jonathon finally spoke up. He said, "Felicia, we would be honored if you and a friend would join us for a night on the town, or just dinner since it's short notice. Could we persuade you to be our guest?"

"Jonathon, I really appreciate the invite, but I have plans."

After studying me for a moment, he said, "Well, I understand. But promise me we'll get together before I leave. Maybe we could all go to lunch or have drinks?"

"That sounds great Jonathon. Sam and I will work it out. You guys enjoy yourselves and don't get into any trouble."

As I prepared to leave, Sam came closer and hugged me. Then Jonathon did the same. He said, "It's been my pleasure meeting you Felicia. I must say you are quite the enchantress."

"Nice meeting you too. See you guys later!"

That's when I felt like Gloria in 'Waiting to Exhale', when she walked away from Marvin switching her behind, hoping he was watching.

When I got on the other side of my door, I started breathing again. I laughed so hard, I had to run to the bathroom before I had an accident.

While washing my hands, I looked in the mirror and realized I looked damn good. I also saw the image of a woman that was somewhat foreign to me, but I liked most of what I saw.

I enjoyed the attention and the hug from Jonathon. Jonathon wasn't as handsome as Sam, but he was extremely sexy. Chocolate with beautiful Locs, flawless skin and an athletic build. I tried very hard not to seem affected by him, but truthfully, from the time I saw him walking toward me, I knew I was in trouble. Again.

Because Tony has been working nights lately, Annette and I have spent the last two nights on the phone. The background checks both came back clean. Benny said he would tail Julia Saunders for a few days, and if anything came up, he would let us know.

Harold made reservations at a new supper club. I was anxious because Carla and Annette and their husbands were also coming. We agreed to go Saturday night and to meet there about eight.

When we got there, Harold had reserved the VIP section for us. Everyone was impressed, but I wasn't quite sure how I felt. I hated to think he was doing that to show off.

Everything was going well until it was time for the girls to go to the ladies room. On our way out, Carla almost ran right into Sam. He said, "Wow, look who's here!"

I froze, but Annette and Carla were thrilled to see him. Carla said, "Hey Sam. How are you?"

"Even better now. How are you Ladies?"

He hugged her and then Annette. Then he turned to me and said, "Hey Miss Felicia. Don't I get some love?"

I hugged Sam and out of the corner of my eye I saw Jonathon

approaching. He hugged me and turned toward Annette and Carla. He said, "Wow Felicia! Do all of your friends look this gorgeous? Hello Ladies. My name is Jonathon."

He took each of their hands and kissed it. I said, "Jonathon, these are my sisters Annette and Carla. Ladies, meet Jonathon, Sam's friend from Richmond."

After a few minutes of small talk, we made our excuses and left them there. As we walked back to the men, all three had their eyes on us. The first to speak was Earl. He asked, "And who the hell were those guys?"

I immediately responded with, "That was my neighbor and his buddy. I introduced them. I hope that was okay?"

Earl looked at Carla and then at me and said, "Oh. Yeah, it's okay."

I turned to Harold and asked, "You wanna dance?"

"Sure Babe."

Later, we noticed Sam with a woman who was dressed a bit sleazy. Harold said, "I wouldn't think he would be attracted to that type of woman."

I thought, here it comes. I asked, "What type of woman?"

"Well, you know. *That* type."

"Harold, you're speaking in riddles. What type are you referring to?"

By then the others were all waiting to hear the answer too. He said, "Nothing, just forget it."

Carla, who never upsets the apple cart, said, "No Harold. I would like to hear what type of woman she is too."

Then Tony said, "Okay, let's not jump all over Harold. It's clear you all know what he's talking about, but you want to crucify the man for telling the truth."

Annette asked, "And what is the truth Tony? Let's hear it."

So Tony and Harold and Earl, all at once, began explaining what type of woman she was. Words like desperate, easy, classless, broke, uneducated, gold-digger, hood rat, etc, etc, etc.

First of all, I was both offended and outraged. I couldn't believe what I'd just heard! Carla seemed undone, and Annette was eating her shrimp. So when she lifted her martini to her mouth and saw my outrage, she asked, "What the hell is wrong with you?"

Carla asked, "Annette. You're not offended by what these men just said?"

She thought about it a minute and said, "Not really. I mean, I'm not surprised."

Now the men were thrilled because they had someone on their side. Earl said, "See Carla. You're always dogging men when there are women that see it too."

It turned into a full blown argument. I finally said, "That's enough!"

Well, Earl and Tony were speechless. Annette and Carla were fuming. I looked at Harold and he looked at me. I said, "Harold, it's time to go."

He turned to them and said, "I feel awful for causing this uproar. Please accept my apologies"

Everyone told him not to worry and it was okay. We soon left.

Once we were in the car, Harold exhaled and I turned to look out of the window. He said, "Felicia, I'm really sorry."

When I didn't respond, he said, "Felicia, I know you're mad at me. If I could undo it, I would."

I slowly turned toward Harold. I asked, "Is it Sam? What is it?"

"Felicia. I admit I was jealous of Sam in the past. My jealousy came from what I thought I saw in your eyes. It was only a moment. But I thought I saw you look at him like you have *never* looked at me."

"You're kidding, right?"

"It haunted me for a while, but..."

"Harold. I have eyes for one man. You. Okay?"

I turned toward the window again. I felt terrible.

When we arrived at my apartment, I asked him to go on home and we'd talk tomorrow. He said okay, but insisted the boys and me have lunch with him the next day at one o'clock. I kissed him and told him we'd be there. He watched me go inside of my apartment and he pulled off.

It was one fifteen a.m. by the time I got my nightshirt and leggings on. I couldn't sleep, so I turned the TV on and opened up my laptop. I heard a text come in. It was from Sam and it read: after Harold dropped you off, he went to the end of the street and parked. He's watching you.

I ran to the boys' room and looked out of their window, and there he was! The *nerve* of him! I was really hoping Sam was lying. I replied and thanked him. I sat on Marcus' bed and felt like walking out of the door and confronting him. That bastard should get a dose of his own medicine.

Why is he doing this to me? How much does he *really* know? He said earlier that I looked at Sam *like I never looked at him*. Hmmm? When was that? That day he caught Sam here? That day, I should have had a look of horror on my face. But maybe, as he said, *for a moment*, maybe he did see…...something.

I paced a while and finally went to bed. By daylight, I was up and ran to the window. He was gone. I took a shower, threw on some sweats and tidied up the apartment.

I was about to fix something to eat when there was a knock on the door. I looked out and it was Jonathon. I opened the door and he said, "Good morning Sunshine! I hope it's not *too* early for a neighbor to borrow a couple of eggs."

"No, come on in and good morning to you too!"

He walked in and I offered him a seat. As I headed toward the kitchen, I asked, "Did you guys enjoy yourselves at the club?"

He laughed and said, "It was interesting. I know you saw that woman with Sam."

"I did. What about her?"

"Didn't you think she lacked…sophistication? Honestly, she didn't really suit my…taste. Now you and your girls, you suit my taste perfectly."

I thought, although worded differently, that's the same shit I heard last night! I asked, "Jonathon, why do me and my girls suit you, but she didn't? Honestly?"

"It's all about class. Now, I don't mean coming from money or being in the right family. When I say class, I mean things like etiquette, being ladylike, having style, attention to detail, stuff like that. To me, those things may sound old fashioned, but I gravitate toward women who care about appearances, because I care about appearances. I think a lot of people think that if they come from a poor family or some dysfunctional situation, their thinking and behavior must also be substandard. But my mom was a single mother with three knuckleheaded sons, and we all did well."

I admit he had a point. I said, "That was a great answer."

"Our lifestyles are sometimes dictated by our income or our exposure.

But most of the time we choose *how* we live. I don't believe you need to have a six figure income to exhibit class or act like a lady."

"And you're right. We all decide how we want the world to see us. Thanks for sharing that with me. I enjoyed our little talk."

"Me too Felicia. And those eggs are about ready to hatch!"

We both laughed and I gave him the bowl I put the eggs in. I asked, "What are you gonna do with *two* eggs anyhow?"

"Well, I planned to make pancakes, but I really think I'd like to go out for breakfast. Interested? We can go and get Sam and be back by ten."

"Actually, I have some things I need to attend to, but thanks anyhow."

Jonathan headed toward the door and said, "Listen, if you change your mind about breakfast, let us know soon."

And out he went. I looked at the closed door for about thirty seconds. I was just given an invitation to be with two great guys and I plan to take full advantage of it. I ran into my room and quickly got dressed. Then I called Sam and told him I was going. He asked me to come on down.

When Jonathon answered the door, he said, "Sam's in his room. Go on in."

I walked in, expecting him to be on his way out and ready to go, but he was completely naked. He turned around to face me, and asked me to close the door. I stood there with my mouth opened. I looked at the door, then at him and back at the door. He whispered, "Felicia, please."

I closed the door but continued to face it. He was behind me so quickly, and had his hands on me so fast, and his tongue was dancing on my neck and I could feel him pulsating behind me, that I didn't know what to do. This was the first time I actually wanted to say no. He said, "Please, just once more…please."

By then he was up against me and breathing so hard and smelling so good and feeling so familiar. I put my head against the door and allowed him to remove my jeans and underwear. I could hear the condom package ripping, but when he attempted to enter me from behind, it just wouldn't go in. He got on his knees and buried his tongue inside of me.

I began scratching at the door, forgetting about Jonathon in the next room. I cried out and melted quickly and almost lost my balance.

He got up and was inside of me. My mind went totally blank. His massiveness had me so stretched, it felt like when I was giving birth. I have no idea how much noise I made or what I said.

When it was over, he held me so close and so tight. He picked me up and carried me to the bed. He said, "Listen, I...."

"Sam, you're better off not making any more promises. We both are."

He laid beside me, and held me in his arms. There was a knock on the door. I panicked and Sam said, "Relax, Girl. It's only Jonathon."

I looked at him and whispered, "*Only* Jonathon?"

He got up and put his sweats on. When he went to the door, I got up but he said, "No, just stay there. It's okay."

So I went under the covers trying to hide my embarrassment. When the door opened, Jonathon came into the room. I was so mad at Sam! I had my back to them, so I didn't realize he had gone out and picked up breakfast. He said, "Rise and shine! We have fresh fruit, bagels, bacon, coffee and more!"

I went further under the covers and said, "Sam, make him go away!"

Jonathon said, "Come on, I thought we were friends."

Sam said, "We'll be out in a little while. Thanks for the food."

When I heard the door close, I popped my head out and saw he was gone. Sam got back in the bed and snuggled with me under the covers. He had his hand under my bra and I closed my eyes and just enjoyed the feel of him. As he descended further under the covers, I could only imagine where he would take me this time. I was in absolute ecstasy.

He asked me to get up, sit on his chest and hold on to the headboard. But first, he went to the head of the bed and propped his head on a couple of pillows. I did as he asked and he said, "Don't let go Baby."

Then he brought me toward his face and took my breath away. We were so engrossed that I never heard Jonathon enter the room, or get on the bed. I never knew he had straddled Sam. But what I *did* know was there was someone behind me with a penis, and they were now kissing me and had their hands under my breasts! I also knew that I was far more turned on than turned off. He whispered in my ear, "Is it good, Enchantress? Shall I continue?"

His tongue was in my ear, and Sam's tongue was already dancing with my G-spot. The two of them destroyed any common sense I had. He said, "I need an answer Love. Shall I proceed?"

My mind was reeling! I had to know what I was dying to know.
"yes"

I screamed so loud, that my voice was unrecognizable to me. Jonathon had taken me off of Sam, put on a condom and entered me from behind. Sam was kissing me and slid under me and began feasting on my breasts. There was so much going on, I feared someone else had joined the party.

Jonathon was magical behind me. He kept saying how great I was. The fire was building so fast, it felt like an avalanche of heat in my groin. My equilibrium no longer worked. My orgasm was so explosive that I feared my heart had stopped. Sam abandoned me, and so did Jonathon.

I was taken off of the bed and put in a kneeling position over the side of the bed. Sam came up behind me and whispered, "I want to take you higher than you've ever been."

He mounted me and I groaned. I grabbed the sheets *and* the air. Anything to keep from losing my mind. Jonathon was suddenly in front of me. He kissed me so sweetly and tenderly. He said, "I need that pretty mouth right here."

He sat in front of me and scooted down so his legs were on either side of me head. I reached in front of me and began to stroke him. I kissed him and licked him and he pulsated in my hand.

He moaned his appreciation. I leaned down and took all of him and he begged me not to stop. Sam behind me went deeper. Fireworks were exploding in my head. Jonathon growled as he came with me. Sam grabbed my waist and released himself inside of me. He kept saying how much he loved me and asked if I loved him too. I don't remember if I answered him. He screamed my name and......

I was certain this would surely kill me.

When I woke up, I was alone in Sam's bed. I looked at the clock and it said twelve fifteen. I panicked. I jumped up and realized I was naked and then I realized I was too embarrassed to face them.

On a tray table next to the bed was an assortment of fruit and bagels, cheese and spreads and some juice and coffee.

I got up and went into the master bathroom. I was so light headed, it felt almost like a hangover. I couldn't even look in the mirror. When I finished in the bathroom, I went back into the bedroom and dressed.

I found my purse, grabbed my cell phone and called Todd. I went back into the bathroom, praying he would answer. Gina answered and told me that Todd and the boys left about twenty minutes earlier.

There was a knock on the door, so I finished with Gina, and hung up. I went back into the bedroom and answered the door. Sam said, "Your son just left. He wanted to know if I'd seen you."

"Oh no, what did you say?"

"Well, I told him I hadn't seen you today."

"Okay, that's good. Anything else? Did he ask you anything else?"

"No, but they saw your car and wondered where you could be."

I went into the living room and looked out of the window. I didn't see them. I asked, "Do you think they're gone?"

"I'll go out and see."

He walked out and I went back into the bedroom. My hands were shaking. I couldn't believe I wasn't there for my kids. And I couldn't *bear* to be in the same room with either of them, especially Jonathon.

I paced until he came back. He said, "There's no sign of them."

"Okay, I need to go home."

I felt awkward, but I managed to say goodbye and ran out. When I was back in my apartment, I immediately called Harold and told him we would probably be late, because I missed Todd when I ran out to the store. He said, "Babe, the boys are here. When you didn't answer the door, Todd called me and I told him he could bring them here."

"They're with you?"

"Yes. You went to the store without your car?"

"Yeah. I went with Carol. I'll be right there."

After lunch, the boys were in Harold's guest room playing with the new WII he bought for them. I was going over in my mind all of the details of the day, because the barrage of questions were soon to come. He sat next to me and asked, "Babe, are you still mad at me?"

"Harold, did you notice I didn't attack you like my girls attacked their husbands?"

"Yes, I did."

"Do you know why?"

"Actually no, I don't. At first I thought I was just lucky, but when we got in the car, I realized you were pissed too. Why was I spared?"

I turned to him and said, "Because I don't believe in making a public spectacle of myself or my man. Nor do I believe in arguing and cussing and carrying on. Truth is, I was as upset as Carla and Annette, but I worry about saying things you can't take back."

"What can I do to make up for this mess?"

I looked at Harold and asked, "Have you been watching me?"

He opened his mouth, but nothing came out. He got up and walked into the kitchen and said, "Felicia, I… Yes, I have. Now you know."

He came back and said, "You have no idea how much I worry about you and those boys! I keep asking you to find a house, but it doesn't seem important to you! When I see the weirdos around here, it makes me crazy! So yes, sometimes I keep watch and twice I even paid someone to keep watch while I was away!"

My mind was going a mile a minute, and I'm sure his was too. We were both trying to decide what to say next. And what not to say. He asked, "Felicia, how did you know?"

"The night you walked Annette to her car, she saw you."

"She saw what?"

"She saw you and some guy, and you gave him something."

"Hmmm…okay, so why didn't you ask me then? Why now?"

"Because *now* is when I decided to ask? I don't know, Harold. I'm really freaked out over this. I was hoping it wasn't true, and you'd give me a perfectly logical explanation."

"Honestly, I thought Sam would have told you, since he was the one I asked first."

"What did you say?"

"Sam. I asked Sam to keep an eye on you and the boys, but he said he couldn't because he worked until midnight. He didn't tell you?"

It felt like the earth was literally moving under my feet. I called myself catching Harold off guard, and he just did to me what Lawrence Taylor used to do to quarterbacks. I was blindsided. Never saw it coming.

I wasn't sure if this was part of his strategy, or if Harold was genuinely coming clean. And my failure to respond (or inability), could have been exactly what he wanted to see. I said, "No, Sam didn't tell me. I guess it's a guy thing, and truthfully I don't talk with Sam that much."

I waited for a reaction, but saw none. I said, "Harold. You and I are gonna have to be on the same page here. I won't go around wondering who the hell is watching me."

"Felicia, I'm *never* gonna stop worrying about you all. But I'll make a deal with you. If you promise to find a house, I'll promise to stop playing security guard."

All I could think about was how to cuss Sam's ass out. I was trying very hard to concentrate on this conversation, but it was extremely difficult. He asked, "Babe, you still have the card?"

"What?"

"The realtor's business card, do you still have it?"

"Yes, I have it. What about it?"

"I promised to stop playing security guard if you promise to find and move into a house, as soon as possible. Okay?"

I thought about that. I also thought about how Sam had betrayed me. No, not betrayed. Used! I was livid on both accounts. I stood and said, "Harold, I will not promise any such thing!"

I felt Felicia Pierce rising up in me! I said, "I will not marry anyone who believes it's okay to lie and control my life! I'm starting to think this marriage thing is a big mistake. I can't marry you. *I can't marry you Harold!*"

Once the boys were asleep, I marched down the stairs to Sam's and knocked on the door. He answered and smiled that famous, gorgeous dimpled smile of his. He said, "Come on in here Girl! I'm so glad to see you! Is everything okay?"

I looked at him without answering. I realized I didn't want to do this in front of Jonathon. I asked, "Are you alone?"

"No, but I think Jon has fallen asleep watching some baseball game in my room. Oh, and Aysia is in her room asleep. What's wrong Sweetie?"

I grabbed his hand and pulled him outside the door. I said, "Sam, you *knew* Harold had been watching me all along and you didn't *tell me!*"

He opened his mouth and I said, "Oh, and you *also* failed to tell me that he asked you to watch us! How could you do that to me?"

"Felicia, you can't possibly know how I agonized over that! I felt if I told you, you'd assume I was making it up to somehow cause a wedge between you two. I worked very hard to keep our relationship free of anything like that. When he asked me, I was stunned. He also asked me not to mention it to you."

Sam's eyes pleaded with me to believe him. I no longer believed *either* of them. I said, "I'm so disappointed Sam. You used me."

"That's not true! I..."

I started to cry and he came toward me. I raised my hands and said, "Don't touch me!"

I backed up and said quietly, "Don't you *ever* touch me again."

I threw my hands up and walked back upstairs.

My phones were blowing up. Harold and Sam. I turned off the ringer on the house phone and put my cell on vibrate. I was drowning in bubbles and surprised I wasn't more upset.

Maybe I was just numb or maybe it was the entire bottle of wine I drank. Or *maybe*, it was the wine that numbed me! I sent texts to Carla and Annette telling them the wedding was off, and that Sam was not innocent after all, like Annette had said.

Annette said she'd be right over and Carla asked what the hell I was talking about. She also said she'd be right over.

So before I got in the tub, I put a spare key under the mat and told them to come on in, since they'd agreed to come together. When they arrived, I asked Annette to keep the key.

I told them I was not leaving the tub, so they would have to endure my stubbornness and nakedness. Annette gave Carla a complete update on the ride over, and she was pissed. She said, "I still can't believe you kept this from me. You know I'm the best when it comes to investigative work. I am a teacher, after all!"

Annette and I cracked up. Annette said, "You don't even know what your own children are up to most of the time! Let alone your husband!"

Annette *really* laughed at that. I stopped laughing. That wasn't funny to me. None of it was funny anymore. I went under the water and wanted to stay there. To hide from the rest of the world, forever and ever. Amen.

What a fool I've been! How do I tell them? I finally came up out of the water, and I began to cry for so many reasons. For falling in love with a man that wants to control my life. For allowing a gorgeous man to use me. And for failing at a marriage, yet still not knowing what I did wrong.

I could never have imagined *me* in a ménage a trois. My imagination didn't extend that far. As ashamed as I was for being so gullible, and as embarrassing as it was to admit it, there was a sensual, erotic woman inside of me that did not regret it.

Felicia Pierce is that woman. She's a full grown woman with full grown needs. Admittedly, she didn't know it until recently, but she's well aware of it now. She has her big girl panties on and is evicting Felicia Wilson.

As my sisters attempted to comfort me, Annette said, "Damn Girl, you smell like a wino!"

Carla said, "It's that French wine. It's potent!"

Annette said, "Okay Licia, what else is going on?"

After telling them every detail, even Annette was speechless. But she managed to say, "I should put a bullet in his fucking head!"

I said, "Nette. It's not like I said no. And not like I didn't…"

They waited for my answer. Eventually Carla said, "You know Licia, I'm not that surprised. They say a woman's libido could spike after a tragedy. You know, like a death or divorce."

"Carla, I honestly think it's because I've been with men who were better lovers. I don't think Todd knew he wasn't reaching me. I didn't even know"

"But Licia, you said Todd satisfied you. What are you saying now?"

"I'm *saying* I was a virgin. I didn't know the difference between good and bad sex. Todd made me feel good Carla. I don't think it was bad sex as much as it was his and my lack of experience."

Annette said, "Carla, it's the reason people cheat. Like Todd. Once he knew satisfaction at a higher level, he wasn't *completely* satisfied with basic sex."

By now, my bath water was cold. And I wasn't as numb as before. I said, "Let's go into my bedroom so I can put some clothes on."

Annette said, "I have some information for you from Benny. He found out something very interesting."

"Annette, how long have you had it?"

"Just today. I was gonna give it to you tomorrow, but after your announcement, I decided to tell you tonight. First of all, the car that was registered to Julia Saunders is actually driven by Robert Covello, her brother. And that address DeLisa gave you is a house owned by Julia too, but rented by Robert. She owns the house and car that he uses."

"Well, that *is* interesting. But I don't see how it helps me."

Annette grinned and said, "There's more. Guess where Robert Covello works?"

I shook my head and said, "Where, I don't know?"

She stood and said, "Bausch and Lomb. On the evening shift."

I opened my mouth, but nothing came out. Finally she said, "Let me summarize. Sam saw you and slithered his way into your life. He learned you were already involved, so he decided to fuck you into loving him. And when Harold asked him to watch you, instead of telling you, he asked one of his buddies to do it, and that way he wouldn't have to worry about your affair being reported back to Harold. What I saw that night was Harold paying Robert to watch you."

As the quiet descended upon the room, I got up and walked over to Annette. I said, "And the lingerie must have come from Sam. He was friends with the owner's brother."

Annette got up and said, "We ought to go down there and beat his pretty black ass! The three of us could tear his ass up!"

Carla quietly said, "No, we've always done things with class."

I looked at Annette and we both fell on the bed cracking up! I said, "I'm sorry Carla. We may be classy ladies now, but you whipped so much ass back in the day, some people are still scared just to speak to you!"

Annette hollered and said, "Yeah, and because I was always in somebody's face talking shit, she had to whip more ass on my account than on her own!"

Annette turned to Carla and said, "But it's all right Cuz. I appreciate you having my back."

Carla took a sip of her wine and choked. She laughed and we started laughing all over again. We talked until eleven thirty and devised a plan that would hopefully get me out of this mess.

Chapter Nine

When I reached my desk the next morning, there was a beautiful arrangement of flowers on it. I assumed it was from Harold, but after what I'd been through, I checked and confirmed it.

As planned, I went up to his department at lunch time. He watched me as I approached his desk. I sat down and sat my ring in front of him. I said, "Harold, we need to figure out a way to end this gracefully. I appreciate the flowers, but I must get on with my life and learn to live it without you."

I put my head down, and prayed this worked. He got up from his desk, grabbed my hand and said, "Let's go outside for a minute."

When all the dust cleared last night, Annette convinced me that Harold was, as she predicted, only guilty of loving me. After all of our investigative work, along with Benny's, we never found him guilty of anything other than watching me.

When we got outside, we sat on one of the benches and he said, "Felicia. You mean everything in this world to me. I admit I screwed up royally, but I also learned a big lesson. My dad told me that when a man truly loves a woman, he sometimes makes the mistake of holding on so tight, that he bruises her beautiful wings. I'm sorry for that."

"Harold. You mean everything to me too. But I can't live my life with someone who wants to control me or worrying about being followed. It's unsettling."

He raised my chin and said, "Please give me another chance. I love you so much. I'll give you all the freedom you need. Please Felicia."

I stared at him. I said, "I'll put this mess in the past if you promise to respect my space."

"I promise Felicia. I can't imagine my life without you."

I looked into his eyes and said, "I'll call the realtor today. What part of town are you interested in?"

He smiled and we embraced. I said, "I don't think we should live together until after the wedding. But, let's get the house now and the boys and I will move in as soon as school is out. Is that okay?"

"Babe, I love that idea! That way you and the boys will already be settled once we're married. I love you so much."

He kissed me and it seemed like forever since I'd been in his arms. As usual, Annette's plan worked perfectly.

By Wednesday, I'd received a total of one hundred and fourteen texts, calls, emails, visits and notes. I responded to none of them. Although I was thoroughly pissed, I felt a sense of sadness for Sam. I'll always fear that Sam will someday decide to tell Harold about our affair. Annette advised me to simply deny it. *Simply?*

There are so many lingering questions I may never know the answer to. Like the hickey. Did he see it? Or when he came over unexpectedly. Were the blinds open enough that he could see inside? Not to mention Sunday, when no one could find me, yet my car was home. And those are just some of the things I'm aware of.

Does Harold love me so much, that even knowing these things he'd overlook them? I don't think so.

I admit I'll miss Sam a lot. He brought a different kind of fun and excitement to my life. A more relaxed, limitless, unexpected kind of fun. He was the one I had sex with, whereas Harold was who I made love to.

Although I did things with Sam I'd probably (did I just say probably) never do again, it was Harold who gave me the courage and confidence to do it. The Pierce in me wonders what else Sam had up his sleeves.

Since sex can be such a powerful thing, I still wonder why it's so often referred to as *just sex*. From the beginning, Harold was very concerned that

I could be used sexually. Because I knew it wasn't my style to sleep around, I totally disregarded his warning.

I don't *really* think it was Sam's intention to *use* me. What I'd *like* to think is that he found me so irresistible, he lost all sense of reality, since that's *my* excuse.

But what I *honestly* think is that he fell in lust with me and no longer wanted to share me with Harold. I think when I turned down his proposal of marriage, he escalated his efforts. And when he saw Harold playing security guard, he decided to use that opportunity to tell me I was being watched.

It's scary to think how close I came to losing Harold, and how conniving Sam is. But I never said no to Sam. That will always be my fault, no matter what he did.

Another thing became very clear to me. Betrayal wasn't something I handled very well. I made a habit of running fast and far from it. Although Harold was dishonest with me, I believed he had my best interest at heart. Sam had his own damn interest at heart! But I was unable to hate him. Just like Todd. I had four houses to look at.

By the end of the week, I had chosen a house. A beautiful new build just outside of Rochester in Gates, NY. Forty six hundred square feet, six bedrooms and six baths. Harold insisted on a lot of space because of his large family.

It was available for immediate occupancy, so when Harold told the realtor we'd be taking possession in thirty days, I couldn't wait for him to get off the phone. I said, "I've been waiting for you to tell me what the down payment and monthly payments will be. I told you I wanted to pay half of the down payment. I've been saving for this."

"Babe, it's all taken care of. The list price was $399,000. We received ten percent off for paying in full. I'm sending a bank check to the builder for $350,000. That's what we settled on."

"Harold, I can't live in a house I have no investment in, in case…"

"*In case?* Are you planning our divorce before we're even married?"

"No. Of course not. But it would be foolish of me.."

"I absolutely agree with you. That's why the house is yours. In your name, as a gift from me. I'm the co-buyer. So don't be looking for another wedding gift Missy!"

He laughed and walked into his kitchen. I said, "Harold that is *so* not necessary. Why don't we just do like most people and pay for it together?"

"Because you'll be busy saving your money for the boys' college funds. That fifty thousand you've saved is the seed money for them."

I opened my mouth, but could think of nothing to say. All I could think of was doing something just as special for him. I decided to give him what he wanted.

When I got home, I was like a little girl. I couldn't believe I was about to live in such a beautiful home. With today being Friday before Memorial Day, we both took a half day vacation. We wanted to take another look at the house before we put in an offer.

Todd and Gina are picking the boys up and taking them to the beach, so they'll be gone until Monday. I began to twirl around and while I was laughing, I noticed my bedroom door opening. Sam came out and said, "Please don't be afraid. I wanted to see you once more before I left."

I was backing up toward the door and he put his hands up and said, "Girl, you don't really think I would hurt you, do you?"

"What are you doing here and how did you get into my apartment?"

"I was worried about you. I know you don't want to see me anymore, but I'm still concerned about you. Are you okay?"

I turned the doorknob and walked out. I headed toward my car, but realized my purse and keys were still in the apartment. Sam came behind me carrying both. He said, "Felicia, wait. Will you at least talk to me?"

I took my stuff and said, "How dare you break into my home! I should call the police!"

I got into my car and he quickly got in the passenger side. I said, "Get the hell out of my car!"

"Damn Girl, I can't believe you won't at least give me a chance to explain."

"How the hell did you get into my home?"

"I admit I got a key made some time ago. Remember when I took your car to get the tire fixed? I also admit this is not the first time I've been in your place. Felicia, please don't hate me. This is killing me."

"You can't possibly think I would believe *anything* you have to say. I trusted you and you shit all over me!"

"That's not true Felicia. I didn't want to lose you."

He turned his head, but not before I saw a tear roll down his face.

I asked, "Why did you treat me like that?"

"I panicked. You had me spellbound."

"As much as I detest what you did to me, I don't hate you. But if you *ever* break in my house again, I swear I will have your ass locked up! And give me my damn key!"

He said quietly, "I left it on your coffee table. And it's true you remind me of Antoinette. I never put it together until you mentioned it that day. Another truth is I would go in your apartment while you were working, just to be in your personal space. I know I sound like a nut. Maybe I am. But I swear, I *never* meant to hurt you. Anyhow, I got a buyer for my house. I've decided to move to Richmond, and Jonathon and I plan to purchase a second Popeye's together."

I looked at this man who so selfishly disrupted my life, and truthfully had me spellbound as well. I said, "I'm happy for you Sam. But I need you to promise me you will never attempt to contact me again."

"I promise Felicia. You're free of me, I swear."

We got out of the car and I asked, "When are you leaving?"

"In a month, as soon as school is out. I gave my two week notice last week, so next Friday is my last day."

"Okay, I guess this is goodbye then. Tell Aysia I said goodbye too."

I walked away feeling a multitude of emotions. He asked, "Did you like it?"

I stopped in my track. I knew *exactly* what he was referring to. I couldn't decide whether to keep walking or turn around and answer him.

When I returned to my apartment, I felt somewhat somber. I guess it's foolish, but I'm *really* gonna miss Sam. I headed straight for the kitchen to get a glass of wine. I noticed the key he left, and the crate of wine he left, which he failed to mention! There was also a note:

> Felicia, I know you're gonna be pissed, but I have a key to
> your apartment. I had it made some time ago. It was my

way of being near you. I'm leaving Rochester soon, so I'll probably never see you again. I'll leave your key on the coffee table. By the way, the wine is a small token to say how very sorry I am. It's an entire case of your favorite....Sam.

I looked around as if someone was in my living room. I'm spooked by the slightest noise now, thanks to Mr. Sam. I tore the note into a million pieces and set it on fire. Then I went into my bedroom, to be sure there weren't any surprises there.

After checking the bathroom and closet, I went back into the kitchen and poured myself a healthy glass of wine. I emptied and washed the bowl I burned the note in, and sat down and drank the wine.

Sam and his tricks. Even while apologizing profusely, he was sitting on one last trick. If I'd come home with Harold, he would have surely seen that note.

Sam's probably expecting me to call him and cuss him out about the note. But I believe my silence is more effective. Like me not answering his question. I wanted to tell him I didn't like it. But he *knew* I loved it. And that knowledge was the last thing he would ever get from me.

I got up and checked the rest of the apartment.

I sent Annette and Carla texts asking them for an emergency meeting. Carla said she needed an hour and Annette knocked on my door ten minutes later. She came in and flopped down and said, "I'm so glad it's Friday *and* we have a three day weekend! So, what's the emergency?"

"Believe me. You'll need a drink for this."

I went into the kitchen and she was right behind me. She said, "I'll get my own drink. You talk."

I told her all that happened. She said, "Girl, I don't know what you got in them panties of yours, but we need to bottle that shit and sell it! Damn Licia! That man has lost his mind over you!"

I looked at her and asked, "Is that a good thing or what?"

She and I both fell out laughing and she said, "It's a blessing he's outta here in a month."

"Don't I know it!"

Annette and I were on our second glass of wine when Carla arrived. We filled her in on the day's events, and she was soon gulping down a glassful herself.

She was concerned we were so laidback. She asked, "Aren't you all worried he's not done with his antics? People like that don't give up until somebody's dead!"

Annette said, "Damn Carla, it ain't that deep! He's pussy whipped, no more no less! Stop being so dramatic and scaring Licia!"

But I was way ahead of her. I already had a plan, albeit an *over the top* plan, but I was determined to do it.

I said, "Nette, I want Benny to follow Sam and put a portable security system in here. Something that has cameras all over the apartment. I can use some of the money Harold gave me for the wedding. He won't know the difference. Do you think he'll do it?"

She looked at me and said, "You know Felicia, I think that's a great idea! Let me call his ass right now!"

He agreed to do it. When she asked about cost, he was evasive but said it would be half price for her.

When she hung up, she said, "Benny doesn't think following Sam will be necessary if your apartment is covered. But if you insist, it could be costly. Otherwise, it'll be about four hundred bucks for material and install. And you can take it with you when you move."

So we called him back and set it up for Tuesday. I also said I would let him know if I still wanted him to tail Sam. In addition, I called the rental office and put in a request to get my locks changed. Annette said she would come over and let Benny in because she could work remotely.

I talked the girls into riding with me to see the house. But first, we put that damn lingerie into the car and took it to the women's shelter. As we pulled into the sub-division, Carla said, "Wow Licia! Who da thunk ten years ago that any of us would be living like this?"

"I know, right. Our parents did well just keeping a roof over our heads and food on the table."

Annette said, "Ain't that the truth! And they worked ten times as hard as we do."

We were all silent for a moment as we thought about our parents' struggles. Both Annette and Carla's dads are deceased. Annette's dad died when she was only two years-old. Finally I said, "Here we are! This is the new Benson home!"

After all the ooos and ahhhhs, Annette asked, "Can we go inside?"

I looked around and said, "I don't see why not!"

I tried the door and of course, it was locked. I said, "I'll go around back and see if I have any luck."

Meanwhile, Annette walked into the garage and turned the door knob leading into the house, and of course, it wasn't locked. So as we entered, it seemed fitting that the two people who had been with me through hell and back, would be the first to enter my new home. I insisted we all go to the front entryway, so that my tour would start at the beginning.

They were both awed by it as much as I was, and so sincerely happy for me. We danced like little girls, as we looked over the second floor loft into the massive two story family room. Then we ran to the other side, looking down at the beautiful entryway. Carla said, "Girl, you're gonna lose your kids in here!"

Annette said, "She has a damn intercom! She's good!"

We all laughed as we descended the stairs and finally left. As we pulled into the parking lot of my apartment, I saw Aysia. She ran over to me and I said, "Hello Aysia. How are you?"

She said, "I'm fine Mrs. Wilson! Where's Todd and Marcus?"

"They're with their dad today."

"Oh, I was hoping we could play in the playground."

She was clearly saddened to learn they weren't home. Sam said, "Hello Ladies! It's good to see you all again."

He had come out of his apartment. Carla and I said, "Hello Sam."

Annette had her phone at her ear, pretending to be talking. She was sucking her teeth at him when he wasn't looking. She waved in his direction and went up the stairs toward my apartment. Carla and I soon followed and we went inside. Annette said, "I would love to shoot his balls off. What a Bastard!"

Carla said, "Annette, you're always talking about shooting somebody. You don't even own a gun!"

"Don't believe it Carla! You don't know *what* I have, Sweetie."

Annette waved us off and went into the bathroom. Carla and I cracked up at Annette. She will forever have a little thug in her. When Annette returned Carla asked, "So, is everyone all set for the cookout Sunday?"

Annette said, "Yes. I'm bringing the baked beans and pop, right?"

Carla said, "Yes. And please remind your mother to bring the potato salad."

We all laughed because Aunt Pat will agree to bring something and then decide not to. I said, "Harold is making shrimp salad and kabobs. Is there anything else?"

"No, that's it. Except please remember to bring chairs and be on time ladies. One o'clock. And Licia, since those kabobs need to go on the grill, you can come a little earlier than one o'clock."

Annette was like, "Listen at Carla trying to sound like a drill sergeant! And excuse me, but you're always late for stuff! I guess you'll be able to find your way into your own yard on time."

We all laughed, even Carla.

That evening, as I was relaxing on Harold's sofa and watching him perform his magic in the kitchen, I decided to do something I don't normally do. I got up and stood next to him. I asked, "What are you cooking tonight?"

He said, "I'm gonna start preparing more nutritious/lower calorie meals. So tonight I'm preparing collards, baked sweet potatoes, and stewed chicken."

"Are you saying I'm gaining weight?"

"Not you Babe. Me. When I met you, I had rock hard abs, but now I have a slight pooch. I used to run most mornings before work, now I often find myself wrapped up in your beautiful body. Who could move?"

He put his hand on my behind and I punched his shoulder. I said, "I came in to help. Can I be your Sous-chef?"

He looked at me stunned. He checked my forehead for a fever. I said, "Okay Dr. Benson, now that you've confirmed I'm okay, can I help or not?"

"Absolutely! But only if you're clear what a Sous-chefs' job is. No matter how tedious the task or bizarre it seems, you must follow directions exactly as instructed. Understand?"

"Yes Sir. I understand."

So I removed stalks from greens, cleaned the potatoes and punctured and oiled them, and kept the work area clean. Then he took six lemons out of the fridge and told me to roll them until soft. He was making fresh lemonade. I began to watch how he sliced this and tore that. I was amazed at the fresh herbs he used. I asked questions and learned a lot.

After dinner, I felt elated. I was excited about learning to cook like a chef. Harold said, "That's exactly how I learned. I would hang around the kitchen and Mom and Dad taught me. By the time I was thirteen, Mom would call home and ask *me* to start dinner, not my older sisters!"

"Do you think I could learn to cook like you?"

"First of all, yes I do. And that brings up something I've wanted to discuss with you, but it would kill me if you took it the wrong way. Should I proceed?"

"Of course Hun. And listen. We have to be able to say hard things to each other, gently, in order for our marriage to work. Okay?"

He shook his head and said, "If you let me teach you to cook, you could become a good cook, like me. But if you also get your culinary license, you can be a great cook."

I never thought of that. He said, "But taking care of us and a house and working a full time job would make that difficult. You don't have to work Felicia."

I *really* never thought of that. "Or you could study whatever you want. I've wanted to offer that option to you for a while, but I was afraid I'd offend you. Please, say something. If I..."

I put my finger on his lip to silence him. I said, "Yes, I'd love to."

I twirled around and laughed out loud. Harold said, "I *never* in a million years expected this kind of reaction. But, please tell me exactly what you agreed to."

"I'll see how soon I can start culinary classes, but I'm not planning to quit my job. At least, not yet. Okay?"

He laughed and said, "Whatever you want Babe"

Chapter Ten

By one o'clock, the kabobs were on the grill and we'd found a nice place under the tent to put our chairs. Harold asked, "Why didn't you tell me she was opening up the pool? I would love a brisk swim."

"Because, it's not warm enough for swimming, and I don't want you getting sick."

"Felicia, its seventy three degrees at one o'clock. It's supposed to get as high as seventy eight. What's the problem? I'm gonna run out and buy some trunks. Wanna go?"

"Honey, please don't do that. I've lived here all my life and when people start acting like its summer beforehand, they get sick."

"You worry too much. I'll be right back."

So off he went. I got up and went into the house and asked Carla if she needed help. She said, "Girl, these kids and that pool are driving me nuts! I told Earl it was too soon to open it, but they're determined to get in. So I told them when they're sick, don't look at me."

I laughed and said, "I just told Harold the same thing. He jumped in his car to go buy some trunks. Men and children. There's no difference."

She and I both laughed and her mom and Aunt Pat came in. I lit up and quickly went over to embrace them. I said, "Looking good Ladies!"

"Felicia, I've been meaning to call you and congratulate you on your engagement. Where is this lucky young man?"

Aunt Pat said, "I still can't believe that silly boy lost you! Well, I'm happy for you too."

I thanked them both and told them that Harold had gone to the store. Harold and I prepared ourselves for this first meeting of my entire ex-husband's family. He seemed unfazed by it, whereas I've been a bag of nerves. But it was inevitable so I'm trying to breeze through it.

I went back outside and over to the grill where Uncle Kenny was holding it down. I said, "Hi Uncle Kenny."

He hugged me saying, "Felicia, it's so good to see you!"

"Same here. How are you guys doing?"

"I'm good and Faye is over there."

I turned and saw her looking right at me. I waved and smiled and she waved back. I turned back to Uncle Kenny and said, "I'll talk to you later."

I stopped to say hi to Faye. I said, "Wow Faye, you look great! How did you do it?"

She said, "Thanks Felicia. I had to because my blood sugar was out of control. I lost thirty pounds! Is it true you about to get married again?"

"Yes, in October."

Just then Harold came up behind me and I said, "Harold, this is Carla's Aunt Faye."

He said, "It's a pleasure to meet you."

Faye said, "It's nice meeting you. I wish you two all the best."

I hugged her and we went to the food table. I said, "Funny, but when I was with Todd, she always acted as if she didn't like me."

"She seemed genuinely happy for us."

"I know. It's weird."

Annette came behind me and asked, "What's weird?"

"You're late."

"I got here before one. I was upstairs with my son because he's scared to get in the pool, but doesn't want his cousins to tease him. I told him he couldn't get in anyhow because it's not warm enough yet."

I looked at Harold and he walked away laughing. Annette asked, "What's his problem?"

"I told him the same thing, but he insists on swimming. By the way, I got the cash for the installation and I'll leave it in the cookie jar."

"Okay, and I'll work on getting that price reduced."

I laughed and noticed Harold with Aunt Pat. Annette said, "Oh shit!"

When we got over there, Aunt Pat said, "Girl, this young man is quite a catch. I told him if I was just a little younger, I'd take him from you."

Annette said, "Mom, quit that. You're gonna scare poor Harold."

Aunt Pat said, "He better be scared! You know, I can still make a man scream like a bi…"

"Mommy!" Annette screamed. "Let's go ask Faye how she lost that weight."

As she escorted her mom across the lawn, she looked back at us and made a face like *what the hell?*

Harold's mouth was wide open and I couldn't stop laughing. He looked at me and asked, "Felicia, was she for real?!"

I opened my mouth to answer, but nothing came out except laughter. I laughed so hard, my side hurt. I finally said, "Now you know where Annette gets it from. Her mom is hilarious!"

While Harold and I were sitting and eating, many of Todd's family members came over and wished us well. Carla and Annette came over and Annette said, "Harold, I'm so sorry about my mom. I can't even blame it on age, because she's only fifty two and has been talking like that for years."

Carla said, "Aunt Pat and my mom are a hot mess Harold. You might as well get used to it."

Poor Harold had no idea where to put it all. He said, "Okay Annette. What was she gonna say?"

Annette started laughing. She said, "Only if you think you can take it, because it's pretty raw."

"Yeah, because I'll wonder forever."

She posed like her mom and said, "I can make a man scream like a bitch, and then act like one. Sniffing and whining and following behind this good pussy."

Poor Harold was floored again! He said, "What! That sweet woman! I don't believe you."

Well Carla, Annette and I were done! We were hollering. All three of us were on the ground crying! Harold looked at us and finally started laughing himself. He said, "You three are too much. I still don't believe it."

Carla called Earl over. As Earl approached, Annette said to Harold, "We're gonna walk away. Ask him what my mom said to him at their rehearsal dinner."

As we watched the exchange between Earl and Harold, poor Harold looked anguished again. Earl was bent over laughing and we went back as Earl was saying, "Man, I was so embarrassed. Like you, I couldn't believe she said it."

Harold said, "Lucky for me, I only heard half of it."

The rest of day was great. We played cards and danced and played horseshoes. Then about six o'clock, everything changed. Sort of. First of all, my son Marcus came running around the corner. I was happy to see him, but not expecting to see him until tomorrow. Then the Todds came out. But what happened next is what caused the uproar.

Gina came out of the house in the skimpiest thong bikini I'd ever seen. It seemed as if the air had stopped circulating. Everyone seemed to stop in mid-sentence. Actually it was beautiful, just inappropriate. Women were whispering. Children were laughing behind their hands. And *all* of the men were gawking. Terribly! I'm sure they couldn't help themselves, but some were just over the top. I looked at Harold and he was mesmerized. I asked, "Harold, are you okay? Harold!"

"Yes Babe, what?"

He never took his eyes off of her. I said, "Look at me Hun."

It took him like six seconds before he could comprehend what I was saying. Finally, he turned to me and asked, "Did you say something Babe? Do you see what she's wearing?"

"Harold, I can't believe you!"

At that moment, Carla, Annette and a few other female cousins went to Gina and asked her to come inside with them. I could only imagine what they planned to say. Todd was looking at it all unfold, so I took that opportunity to call him over. I asked, "Todd, what was that about?"

"What do you mean?"

"You don't think that was inappropriate?"

"I think she looks great!"

"She does look great. But for your eyes. Does she make a habit of dressing like that around our sons?"

He looked at me as if a light came on. He said, "I'll be back!"

I looked at Harold and said, "Me too!"

I went behind him and we both went into the house where Gina was standing with her hands on her hips and Annette was in her face. Todd ran and stood between them and said, "It's my fault! She didn't want to, but I begged her to. She did it for me."

He turned to Gina and said, "I'm so sorry Boo. I didn't think it through. I was so…"

He turned to us and said, "Please don't blame her. It's my fault."

He escorted her to the car, and I decided to follow them. Once Gina was seated, I said to her, "Gina, you look amazing. I had no idea you were stacked like that Girl!"

She finally looked at me. She was obviously embarrassed, but managed to say, "Thanks Felicia, and I assure you the boys never see me like this. Todd was so adamant about it, and I was concerned about the kids and…."

I stopped her and said, "Listen, I used to be married to that man. I know how persistent he can be. No explanation needed."

She chuckled and I whispered, "Girl, you almost killed my fiancée! I thought I would have to call the paramedics!"

She looked at me and we both laughed.

Todd Jr. came running out and asked, "Mom, can we stay?"

"Yes, Todd."

Gina said, "I thought we were gonna go to Friendly's for ice cream and you would go home tomorrow."

She seemed so disappointed. He looked at me not sure what he wanted. So I said, "Let's make a deal. Let's all go to Friendly's later and you guys can go back with Gina."

I looked again at Gina for her okay, and she nodded enthusiastically. Todd went back and I reached in and hugged her and said, "I'll always love you for loving *our* sons. They love you Gina. Thank you for all you do."

She began to cry and said quietly, "I can't have kids Felicia. Your boys have given me so much joy. Thank you for sharing them." After hugging her again I said, "Remember, they're our boys."

When I was back inside, Annette said, "I hope you told that trick how inappropriate she looked in front of our husbands and children. And personally, I didn't appreciate seeing her stank ass either."

"She did it for Todd. Granted, she should have considered her audience and told his ass no, but sometimes that's easier said than done. I use to be married to Todd, so I know how he is."

Todd asked, "How is he?"

Unbeknownst to me, Todd had entered the room behind me. He asked me again and Carla said, "Todd…"

"No Carla, I'll answer him. Privately."

I grabbed his hand and practically drug him into the study. I said, "I can't believe you put Gina through that! Totally humiliating her, just like you did me. When are you gonna grow up and stop being so fucking selfish Todd!"

"Wait a minute Licia! What the hell did I do that humiliated you? Yes, I screwed up our marriage, but I never did anything to you!"

"You're unbelievable! You really are a piece of work. So self-absorbed that you're blinded by how your actions affect the people around you. Let me ask you a question. How would you feel if you found out Gina was screwing another guy?"

"I'd put her ass out."

"I didn't ask what you would do. I asked how you would *feel*."

He looked at me, crossed his arms and said, "I would feel betrayed and hurt. And mad as hell."

"Would your manhood be bruised? Wouldn't you wonder, *what does he have that I don't?* Or people thinking, *damn Todd can't satisfy his woman.*"

"Honestly, yes I would."

"That's what I went through Todd. Stop and think how your selfishness affects your loved ones. Gina doesn't deserve to be remembered like that. I'd hate to see you lose her too."

"You really like her, don't you?"

"I really do. I couldn't ask for a better stepmom for our boys. And by the way, marry her!"

"You think?"

"Absolutely!"

As we were walking out, Todd stopped me and said, "Felicia, I apologize for treating you that way. I know I said it then, but I understand now what I really did to you. I'm really sorry."

"Thanks Todd. I appreciate that."

We finally rejoined the others and Annette and Carla had gone out and convinced Gina to come back in. The men were swimming with the kids, so Harold barely missed me. Gina put on different clothes and the girls hung out in the living room. The wine was flowing and Aunt Pat said, "So Gina...."

Annette and Carla said, "Not today!"

Aunt Pat opened her mouth and started laughing. She put her drink down and laughed some more. Aunt Debra asked, "Pat, what the hell is so funny?"

"Debra, you should have seen the look on Harold's face when I told him I was gonna take him from Licia. Girl, you would have pissed your pants. That Black man turned six different colors. I *did* piss *my* pants!"

Everybody lost it. We all laughed again at poor Harold's expense, but it was all in fun. Anything to keep Gina's name out of Aunt Pat's mouth. Soon the men came in and we all decided to go to Friendly's. I told Carla her boys could come too.

That's when Todd announced that after ice cream, all of the boys could stay at his house tonight. All of the parents said yes with no hesitation. I looked at Gina and she said, "Wow, five boys! Who wants to camp out?!"

All of them, including Gina were jumping up and down. We all looked at them and Annette said, "Licia, I think I like her too."

By nine thirty, Harold and I were sitting up in bed. He was watching baseball, and I was on my laptop. The phone rang, and it was Gina. She said, "Felicia, I'm sorry for calling so late. Everything is fine. I just wanted to thank you for today."

"Gina, your welcome. I meant every word."

"I don't know what you said to Todd today, but he's a different man. Carla said you told him not to screw up with me like he did with you."

"Yes, that pretty much sums it up."

"Felicia, he asked me to marry him. Do you believe it?"

I sat up and screamed. I asked, "What was your answer Gina?"

"I said yes. I'm so happy Felicia. I've wanted this for so long, but he said he wouldn't marry again. Do we have your blessing?"

"You absolutely have my blessing, and if there's anything at all I can do to help, please don't hesitate to ask."

"Thank you again. We'll talk soon. Goodnight."

I told her goodnight and we hung up.

I turned to Harold and he asked, "What happened?"

"Todd finally asked her to marry him. Thank God he finally did the right thing by her."

"Wow, that's great news. I've been meaning to ask what you and Todd were arguing about earlier. I came in and Aunt Debra said you were telling her son off and told me not to interfere. She said he needed to hear it. So I did as I was told."

"I told him his selfishness was gonna cause him to lose her. Making her wear that bikini and humiliating herself. I wanted to slap his face!"

Then I made a face and with plenty of attitude I said, "Oh and by the way, I owe you a slap too! Looking at Gina like she was a stripper! I thought I was gonna have to call EMS."

"Babe, I was stunned."

"No. You were drooling."

"I'm sorry Babe. I couldn't believe what I was seeing."

"You *liked* what you were seeing. I understand women are beautiful and should be admired, but gawking is disrespectful and highly offensive."

"I'm really sorry Babe. I'll look, but not gawk. Okay?"

"We'll see Mr. Benson."

I felt frisky, so I got up and grabbed a piece of butterscotch candy off of my dresser. Then I removed his boxers and crawled between his legs. I opened the candy and put it in my mouth. He asked, "Are you punishing me Felicia?"

I shook my head no and slowly licked my lips. Then I began licking him, slowly from bottom to top. When he was reaching the edge of his patience, I finally inserted it in my mouth. I removed the candy, but I continued enjoying him. I could tell he was resisting, so I increased my pace and he let it go. He touched my hair and said quietly, "You're incredible. I love you so much."

"I love you too. Very much."

"I always seem to want you more when it's your time of the month."

"Really? Why is that?"

He groaned and said, "I wish I knew."

We lay there quietly for a while, until he started yelling "It's gone! Jeter just hit a two-run home run!"

He scared the shit out of me. He was totally engrossed in the Yankees, as they were putting a whipping on the Red Sox. I got up and went into the kitchen for a snack. I grabbed two of the ice cream sandwiches we bought at Friendly's.

When I returned, I asked if he'd always been a Yankee fan. He said, "Yes, I've always loved the Yankees! That reminds me. We need to plan a weekend getaway to NYC to see a game. Would you like that?"

"I'd love it! But the boys will be quite jealous. Although they're Mets fans, they've never seen a big league game before."

"Then we'll take them with us! And maybe Todd and Gina would like to go. Our engagement gift to them. What do you think?"

"I love the idea, but maybe it's too much."

"I could even check the schedule to see when the next series between the Mets and Yankees is this summer. If it's not sold out, I could go ahead and snatch the tickets now!"

There went my other son. He was so excited and clearly didn't hear a word I said. He came back with his laptop and began his search. As we were looking at the Yankees' website, a huge smile crossed his lips.

He grabbed his phone and made a call. He said, "Hey man, I know it's late, but I want to first congratulate you and Gina. And secondly, we'd like you all to be our guests at a Yankees/Mets game in NYC next month. Our treat as your engagement gift."

I sat there with my mouth opened! He said, "You would! Great! I'll call you tomorrow with the details. Yeah, I know you and the boys are die hard Mets fans, but the Yankees don't care and neither do I!"

I couldn't believe what I was hearing. They soon hung up and he said, "It's all set Babe. He's as excited as I am. He said he'll tell the boys when their cousins leave."

I wondered what the hell just happened. He was busy typing away on his laptop. I asked, "Excuse me, what does *all set* mean?"

"I just purchased six tickets for Saturday June twenty third. The game starts at three o'clock."

"Did you forget we're supposed to be moving next month? I have a lot to do."

"Babe, the movers will do that."

"What movers?"

He looked at me and realized what he'd done. Again.

"I'm sorry Babe. When you said you wanted to move as soon as school was out, I hired a moving company."

"Okay?"

"They do everything Babe. Pack, move and unpack. Everything."

"Really? So, what date did you give them, Mr. Benson?"

"I'm always in trouble when you call me that."

He started typing again. He went to his email and opened the one from the moving company. He said, "The date is June thirtieth. I figured that would give you a week after school was out, unless you want another date."

"No, that's fine. But Harold...."

"I know, I should have told you. I forgot. You mad at me?"

"Well, yes and no. Yes because you didn't tell me and no because you did a good thing. I am concerned about something else though."

"What's wrong?"

"You must know I'm not accustomed to the kind of financial freedom you've known."

"I knew this conversation was inevitable. So I'm gonna tell you what you need to know. My net worth is about four million. But I earned it. Our parents paid for our education, our first car and first home, but the home would be a wedding gift. When we turned twenty five, we each received a hundred thousand dollars for investment purposes only. That's how I acquired most of my wealth. And I assure you I don't spend carelessly. The only time I spent money was when Tara and I went on a three month road trip across the country."

"Wow. That's a lot to absorb. I don't want my life to be different. And I feel useless when it comes to money because you pay for everything."

"Soon, it'll be *our* money and *we'll* pay for everything?"

I laughed and asked, "Harold, why do you work? And how much do you make?"

"I work because I enjoy my job. I currently earn ninety two thousand annually with IBM. Through the family business I have stock and I'm employed as a consultant. I have my personal investments. All of that comes to about eight, maybe nine hundred thousand annually."

We talked for another hour or so, and it seemed the more he told me, the more my head was spinning. Eventually, we finished watching the Yankees kill the Red Sox.

Chapter Eleven

It was Memorial Day and strange that my kids weren't going with me to the parade Rochester has every year. I talked to Todd this morning and he's planning to take all of the boys. This is Harold's first parade, so I was more excited for him than myself.

We got there an hour early and found a great spot on the corner of Main and State. After setting up our chairs, Harold walked to a nearby vendor and grabbed breakfast sandwiches and coffee.

Soon the crowd was huge and the parade had begun. About halfway through, someone tapped on my shoulder. When I looked up, it was Aysia.

She said, "Hi Mrs. Wilson! I saw you from over there. See my dad and my aunt are waving."

I looked over and sure enough there was Sam and Cynthia. Harold and I both waved and Aysia asked, "Where's Todd and Marcus? I never see them anymore."

"They spend a lot of time with their dad, Sweetheart. They're here somewhere."

"Oh, okay. I have to go back. Bye Mrs. Wilson."

Then she hugged me so tight, I almost cried. I said, "Goodbye Aysia. Be careful getting back."

I watched her get back safely. Harold made a point of kissing my forehead and putting his arm around my shoulder. I guess he'll always feel insecure when it comes to Sam.

After Harold dropped me off, I remembered I had no food and realized it was my only free moment the entire weekend. But not for long. So I grabbed my purse and keys and went out the door.

While checking out, of all people, Jonathon was heading my way. I thought I'd successfully avoided a confrontation with him. He said, "Hello Felicia."

"Hi Jonathon. I didn't know you were still here."

"Actually, I came back yesterday. How have you been?"

"Fine, thank you. And you?"

"Really good, actually. I can't tell you how much I enjoyed our last meeting. Did you like it?"

"Jonathon, I'd rather not discuss that, if you don't mind."

I continued checking out and eventually left the store. As I was loading my bags in the car, he came over and said, "Felicia, I didn't mean to upset you. I realized I embarrassed you. I'm very sorry."

He started helping me with the bags. I said, "Frankly, I'd like to forget it ever happened, okay?"

"No problem. You take care."

By the time I was in the car, I was shaking. Why did I have this feeling they'd never allow me to forget it?

By the time the boys were fed and bathed, they asked me for the tenth time about the Mets game. I said, "You guys have only a few more weeks left of school. Then we'll get ready for the game, okay?"

They both said okay and we went into their room. I asked, "How do you feel about having your own rooms?"

Todd Jr. said, "That would be great Mom!"

But Marcus wasn't as thrilled. He asked, "Would I have to sleep in the room by myself Mommy?"

"Yes, but now that you're a big boy, you'll be just fine. Okay?"

"I guess so Mom."

"We've picked out a house, and we'll be moving soon. You guys will have rooms right next to each other, and right between your rooms is a bathroom. So you can visit each other by going through the bathroom. Doesn't that sound like fun?"

Marcus lit up then and now Todd wasn't thrilled. I had a copy of the floor plan. While they were looking at it, I asked Todd to come into the kitchen.

I said, "Your brother looks up to you, so maybe at first you guys can keep your doors opened between your rooms, until Marcus is used to being alone. Would you do that?"

"Sure Mom. I'll take care of him."

We talked a while longer, and they went to bed. By the time I got myself ready for the next day, it was almost ten o'clock. I'd showered and put on a sundress.

I went to the cabinet and took down the cookie jar and made sure the money was still there. I hid it in case someone was looking for cookies. While in the kitchen, I saw the two bags of trash I'd forgotten to take out. I really needed to get them out of here.

I grabbed my keys and went down to the dumpster. Thank goodness it was well lit and in the open. As I was coming back up the stairs, I saw him again. He said, "Hey. What brings you out tonight?"

I pretended to be at ease and said, "Just putting out the trash. What brings you out?"

"Searching for enchantment. And I found it."

I laughed as I continued toward my apartment. I said, "You *are* a charmer Jonathon. Have a good night. It was good seeing you again."

I was almost there. He said, "Earlier, I asked if it was good. Maybe I should have asked how good was it."

I was in front of my door. I had my key and was about to put it in the lock. He stood behind me and put his hand over mine and put the key in. I froze. I didn't know whether to scream or continue my pretense. I turned my head and said, "Thanks Jonathon. I got it."

He leaned into me and said, "You didn't answer my question."

I could feel him harden behind me. His breath was on my neck. He was throbbing and rubbing my behind. He asked, "You want some company?"

"My sons are..."

His tongue was leaving trails of heat on my neck and now was in my ear. His hand went from my thigh to under my dress. I said, "Please Jonathon…."

He whispered, "Shhhh...."

He discovered my nakedness and groaned. I didn't want him to stop. He inserted two fingers and began to grind against me. He pinched my nipple and my muscles convulsed around those fingers. He moved them vigorously. My head went back and shamefully, I melted all over them.

My legs were shaking and I was dripping wet. He came too. Violently. His head was resting on my head. His breathing was labored. He removed his fingers and put them in his mouth.

I had my head against my door. He moved my hair and kissed me gently on my neck. He eventually walked away.

I called Annette at lunch time the next day, and she said everything was going fine. So I went to grab some lunch and ran into Harold on the way back. I said, "I thought you had a meeting?"

"I did. We finished early. What did you get to eat?"

"I went to Wegman's and got a salad"

We sat outside and ate the salad together. I asked him if he'd finalized the details for the men, and he had. I told him everything else was being handled by Stephanie, the wedding planner. He said, "She's also handling the honeymoon. I asked her to take care of it for me."

"What honeymoon?"

"I'm not telling you where. It's a surprise Babe."

"You know I don't like surprises Harold."

"Sounds like a personal problem."

He finished my salad and took the remains to the trash. He came back and began telling me when his parents, the cooks and his sisters would be arriving. I said, "I would like to go back to the honeymoon and me having a personal problem. Any *personal problem* I have is a major problem for you, Mr. Benson."

"You don't scare me Mrs. Benson. However, I *am* scared of Aunt Pat. Real scared!"

We laughed again and went back to work. When the day finally ended, I zoomed home. Annette left me a key under the mat. I went inside and all of the info was in my room on the dresser.

I went to the cookie jar, and there was two hundred dollars there and another key. I requested three keys and asked her to keep one, just in case. I looked around and saw no evidence of cameras. It seems he did a good job, but I wouldn't really know until I began using them. Benny explained it all to Annette, and she planned to come over tonight to explain it all to me.

Once the kids had eaten and washed up for bed, I quizzed Todd again on his spelling words. Finally at eight thirty, I sent them to bed.

Annette got there exactly at nine. After I understood how to use the equipment, she said, "You can tape you and Harold getting it on!"

"He ain't never gonna go for that."

"He doesn't have to know Licia. By the way, did you ever become an owner and operator of a vibrator?"

"No Annette. And what does that have to do with anything?"

"It has everything to do with this. It's perfectly normal *and* natural to pleasure yourself Sis. And watching your man sex you can be very erotic. Part of the reason you're unable to rid yourself of Sam is because he brought something to the party that Harold doesn't. I'm sure Harold is great, but remember our conversation about the different levels of sexual satisfaction?"

I nodded yes. She said, "For instance, now that you've experienced a threesome, and loved it, you will always want to do it again (She would have to mention that). I'm concerned because you haven't learned how to create boundaries. Just because something is good to you, doesn't mean it's good for you. There must be a point when you say no and mean it. I'm not telling you not to do your thing Licia, but I am concerned that you haven't perfected the art of it."

"So what should I do. I don't want to cheat on Harold anymore."

We went into the kitchen and got some wine. She said, "You weren't cheating on Harold as much as you were chasing Sam's penis. First of all, your cheating was not for the sake of cheating, which is not common because that's why most women cheat. They're usually devastated because their husbands cheated, or did something horrific to them. *Your* cheating was *just sex*, which is usually why *men* cheat. Very dangerous Chica."

"Dangerous?"

"For several reasons Licia. First of all, you don't know what you're doing. You're sloppy and you allow yourself to get used. It's your show, not theirs. And you must learn to hit it and keep it moving. A real playa doesn't catch feelings and has full control of her pussy."

I looked at her and wondered if I would ever get past this. She said, "Now, back to the vibrator. By pleasuring yourself, you don't have to depend on anyone else. And you learn more and more how to control that desire."

"Nette, you've cheated for years. Have you really changed?"

She laughed and said, "More like I've evolved. When I pleasure myself, I make it a cheat session, so I'm cheating without cheating. I had to come to grips with the fact that the thrill for me was not conquering men, but the cheating. Pleasuring yourself is another level of satisfaction. So now, I don't have to cheat anymore. It may sound silly, but it works for me."

"So how do I learn to pleasure myself? I've done some things with Harold, but nothing alone. It seems so weird to me."

"If you're more comfortable with Harold, then start with him."

She started laughing and said, "I swear, you are something else. You freak two men at once, yet you can't do yourself. Not to mention, you still can't speak freely with your hubby-to-be. I want you to tell him that you want to try different things. That will thrill him, I'm telling you. Ask him about a trip to a toy store. Tony loves it when we go to the toy store."

I cringed at the thought of talking to Harold like that. But she was right, and I knew it. And I was missing me some Sam McElroy. That man lit fires in me I don't think Harold ever could. I said, "Annette, I miss Sam so much. What am I gonna do?"

I began to cry and said, "I have to tell you something."

I told her about Jonathon. I said, "I have no control Nette."

She grabbed my hand and then her keys. She said, "Let's go!"

When we got to Adam and Eve's, I was so ashamed. I cried halfway to the store, partly because I left my children alone and partly because I was feeling some kind a way about Sam and Jonathon. She parked and said, "Listen to me dammit! We're going in there and buy you a Sam. Do you hear me?!"

I just shook my head. She said, "Look at me Felicia Pierce! You will get over them! Think about that wonderful man who lives only to please you. He's the one who sees your essence, not just how horny you are. And..."

I couldn't believe it. Annette was crying.

I started to speak, but she put her hand up and said, "I have to say this. I will not allow those fools to fuck you into losing the best thing you've ever had. You deserve Harold, and you're going to recreate him just like I've done with my husband. And even though my sexual appetite exceeds Tony's, I've learned to creatively bring out in him what I need him to be. So, play the hand you're dealt. You've got the nuts Licia. You just have to learn how to slow roll it."

I reached over and hugged my sister and told her how much I loved her. Then I asked, "How did you become so wise?"

She just said, "Girl, get out of the car and let's do this."

When we got to the door, I asked, "What are the *nuts* and what does *slow roll it* mean?"

She hollered laughing.

I was clearly a newbie to toy stores. I looked at everything. Annette said, "Come over here. I wanna see what Sam looks like."

As we were looking at the vibrators, I couldn't help but giggle at the sight of some of them. But then I saw it. Sam. That was so funny to me, because I was imagining using it and Harold hearing me call it Sam. That wouldn't be pretty. I asked, "How do I explain it to Harold?"

"Just tell him you've always had it. He'll be intrigued and soon he'll be using it on you. You'll love it and so will he."

"That's hard for me to fathom. Harold's not that type, at least I don't think he is."

"They're all that type!"

On the way home, she told me why there was still two hundred dollars in the jar. She said, "I told him he still owed me and that he was only getting two hundred. He asked me when he would be done making it up to me and I told his ass never!"

"What did he do Nette?"

"That bastard taped one of our sessions without telling me. His mistake was playing it when we got together again. I took it out and told him I was gonna send it to his wife. I ran out with it, so he has no idea where it is or if it still exists. He'll always wonder if it'll show up on his doorstep one day!"

She was cracking up. I asked, "So, where is it?"

"I ripped it to shreds and burned it! I'm not crazy!"

When we arrived back at my place, I checked on the boys and they were fine. Annette explained to me that *the nuts,* is when you have the best possible poker hand. And *slow rolling it* means not going all in, just betting slowly and dropping the bomb at the end.

I know a little about poker, but Annette and her family play all the time. She said, "I want you to thoroughly clean that vibrator and do what comes naturally. I want a report tomorrow."

I laughed and asked, "Are you serious?"

"Absolutely! Because unless you're in love with Sam, this will cure you of him. I guarantee it."

By mid-week, Harold, Earl, Carla's two boys Earl Jr. and Evan, and some of the other family all had colds. Harold was a miserable patient. I insisted he stay home from work on Wednesday but he refused. By Thursday, he couldn't get out of bed.

I made an attempt at chicken soup. It was okay, but not delicious like his. I called his mom and asked her how she makes it. She said, "The secret to good soup is simplicity. I'll email you the recipe right away. Can I speak with that hard headed son of mine?"

I smiled and said, "Okay Mom. And thanks. Here he is."

I handed him the phone and retrieved his clothes to wash them. When he hung up he said, "My mother thinks you're a saint. She said as particular as you've been all of your life, you chose Felicia. For a reason! Then she said the Bible says when a man finds a wife, he finds a good thing! So you must trust her instincts and advice. Understand?"

He laughed again and said, "When she starts quoting Scriptures, you don't want to mess with her."

"Hun, will you please tell me about this honeymoon? I need to prepare for it. And when exactly are we going?"

He sat up in bed and said, "We're going Sunday after the wedding. It's a warm climate, so just pack bikinis. By the way, Stephanie told me you tried to pry it out her. Leave her alone."

I laughed and said, "I don't appreciate being kept in the dark."

"You'll get over it."

I rolled my eyes and said, "I need to get home to meet Todd with the boys. Are you sure you have everything you need?"

"Yes, I'm sure. Go on and I'll call you if I need anything."

I leaned over and kissed his forehead. I said, "I can't afford to get sick, so that's all you get. Goodnight Honey. Love you."

"I love you too Babe."

As I was leaving, he said, "Oh Babe, look in the drawer in the kitchen next to the stove and get that spare key. I've been meaning to give it to you. And I should have one for your place too, even though you won't be there much longer."

"Okay Sweetie. I'll get the key and be on my way."

I really wasn't comfortable giving him a key, but I couldn't come up with a legitimate excuse to deny him.

About eight thirty my phone rang and it was Harold. I'd just put the boys to bed, took a shower, and was in the kitchen cleaning up the dinner dishes. I quickly answered, hoping everything was okay. I said, "Hi Hun. You okay?"

"Yep, I'm watching baseball. What are you doing?"

"Just cleaning up after dinner. I still need to find a dress to get married in. I don't think jeans and heels would be a good look."

He laughed and said, "Mom just called hoping you were still here. Dad wants to know if you'd be willing to do something a little sentimental."

"What would that be?"

"There's a bracelet that's very special to him. When my grandmother was ill, my grandfather took most of the money he had and bought it for her. She'd been admiring it for some time, so when her birthday came around, Granddad presented it to her. It's very special to Dad."

"So what does Dad want me to do?"

"Well, when Tara and Danielle got married, they wore the bracelet as *something borrowed* and Dad wants to know if you'll also wear it?"

"I'd be honored. Should I call him tomorrow?"

"Yes, Dad would like that. Also, I totally forgot that Tammy is graduating from high school next Saturday. She would have a fit if I'm not there. I would like you to come with me. We could fly in Friday evening and come home Sunday. What do you think?"

"Wow, I guess so. I'm sure the kids can stay with Todd and Gina."

"Why don't we bring them?"

"Let me think about it and let you know tomorrow. Can you get a flight at this late date for all of us?"

"I'm checking right now."

"Harold, the boys have never flown before. Maybe it's not such a good idea."

"They have to do it sometime Babe. Now is as good a time as any. Plus, it's better not to tell them until it's time to go. That's what my parents did, so we wouldn't have time to think about it. I think we should go for it. As a matter of fact, there's a flight leaving Rochester at four thirty on Friday. There are several seats available. I need to know as soon as possible Babe. Okay?"

I was deep in thought and he asked, "Felicia, are you still with me?"

"Yes Hun, I'm here. I'm just wondering how they'll react to this. As a mother, it pains me to put them in a frightening situation. The thought that they might cry upsets me. I really have to figure this out."

"I understand. But I also think that just like they had to learn to walk, and I'm sure they had some spills during that process, they also have to learn other unpleasant things. I think you're putting the cart before the horse. If we present this experience as a fun adventure, maybe they'll see it that way too. Okay?"

"Let's talk tomorrow. I need to sleep on it. Have a good night Hun."

"Babe. I need to ask you another question."

"Honey, I don't want to talk about it right now."

"No Babe, not that. Something else."

"What?"

He chuckled and said, "First of all, I'm not sleepy. I slept all day. Secondly, I want to talk you. Can't you spare a few more minutes for me?"

"Okay. Let's talk."

"I want to do something for your dad, but I remember you saying how proud he is."

"Harold, what are you up to?"

"The last time I spoke with your dad, he was telling me that his car was giving him a lot of trouble. He also said because he's still paying for your mom's car, he can't afford to buy another one. He was concerned it wouldn't last another two years, which is how much time he still has left to pay your mom's car off."

"Your point?"

"Well, my first thought was to just buy him a car. But I realized that wouldn't be a good idea. Then I thought if you offered him *your* car, he might go for that...easier."

"And what would I drive?"

"Whatever you want. Wouldn't you like a new car?"

"Harold, my car *is* new. I bought it less than a year ago. And my dad can't afford another car payment. We just established that."

"I'll pay your car off, so it'll be free and clear."

"So in reality, you would buy two cars. That's insane."

"I'm paying your car off anyhow. I don't believe in paying interest. I realize most people don't have a choice when it comes to big ticket items. But Babe, you are no longer most people. Your thinking has to conform to that. Okay?"

"Um-hum. I hear you. But my dad won't go for it."

"I think he will because it's coming from you, not me. Tell him that I plan to buy you a....what car do you want?"

I laughed and said, "Harold, this is crazy. Are you serious?"

"Felicia, tell me."

"Well, I've always wanted a Volvo. I could never...."

"Okay, a Volvo it is. Find the one you want, and we'll get it when we return from Detroit. By the way, that's a great choice. Very safe and they last forever. You simply tell your dad I'm gifting you with a Volvo because you told me that's something you've always wanted. Then tell him your car is paid off. Make him think it's your idea."

"I'll tell you what. I'll give it a whirl. I don't expect him to go for it, but I do think if I say I can't drive two cars, he'll probably offer me something for it. That'll make him feel better. Then what do I do?"

He paused and said, "Tell him one hundred dollars."

We both laughed and I said, "Harold you have got to stop! You're spending so much money. Fifty thousand on the Volvo and almost thirty to pay my Honda off. You're starting to scare me."

"Babe, I know it sounds like a lot, but these are necessities. And honestly, how can we ride in good solid vehicles, and know that our parents are struggling to keep their car going. It's sinful. I had to do something."

"You are a gem, my love. I can't imagine how you have any money left. Thank you for this, and I'll work really hard to make this happen."

"Good. Now I'll let you go. Even though it's only nine thirty."

I decided to ask him something. "Are you sure you're not tired?"

"I'm sure Babe. The game is on rain delay, so I'm just sitting here."

"I have a question for you, but it's not easy for me to ask. Will you indulge me?"

"Absolutely."

"Do you….um, masturbate?"

He laughed and said, "Of course I do. And since meeting you I can't stop!"

He was cracking up. I asked, "Are you laughing at me?"

"Of course I am. So, why the question? Does it bother you?"

"No, not at all. It's just not something we've talked about. I know you like to watch me do certain things, but we've never dealt with you and masturbation."

"Since we've been together, my sex drive is through the roof. So when I can't have you, I have to take matters into my own hands."

I was quiet for a moment, and then I asked, "Do you watch movies?"

"Felicia, where is all of this coming from?"

"I just want to know what you like and don't like to do. I'm not offended or intimidated by any of it, I promise."

"Okay. I do like to watch movies. I'm probably like most men, with my fantasies of beautiful women. I participated in an orgy once in college. I couldn't wait to do it, but I was totally disappointed. Let's see. I had one relationship that was almost serious, until I found out she lied about everything she told me. What a piece of work she was. I think that's it."

"Wow, that's….interesting. An orgy, huh?"

"Yep, but I realized some fantasies should remain just that. Fantasies. Because they rarely live up to our expectations."

"Is there anything else I need to know about this *almost serious* relationship?"

I shook my head no and he buried himself inside of me. He asked me to make him happy. I put my hands on his shoulders and began to move at the pace he likes. I leaned closer and put my tongue in his ear, continuing to move.

I knew he was close, so I released his ear and offered him my nipple. I knew my orgasm would make him come, so I brought his head closer, urging him to suck harder. I said, "Open your eyes and watch me come."

I dug my nails in his forearm and began to throb all around him. He buried his head between my head and neck and exploded. We were so exhausted, we both fell asleep.

The following day at work, I was in a daze. He went home about six that morning and stayed home from work. About eleven o'clock, he called me. He said, "Good morning Babe."

"Good morning. How are you feeling?"

"Incredible. I can honestly say I'm pussy whipped."

I laughed and said, "Harold, I've never heard you talk like that."

"Well, I've never felt like this before. Did I offend you?"

"No, of course not."

"So, how do you feel?"

"Fabulous. A little tired, but I feel like I'm on top of the world."

"So do I. It's like we reached some new plateau. Why is it you never told me about that?"

"I don't want to talk about that now. Let's talk later."

We agreed to end our conversation, and I went back to work. I sat there and smiled. I learned recently that I have to wait until the fall to start school. I was disappointed, but hopefully my other plan will come to fruition a little sooner.

He never said a word about us not using a condom. I did it on purpose, but I'm not sure if he even thought about it. We did talk briefly about another form of birth control, but we never settled on anything.

Maybe he thinks I took care of it. I just hope to be pregnant by the wedding. I have no interest in waiting. I want to have this baby and lock it up by my twenty ninth birthday.

Chapter Twelve

As June began to heat up Rochester, the kids were getting more and more excited. School was ending soon for the summer, they were about to attend their first Major League baseball game, moving to a new house and now, taking their first flight.

As we entered the airport, the boys were awed by it all. Marcus said, "Mom, everything is so big!"

"I know Marcus. Do you need to go to the bathroom? Either of you?"

They both shook their heads no. When it was finally time to board, Harold and the boys were so excited. He was right about me being overly concerned. Harold said to them, "Guys, we'll be there in just over two hours. Isn't that great?"

Marcus asked, "Mom, is the car getting on the plane too?"

"No Marcus. Once we get there, we'll rent a car and drive to Harold's parents' home. That's where we'll be staying."

Once on board, I found out of course, we were in first class. That made *me* excited. I said, "Wow, I've never flown first class before."

Harold said, "Me either. But I thought it would make the boys' first flight more pleasant and secretly, I've wanted to check it out myself."

Once we were settled, Harold whispered, "Wasn't I right?"

"Yep, you sure were. Thank you."

He caressed my hand and looked at my ring. He said, "I can't wait to show you off. My chest will be sticking out the entire time I'm there."

"You need to quit. Why do you say such things to me?"

"Because it's true. I can't believe Todd ruined your marriage. He couldn't possibly have known what a hidden treasure you are."

I leaned over and kissed him. Marcus and Todd were in front of us, so they couldn't see it. Harold said, "Babe I know you're uneasy about us staying at the house, but my parents aren't prudes. They would've been so hurt if we stayed in a hotel. Mom can't wait to teach you to make soup. And Dad is so excited about the boys coming. They only have granddaughters, so he is really anxious to play with them. He was disappointed that the Tigers aren't home this weekend, because *he* would've taken them to their first game. He was thrilled to hear they're baseball fans."

"Well, there's no better feeling than being welcomed in such a nice way. You have a wonderful family."

"*We* have wonderful families."

Harold kept an eye on the boys, because I went right to sleep. I woke suddenly, and looked frantically for my sons. Harold said, "Go on back to sleep. I can watch them."

That was the last thing I remembered until Marcus said, "Mom, wake up! We're here!!"

When we got inside the airport, Harold's sisters Karen and Tammy came over to greet us. Karen said, "Dad asked us to come and get you so you wouldn't have to rent a car."

Harold said, "Then I need to cancel the car. It'll only take a minute."

Karen took the boys to get bubble gum. I asked, "Karen. Are you gonna give them your teeth when theirs fall out?"

"Yeah Girl. I don't need these things. But I should've asked. I hope you don't mind too much."

"No, not too much. And thank you. You're very kind."

"Don't mention it. They're my new nephews!"

She reached out and hugged them heartily. Harold finally returned and we were on our way.

When we arrived, the house was exactly as I expected. Spectacular! Sprawling lawns, on at least two acres, and beautifully manicured. I feared it would be over the top with servants and whatnot, but surprisingly it was just like anyone else's home. Just bigger. Much bigger! I would guess there was about ten to twelve thousand square feet of living space, if not more.

The boys were a hit with everyone, but Grandma fell in love. She told Harold to take us to our *rooms* so we could get settled, and to make sure the boys bring their swimsuits when they come back down. Marcus asked, "Dad, are we going swimming?"

"We have a pool out back. Would you like to swim later?"

Both boys yelled, "Yes!"

Recently Todd, Gina, Harold and I discussed something that had come up. The boys asked me if they could call Gina, Mom. I didn't have a problem with it, but I also needed Todd's permission to allow the boys to call Harold, Dad. Most people would think that was absurd, but for the four of us, it really worked. All four of us loved them and would do anything for them. And the four of us got along so well. We all agreed they were super blessed to have two moms and two dads.

When Harold's mom heard the exchange between Harold and the boys, she went around the corner into the massive kitchen. I went behind her because she was crying. I immediately went to her and asked, "What's wrong?"

"I'm so happy for Harold and you and those boys. I never thought in a million years he would get married. And he's so happy!"

She reached for me and held me and I held her too. I said, "Mom. He's been like a knight in shining armor for me. He rescued me from such sadness. I never thought I would love again."

She and I were both in tears. Then we both smiled and began to laugh at ourselves.

She said, "We sure are silly."

"I know, right. I'm a wet blanket. I cry at any and everything."

"Me too. And I've fallen in love with your mother, Felicia. She's become one of my dearest friends."

We heard the boys coming down the stairs and she said, "I'm sure you all are hungry. Please tell Harold to announce dinner."

I looked at her and she laughed and said, "He'll know what I mean."

So I met Harold and the boys in the living room and said, "Hun. Your mom wants you to *announce* dinner."

He laughed and said, "Okay."

He went to an intercom in the foyer and said, "Dinner is served."

All of a sudden people were coming from everywhere. I wondered where we would all sit. I followed Harold and his sisters to the dining room. But mom told us we'd be eating poolside. And before long, Harold's dad came home.

Harold went toward the foyer to greet him, and the boys ran after him. Mom and the girls were getting dinner, so I began to help and Mom said, "No, go and greet Harold. He's anxious to see you."

I went toward the foyer and saw both of my sons in his arms. He was carrying them. I was outdone! He and Marcus were having a conversation. Marcus said, "I have two moms and two dads. Did you know that?"

"Yes, I know."

"Granddad, we have three grandmothers but only two granddads. Our other granddad went to heaven. Granddads are nice."

Dad was clearly enjoying this conversation with the boys. Harold and I retrieved the boys from Dad. I said, "Guys, let's not be too bothersome. Granddad has had a long day at work."

Dad said, "Nonsense. I'm enjoying them."

He reached for me and hugged me and kissed me on my cheek. He said, "Hello Beautiful. You and these boys have stolen my heart. Marcus almost made me cry, talking about how nice granddads are. I remember my grandfather. He was a pistol. Hahaha. Gave my grandmother fits. He liked to drink a bit too much and would get his rifle and shoot at the stars!"

We all cracked up. As we filed outside, the girls were busy preparing everything, and I began to help. Karen said, "Felicia, if you don't sit your ass down somewhere, we'll have to endure the *Jackie lecture*, and ain't nobody tryna hear her mouth."

For some reason, I was shocked to hear her talk like that. I hollered laughing and they looked at me and started laughing too. Melissa said, "Felicia, my sister is a thug. We've been holding our breath waiting for her to say something ridiculous. We all thought you'd be Miss Perfect, because Harold is so damned particular."

I laughed and said, "Honestly, I thought the same about you all for the same reason."

Karen said, "Girl, you must have really put it on him, 'cause we thought he would forever be a playboy."

Melissa said, "Don't pay any attention to Karen's crazy ass. He just dated without any interest in getting serious. The women loved him because he's good looking and so charming."

The chimes rang again announcing the rest of the family. Karen walked over to me and whispered, "At about midnight, we want you to meet us downstairs. We're planning a pajama party for you. You're not an early bird, are you?"

I hesitated and said, "No, I'm not."

"You look worried. We're not gonna put you through an initiation or anything. It'll be fun."

She laughed as we greeted her sisters. I said, "Okay, I'll be there."

As the evening began to wind down, the long day began to catch up with us. All of the kids swam themselves into oblivion. Marcus was asleep on Mom's lap and the girls were in the family room asleep. Todd was hanging tough. He and Danielle's husband Cliff were talking baseball.

Cliff couldn't get over how knowledgeable Todd was about Mets trivia. Harold was asking Tammy why she hadn't decided on a school yet. She said, "Because I want to be in a warm climate, but the school I like best is in that cold city you live in."

I asked, "What school Tammy?"

She said, "RIT. Are you familiar with it?"

"Oh yes. RIT is one of the best engineering schools in our area. Are you planning to be an engineer?"

"Yep, just like my brother. I want to be a Software Engineer too."

"I'm sure you'll do as well as your brother."

He smiled at me and caressed my shoulder. Then he said, "I think it's time we put these boys to bed."

Todd said, "Aw man. Do we have to?"

"It's ten thirty Todd. It's been a long day. We'll get up tomorrow and do some fun stuff, okay?"

"Can we go and see Comerica Park? And Mom, can we get one of those cameras at the drugstore for five bucks? I have money in my piggybank, so I'll pay you back!"

"We'll see Todd. Say goodnight to everyone."

"Mom, can I call Dad and Mom before going to bed?"

Harold went in his pocket for his cell phone. He called Todd and gave him the phone. Todd spoke with his father, he kissed and hugged his new grandparents and we took both boys to bed.

Later, I heard noise in the kitchen, but everyone was accounted for. I thought to ask the sisters about cleaning the kitchen, but decided against it after what Karen said about the lecture. Finally I asked Harold, "Who's in the kitchen?"

"Mom hires her students when she has large gatherings to clean up, so they can make a little money."

"Oh, okay. That's so nice of her."

"Dad says it's a wonder we have any money left."

The men announced they were about to leave. They gathered the girls and put them in the SUV. Harold asked his sisters, "Are you ladies staying?"

Tara said, "Yes, is there a problem?"

He laughed and said, "As long as you don't try to invade my privacy, I don't care."

"Boy, nobody wanna be nowhere near you except Felicia."

The two of them continued with their back and forth, and Karen took that opportunity to remind me about later. Soon he and I went up to bed.

By eleven forty five we'd showered and were in our pajamas. I asked, "Where do you shop for your clothes?"

"Why? You wanna buy me something?"

"I was just asking. You have such nice pajamas. Where do you shop?"

"I usually order them from Brooks Brothers. I'm not a big shopper, but I like quality."

I cleared my throat and said, "Don't be mad, but your sisters have invited me to sleep down in the playroom with them. They're having a pajama party for me, so I'm expected to be there."

"Oh hell no! I want you here with me!"

"Hun. I won't get an opportunity like this for a long time. It's my chance to get to know your sisters better."

He pouted and put my hand on his lap. He was hard and acting spoiled.

I reached in his pajama pants and I laid my head in his lap. I looked up at him and he was smiling. When I walked out, he was happy.

I could hear the sisters from the second floor. By the time I reached the playroom, it was on and poppin'. The wine and liquor were flowing, the music was on and I would swear I smelled pot.

When they saw me, Melissa said, "We thought Harold had you on lock down. We were gonna come and get you, but decided against it."

I laughed and said, "I admit it wasn't easy. He's a little spoiled, but he usually lets me have my way."

Karen said, "That's hard to believe. Harold *always* gets his way! What the hell did you do to my brother?"

Everyone laughed, but I wasn't sure if that was all that funny. Tara said, "Felicia, don't give any thought to what Karen says. She's a pot head!"

Karen said, "You want some? I know this guy…"

Danielle said, 'I'm sure Felicia's drug of choice is not anything illegal Karen."

I laughed and said, "No, thanks. I'll go over here and make myself a martini. Anybody else want one?"

Everyone got up and came over to the bar where I was. We all fixed drinks and got food. Tara asked, "So Felicia, did you finally find a dress?"

"Sadly no. I've narrowed it down to five though."

"Danielle said, "Five! You do realize your window is closing. What are you waiting for?"

"I don't know. For some reason I don't seem to recognize the urgency. Everyone else does, but I'm just cruising along like I have forever. I originally wanted to have a spring wedding next year, but Harold insisted that he wanted to get married sooner."

Karen said, "Unconsciously, she's making him suffer for forcing the wedding on her too soon."

Everybody said, "She's a Psych Major!"

We all fell out laughing and then I said, "I realize it's late in the game, but Tara, Danielle, would you consider allowing Mya and Cheyenne to be in the wedding? They're so precious and Todd and Marcus would have someone to escort down the aisle."

They looked at each other and shook their heads yes. I said, "I'm sure the bridesmaid dress will be appropriate for them too."

Tara agreed to order them for both girls. Danielle opened her laptop and said, "This is so exciting! Okay Miss Thing, show me the dresses. We're gonna pick this dress out tonight."

I said, "Why don't we have a vote. I won't commit to choosing what you all pick, but I will definitely put it high on the list."

So we looked at the five dresses and the winner received four votes. I said, "Wow, you all really like this dress. Why this one?"

Melissa said, "I think it's gorgeous and will show off your curves. Everyone's not made to wear a dress like that. You'll look like a mermaid in that dress!"

Everyone concurred. Karen said, "That also means you can't gain one ounce if you choose it. And whatever you do, don't get pregnant before the wedding!"

My heart skipped a beat. Because of my silence, Tara asked, "*Are* you pregnant?"

I looked at them and said, "No, no I'm not pregnant. But to be honest, we hit a rough patch when I told him I didn't want more kids. But I later decided to surprise him with a child. I figured if I get pregnant between now and the wedding, it won't be that big of a deal. But Karen is right. I have to be careful in the event I get pregnant."

Danielle said, "Don't worry yourself over it. It'll happen when it happens, and if you have to get the dress altered, then so be it. Order it two sizes too big. Problem solved."

I thought about that and said, "You're right. I won't worry about it."

I suddenly realized Tammy is only seventeen. I felt terrible speaking so bluntly in front of her. I said, "Tammy, I probably made a mistake saying that in front of you."

Tammy said, "With four sisters and a cool mom, I've heard it all."

They all shook their heads and Tara said, "We're very open about sex in this family. Mom told us if any of us got pregnant, she'd kill us!"

Karen said, "When we turned sixteen, she made us get a shot every three months and supplied us with a boatload of condoms. She wasn't playing!"

Tara laughed and said, "She also gave Harold condoms, and asked him if she needed to show him how to use them. We died laughing!"

Danielle said, "He was so outdone, he called Dad. Dad came home immediately and told Mom he'd handle it and not to touch poor Harold."

By two o'clock, we were drunk as skunks and laid out on the floor. We had air mattresses, but no one had the energy to open them. Karen went outside and had another joint and tried to persuade us to join her. We were still drinking and eating. I said, "These crab cakes are so good. Did your mom make them?"

Melissa said, "Actually, Dad made them. No one makes crab cakes like Dad. When you and Harold went upstairs, we went into the kitchen and drug him with us."

I asked, "Ladies, would you be upset if I went upstairs and crawled into bed with Harold?"

They said, "No, not at all!"

I said, "Thanks for everything. I'm glad we had the opportunity to get to know each other."

Danielle said, "Yes, that was the plan. We realized things will start to get busy, and we wouldn't have the chance to kick back and get to know our new sister."

I got up and hugged them. I said, "Goodnight Ladies and thanks again. And remember. My hope to surprise Harold with a child is a secret."

Melissa said, "Don't worry. One thing we do well is keep secrets."

Breakfast is served, was announced over the intercom. That was so funny to me. As we entered the dining room, the sisters were still in their pj's and looking hungover. Cheyenne and Mya were also there.

Dad asked, "So Felicia, did you enjoy your pajama party?"

"Yes Sir, I really did. And those crab cakes were to die for."

"I'm glad you liked them. As a matter of fact, Jackie asked me to make more."

He unveiled a platter full of crab cakes. Harold said, "I was just about to complain because you know how much I love crab cakes."

Mom said, "I knew once you heard the girls had them, you would have a fit."

Dad asked the boys, "What is your favorite food?"

They both said, "Pizza!"

He laughed and asked, "Would you guys like to go with me and help make your *own* pizza?"

They both said, "Yes!"

Marcus said, "Granddad, I thought you had to go to the pizza store to get pizza."

Everyone groaned and Dad said, "No Son. We make our own."

Tammy said, "Daddy, please spare such a small child the lecture. It's my Graduation Day!"

We all laughed and Dad turned to his granddaughters. He asked, "Would you ladies like to go for a ride with the boys and me?"

They both said, "Yes!"

We took the boys upstairs to get them ready for their adventure, and Harold asked me, "What would you like to do today."

"Let's help get the house ready."

"Okay, but let's take a tour of Detroit's highlights first."

"Okay, that sounds like fun."

We took the boys back downstairs and they all went with Dad.

When we returned, the house had been transformed. There were banners and balloons and Mom had hired more of her students. She refused our help, and suggested we go and have a swim.

We went upstairs and I said, "You swim. I don't want to."

"You do know how to swim, don't you?"

"Of course, but I've never really been a fan of it."

"Okay, but will you at least put on your swimsuit so I can have something to look at?"

"I didn't bring one. But I'll put on some shorts? How's that?"

He smiled and said, "Okay that works!"

While we were out back, the students and sisters were in and out. Tara brought us some iced tea and Karen brought out vodka to go in it. She said, "You're a girl after my own heart. I know damn well you're ready for a little something!"

She went back inside and I laughed and poured vodka in my tea. Harold came over dripping wet, and I asked him if he would like a shot in his. He said, "My wino sister always has something to alter one's brain."

He got back in the pool and I went back to my laptop. I wanted some water, so I went inside.

As I approached the kitchen, I heard one of the students ask Karen, "Is that your brother in the pool?"

"Yes, do you know him?"

"No, but I'd like to. Would you introduce us?"

"Girl, hell no. He's engaged."

I walked in and spoke to them. The student asked me, "Would you introduce me to your brother?"

"Excuse me?"

As if right on cue, Harold came into the kitchen. He asked me, "Why did you leave?"

"Harold, this young lady would like to meet you."

She went over to him and said, "Wow Harold! I didn't know Mrs. Benson's son was so handsome! It's nice to meet you. I'm Wanda."

Harold laughed and said, "Wanda, it's nice meeting you too. Have you met…?"

"Yes, these are your sisters, right?"

He pointed to Karen and said, "That's my sister Karen."

Then he walked over to me and "And this is my fiancée, Felicia."

Karen fell out laughing and left. Poor Wanda was so embarrassed, I felt sorry for her. She said, "I'm really sorry."

I said, "Don't worry about it. No harm, no foul."

Harold and I went back outside, and Karen was already out there having a drink. She said, "That shit was hilarious! But I would've whipped her ass for hitting on my man!"

Harold said, "I guess you know by now that Karen is a thug."

I said, "Stop Harold. She is not. I'm tired of people saying that. Now take your pretty Black ass upstairs and put some clothes on."

The graduation and party were great. The next day was bittersweet. The boys and their cousins were playing in the yard. All of the sisters, the husbands, Mom and Dad and Harold and me were relaxing after a wonderful brunch.

Earlier, Mom insisted that we all go to church. It started at eight o'clock, and when we returned the brunch was waiting for us. She'd ordered it from one of their restaurants.

We had to be at the airport by one o'clock, so it was soon time to get ready to leave. As I went upstairs, I looked back and realized I was really going to miss them. I started to get anxious about seeing them in October. Especially Karen.

When we were all in the foyer saying our goodbyes, Marcus went over to Cheyenne and hugged her. She said, "I love you Marcus."

There wasn't a dry eye in the house. Todd said, "Granddad, I had a ball yesterday. Thank you for taking us to Comerica Park and letting us make pizzas. Oh, and thank you for the camera."

He looked at me and said, "Mom, I told Granddad I would mail him the money for the camera. He said I didn't have to, but Dad said a man always pays his way, right?"

"Yes Todd, that's right."

Before leaving, Karen drug me upstairs to her room. She hugged me so tight, it was as if her life depended on it. She said, "I love you Sis. I'm so happy you're a part of the family."

"I love you too Karen. I hate to have favorites, but you're it for me. That has to be our secret. And I can't wait to see you in October."

"Hell no, I'll be there in September for the bridal... Oh shit!"

She whispered, "Please don't be mad. Your friend Annette has planned a surprise bridal shower for you. She said you didn't want one since you'd already been married. She's a girl after my own heart, because she said she didn't give a shit what you wanted!"

I cracked up. I said, "Although I really don't want a shower, I'm so happy that I'll get to see you guys again so soon."

We all napped on the plane ride home, although we made time to eat. When we dropped Harold off, he said, "Call me later and make time to go online and look for that *thing* we talked about."

The boys told him goodbye and he came around to the driver's side and kissed me on the cheek. He asked the boys, "Did you have fun?"

They said, "Yes!"

Todd said, "I can't wait to call my cousins and tell my friends at school. It was the greatest Dad!"

Harold waved and went into his apartment. I think I saw him tear up.

Once we were home, I called my parents and told them we'd landed. They wanted to know all about it, so I was on the phone with them for an hour. Then I called Annette and told her I'd decided to spend the money and have Benny tail Sam, and to find out how soon he could start."

"What has that bastard done now? I swear I will kill his ass if he doesn't leave you alone!"

"He hasn't done anything that I know of. I would just feel better."

"Okay, I'll call him later. If you don't hear from me tonight, I'll call you tomorrow."

We hung up and the boys asked if they could play on the PlayStation. I asked, "Aren't you all tired?"

Todd said, "No Mom, we're not tired. It's only six o'clock."

"Okay, but just for an hour."

I sat on the sofa, exhausted. Before I knew it, the boys were waking me up. They had on pajamas and I asked, "Did you take your showers?"

Todd said, "Yes, I used your bathroom and Marcus used the other one. You were asleep, and we didn't want to wake you."

Soon the boys were in bed and I was reaching for my phone calling Harold. When he answered, he appeared to be asleep. I said, "Honey, I'm sorry I woke you. Go back to sleep and we'll talk tomorrow."

"Okay Babe. I guess I was more tired than I thought. Love you."

"I love you too. Bye."

We hung up and I was alone and wide awake. I decided to take a shower and get in bed with my laptop. I turned the TV on and then remembered the cameras.

I got up and went to the main panel and looked to see if there was any activity. There was nothing. Thank God. I don't know what I'd do if something was on there. I went back to the laptop and looked again at the dress that the sisters selected.

Before going to Detroit, Harold gave me a prepaid Visa card for twenty thousand dollars. The name on it was Felicia P. Wilson-Benson. He asked what name I planned to use after we were married. I hadn't thought about it.

But after seeing the card, I really liked his choice. When I married Todd, I dropped my middle name, Shiree. I didn't want to drop Wilson, because I wanted to have the same name as the boys.

I decided to check and see if any local stores carried the dress. There was one store in Victor, N.Y. at Eastview Mall. I decided to text Carla and Annette. I asked them if they were available tomorrow to go after work with me.

It's about a half hour drive, so hopefully after they feed their families and get them settled, we could go about seven o'clock. Carla responded immediately, saying yes she could go. I never heard from Annette.

The following day after a staff meeting, Harold was in my department speaking to one of the managers. He came over to my desk and said, "Good morning. Did you get enough rest last night?"

"Good morning. I did. How about you?"

"I got plenty. Did you find a car?"

"Damn, I knew I was forgetting something."

He gave me that look and said, "I need you to take care of that today Babe, okay?"

"Yes Sir. I promise."

He laughed and I said, "I'm sorry. I spent my time looking for a dress. I *must* get that off my list."

"All right. I have someone waiting to hear from me on it. He's a friend of Dad's who agreed to sell it to us at cost."

"Why don't you pick it out? The only thing I'm sure of is that I want it to be a pearl color inside and out. And with a sunroof, if that's okay?"

"Okay, I'll handle it. I'll call you later with the details. Gotta go."

He walked away and I got a little giddy as I realized I was about to have the car of my dreams.

Later that day, Annette called. She said she *really* needed to talk to me. I told her I would call her back in five minutes. I told Trina I needed to get something from my car, and I'd be right back.

I called her and she said, "Licia, Tony walked in on me talking to Benny last night."

"Oh no! What happened?"

"Nothing really. He wanted to know who I was talking to and I waved him off. He wouldn't leave it alone, so I cussed his ass out. But I couldn't get that information to Benny until today."

I laughed at Annette's crazy ass. I asked, "What did Benny say?"

"He said he could start today, but he wanted me to warn you that it costs a hundred and fifty dollars a day. And that's with my deep discount. Are you sure you wanna go through with this?"

"I do Nette. Hopefully, it'll only be for a week."

"Okay. I'm home today. I feel like it's time for a vacation."

"I know the feeling. Even though I just got back from Detroit, I still feel like I need some me time."

"Girl, let's do it! Let's plan a long weekend getaway. I'll get with Carla and ask if she wants to join us. Please Licia, I really need this."

"I'd love to, but I can't. Not for at least thirty days."

"Why?!"

"Because I'm moving on the thirtieth and we're going to NYC on the twenty third. And I have to get back Nette. Let's talk more later, okay?"

I hurried back to my desk and began going through emails. There was one from Harold. I opened it and saw the car. It was perfect. I should have known it would be. The cost was blacked out. I replied and told him I loved it. He replied and said it should be here in a few weeks.

When I got home, there was a message from Gina. She was missing the boys and wondered if they could come earlier than Friday. I called her back and she said, "I was hoping tomorrow. I'm off from work until late August. The school system changed their vacation policy so we can't carry over anymore. I had to take it."

Before hanging up, she agreed to pick the boys up tomorrow after school and keep them through the weekend. I still haven't shopped, so I told the boys we were going out to grab dinner. When I opened the door, Harold was just about to knock. He asked, "Where are you going?"

"We were gonna grab some dinner. Wanna come?"

"Sure, let's go."

As we were getting into Harold's car, Sam and Aysia pulled up. We all spoke and Sam said, "We're moving on the twenty third to Richmond. If we don't see you all, it's been really great having such nice neighbors."

I said, "That's great Sam. And thanks again for all the wine."

Harold said, "Man…"

I interrupted and said, "We really should be going."

Harold looked at me and decided to take my lead. We said goodbye and off we went. He eventually asked, "So what does everyone want?"

I said, "Let's do a buffet."

While the boys were getting dessert, Harold asked, "So why did you interrupt my conversation with Sam?"

"I was afraid you were gonna tell him that we were also moving, and I didn't want him or any of our neighbors knowing our business. My dad always said it wasn't good for people to know when you were going on vacation or moving."

"I guess that makes sense. But since he's moving in a week, I guess I really didn't think about it."

"He's a nice guy and all, but I really don't know him like that. I guess I'm just very cautious about those things."

"Well, it's better to err on the side of caution. I would rather you be that way than too trusting of people. I plan to get the best security system available for the house. By the way, do we have any furniture yet Missy?"

"Why the hell do you call me that?"

He laughed and the boys returned. He said, "Because that's what my dad would say to my mom when she was in trouble. And you seem to be in trouble. Why don't we go out tonight and start getting some things."

"I can't. I have to go to Eastview Mall. I'm meeting Annette and Carla at seven o'clock at my place. Oh no…"

I grabbed my phone. She answered quickly. "Annette, did I ask you about going tonight? I'm with Harold and the boys."

"I just talked to Carla and she and I will meet at your place at seven."

"Okay, I'll be there. Bye."

I looked at Harold and said, "Hun, I *really* need to get this done and out of the way."

I looked at the boys and asked, "Guys, would you go and get Mom a chocolate ice cream cone?"

Todd said, "Okay Mom. Come on Marcus."

I turned to Harold and said, "The boys don't know yet, but Todd and

Gina are taking them tomorrow to a festival and will be keeping them for the rest of the week. That will give us some time to shop for furniture, okay?"

He shook his head and said, 'That's fine Babe. Let's finish up here so I can get you back in time to meet the girls."

"I'm gonna need a favor?"

"What do you need?"

"A babysitter. Can the boys stay with you until about eight thirty, nine o'clock?"

He laughed and said, "Sure Babe."

On the way to the mall, I asked Annette if everything was cool at home. She said, "Yeah Licia. After I told his ass off, he's been a different person."

Carla said, "He and Earl were down in the basement and I heard Tony say, "Man, she was *not* playing! Women can be so sweet, but don't fuck with 'em! They're like beasts!"

Earl said, "Listen, you're talking to a man who knows. Carla actually grabbed me by the balls once and said, Negro, you will wake up a castrated motherfucker if you *ever* do that to me again!"

Annette and I screamed laughing. I asked, "Carla, what had he done?"

"That was when he said he was going to Mississippi with Donald."

"Oh yeah, I remember that. He actually went to Atlantic City with some chick and your co-worker saw him and called you."

"Yep, and when he went to sleep that night I got the biggest knife in the house and grabbed his nuts and said, Wake up, you Son of a Bitch! I'm sure he saw his life flash before him, because all he could see was the glitter of that knife in his face. I showed him the picture Terry sent me. Girl, you had to be there to see the look on his face."

We all cracked the hell up. My girls are hilarious, that's for sure. I said, "I already know Harold has issues, but I wonder what kind of new crap he'll bring to the table? So far, his only crime is that he wants to be so damn controlling. But he's really calmed down lately."

Annette said, "Yeah, for now. I don't see him changing his ways Licia. He's being a good boy now, but you need to prepare yourself for a controlling husband."

"I know you're right. But I think I've figured out how to handle that."

Annette said, "Before I forget, Benny said he started tailing Sam today. He said he saw you all when you went out."

"Wow, that was just a couple of hours ago."

"I know. He's already on the job."

The dress was magical. Annette and Carla stood there with their mouths opened. I asked the salesperson how long it would take to order. She said two to three weeks. I asked about a head piece so we went over and found the perfect match. Both had lace and sequins.

The dress had one inch sleeves, just off the shoulder. It had a deep V in front and back, and was fitted past my thigh, with a high/low feature. The bottom in back featured a short one foot train. Like Karen said, I looked like a mermaid. I was concerned because I couldn't wear a bra, but the dress had one built in and the girls said it looked fabulous.

While we were there I found shoes, garters, panties, thigh high stockings, and lingerie for my wedding night. I called Karen and asked her what size shoe she and Tammy wear, and I ordered theirs and Carla and Annette's. That was my gift to each of them. Danielle and Tara insisted on taking care of the girls accessories.

When we were done, I asked the salesperson to wait a minute before she completed the sale. Then I asked Annette and Carla to leave out because I wanted to do something I didn't want them to see.

When they left, I asked the salesperson about some garters I saw that were monogrammed. I gave her the names of everyone in the bridal party. Then I decided to get one for our mothers and the other sisters as well. And one for myself, of course.

When I got outside, they looked at me funny. I said, "Everyone likes a little mystery, right?"

Annette said, "Whatever Felicia."

I said, "Come on. I gotta get my kids!"

With mid-June approaching, I realized I had two weeks to pack. I didn't even have a box. With the moving company doing the work, it dawned on me that my attention needed to be on the new house.

Although the builder had custom blinds installed, I remembered the sliding glass door had nothing covering it. I needed to get with Harold and go back and see what else was needed.

And of course, the Yankees/Mets game is next weekend. Harold and Todd seemed to have it all arranged. We'd leave Friday, taking Harold's Navigator, stay two nights and return to Rochester on Sunday morning. There appears to be no rest for the weary.

Tuesday after work, Harold and I entered our new home. As I entered the kitchen, I realized there was construction going on in the backyard. I asked, "What are they doing back there?"

That's when I realized I was looking out through French doors and not a sliding glass door. He said, "I asked them to put in a pool. It should be ready in another week. I also asked for an enclosed deck. What do you think?"

I walked up to him and asked, "What does it matter?! If you make one more decision without consulting me, I will end this relationship!"

I walked out and got in the car. I was fuming! He came out and said, "Felicia, I wanted to surprise you. I'm sorry Babe."

"Harold. A surprise is a bouquet of flowers or a box of chocolates. Not a permanent structure on the house or property! I told you once that you need to learn what it means to be a couple. This is getting out of hand!"

I was so damn mad at him. He said, "I didn't mean any harm. I'm sorry."

"Harold, you treat me like I'm a child. I will not accept you making decisions for both of us. I'm a grown ass Woman! And you need to know that I am not impressed by your money nor am I intimidated by it. I made it just fine without it, and I can continue to do so."

"I know that Felicia. I promise to do better."

"No, better is not good enough. I need you to stop! I would never consider making a decision like that without consulting you."

He sort of laughed and asked, "Can I come clean?"

"Clean?"

"Yes. It seems every woman I've ever dated eventually showed themselves as a gold-digger. Yet, even when you learned I had a little money, you were never fazed by it. I remember your concern about my parents when you learned they paid for our engagement weekend. And how you fussed over not helping to pay for this house. You have never, not even once, asked me for anything."

I continued to be silent. He said, "Okay, I'm coming cleaner. It worries me because somewhere in my psyche I have this unsettling feeling that you don't need me. That's troubling, because I can't imagine being without you. I would give away every cent I have if it meant you would be lying in my arms every night."

"What else have you done?"

"I haven't done anything else, but Annette....oops!"

"Annette?"

"Felicia, she'll kill me if I tell you."

"I'll kill you if you *don't*."

"She's planning a surprise bridal shower and…."

"I already know about it."

"Who told you?"

"Drunk ass Karen!"

He bent over laughing. He finally said, "Thank God I wasn't first. I'm so sorry. Please get out of the car Babe."

I hesitated, but I got out. He asked, "Will you please forgive me?"

"Um-hum. But you're on punishment."

I walked back in the house and went back into the kitchen. I turned and asked again, "Are you sure you haven't done anything else? Because I don't remember double ovens?"

"You're right. I honestly forgot about the ovens. The fridge and stove are different too. Sorry."

I turned to look at the fridge and it was huge. The stove was now a six burner gas stove. I put my hands on my hips and said, "You have one last chance to tell me what else you've done."

"Babe, as the son of a chef, I'm used to having things a certain way. I never even thought about it. Give me a little slack."

"Um-hum. Okay. But as we go through the house, you better try to remember."

As we went through the bedrooms, I didn't notice any changes. We made our notes and made decisions on what to get for this room and that. When we reached the basement he said, "Okay, I had the doorway that was over there changed to French doors. That way we can more easily go out to the pool area from down here. And I asked them to turn the storage room into a shower/changing area. You mad?"

I walked over and admired the French doors. Then I opened the door to what used to be storage and it was a beautiful room with two shower stalls and two changing areas. I turned back to look at him and asked, "Anything else?"

He pointed to the media room. I sashayed over to the media room and looked in. I couldn't see any change. I opened the glass doors and tried to see what he'd done. I turned and said, "I don't see it."

"Look over there."

I turned and there was a popcorn machine in the corner. There was also a wine fridge and a regular sized fridge. I asked, "What else, Mr. Benson?"

"Damn, I feel like a murderer telling the cops where to find the bodies. I don't know. That should be all, but I'm not sure. I'm sorry! I love you and I thought these things would make you happy!!"

He went upstairs and I started after him. Then Felicia Pierce stopped me. She said let him fume and let him be upset. He'll get over it.

I went upstairs after looking at the popcorn machine and refrigerators. He was in the kitchen looking out into the backyard. He said, "Felicia, you're the best thing that's ever happened to me. I came up here and realized I *am* a spoiled brat, just like my sisters have said. I think I should have my way because I'm a *good guy*. But it's all been at your expense. I'm sure you're tired of my apologies. And I'm tired of giving them."

I went over to him and lifted his hands to my lips. I kissed them and said, "If this is as bad as it gets, we should easily survive it."

He brought me into his arms and we held each other for a long time. He finally released me and said, "I have *really* learned my lesson. But no more promises. I might make mistakes along the way because I'm still a work in progress."

I remained silent as we locked up and left the house. I loved all of the changes he made, but I had to put him through this so he would learn his lesson. Hopefully.

Chapter Thirteen

As we entered the Big Apple, we were all awed. None of us had ever been there before. So many people and they were everywhere. And the buildings! All of them so high, you have look into the sky to see the tops of them.

When we finally reached our hotel, it was almost ten o'clock. We grabbed some take-out and retired for the night.

The next day, we were up early and the boys wanted to go out right away. We agreed to have breakfast at the hotel and Gina and I went walking in one direction while the fellows went toward Times Square.

We agreed to be back by noon. I made the men promise to hold the boys' hands and not let them out of their sights.

Gina and I did a lot of looking and finally decided to stop in a little shop. We were floored at the cost of things. A pair of shoes cost a thousand dollars. We looked at each other and left.

We laughed and she said, "Felicia, I've been meaning to tell you. We decided to have a small ceremony after church next month. We would really like it if you all would come. It's on the fifteenth of July."

"Do you have any family in Rochester?"

She looked away and said, "No. I'm from the Syracuse area, but I ended up in the foster care system in Rochester."

"Oh, I didn't know. Do you know your family?"

"Yes, but we don't really have a relationship. My foster mom adopted me. She'll be there."

She paused a moment and then said, "You see, when I was eleven, my mom's boyfriend raped me repeatedly over a four month period. He told me if I told, he would kill my mother and then me."

My mouth suddenly went dry and I had trouble breathing. She continued. "One day my teacher took me to the bathroom because I was bleeding. She assumed I'd started my period and she said, "Let's go to the nurse's office Sweetheart."

I said, "No, I can't! He said if I tell, he'll kill Mommy and then me!"

"Who is *he*?"

"Freddie."

"So what is it you're not supposed to tell?"

I started to cry and said, "Miss Taylor, he hurts me. He makes me open my legs and he puts his thing in me."

I gasped loudly. I was horrified! I said, "Gina, my God!"

She and I were both standing on the street in New York City with tears streaming down our faces.

I found a bench and suggested we sit. I looked around and saw a vendor, and got a couple of bottles of water. I gave her one and asked if she was okay. She said, "Felicia, you are one of very few people I've ever shared that with."

"So what happened?"

"It all seemed to happen so fast. Miss Taylor took me to the nurse and soon the principal came in with the police. A female officer took me to the hospital. She was so nice. She stayed with me and held my hand the whole time I was examined. I kept asking for my mom, but the next thing I knew, I was at this house with other kids. After about a week I was taken to see my mother in jail."

She turned away but continued. "Then these people kept asking me if my mom knew. I told them I never told her because I was afraid Freddie would kill us. A few weeks later, they let me go home. My mom kept telling me to tell the police I made a mistake and that I fell. She said, "I need you to do this so Freddie can come back and pay these bills. He won't mess with you anymore, I promise."

I did what she said. The tests from my exam proved I'd been violated repeatedly. That's when they came and arrested her again, and took me away again. I was brought to Rochester because they didn't want anyone to know where I was. I learned much later from my foster mother that they used my taped testimony against Freddie and my mom. They both went to prison."

She looked at me and said, "About five years ago, I made an attempt to reconnect with my mom. She didn't want anything to do with me. Mainly because she'd become addicted to drugs and she didn't want me to see her that way. She apologized to me and said, "You deserve better. I should've protected you. I suspected it, but my need caused me to turn my head to it."

I just looked at Gina. I couldn't believe what I'd just heard. I asked, "How in the world did you become such a kind, loving person after such a horrible experience?"

"My adopted mom is a kind, Christian woman who loves me very much. When I was fourteen, she told me that I'd had a hysterectomy. Freddie really tore me up, and that's why I never had a period and will never have children."

"Have you considered adopting?"

"Yes, but I don't know how Todd will feel about it."

"Have you told him about being raped?"

"Yes."

"You should give it a whirl. He loves you to pieces."

She smiled at that. We realized it was time to return. She said, "Felicia, please don't say anything about this to anyone."

"Don't worry. I promise to keep it to myself."

Gina and I were looking at these men and cracking up. By the fourth inning, she and I were ready to roll. It was hot and the Mets were getting killed by the Yankees.

Harold was in heaven. Hollering and jumping up and down, like he was twelve. Todd and the boys weren't much better. Even though their team was losing, they hollered at any ray of hope. A strike out, a pop up, anything. It was sad. Gina said, "Felicia, let's go and indulge in a beer or something we don't need."

"I'm right behind you."

So we walked around Yankee Stadium and ate veggie burgers and drank beer. We returned during the eighth inning and they were still at it.

The Mets finally scored. Now they were only *six* runs down! At the top of the ninth, the Mets hit back to back home runs. The first one was a three run shot. So now they were down two runs with two outs. The game was finally exciting. But the batter struck out and the game was over. The boys were so disappointed. I thought Marcus was gonna cry.

I said, "Wow, what a game! You guys have great stories to tell your friends! And the Hall of Fame players you saw! You saw the great Mariano Rivera, and you saw the great Carlos Beltran hit a homerun against him! Not many people can say that!"

Todd said, "Yeah Mom. And after David Wright hit the three run homerun, it became a save situation. So Mariano came in and Carlos knocked it over the center field wall on the first pitch!"

"So you guys got to see history."

Marcus asked, "What's that?"

Big Todd said, "It's when something happens that's never happened or has only happened a few times. We were lucky to be here to see it!"

Marcus finally began to smile. As we filed out, Gina looked at me and I looked at her. We were holding our bellies. I asked, "Do you feel sick?"

"Yeah, my tummy is rumbling."

We both headed toward the restroom. We emerged about ten minutes later, after puking our guts up. By the time we got back to our room, she and I were both running for the bathrooms again. This time it was coming the other way. It was awful! We convinced the guys to go out to dinner, but to first bring us some crackers and ginger-ale.

After a couple of hours, we were feeling better. We took showers and were in our pajamas when they returned. We were watching a movie and nibbling crackers and sipping ginger-ale. I wanted some real food. Gina asked, "So what did you guys eat?"

Harold said, "Well Todd and I each had a slice of pizza. We had to know if it really was as good as New Yorkers claim. And it was!"

Todd Jr. said, "Me and Marcus wouldn't touch it because Granddad said not to."

Harold said, "I can't wait to tell Dad!"

I asked the boys, "What did you eat?"

Marcus said, "We had Chinese food! Mom, it was great! Daddy and Dad had it too!"

Gina asked, "You all had two dinners?"

They looked at each other and Todd said, "We had to make sure it was okay for the boys to eat!"

We all laughed and Harold asked, "You feeling better Babe?"

"Yes, but I'm really hungry."

"Gina said, "I am too!"

"But I guess it wouldn't be smart to eat anything."

She agreed. Todd said, "Why don't you two go on to bed and we'll put the boys down. They can have showers in the morning."

I was up and on my way before he finished the sentence.

When Harold joined me later, he cuddled up to me and said, "You know, we had lots of food but none of us got sick."

"You probably got yours from a different vendor."

"I had the time of my life today. I'm such a kid."

He reached inside of my nightgown and began massaging my breasts. As much as I was enjoying it, I said, "You will have to wait for that."

He groaned and said, "I know you're not feeling well. And I know this isn't the best place for it, but that's what makes it so exciting. I want to make you feel better."

He trailed his tongue along the length of my ear lobe. He spoke very quietly and very slowly. *"I like to feel you quiver and hear you scream and moan. I like when you part your luscious thighs and caress my face with them. I also like when you press your sweetness against my tongue...umm. I like...when you squeeze my head with those thighs and move against my face until you come. You scream....and you come."*

By now I was unable to think. I was boiling and wet and he knew it, because I couldn't keep still. He said very quietly, "Open your legs."

I opened my legs and he moved under the cover. He rubbed my thighs and they began to shake. He licked me like a child would a lollypop. I reached for his face and brought him to my desire. He loved me so well, I cried because I couldn't scream.

And just when I thought it was over, he crawled on top of me, kissed my neck and suddenly I was filled with his hardness. Neither of us lasted ten seconds.

He blew me away.

Gina continued to be nauseous, but I was better. I gave her more ginger-ale and more crackers. I had dry toast and plain scrambled eggs. I said, "Maybe you should try the toast."

She did, but she didn't feel any better. We got on the road, and I feared the ride would upset her tummy even more. I insisted she lay down in the middle seat, while the boys and I sat in the rear. She took a long nap, and woke up about an hour before we got home.

She said she was finally feeling better. I gave her a little more ginger-ale. She is such a sweetheart. I sometimes can't believe this is the woman who is sleeping with my ex-husband and about to become his wife. I understand why he loves her, because I do too. Anyone looking would truly think we're all nuts.

When we got home, there were two cases of wine and a note at my door. It read: The movers couldn't move it and my car was full.

I went down the other stairs to retrieve my mail. My hand was still shaking when I went inside my mailbox and found another surprise. There was a note inside saying my neighbor Carol had signed for a package. What the hell?!

I knocked on her door and she answered. She said, "Hi Felicia! I have a package for you."

"Hi Carol. I appreciate it. Thanks."

She handed me the package and it was from Detroit. I exhaled. It was addressed to Todd Wilson Jr. from Harold Benson Sr. I looked toward my door and Harold was waiting for me.

He seemed unnerved too. That fucking Sam. I'm sure my discomfort was obvious to Harold.

I'd called Dad Benson after returning from Detroit to tell him that Todd had given me the money for the camera. He said, "Put it back in his piggy bank. I'll send him a note saying I got the money."

I gave the package to Harold and walked inside. He said, "Todd you have a package."

Todd ran into the living room and asked, "Wow Dad, it's for me?"

"Yes, open it!"

He looked at it carefully and said, "It's from Granddad in Detroit!"

Marcus was watching and feeling left out. When he got it opened, he said, "Wow! A real camera!"

He took the note out and read it. It read: Todd, thanks for the money. I'm very proud of you because you kept your promise. A good man always keeps his word. There's a camera for you and one for Marcus. Enjoy your summer and take lots of pictures. Granddad and Grandma love you both.

Todd looked inside and there was another package unopened. He gave it to Marcus and he lit up. Marcus opened his package and saw his camera. They were ecstatic, and I told them to take them to their room.

I looked at the wine and wondered how long it would take to consume it. I had enough reminders of my time with Sam. I didn't need any more. I prayed I would never, *ever* hear from him again. He was a huge mistake that I still don't regret.

I went in the kitchen and poured myself a glass of wine. I knew I was taking a chance with my sensitive tummy, but at that point I didn't care. It was worth puking, if I must.

Last week Harold and I went out and purchased lots of furniture. We also ordered lots of furniture. I told Harold I wanted to take my time to furnish and decorate certain spaces in the house. He backed off and allowed me to do what I wanted.

After our experience in New York City, he asked me how I felt about sound proofing the master suite. He said he didn't want our love making stifled because we didn't feel free to make noise. I knew he was really talking about me. He said, "Babe, we only have a week. What do you say?"

"Yes. I would like that."

Gina offered to go to the new house and wait for furniture deliveries, cable installation, and other things I couldn't be there for. She also kept the boys so they didn't have to go to daycare. Carla, also out for the summer, offered to go over and help me clean the bathrooms and kitchen.

During the week, I took the plants over and other things I wanted handled with care. By Thursday, although things were chaotic, everything seemed to be on schedule. I took Friday off, and spent most of that morning thoroughly cleaning the apartment.

Harold also took off, and took some of the heavier items I didn't want on the truck like my grandmother's china. He and my parents were at the new house.

Carla was at the apartment with me. She said, "Girl, that house is beautiful. I'm so happy for you!"

"I remember when you got your beautiful home, and how happy we all were."

"We've always celebrated each other Licia. There's nothing like great friends."

"They're priceless, that's for sure."

We smiled at each other and she said, "I know you're glad *you know who* is gone."

"Yes, I really am. I had to take my equipment down last night. I hope I got it all!"

Carla laughed and said, "I know, right. It wouldn't be good if you had to explain that to Harold."

"I know. I told my dad I'd had it installed when I moved in, and asked him if he would keep it for me. He was glad I had the foresight to do it."

"What about Benny? Did he have anything to report?"

"Not a thing. He told Nette he was *not* following that dude to Virginia, so she better not ask him to!"

We both cracked up and she said, "You should write a book! That shit was unbelievable!"

"What was unbelievable?" Annette walked in and looked at us and repeated her question. Carla said, "I was referring to Licia and Sam. Oh, and Jonathon! Ha-ha."

Annette said, "I know that's right! At one point, I really thought I was gonna have to shoot that fool!"

Carla and I just looked at each other. Annette got a bottle of water from the fridge and I asked her, "What are you doing off so early?"

"I had to get the hell outta there! It's hot and it's Friday. I only left an hour early."

I looked at the time, and it was four thirty. Where on earth had the time gone? I asked Annette, "So did Benny tell you what my total came to?"

"Yeah, it's taken care of."

"What the hell do you mean it's taken care of?"

Annette went into the living room, opened her water and said, "I don't want this water. You got any wine?"

I walked into the living room and asked, "Annette, where's my bill?"

She laughed at me and said, "You better get outta my damn face."

She sashayed back into the kitchen and began looking for wine. I went behind her and grabbed her arm. I said, "Nette, you must've forgotten that you can't fight! Tell me or I will whip your ass up in here!"

She laughed again and said, "Okay. I gave him a big o kiss and he said the bill was paid in full."

Carla and I looked at each other and Carla asked, "Just how big was the kiss?"

"Oh, about two minutes. He was always quick! Ha-ha."

I yelled, "You gave him a blow job to pay off my bill?!"

"No Silly! I gave him a blow job because he gave *me* one. Yum!! Can't nobody beat Benny giving head."

I was floored. I couldn't even speak.

Carla was cracking up and Annette said, "Calm down Licia. This is what happened. I went to pay him like you asked me to."

"No, I did not!"

"Well, that's the story I gave him. Anyhow, he asked me when his debt would be paid off. I told him if he put his head between my legs, he'd be paid in full. So he did. Quite well, I might add."

I shook my head and Carla was still laughing. Annette said, "Then I told him that also included payment in full for Felicia. He was okay with that too, but he said it wouldn't be very nice of me if I left him in that state. So two minutes later, it was a wrap."

I shook my head at my crazy ass sister. I said, "Girl, what the hell! So should I thank you or pay you?"

"Believe me, the pleasure was all mine. I *will* take a glass of wine though."

I'd put a bottle of red wine under the counter and white in the fridge. I told her I only had paper cups, and she cringed.

She went into the dining room where the glasses were lined up for the movers to pack, and got one. She said, "I'll wash it. I just can't drink out of a damn paper cup!"

Carla asked, "So Nette, what happened to your pledge not to cheat anymore?"

"I did not have sexual relations with that man!"

We cracked up. That girl is crazy as hell.

Harold was knocking at six a.m. He said, "Good Morning! Why is it you never gave me a key? What are you hiding, Missy?"

He had breakfast cooked and it smelled heavenly. I asked, "What did you cook?"

"You didn't answer my question."

"Shut up Harold. I never even thought about a key."

He laughed and said, "We have French toast, boiled and scrambled eggs, and sausage. Where are the boys? They need to be up."

"Todd came and got them yesterday. He's keeping them until Sunday, so we can spend the first night together alone."

"I must call that guy and thank him."

When I'd finished eating, I threw away the paper plate and fork I'd used. I asked Harold to eat up so I could get some last minute stuff done. He came up behind me and said, "I'd rather eat you. We still have over an hour before the movers get here and there's no one here."

I turned around and asked him, "Have I told you lately how much I love you and how much I appreciate all that you've done? I plan to spend the rest of my life making you happy."

"Aww, I bet you say that to all the guys."

He pulled me into his arms and kissed me lovingly.

After the kiss, he looked at me and said, "Babe, you never told me what kind of birth control you settled on. I love not using condoms. Did you settle on the shot?"

"Yes, I took care of it."

I retrieved his plate and threw it away. He went into the bedroom and was removing his clothes. He said, "Come here. Where's your vibrator?"

"It's at the house. I certainly didn't want the movers to find it."

He laughed and said again, "Come here."

I went over to him and kissed him. I said, "If we make love, I won't have the energy to do all that needs to be done today. Let's wait and make love all night, okay?"

"I know you're right, but whenever I'm around you my little head becomes the master. He wants to know if you'll give him a kiss. Please?"

I looked at him and said, "Something tells me I'm going to regret spoiling you like this. You are so greedy Harold."

Just before leaving, I looked around to be sure I hadn't forgotten anything. Harold will be here and I'll be at the house. It's hard to believe I won't live here anymore. I finally gave him a key.

When the evening sun was setting, Harold and I were in the family room after enjoying a wonderful dinner he prepared. His mom surprised me with a beautiful set of cookware, dinnerware, drinking glasses and very nice everyday silverware.

Earlier while helping me in the kitchen, Mom said, "Sweetheart, you will need a lot of new things for your kitchen. I'll take you out next week and buy you some things. From your dad and me, okay?"

I laughed and asked, "Are you saying my stuff is dated and cheap?"

We both laughed. I said, "Ok Mother, it's a date."

We have furniture in the family room along with a big screen TV, which Dad and Harold mounted on the wall yesterday. The living room and dining room are empty for now. We ordered the living room furniture, but I'm still looking for the dining room furniture. We have a new kitchen table with eight chairs. We also bought four bar stools for the breakfast bar attached to the large island in the kitchen.

The boys each had complete bedroom sets, already set up. When I moved into the apartment, I bought two twin beds for the boys. They were still in good shape, so we put them in one of the guest rooms. Another guest room had my almost new queen size bed in it. None of the guest rooms had any other furniture.

For the master suite, we ordered a king sized bedroom set, but only the mattresses, a pair of chairs and a vanity for the dressing room had been delivered. The master suite has two large walk-in closets, a dressing room and en-suite. The en-suite has two separate vanities and a large jetted tub between them. The entire right side is a large walk-in shower. We installed a big screen TV above the fireplace in our room. There's a loft area upstairs, so we opted to put a TV there, and not in the boys' rooms for now.

Harold was lightly snoring when I went into the kitchen to make sure everything was in order. I looked out into the backyard and saw the beautiful pool, and wondered how much trouble that was gonna be. It was nice to be able to go out on the enclosed deck and not be affected by the weather or insects.

I remember a spring night some time ago, when I was standing on a deck and feared my husband was cheating on me. I remember the heartbreak and betrayal I felt when I learned it was true. How my life has changed since then.

As I stood in the kitchen, I turned to see Harold still asleep. All of a sudden Sam danced across my mind, and I bumped into the table and woke Harold. He asked me if I was okay, and I told him I was fine and to go back to sleep. He got up and stretched and said, "Come on Babe, let's go to bed."

We made sure everything was locked up before going to our room. As we ascended the stairs, I prayed that Sam would do his dancing elsewhere. Harold said, "Babe, get undressed and let's enjoy the tub tonight."

I went in and put a drop of Amazing Grace in and then turned on the jets. It smelled heavenly, and I hurried to undress and get in. Harold got in behind me and we sat with our heads back, enjoying the quiet and massage of the jets.

Harold was so quiet, I assumed he'd gone back to sleep. I picked up his hands and put them under my breasts. A moment later he began to chew on my neck and touching me between my legs.

He stood up and said he wanted to get in the shower. After some adjusting, we found the right pressure and temperature we liked.

He sat on the built in bench and pulled me to him. He reached up and unhooked the handheld showerhead. He began kissing my naval and then he put that water between my legs. It was so intense.

He told me to hold on to the handrail and put my foot on the bench. He pulled me closer and began to taste me. He got the showerhead again and the two things going on at once were more than I could take.

I instinctively went to my knees. He told me to turn around. I was hesitant, but I turned around and he entered me from behind. Then he raised one of my legs and hit me with that water again.

He was so deep inside of me and that water was so intense, it had me seeing angels. I exploded. For an eternity.

The last thing I remember was looking down and seeing the showerhead flopping around on the floor of the shower.

The following morning, Harold was kissing my neck and running his hands through my hair. I asked, "What the hell was up with the water?"

He laughed and said, "Many women use the jets to masturbate. You didn't know that?"

I just laughed and he asked if I was okay. I said, "Yeah, why?"

"Because you passed out for about thirty seconds. I had carry you to bed. You don't remember asking me what happened?"

"No, not really. I sort of remember you carrying me though."

He smiled and asked, "You hungry."

"No, I'd rather lay here and sleep some more."

"Me too."

So we slept off and on until noon.

The next couple of weeks we continued to organize and the rest of the furniture was delivered. Harold and I were doing much better. He stopped being so controlling, and I'm slowly getting over Sam. Harold continues to take me higher sexually, and I admit it was unexpected.

The summer was moving quickly and before we knew it, it was Todd and Gina's wedding day. It was a *beautiful* ceremony. Gina asked Carla to be her matron of honor and Tony was Todd's best man.

The boys were junior ushers. Her mother was there, and she's a beautiful woman who clearly loves Gina. While looking into her mom's face, I could tell that as much as Gina needed her, her mom needed Gina just as much, if not more.

One day about a week later, I noticed a car in the driveway when I came home from work. As I got near, I realized it was a beautiful pearl colored Volvo. I was beside myself.

As I was getting out, the garage door came up and Harold stepped out. I ran to him and hugged him and asked, "Is this really mine?"

He just smiled. I asked, "Can I drive it?"

"I'm thinking that's why we got it Babe."

He went in his pocket and pulled out the keys. I snatched them and ran to the driver's side and opened the door. I was about to get in, but I ran back, kissed him and went back. I suddenly stopped and said, "Thank you Harold!"

I got in and just looked at it all. I touched everything like it was silk. I turned the key and thrilled at the sound of the engine. I looked up at him and he was leaning against the wall of the garage and smiling. I began to come back to reality. I got out and said, "Let's go for a ride."

I handed him the keys and said, "You drive."

He laughed and said, "Babe, I drove it here."

I was feeling, I don't know, some kind a way all of a sudden. I've been feeling that way since moving too. It's like these things aren't *really* mine. I'm having this extremely long dream and I'll soon wake up to learn none of this is real.

My eyes welled up and all of a sudden I began to cry. He ran to me and brought me into the garage. He asked, "What is it? What's wrong?"

"I'm afraid I'll wake up one day and you'll be gone. I feel like Cinderella, and at midnight everything will return to the way it was."

He took me into the house and poured me a glass of wine. I looked at him and asked, "Are you really in love with me?"

He sat next to me and said, "With all of my heart Felicia. Didn't you see the joy on my face as I watched your excitement over that car?"

"This is new for me. If nothing else, I've always been confident in myself. And I've never had anyone love me like you."

"I've always feared what you're now afraid of. I've never had anyone love me like this either."

That's when I realized it was soon time for my period. I said, "It must be PMS. With so many things going on, I'm just emotional."

"That's right. You're due in a few days."

Even that upset me. That means I'm not pregnant. But at least I feel better knowing that I'm not losing my mind. I said, "Let's go over Annette's! She'll fall out when she sees the car!"

"Okay but remember, not a word about our plan."

"I promise. Not a word."

Chapter Fourteen

My girlfriend Alice used to say, "It's hot as peppa out here!"

That's how August feels in Rochester. Harold and I created our first joint checking account shortly after I moved. We looked at our monthly income and monthly expenses, and he explained to me how he wanted the money handled.

Then he said, "I know you have credit cards. Felicia, paying interest makes my stomach hurt!"

I laughed so hard, I had to run to the bathroom! When I returned, he was laughing and said, "Babe, give me the damn bills! I'll pay them off and you can burn the cards in the fireplace."

"Harold, I don't like the thought of you sweating me about how much I pay for clothes and maintenance. I can't have you questioning how much I pay for a manicure or saying I have enough shoes."

"I will say this again. I have five sisters and a mother, and excuse me, but I pay two hundred dollars for a pair of pajamas. I realize women like nice things and lots of those things, and I want you to have those things. I have no interest in stifling your desire to shop and look good."

He looked to heaven and said, "Lord, I pray I don't regret saying this, but Babe, buy anything you want. Just don't overdraw the account and do *not* use any more credit cards. Okay?"

"Okay, I promise to try this your way. But don't you think we should have at least *one* major credit card?"

"Absolutely."

He went into his briefcase and gave me a Visa Card and an American Express card. He said, "I got these for you. They should be left at home unless we go away. They're for emergencies, car rentals, plane tickets, etc. They're joint with mine."

I was trying hard to adjust to all of this.

By mid-August while sitting at my desk, I realized something. Back in July when I had PMS, my period never came. I was so busy with work and the kids being off and the new house, that I never missed it.

I couldn't remember having one in June either. I remember the one at the end of May, because that's when Carla had the cookout. But, for the life of me....

After work I stopped at the drugstore. I was so nervous, I couldn't think straight. I ran to my bathroom and read the instructions and realized I had to wait until morning.

My dress was tucked away safely at Carla's, because I didn't want Harold peeking. I began to worry about it now. If I'm pregnant, I'd be almost four months at the wedding! Hopefully, I did have a period in June. I was a wreck.

I went for a glass of wine and realized I couldn't drink. Now I understood why I'd been so weepy. I spoke to Harold briefly and told him I was tired and I'd see him the next day.

When we hung up I went upstairs and the boys were playing in the loft. Todd asked, "Mom, can't I have a TV in my room? I'm tired of watching what Marcus is watching."

"I'll think about it Todd. It's late guys. Let's pack it up and get ready for bed."

When I finally got in bed, I tossed and turned all night.

I got up and hurried into the bathroom. I had everything sitting on the vanity. I did my thing and waited. I went downstairs and made coffee and realized again, that I couldn't drink it. I went back upstairs and looked at the results. I'm not sure how I felt.

About ten thirty, Harold came to my desk. He smiled and asked, "How are you feeling today. You still look tired."

"I'm okay, but I didn't sleep well."

"I'm sorry Babe. I'll come over tonight and make shrimp scampi and asparagus. How's that?"

"That sounds great! Thanks Hun."

He knows that's my favorite and it's been a while since he's fixed it for me. I asked, "Harold, can we go away this weekend? I just want to get away and relax and not have to do anything."

"It's short notice, but maybe I could get us a room at Geneva on the Lake. How does that sound?"

"Actually, Geneva on the Lake is perfect."

After he left I began wondering just how to tell him he was about to be a father.

I called my gynecologist at lunch time and she said I could come in after work. I called Gina and asked her if she would please get the boys and she said she would gladly get them. She asked if they could stay overnight. I told her yes.

After leaving the doctor's office, they confirmed my pregnancy. I was about six weeks. Now that Harold had what he wanted, I realized I was unmarried and pregnant. That could *never* have been me a few years ago.

I'd really put my trust in this man. Would our parents be disappointed? I'll tell Harold it'll be our secret until we're married, for the sake of our parents.

Harold came by about six o'clock and went right into the kitchen. I asked what he wanted me to do, and he showed me how to clean the shrimp. I was getting really good as a Sous-chef, and we enjoyed cooking together.

But that day, I was preoccupied and making mistakes. He said, "Why don't you go up and take a shower and come back when the food is ready."

"No, I want to help. I promise to do better."

"Oh, I got us a room for this weekend."

"Great! When do we leave?"

"Friday after work. I have an important meeting Friday afternoon, or I would suggest just working a half day."

I was so excited that I went to the fridge and reached for the wine. I stopped myself, and went for a bottle of water. I asked Harold if he wanted something to drink. He opted for water too.

Two days. I had two days to wait.

Friday finally came and we were in the car and on our way. I couldn't seem to contain my excitement. Of course, he thinks it's the weekend away.

I started taking prenatal vitamins yesterday. I'd succeeded in avoiding the subject of wine. I'd decided that after dinner, but before going to bed I would tell him.

When we were checking in, the owner came out and spoke to us. She remembered us, I'm sure because it's not everyday someone rents out the entire bed and breakfast. She smiled and said, "Mr. and Mrs. Benson. We have the same room for you. I hope this continues to be where you come for your getaways."

Harold said, "Thank you very much. We thoroughly enjoyed our last stay, and we're looking forward to a quiet weekend."

She came over to me and said, "Mrs. Benson, how are you?"

"I'm well thanks, how are you?"

"Things couldn't be better, thank you. Are you still enjoying your engagement, or have you gotten married?"

"The wedding is October fifteenth."

"That's wonderful. I don't believe in long engagements. Enjoy your stay and if you need anything at all, please let me know."

Once we were settled, Harold went to the store to get of all things, a bottle of wine. I hurried downstairs and asked about having dinner delivered to our room. She said, "Absolutely! Are you having a baby?"

I was stunned. I asked, "How did you know?"

"Many wives come here to announce fatherhood. Does he know yet?"

"No, I'm telling him tonight. I'm so excited!"

"Okay, mums the word. I'll send dinner up shortly, and non-alcoholic champagne up at eight thirty, okay?"

I hugged her and thanked her. I went back upstairs and changed into a lounging dress.

When Harold and I were finishing dinner, he said, "I'm glad you suggested we stay in for dinner. This is a great start to a relaxing weekend."

"Me too. I'm enjoying the solitude of just you and me and not having to deal with other people."

I glanced at the clock and saw that it was five minutes after eight. I said, "Harold, have you ever gone back to that night many months ago when we first shared our love for each other?"

"Yes, I have. That was a trying time for us."

"Yeah, mainly because we found out we wanted different things."

"Felicia, I know you've been having your doubts lately. And if you're thinking about me wanting children, I'm going to stop you right now. I love Todd and Marcus. They are truly enough."

I got up and said, "Well, I've thought about it too. And I think we should do something permanent about it."

"Like what? Are you having problems with your birth control?"

"No, not really. I *am* having a problem with something though. As a matter of fact, I've had a problem with it for a while. So I took it upon myself to resolve it."

He got up and stood in front of me. He seemed very worried so I decided to end this charade. He asked, "What's wrong?"

"Well, my problem *was* the fact that you are the most wonderful man in the world, who I felt I didn't deserve. You said to me recently that I'd never asked you for anything. Well, the same goes for you. And I know that a child would be something you would ask for, right?"

He closed his eyes and asked, "Felicia, why are you doing this?"

"Harold, would you please answer my question."

"Yes. If I ever asked anything of you, that would be it."

I smiled and walked over to him. I said, "Then ask me."

"Are you sure about this Babe? It wouldn't be right if you did this just for me. You would have to want it too. Do you?"

"Ask me and find out."

"Babe…"

He turned and walked into the bedroom. I went behind him and he turned to me and said, "I love you so much more than my need for a child. But a child would…."

"Harold. You've been a great dad. Are you ready to be a father?"

Unable to speak, he nodded his head yes and sat down. I walked over to him and raised his face to mine. I said, "Good. Because your son or daughter will be born in about seven months."

He looked at me with his mouth opened. He finally asked if I was sure. I told him my doctor said I'm about six weeks pregnant. He continued to look at me. I said, "Say something Hun!"

There was a knock on the door and I glanced at the clock and it was eight thirty one. I grabbed my wallet, got a five dollar bill and opened the door. The maid handed me the champagne and I thanked her and gave her the tip. I went back into the bedroom and he hadn't moved. I asked, "Are you okay?"

"I don't understand something. Weren't you using birth control?"

"No. I let you think that because I wanted to surprise you."

He got up and asked, "Surprise me? You planned this?"

"Yes. I even told your sisters. I decided…."

He picked me up and asked, "This is real? You're absolutely sure?"

"Yes, and put me down! You have to be more careful with me now."

He slowly put me down and gently kissed me. He wrapped his arms around me and twirled me, picking me up again. He looked into my eyes and said, "You have been such a blessing to me."

He unexpectedly welled up, and put my head on his chest and just held me. Then all of a sudden he said, "Felicia, I have to call my dad!"

"Wait! That's something else we have to talk about. I haven't told anyone yet. I know it sounds old fashioned, but I'm pregnant and unmarried. I don't want our parents to know until we're married."

"Felicia! No! I can't wait that long. Let's get married tomorrow then."

"Harold, no."

He seemed so disappointed. He said, "My parents are different from yours. I'll tell them not to tell your parents. Please Felicia."

"Harold, let's discuss this tomorrow. I'm sure we'll come up with something that will work for both of us."

He looked at me and said, "Okay Babe. Let's discuss it tomorrow."

There was something about the look on his face that said he was up to something.

We had a beautiful night making love and wondering what we would have. We both said it would be nice to have a little girl, but Harold said, and it never dawned on me, that a boy would continue the Benson name.

The next morning, Harold woke me up at six o'clock. He said he had a surprise for me. While I was in the shower, he packed my stuff. He ran into the bathroom and grabbed my toiletries. He said, "Come on, we're going to Detroit!"

"Harold, what!?"

"You and I have a flight to catch in two hours! We'll be back tomorrow and no one will know we went anywhere except here."

"Harold, you're doing it again. Please don't start that again."

"You just don't understand. My family has wanted this for so long. It would be a sin to make them wait. Remember when we were there and my mom said she never thought I'd marry or have children? My dad was scared to death that Benson would die with me. So even if we have a girl, she'll be born a Benson."

"You know what. I'm gonna do this for you. But you've got to promise not to tell anyone else."

"I promise Babe."

We landed in Detroit just after eleven o'clock. We rented a car and drove to *Benson Manor*. Harold went to the intercom and announced, "Harold and Felicia are here!"

People came from everywhere and wanted to know why we were there. We all went into the kitchen and Mom asked, "Are you hungry? I can make you all a sandwich or something."

"No Mom. We're good. We have great news and I didn't want to tell you over the phone."

"What is it! I love great news."

"In about seven months, Felicia and I will be having a baby!"

She put her hands over her mouth and the tears just flooded her face. She sat down and Harold held his mother lovingly. Finally she looked at me and opened her arms, inviting me into them. I cried as I reached her and soon the sisters were all around us in tears.

That's when I realized he was right about coming. It meant so much to them. I've known Harold for eight months and never saw him shed a tear. Now I've seen him cry twice in twenty four hours. Mom finally said, "Melissa, please hand me the phone. I have to call your dad."

Harold said, "Mom, please let me tell him."

"That's fine, but I still need to talk to him."

She called Dad and said, "Your dad said he has a quick stop to make and will be right home. Felicia, come here Child."

She put her arms around me again. She looked to heaven and began to pray for me and her grandchild. She looked at me and said, "Felicia, I know you were raised a Christian. Please promise me you will pray daily for yourself and this child."

"Mom, I promise."

The chimes rang, and Tara and Danielle came in with both girls. They immediately ran for Harold and had him in tears again. As Karen and I entered the foyer, both sisters seemed delighted to see me. Tara said, "Be careful Sis. You're carrying precious cargo."

I laughed and finally was in their arms. Danielle said, "See Felicia. I told you not to worry."

Mom came in and said, "Felicia, you need something to eat Dear. Is anyone else hungry?"

Mom made me a salad and everyone else grabbed a snack. She put a glass of milk in front of me and said, "Drink up Dear."

I told her I didn't like milk, but she smiled and kept nagging me to finish it. Everyone was laughing and talking and then it happened. The chimes rang again. Mom said, "Let's wait for him to come in here."

He walked into the kitchen, and his eyes almost popped out of his head. He asked, "Benny, what are you doing here? And Felicia, it's so good to see you Darling. Is everything okay?"

He came over and hugged both of us. I'd never heard anyone call Harold Benny before. My mind immediately went to Annette's friend. I chuckled and Harold asked, "Are you laughing at my nickname?"

Still laughing, I said, "Yes I am."

Everyone was waiting for Harold to tell him. He said, "Dad. Felicia and I decided to come on the spur of the moment. And no, nothing's wrong. How are you?"

"I'm good Son. Where are the boys?"

"They're with Todd this weekend. Dad, would you come over here. I want to show you something. Babe, will you come over here too."

I said to myself, *he's making too much of a production out of this.* He said, "Dad, Felicia and I would like to tell you something interesting. She and I almost broke up back in February when I told her I loved her. She said she loved me too. But my mistake was telling her that I wanted more children and she was horrified. Anyhow, she couldn't resist me so she kept seeing me and loving me. As you know she accepted my proposal of marriage, but I never told you all she didn't want any more children. But I accepted it. Dad, do you know what she did?"

"I'm sure you're going to tell me Son."

He laughed and said, "She devised a plan to surprise me. She told me she handled the birth control issue because she knows I can't resist her."

Dad smiled and said, "Son. You're a lucky man."

Harold kissed me on the forehead and said, "Yes I am Dad. Because the surprise is that she never used birth control. She told me yesterday..."

He choked and welled up. "That we're expecting a child in seven months."

Dad's head went down and he cried. Harold embraced him and Mom came over and held him too. Anything present with a heartbeat was crying.

I had never in my life seen so much emotion in a family before, unless someone had died or some other terrible thing had happened. But tears of joy from men, was foreign to me.

He looked up and walked over to me and said, "Daughter, we were so stunned that someone, *somehow* was capable of stealing his heart. We knew when we met you in April that you had actually done just that. I also knew when I met you, like me with Jackie, my son didn't stand a chance."

He hugged me again and kissed my forehead. He looked at his family and said, "We all worried the Benson name would fizzle because Harold was never going to find anyone worthy of him or his name."

They all laughed and agreed. The kids came in and asked, "What are *we* gonna eat?"

Everyone began to scramble and we all helped with lunch. I looked around and Dad, Mom and Harold had disappeared. I also noticed that Danielle was gone. I asked Tammy where they were and she asked, "You being nosey?"

She laughed and said they were in the study, and began pouring milk for her nieces. Harold came back and asked me to join them. He said, "Dad and Mom want to see you. Are you okay?"

"Yes, I'm fine."

"I've been meaning to ask you how come you haven't been ill or had morning sickness. When does that happen?"

"I had it with Todd but not Marcus. My pregnancy with Marcus was a breeze. I'm hoping that will happen this time too."

When we went into the study, Dad and Mom were looking at some papers and discussing something. Mom looked up and said, "Baby, sit down. You've had a long day."

Dad said, "Harold told us about your concern about being unmarried. We definitely respect it and promise to keep this between us."

"I really appreciate that. My parents aren't as open about sex. They've always expected decency from me, and I'm not real sure how they'll take this. They probably assume we're intimate, but unlike you all, we never discuss such things."

About fifteen minutes later, there was a knock on the door and Tammy came in. She said, "Danielle just pulled up."

Mom jumped up and said, "Great! She has a surprise for us."

We all went toward the foyer and the chimes sounded. When I saw who walked in, I almost fainted. Coming in the door were my mother and father.

Harold looked at me and said *surprise* very quietly. I continued to stand there with my mouth opened like a deer caught in headlights. I found my legs and voice and asked, "What on earth are you doing here?"

My mom came over and put her arms around me and said, "Harold and Jackie invited us. Actually, they wouldn't take no for an answer."

Daddy said, "I've always wanted to come to Detroit. He and Harold's dad shook hands. Daddy asked, "We're still on for tomorrow, right?"

Dad Benson said, "Calvin, I'm looking forward to it."

I asked, "What's going on?"

Daddy said, "We're going to see the Tigers."

Mom said, "Come with me Barbara. I'm sure you're…"

I said, "There's something you all aren't telling me. I want to know right now."

Everybody stood still and quiet. Harold said, "Okay Babe. The truth is, I told Mom your concern this morning. I asked her if she could get Pastor Floyd to come over and marry us. He said yes, but Mom said there was no way she would be a party to this without giving Calvin and Barbara the chance to be here, so she called them. She simply told them that we were having a private ceremony tonight and if they could make it, there would be tickets waiting for them at the airport. We were careful not to book on the same flight."

Daddy said, "Daughter, your mother said two weeks ago she suspected you were pregnant. She said she could see it in your eyes. It's the same way you looked when you were carrying the boys."

Mommy said, "Baby Girl, you've never done anything to bring us shame. We're *so* proud of you. If you *are* pregnant, we're happy for you."

I looked at her and my lower lip began to tremble and I nodded my head. She and Daddy came to me and embraced me like I was a little girl. I cried and said, "I was so afraid to tell you. I'm so sorry."

Mommy said, "I told your daddy I didn't think you even knew it. The way you were carrying things and running around."

Harold said, "She found out earlier this week that she's about six weeks pregnant. Maybe more, we're not sure yet."

Mommy said, "She's closer to eight weeks, I would say."

I said, "Mom, do you really think so?"

She said, "You're my only child. Didn't I know every time before?"

I shook my head yes. Mom Benson said to her husband, "Harold, call your manager at Benson's South and order dinner for us please. This is a celebration!"

Everyone began to go in different directions. I said, "Wait a minute! Did I understand we're having a wedding tonight?"

Everybody stopped again. Harold said, "Well, yeah Babe. Isn't that what you want?"

I looked around at the faces of my loved ones. I tried hard to figure out what getting married here would mean. I said, "What about the wedding in October?"

My mother said, "You can still have it. No one has to know about this ceremony."

I thought about that. I also felt like I was being rushed. I said, "I need a minute alone."

I went upstairs and got Annette and Carla on three-way. I told them everything. They reminded me I didn't want to have any regrets. I said, "I kinda feel that doing it now would take away from doing it later. It won't be special and you guys aren't here and I would always feel like my *real* anniversary is today's date. I'm gonna wait."

Carla said, "Good! Please give us a girl! We're so happy for you."

And Annette said, "Yes we are! Hurry home so we can spoil you! Love you Sis!"

I said, "I love you both too! So much."

Harold came in and asked, "You okay? You mad at me?"

"So you told your mom this morning?"

"After I made the reservations, I called her and asked if she would call the pastor because we needed to get married and that we would explain when we got here."

He just couldn't help himself. I got up and kissed him. I said, "I'm not mad Harold. I guess I'll have to get used to being a Benson."

We all had a grand time that night. And the next day, Mom Benson showed me how to make chicken soup.

Chapter Fifteen

It's almost time for school to begin. Marcus is both excited and apprehensive. He asked a lot of questions and continued to ask if I thought he was smart enough to go. I assured him he was.

Todd Jr. is concerned because he's going to a new school and will not only miss his old friends but will now have to make new ones. They've both driven me crazy.

Admittedly, I was also apprehensive about starting school. My two classes begin mid-September, and I hadn't been inside a classroom in years.

When my parents returned from Detroit, Harold and I paid them a visit. We were on the front porch and I announced that Harold had bought me a Volvo. They were both excited about it, mainly because they knew it's the car I'd wanted for years. I said, "So Daddy, I now have two cars."

"You didn't trade in your Honda?"

"No. Since it was already paid off, I really want you to have it."

Mom was elated and looked at Daddy. But he didn't show any emotion at all. Finally he said, "I can't just take your car Daughter. I have to pay you something for it."

"How much would you want to pay for it?"

"Let me think about it and I'll let you know."

Mom said, "Calvin, take the car. She clearly wants to give it to you. I swear, you don't know a blessing when you see one. Look at how that would help us. In two years we would be car note free. Take the damn car!"

I couldn't believe my ears. My mother *never* says bad words. I looked at her sideways and she laughed. She said, "That father of yours and his silly pride! He causes me to sin more than anybody."

Harold started laughing. He said, "Mr. Pierce, your daughter is going to get on my nerves all week if you don't take that car. She's been saying for the last couple of days how excited she was that she could finally give you something like that."

Daddy smiled and stood up. He said, "Okay."

My eyes got big and I asked, "Does that mean you're actually going to take it without trying to pay me for it?"

"Yep, I am. Your mom is right. I need a car and I do allow my pride to cause me to lose out on things. And I thank you both for this."

He walked toward the front door and said, "You're good kids. We're blessed to have you."

I asked, "Daddy, where are you going?"

"I have something for you. Wait right here."

When the door closed, I asked Mom, "What's he up to?"

"Girl, I have no idea."

She put her hands together and said, "Thank you both for this. He and I were just saying that it would be so nice to be car note free. And you two come over here and practically hand it to us. What a blessing!"

When Daddy came out, he had a small worn box in his hand. He said, "Daughter, when you were born, I went to the store and bought you the prettiest dress I could find. Most people, including your mother, thought I was disappointed because you were a girl. Anyhow, your mother said it was too cold for you to wear that dress home from the hospital. So she sent me back to the store and told me to get you some warm clothes. Well, I knew that by the time it was warm, you'd be too big for that dress. Your mother never knew, but I would put you in that dress in the winter time and play with you when she was working. I took pictures too. I never told Barbara."

He turned to Mommy and continued. "You see, when a man looks at the woman he loves, he thinks she is the most beautiful, and most precious thing in the world. He loves to see her smile, and hear her laugh. He marvels at how she matures from a budding flower to a lovely rose. He admires her grace and her elegance. He etches those moments in his mind, because those are the times most dear to him."

Then he turned back to me. He said, "So, I want you to know that I was never disappointed you weren't a boy. I was thrilled that I would get to see Barbara all over again."

He handed me the box and inside was a beautiful tiny dress. I took it out and saw the price tag still on it. Then I saw three pictures of me in the dress. I looked at my father and said, "Daddy...."

I went into his arms and I cried. I said, "Oh Daddy. There is nothing in this world that has warmed my heart like this. I will cherish my dress forever!"

Mom was floored too! She said, "Calvin, that was so sweet Baby!"

"You've always been the apple of my eye Barbara. When I look at you, caterpillars become butterflies."

He and Mom both smiled and a tear came down Mom's face. It seemed to be something private between the two of them. Mom got up and kissed her husband on his cheek. She said, "If you keep talking like that, you might end up with another daughter!"

I was done! My parents never talked like that around me and my father had never expressed his feelings like *that* before. I almost feared something might be wrong. Harold tapped me on my shoulder and whispered, "We should leave."

I said, "Daddy, this has been such a special moment for us. Thank you for your sweet words and my wonderful gifts. And Mom, take care of my Daddy. We're gonna go around the corner and get the Volvo. We parked it there hoping we'd be able to leave the Honda here."

By the end of August my doctor said based on the size of my uterus, I was probably close to ten weeks. That was good news and bad news. I'd never get in my dress unless I stopped eating until after the wedding. Even if I had it altered, it wouldn't be the same. A little depressed, I went over Carla's house. I asked her if I could see my dress. She said, "Come on, let's go upstairs."

We went into her room and she went into the closet and pulled it out. I slipped it on. She said, "You were smart to get it too big."

It was still too big and my tummy wasn't showing through yet. I said, "Carla, I will never make it to October. I was just told that I'm ten weeks pregnant. By the wedding day, I'll be four and a half months!"

Carla said, "Don't upset yourself Licia. This is nothing compared to some of the stuff we've gotten through."

She was right about that. I asked, "Honestly, would this dress look good on a fat girl?"

She hollered laughing and said, "Honestly, no it would not look good on a fat girl. It's designed for a curvaceous body, which you have. It would even look good on a larger sized curvaceous body. The only thing that would take away from it is a large waist or a protruding stomach."

"I could conceivably have both in a few weeks."

"Yes you could. Or, you could carry little Carla in your big ass like you carried Marcus. No stomach until you were almost six months, remember?"

Again, she was right. My behind was so big, you could sit a drink on it. Carla said, "I know what you can do. Go back to the bridal boutique and find another dress. The first one hasn't been altered so if you must, you can return it. Depending on where you carry the baby, you still might be able to wear the first one. Then you can return the second one."

"Can you go with me tomorrow?"

"Yeah, I'm free all day. Are you going to work?"

I thought about it and said, "I'll take a half day. Let's plan on one o'clock. I'll pick you up."

Later that evening, Harold and I had spinach salad and baked chicken for dinner, which I prepared. He was telling me how much improved my skills had gotten. We were surprised when Tony and Annette stopped by on their way home.

We offered them drinks and Tony asked if we had plans for Labor Day. Harold said we decided to have a quiet one because of school starting next week. Tony asked, "Harold, can I see you a minute?"

"Sure man. Let's go out on the deck."

I watched them leave and I asked Annette, "What's that about?"

"I'm not sure, but I think they're planning a bachelor party for him. You're okay with it, aren't you?"

"Absolutely! That's very nice of them."

I got up to get a glass of spa water. I asked, "Have you ever had spa water before?"

"You mean that water with the cucumbers in it?"

"Yes, it's really good. A woman at the doctor's office said I should drink it throughout the day. But you can put more than just cucumbers in it. See, I have orange slices and strawberries in mine."

"Give me a little bit of that. It looks good."

"What are you doing tomorrow about one o'clock?"

"I'll be at work. Why, what's up?"

I handed her a glass of water and said, "I need to pick out another dress. That dress I bought is designed for a flat stomach and narrow waist, and although I have those now, I won't in a few weeks. Anyhow, Carla agreed to go with me tomorrow afternoon. I was hoping I could talk you into coming."

"Okay. I'll meet you at Carla's at one."

The fellows came back in and Harold said, "I'm having a bachelor party! How do you feel about that Babe?"

"That's great Hun! Tony, that's really nice of you guys. Thanks a lot."

"Actually, it just gives us fellas an opportunity to get drunk and stay out late without having to fight with our wives!"

Annette looked at him and shook her head. She said, "Licia, we'll be planning a bachelorette party for you too, although in your delicate condition, a stripper might not be on the menu. Damn!"

We all laughed and Harold asked Tony, "Will we have strippers?"

Tony looked at me and then his wife and said, "No Doubt. What's a bachelor party without hunnies?"

Annette said, "Sorry Felicia, but they will not outdo us. We *will* be having strippers!"

We all laughed and Tony said, "Listen, we need to get out of here and go get Tony. We'll be talking to you guys soon. And if we decide to do anything this weekend, or if you all do anything, let's get together."

We all agreed and they left.

Harold said, "Babe, I can't believe you're okay with strippers."

"Why would you say that?"

"Most women are opposed to their men being around strippers, hookers, you know, women who get paid to do what they do."

"Yes, I suppose that's true. But my stance has always been if my man was going to indulge, he was going to do it whether there were strippers in his face or not."

"So have you seen male strippers before?"

"Yes, I have. And I'm sure you've had your share of strip clubs"

"Yeah, on occasion. One thing that probably makes me different from many men is that I'm not ultra-intrigued by strippers. Some men are so obsessed, they'll miss work to go to strip clubs. After establishing a woman is pretty and sexy, my intrigue is then what's beneath the breast and above the neck."

He smiled and said, "When I saw you the first time, you were talking with a coworker. As I was passing by, I saw this fine ass woman and I paused. Actually, I saw your ass. Damn! Then I observed you, and your head went back and you laughed."

"You never told me that."

He came over to me and kissed me on my forehead. He said, "After recognizing your beauty, it was your mind and heart that kept my attention."

I smiled and asked, "So, are we ready for this wedding? Stephanie says all details *appear* to be in order."

"I'm sure they are. She seems good at what she does."

"By the way Hun. I think we should postpone the honeymoon."

He looked at me and seemed sad. He said, "I really want us to have something to remember Babe. What if I let you choose the destination?"

I thought about that and asked, "Where were we going?"

"Jamaica, but after your announcement, I was concerned about you being too warm and away from the states in the event you needed a hospital, so I thought about Miami Beach."

"Let me think about it some more. Miami Beach sounds great."

"Good. I'll email Stephanie and ask her to make the changes. Sound okay?"

"Yep, that sounds great."

When we arrived at the bridal boutique, there were no other customers. And luckily, the same salesperson was there. I explained to her my dilemma. She said, "If you're interested, we have a line of maternity dresses."

I thought about that and then something dawned on me. I asked, "What if I order the same dress, a size or two larger. Then when the time comes, I could have one altered and return the other."

"Sure. You could do that."

After leaving, Annette said, "Girl, you spent some cash up in there today. I'm surprised you still had money left from that five thousand Harold gave you."

"Actually he gave me a prepaid card after that for the remainder of the expenses."

"Damn, how much was that?"

I hesitated then said, "Twenty G's."

She and Carla both looked at me and said, "What!"

Annette asked, "Who the hell does that?"

I told them about Harold's family being loaded, but not much about his wealth. Annette said, "If that man dropped twenty five G's on you with no hesitation, you're buying lunch Trick."

The second week of September was a trying one. While standing at the copier at work one day, I became very nauseous. I stood there a moment, hoping it would pass and that was all I remembered.

When I regained consciousness, I was in an ambulance with Harold holding my hand. He said, "Babe, you're okay. You're on the way to the hospital. Do you know what happened?"

"Not really. I was at the copier and feeling sick."

"Well apparently you fainted."

The attendant in the ambulance asked Harold to step aside and he checked my vitals. He asked, "Ms. Wilson, how do you feel?"

"A little groggy, otherwise okay. Is the baby okay?"

"Yes, we're getting a nice heartbeat. Baby seems fine."

"Thank God. What happened to me?"

"Tests will tell us more, but it seems you simply fainted. Do you remember getting up too fast or do you have a history of fainting?"

"No I've never fainted before."

"All of your vitals are normal. Sometimes pregnant women faint for no apparent reason. We'll check you out and make sure all is well. Okay?"

"That sounds great. Thank you very much."

By the time I was discharged, I had been poked and prodded, had given all kinds of body fluids, and everything came back well. I was relieved and Harold was a mess.

He was on the phone with Gina thanking her for getting the boys from after school care. My parents were out front waiting on us, along with Carla and Earl.

Daddy was a mess like Harold, but Mom was fine. She said, "Felicia, I think you're doing too much. You need to slow down and you'll be fine, okay?"

"Yes Mother."

Since we didn't have a car, my parents took me home. Carla and Earl were there to take Harold to get our cars.

Daddy was quiet, while Mommy talked the entire time. She said, "You know, girls do that to their mothers. I saw about a week ago that you are carrying a girl."

"Really Mom?"

"Yep. But since then I *also* saw a boy."

"So you're still not sure?"

"Oh I'm sure Felicia. I see one of each."

I looked at Daddy and he looked at me, and I think we both were thinking the same thing. Mommy has finally lost her touch. Surely my doctor and even the hospital would've seen twins. Right?

When we got home, it was about seven o'clock. I'd been at the hospital for four hours. I was tired and hungry. Mom said, "I made some of Jackie's soup yesterday and I brought you some."

The three of us sat down and ate soup and Daddy finally asked, "Daughter, you feeling ok?"

"Yes, Daddy. I'm feeling much better."

"You know that fiancée of yours doesn't want you to step foot back in IBM until that baby is born."

"Did he say that?"

Mom said, "Calvin, that is not our business. I told you not to get in it."

Daddy said, "Daughter, the only reason I'm telling you is because I know how you love your job and I didn't want you and Harold fighting over this. He's a good man Felicia. And he's scared to death for you and that baby. At least hear him out, okay?"

I sat there for a moment and said, "I know Daddy. He's a good man. But, sometimes I think he wants to control too much of my life. We've been working through it and things are a lot better, but sometimes he lapses into thinking he's my father, and I'm not gonna let him do that."

"Men are natural protectors, so try to be understanding."

"Okay Daddy. But I'll never allow Harold or anyone to control me."

I got up and started clearing the dishes off the table. I said, "So Mom, what do you think of the dishes we picked out? They look great, don't you think?"

"Yes I do. They go very well in your kitchen."

"I really appreciate my new stuff Mom."

She smiled and said, "You're welcome. I enjoyed doing it."

Soon the front door opened and Harold, Earl and Carla came in. Mom said, "Harold, I made some of Jackie's soup. Want some Son?"

"Yes Ma'am. I'd love some."

Carla came over to me and asked, "Girl, you okay?"

"Yes, I'm fine. I can't believe I fainted. Who does that?"

She laughed and said, "By the way, your dress came today."

Earl asked, "Who buys two wedding dresses?"

I said, "A pregnant woman, that's who."

We all laughed and Harold and I thanked everyone for their help. Soon the house was empty and he asked if I wanted a snack. I said no and went upstairs.

Later, we were in our room and he asked, "Babe, you need anything"

"No Hun, I'm good."

"I'm going to get a snack. You sure?"

"Yep, thanks Hun."

When Harold returned, he had a bowl of ice cream and a beer. I asked, "Am I pregnant, or are you?"

We both laughed and he said, "I brought the ice cream for you and the beer is for me."

"Why would you do that when I told you I didn't want anything?"

"It's your favorite. I bought it for you yesterday. Don't you have any cravings?"

"I crave to be a size eight again by the time our child is six weeks old. I know your intentions are good, so if you want to give me treats, give me fruit or veggies. Okay Precious?"

He laughed and looked at me lovingly. He said, "Babe, you really scared me today (here it comes). I hate to admit it, but I don't remember ever being that scared."

"I know Harold. But it's over. My body is doing what pregnant bodies do. It's conforming to the changes occurring."

He stood up and said, "I'm really having a hard time here. I could use your help."

He came over to me and said, "I want you to stay home and off your feet until the baby is born."

I looked at him and said nothing. He said, "Felicia, I'll hire help and you can take it easy."

Still, I said nothing. Then he said, "If anything happens to you or that child, it'll kill me. Literally."

I got up and went into the bathroom. I sat on the side of the tub and thought about what he'd said, and what my father said earlier. I knew I wasn't interested in hired help. I also knew he would drive me nuts if I didn't give him *something*.

I went back to my chair, still silent. He said, "I know you wanna kill me Felicia. And I know you're thinking I'm trying to control you. But my *everything* is right in front of me. You, those boys and that child are *everything* to me. I don't know what to do."

"Harold, sit down."

"Babe, I..."

"I listened to you, now listen to me. I will *not* quit my job. I *will* however, leave at the end of September and return after my maternity leave. There's a chance that someday I'll consider leaving permanently, but that will be my choice and no one will have a say in that, not even you. I worked very hard to get to where I am, and I will not throw it away because my husband can pay my bills. Even you work because you love your job, not because you need to, right?"

"You're right. I can't argue that. And..."

"I'm not done. I will not allow *anyone* in my home as help around the house, do you understand?"

"I was just concerned…."

"*Harold*, do you understand?"

"Yes."

"IF…you decide to surprise me with a damn maid, I will leave and not return. I mean it."

He looked at me and I think it sunk in that I meant business. He said, "That's another thing I love about you. You don't give me drama. I've heard stories from married men about their wives screaming and cussing them out. You've never given me grief like that."

"What does that have to do with this discussion?"

"Everything! I honestly had no idea how to approach you with this. I fully expected to see a side of you I hadn't seen, yet you listened, thought about it and answered me. And thank you for giving me some relief Babe. I'm happy you'll soon be home."

At that point, I was certain he was gonna be more trouble than the new baby.

Chapter Sixteen

Both of my babies are in school now. And I'm really excited about my class tonight. My classes are Tuesday through Thursday. I didn't have any more episodes and Harold was counting the days until September ends. I spoke with my supervisor and she said, "Felicia, my husband wanted to carry me to the bathroom. I understand, believe me."

I laughed and she said, "We look forward to your return, and I appreciate your offer to train a temp."

By the end of the week, I admit I was exhausted. I came home Friday and crashed. Annette has helped me by getting the boys when she gets Tony, and Harold picks them up and feeds them while I'm in class. Today, Harold got them for me and took them to Todd's. Annette called and woke me up. She said, "Girl, those classes are kicking yo ass, huh?"

"Yes they are. But I'm hoping since I'll soon be home during the day, it'll get easier."

"I hope so Licia. Any plans for the weekend?"

"Not really. We're thinking of going to the farmer's market, since its cooler now. Harold wants to teach me how to purchase and use herbs."

Annette laughed and said, "Wow, that's so exciting."

I laughed and said, "Don't get smart Nette. I really want to do well, and Harold helping me will help to jumpstart that."

"Girl, I'm just teasing you. I'm really proud of you."

"Thanks Nette."

"I'll talk to you later. Go back to sleep."

After my nap, I went to the bathroom and decided to take a shower. Soon Harold was knocking on the door asking if I was okay. He came in the bathroom and I said, "Yes, I'm fine."

He glanced down and said, "I finally see it. You're starting to show."

He got on his knees and put his hands around my waist. Then he leaned forward and listened to my stomach. He kissed my navel and looked up at me. He said, "You're so beautiful. I never thought you could be more beautiful, but you are."

I smiled at him and caressed his face. I said, "I bet you say that to all the pregnant girls."

He laughed and asked, "What do you think it is? I keep wondering, not because I have a preference, I just want to know."

"My ultrasound is soon, so you can find out then. But I don't want to know. I never knew with my other two either."

"I love the element of surprise, but I know it would drive me crazy wondering."

He parted my thighs and kissed me between them. He picked me up and carried me to the bed. He seemed to be starving, the way he sated himself. I could feel that familiar fire building deep inside of me. And just as I was ready to release it, he stopped. He got up and removed his slacks and boxers and returned to me. I said, "That wasn't very nice."

He snuggled up against my neck and began chewing and licking my ears. He said, "I'm sorry Babe. I want us to come together."

He went to my chest and said, "They're so big. Ummm, there can't be anything sexier than a pregnant woman."

He put his hands underneath my breasts and felt their heft. He brought them together and inserted both nipples into his mouth. I reached down and inserted him. And he soon got his wish.

The phone ringing caused us to stir. Harold got up and answered it while I got up to go potty. When I returned he said, "That was Carla. She asked if we wanted to come over. Annette and Tony will be there."

"I really wanted to rest tonight, but that does sound like fun. You wanna go?"

"Yeah, let's go. Why don't you call Carla back and ask her what we should bring."

The next morning, he woke me up about eight o'clock. I really wanted to sleep later because we stayed at Carla's until after midnight. It's so nice how Earl and Tony have embraced Harold.

We had lots of great food and had a great time. He said, "We should get to the market early so we don't miss out on the good stuff. And, I was thinking we need a freezer so when the weather gets bad, we'll have a supply of food if we can't get out. What do you think?"

"I was thinking the same thing. Especially when things are on sale, I could stock up and freeze them."

"Why didn't you buy one, or ask me to?"

"Because you've done so much. I don't want to appear like, I don't know."

"Felicia, don't do that. Please Babe. It's not fair that you get mad at me when I make decisions, yet you won't make *any* decisions."

"Okay. And you're right. I promise to do better."

"So we'll go to the market and then shop for a freezer, okay?"

"Sounds like a plan. And..."

He looked at me and said, "And?"

"Could we also get a set of lounging chairs for the deck? I need something that reclines so my feet won't swell. And I want two so you can be out there with me."

He looked at me and said gently, "Don't ask me Babe. Tell me. How are your feet? Do they hurt?"

"No Hun, I'm fine. I just don't want it to happen."

"Okay, let's go."

By the time we returned, I was tired but on top of the world. The weather was great and we did a lot, but not too much. He tried to convince me to start buying maternity clothes. I told him I didn't start wearing that mess until my eighth month. He just wanted me to look pregnant.

When we pulled into the driveway, for some reason the garage door wouldn't open. We tried several times and finally he said, "Let's just go in through the front door and see what the hell is wrong."

Harold drove a Navigator, so we were able to get everything in his truck except the freezer. I grabbed a couple of cushions and he grabbed the two chairs and then he came and unlocked the door.

When we opened the door, everyone whispered *surprise*, and I froze. I needed my mind to catch up to what was in front of me. I refocused and looked again.

Everyone I knew in this world it seemed was there. The first on my radar was Tammy. She came over to me and said, "Hi Felicia! Are you surprised?!"

I opened my mouth but could only cry. Harold's mom came over and said, "Come on over here and sit."

Annette brought me a glass of spa water and Gina came over and kissed me on the cheek. Gina asked, "Are you okay?"

I chuckled and said, "You guys got me good. And yes, I'm fine."

I sat there while each person came and greeted me and decorated me. Finally Harold came over and said quietly, "You forgot, didn't you?"

"Yes. Why didn't you remind me?"

"Oh no. I wasn't about to do that."

He kissed me and brought me to my feet and embraced me. Then he asked Carla, "Are the guys outside?"

"Yep, they're here."

The men had all of the cars around the corner so I wouldn't see them. The garage door opener didn't work because Harold had removed the battery. I was set up big time. He said, "We'll be at Tony's for the day. Now you all take care of my baby. Both of my babies!"

Everyone laughed and he left. The men were bringing the cars and parking them close to the house. Eventually Daddy came in and asked, "Daughter, were you surprised?"

"Yes. And why didn't you tell me?"

"Look at all these women. They would've crucified me!"

Karen came over and said, "Come on Sis, you ready to party? Everyone's waiting for you."

I turned to my father and kissed his cheek. I said, "I gotta go Daddy."

I was still in the foyer, so I hurried to see what was going on. When I went into the family room, my home had been transformed.

Stephanie was there and directing people to do this and that. She looked up and saw me, and rushed over to see me. We hugged and she said, "Your family and friends are the best. You know, we were here last night?"

"When?"

"When you and Harold went to Carla's house, your sisters and moms and me came and set up some things. Then Harold made sure you got in late and left early so you wouldn't notice."

Annette said, "We got you pretty good, huh Trick?"

"Annette, don't call me that in front of people."

Stephanie said, "Don't worry. She's already called me worse than that! We've been having a ball!"

I looked again at the transformation. The family room, kitchen and deck were all decorated. And the backyard was beautiful. I looked outside and noticed coworkers, old friends, and my other sisters-in-law, and many from Todd's family.

Melissa and Gina were in the kitchen preparing asparagus and other vegetables to grill. I walked in and said, "Yum, when will that be ready?"

Gina said, "When it's time to eat, I'll put them on. They only take a minute to cook. No overcooking veggies, remember?"

I shook my head yes.

Then I went on the deck and my moms were there. I went and hugged each of them very tight and sat between them. Mom Benson asked, "So you're taking an early leave?"

"Yes. My last day is this coming Friday, but I refuse to quit my job."

She said, "Good for you. I had an episode like that with Karen. Now I know why."

We all laughed. We looked up and she was coming to join us. She asked, "Sister, where are the men in this town? Stephanie took us out last night and they were a bunch of wall flowers. What's up with that?"

The moms and I were cracking up. I said, "I guess that's why I ended up with a Negro from Detroit."

"Yeah Girl, they come right at you. I'd rather fight them off than wonder if something's wrong with me, like bad breath or something."

"When did you all get here?"

"We flew in yesterday afternoon and we're leaving tomorrow."

"Why don't you all stay a few days. It's so nice seeing you all."

Mom said, "Dad has to get back."

I turned and asked, "Is Dad here?"

She laughed and said, "He sure is. He and I are staying at the hotel while the girls stay here."

"No Mom. Please stay here. You and Dad can have my room."

"Barbara, tell our child something."

Mommy laughed and said, "They don't want to be around you kids. It's an opportunity for them to be alone."

Karen laughed too and said, "Girl, let them stay there. Mom can't have any more kids, so we're good."

Then she turned to her mother and said, "So Mom, is a man Dad's age still interested? I mean, maybe I should date an older man."

Mom Benson said, "Your dad has never lost interest. Finding the time is our problem."

Then my mother said, "And now that Calvin is retired, I can't keep him away from me!"

I said, "You know what. This is *way* too much information for me. I'm going outside."

I could hear them laughing at me even after I was down by the pool.

Ever since my mom met Harold's mom, she's been a different woman. Cussing, telling Dad off, and talking about things of a sexual nature. Although it's a bit unsettling, it's also refreshing. I like this Barbara.

It's also interesting that I've not been the same person since I met Jackie's son. It's *almost* as if that family has some kind of spell on us. Like Dad and Mom showing up in Detroit and staying a whole week. That really was strange. My parents have never done anything like that. What has gotten into everybody?

Later, when only the family was left, Danielle asked, "So, when do we find out the baby's sex?"

Carla said, "She never wanted to know what her kids' sex was. You're not gonna tell us, are you Licia?"

"Harold's going with me when I have my ultrasound. Then he can tell all of you, as long as no one tells me. I love being surprised."

Soon the men returned and the party started all over again. I was so happy to see Dad Benson. He came over to me and said, "Little Girl, you doing okay Baby?"

"Yes Sir, I'm doing just fine. He embraced me and held me close. Then he said, "Your parents tell me you're planning to quit working for a while. I'm glad because some things aren't worth your health. Take it easy. You'll be glad you did."

Mom Benson came over and asked Dad, "What did you all do Love?"

"Well, we had what is known as a Groom's shower. Harold got gifts and we quizzed him on what it means to be a husband. He failed miserably."

Harold said, "Dad, I did not. Mom, I got a ninety two."

Mom asked her husband, "Did he Harold?"

"Yes, he did very well. I was just joking. Apparently, he and Felicia have had some trials, and he learned how to respond in certain situations."

Harold said, "I learned a lot. Specifically, that a man should be constantly thrilling his wife. He should never become lazy in loving her, in or out of the bedroom."

Mom and I were both speechless. We looked at both Harolds and were amazed. I finally said, "Wow. That's incredible. I'm really amazed and happy that a man told you that."

Everybody was drinking and eating and still having a great time. New friendships were made, old ones renewed. The dads eventually slipped out and the moms were back on the deck, now enjoying the new chairs. Harold and I were sitting on the barstools, interacting with everyone.

Harold said to me, "Todd was with us today."

"I wondered about that. Did he feel out of place?"

"I actually called him and said, "Man, you do know we miss you here. If you can get a sitter, come on over and have a drink with us."

I smiled. What a blessing that we all get along so well. So many exes fight like cats and dogs and spend time and energy hating each other. They apparently forgot they used to love these people.

The next morning, the house was abuzz. I strolled downstairs and Mom said, "Good Morning. How are you Baby?"

"I feel great. How are you this morning?"

Karen said, "Please don't ask. She and Dad have been acting like love birds all morning."

Mom looked at me and winked. And Dad came over and patted her behind. Harold came down and Dad asked, "Harold, did your mom tell you her news?"

We both looked at mom and waited. She smiled and said, "I'm pregnant!"

She and Dad cracked up. No one else thought it was funny. She said, "Okay, I'm retiring. At the end of this semester."

Harold went to his mother and said, "Mom, I didn't think you'd ever leave. Congratulations!"

He hugged his mother and kissed her. We spent the rest of their visit around the house. Before they left, Karen and I took a walk around the house. She laughed and said, "By the way, you did a good job pretending to be surprised."

"I know you're not going to believe this, but I totally forgot about the shower. And I never knew the date."

We laughed and continued to talk for another fifteen minutes or so. Eventually, she lagged behind me and smoked a joint.

In the days to follow, I tried to remain focused. But with training the temp at work, my classes in the evening and counting down to the wedding, it started to get stressful. By Thursday, I couldn't *wait* to leave IBM for a while. I rode in with Harold because I was too tired to drive.

Harold called me later that morning and asked if I wanted to grab a salad for lunch. I'd been staying in during lunch to work with Linda the temp, and to help my supervisor with the distribution of my assignments.

I decided I would take a short lunch today so I told him yes. He came to my desk about eleven forty-five and when I looked up and saw him, he had a devilish grin on his face. He asked, "You ready?"

"It's too early. I really shouldn't leave yet."

Lenora my supervisor and Linda walked up. Lenora said, "Go on Felicia. You haven't taken a lunch break all week."

Then she turned to Harold and said, "Hello Harold. How are you?"

"Doing great. How are you Lenora?"

"Not bad. Except for the fact that our girl Felicia is leaving us. We're really going to miss her. By the way, this is Linda. She'll be our temp while Felicia is on leave."

Harold reached out and shook her hand. He said, "Linda, it's a pleasure to meet you."

I said, "Linda, this is my fiancée. He works on the fourth floor."

I noticed a brief exchange between Lenora and Harold. He said, "Let's go Babe. I need to get back for a one thirty meeting."

While in the car, I couldn't shake the feeling that something was up. Then it dawned on me. They must be trying to surprise me with a shower or something. We went to Ruby Tuesday's and were having our salads when Harold said, "I have some news Babe."

I looked up and said, "Good news, I hope."

"Yeah, I think it's good. I hope you will too."

I dropped my fork and said, "Harold don't play with me. What is it?"

"Do you recall the weekend we went to the bed and breakfast, and I had to wait to leave because I had an important meeting?"

"Yes. You couldn't take a half day because of it."

"I learned in that meeting that Victor, the VP of my division wanted me to take a new position."

"That's great, as long as it doesn't involve relocation."

"No it doesn't. But the position is the manager of your entire department. I would be your boss."

I laughed and said, "Oh, hell no. What?!"

He laughed too. He said, "When I told him of our upcoming nuptials, he said it would be a conflict of interest."

"Harold, why didn't you tell me then?"

"Because that was the weekend you announced your pregnancy, and it became insignificant because I couldn't take the position anyhow."

"So why are you sharing now? What's different?"

"Victor and I met again today, along with Lenora."

"Lenora?"

"Yes. I learned today that before your announcement of an early leave, you were about to get a promotion."

"What?! Really?"

He smiled and said, "Lenora has accepted a position in another division of the company. She will soon be a manager, and has requested to bring two of her people with her. Your co-worker Trina has accepted and will be a team leader."

"Lenora and Trina are leaving! That really saddens me, but I'm happy for them. I can't believe they're leaving me though."

"Yes, Lenora speaks very highly of Trina. And *you*. That's why she wants you to supervise the department."

"What? Me?"

He laughed and said, "Yes, you. I was also offered the managerial job again today, and I accepted it, with conditions. So technically, I'm your boss today. That puts me in position to present this job opportunity to you. Lenora, Trina and you would relocate to the downtown office, and would no longer be in *my* division. That means I could take this job with no conflict of interest. However, I do not want you to make your decision with that in mind. I feel confident that other opportunities will come along for me."

"What happens if I turn down the job?"

"You still win. The girl Linda you're training has been offered a permanent position. You would take Lenora's position as supervisor."

I was stunned. I already knew what I wanted. I said, "I guess I should pack my bags then. I'll be going with Lenora and Trina. Congratulations Honey!"

When we returned, Harold said, "I didn't really have a meeting at one-thirty. I made that up."

We were in the elevator, and I asked, "Why did you make it up?"

As the doors opened, there was a loud *surprise!* I put my hands over my mouth and looked at him and he said, "That's why!"

I got off the elevator and all of my co-workers were there, offering congrats and hugs. I looked at the banner and it read, 'Happy Nuptials and Happy Baby Felicia!'

Lenora and Trina came over to me and asked, "Did Harold tell you?"

I looked sad and said, "Yeah, he told me."

They looked at me, and Trina asked, "Felicia, you're not taking it?"

"Well I thought about it and….Hell yeah, I'm taking it!"

We all jumped up and down like little girls. I said, "Lenora, how can I ever thank you for this?"

"Listen, when you have a great team, you don't want to break it up. Together, we did our thing over here. Now it's time for all of us to move up and make some history downtown. Are we ready?"

Trina and I both said, "Yes!"

By day's end, I was exhausted. Lenora said, "You worked enough this week for six days. Go home and enjoy your wedding and baby. I'll be in touch."

We hugged and I became very emotional. Harold loaded all of my gifts into his truck. He said he would have someone clean out my desk and he'd bring my things home next week.

On the drive home he said, "Babe, I have to go on a business trip to Chicago Monday morning and I'm returning Tuesday evening. Wanna go?" "I don't think so. Besides, I would miss my class."

"Oh, that's right. Also, I'm gonna start moving my things into the house. The apartment was furnished, so I don't have any furniture to move."

"Okay. That's a good idea."

I suddenly realized he wouldn't be here Monday. I said, "You're gonna miss the ultrasound on Monday."

"Oh no, I really wanted to be there. Can you postpone it?"

"There's usually a two to three week wait. I *really* need to know my true due date."

"How will I know the sex? Can you ask the doctor or whoever, to write it down and place it in a closed envelope?"

"Sure, I'll ask them to do that for you."

Monday morning, I got up and fixed breakfast for my sons. I took them to school and came back home. Harold stayed at his apartment last night to prepare for his meeting in Chicago. My appointment was at ten o'clock, so I came home and dressed and was on my way.

The attendant was a female, so she and I made small talk. I told her because I couldn't remember the date of my last period, I was anxious to know my true due date. She was very nice and was making notes and smiling. She asked me if I felt activity yet. I told her I felt movement, but no kicking yet.

She asked me if I wanted to know the sex of the baby. I said no, but I was curious if she was able to determine it. She said, "Yes. I'm sure of the sex. Do you have a preference?"

"No, not at all. Please don't tell me."

She smiled and said, "I won't tell you the sex, but I'm sure you want to know you have twins. Congratulations!"

My mind went completely blank. The room was spinning and I was trying to absorb this information without fainting again. I finally asked, "Dear God, are you sure?!"

"I'm very sure. If you turn toward the screen, and I'll show you your babies."

I turned my head and I saw two blobs. She asked, "Are you sure you *still* don't want to know their sex?"

I opened my mouth, but it was so dry I couldn't talk. Finally I asked, "Is one of them a boy?"

"Yes, there is a boy."

"Good. I don't want to know anymore. Except, are they okay?"

She smiled and said, "They're great. Everything seems to be as it should be at this stage."

She also told me that based on their size and the info I gave, she was confident I got pregnant around the second or third week of June. That put me at fifteen weeks, and since twins don't usually last full term, I was looking at a due date around March tenth.

When I left, I was still in a daze. I didn't know what to do or where to go. I opted to go and see my mom. I looked at the envelope with the sex of my other baby and put it safely inside my purse. I didn't really need it though. Mommy already told me it's a girl.

When I got out of the car, I was sort of glad to see the Honda not there and my mom's car was. I walked in and said, "Mom, it's me."

"I'm in the kitchen. Come on in Felicia."

I walked in and said, "Hi Mom. What are you cooking?"

She said, "I had a taste for some collards and corn bread."

"Yum. That sounds good."

"I forgot you're off now. I'll fix you some and you can come back in a couple hours and pick it up."

"Mom, what made you say I was having twins?"

She screamed laughing and dried her hands on a towel. She said, "Girl, you found out it's true, didn't you?"

"Mommy…"

She hugged me and we both cried. She said, "Lord, Thank You. This is a joyous day!"

Then she released me and said, "You know the only person who believed me is Jackie. I know you and your daddy thought I was nuts, but I know what I saw."

I laughed and said, "Yep. I thought you had finally lost your touch."

"So, so tell me. It's one of each, right?"

"Mom you know I never want to know the sex, but I did ask her if there's a boy up in here and she said yes."

I reached for my purse and said, "The other baby's sex is in this envelope. It's for…"

"Girl, give me that damn envelope!"

"Mommy! What's up with all this cussing! You stand there and thank God, and in the same breath, you're talking like a sailor."

We both laughed and she said, "Hand me that envelope before I whip your behind Girl!"

I handed it to her and I said, "Whatever you do, show your poker face. As a matter of fact, I'll go to the bathroom and you look and put it back in the envelope, okay?"

She said okay and I went to the bathroom. When I returned, she was at the stove, putting her greens in the pot. She asked, "Are you getting excited about the wedding?"

"I guess so. Right now I just wanna get it over with. Did I tell you we're going to Miami Beach for a week long honeymoon?"

"I thought you were going to Jamai…oops. I hope I didn't spoil the surprise."

"No, he told me because I wanted to postpone it. I'd rather wait until the babies are born. Wow, that sounded strange coming out of my mouth. Babies. Do we have any twins in our family Mom?"

"Yes, on both sides."

My cell phone rang and it was Harold. I answered and he said, "Hey Babe, how are you?"

"I'm fine. How's it going there?"

"Very good. How did it go?"

"It went well. I'm at Mom's and she opened the envelope. I have no idea what she saw, but she's smiling."

"Put her on the phone Felicia!"

"Okay. Calm down."

I whispered to Mom, "Tell him it's a boy, okay?"

She said okay and took the phone. She said, "Hello Son. Yes, she went out to get something out of the car. It's a boy! Are you happy? Well, she's coming back in. Don't give it away. You're welcome, and safe travels back home. Here she is."

I asked, "What time will you be landing tomorrow?"

"Five thirty, but I'm trying to get an earlier flight."

I told him the due date and he said, "I love you Babe."

I told him I loved him too, and we soon hung up. I said, "Mom, you did that too well."

We cracked up and I said, "Please don't tell Jackie. Believe me. Harold will want to do that."

"I'll let Jackie tell me. How's that?"

"Perfect. And you can't tell anyone else yet either."

She laughed and said, "I wish I could see Harold's face when you tell him."

Chapter Seventeen

By Tuesday afternoon, I was a mess. I had my first test that night, which I could barely study for. My mind was twirling with the knowledge that I had two babies. Two!

I wanted to cry, but the tears refused to come. I was totally feeling sorry for myself because I didn't even want *one*. I kept trying to convince myself that it was meant to be, and Harold was going to be ecstatic. And to know that he might have *two* sons, I might need to call the paramedics *before* I tell him.

But what about me? When would I be able to resume working? How could I put two babies on my mother? Even though she seemed delighted, it didn't seem right. Or fair.

Harold's mom called just as I was getting in the house. She said, "Felicia, I'm concerned that a couple of our friends didn't get invitations. Could you kindly ask Stephanie if they're on her list?"

"Sure, what are their names?"

She gave me the information and asked, "So, did you have your ultrasound yesterday?"

"Yes Ma'am I did. My due date is March tenth."

"And the sex?"

"I don't know. But when Harold comes in tonight, he'll let you all know. The results are in a sealed envelope, because I don't want to know."

She was quiet but then she asked, "Are you sure you're okay Child? You sound tired. And have you been praying daily?"

"Yes Ma'am, I pray every day. I am a little tired. But as I told Harold, I'm having trouble sleeping because my body is changing so rapidly."

"I'll send you a body pillow. Are you allergic to feathers?"

"No, I don't think so."

"Good. I'll go online and order it for you tonight. You should have it in a few days Darling."

"Thanks Mom. That's really kind of you."

"Don't mention it. No need in suffering any more than you have to."

Just before we hung up, Harold walked in. I told her he was here and she asked to talk to him. I whispered, "It's your mom. She wants to know the sex of the baby and I told her that it's in a sealed envelope."

He kissed me and said, "Okay."

He took the phone and said, "Hello Mother."

He went up the stairs and I heard him close the bedroom door.

When I returned from my class, I was tired but excited about the news I was about to drop on Harold. The boys were in bed and he was cleaning the kitchen. He said, "Mom's concerned because she said you don't sound happy to her. Are you unhappy?"

I thought about that and said, "I'm just anxious to get past some of this stuff. Like the wedding. I do have something to tell you though."

I went into the kitchen and poured a glass of juice. I wished it could've been a tall glass of wine. He came behind me and asked, "Nothing's wrong is it?"

I turned and said, "Oh no, nothing like that."

"What is it?"

"I confess that I know Mom told you we're having a boy."

"Oh Thank God! It was lonely having to enjoy that by myself."

"What she didn't tell you is that your son has a twin."

Harold blinked two times and asked, "What did you say?"

I could see him reaching backwards for a chair. I could see his eyes looking upward. And then I saw him fall. I hurried over to him and asked, "Harold, are you okay?"

He laughed and said, "Babe I thought there was a chair there."

He got up and looked at me real strange. He asked, "Babe, did you really say my son has a twin?"

"You know what. You need something."

I went to the bar and poured him a shot of scotch. I said, "Come on."

We went out on the deck and sat on the sofa, next to each other. I said, "I learned on Monday that yes, we're having twins."

He put his head down and then looked up at me. He asked, "How are you dealing with this Felicia? You gave up so much to give me a child. Are you doing all right?"

"I'm better. I've had two days to deal with it. That's why I went to Mom's. I was in shock. Like you are."

He laughed and said, "Since I've met you, my life has truly been a roller coaster ride. I don't know what'll happen next."

"How are you? Are you happy about this?"

He laughed again and asked, "Are you kidding? This is the best news in the world to me. So, what is the sex of the other baby?"

"I don't know. When the lady told me there were two babies, I almost fell off the table. I asked if one of them was a boy. She said yes, so I asked her to put the sex of his twin in the envelope."

Harold emptied his glass. I laughed and said, "The night I went to the hospital, when my parents brought me home, my mom told me I had twins. Daddy and I thought she had lost her mind, so we ignored her. So yesterday when I went to her house and told her, she asked about their sex and I allowed her to open the envelope. It's in your top right drawer."

"Wow, how does she do that?"

"I guess God gave her the gift to see my babies. She doesn't see other women's babies, just mine."

"Would you go with me so we can see it together? Please."

"I don't have to. Mom told me six weeks ago that I was carrying one of each."

I threw my rule out of the window, and gave in to my husband-to-be. I rationalized that if Mom was wrong, I would be very disappointed. And if she's right, then the element of surprise is gone anyhow. So he said, "I'll go up and get it, and I promise not to look until I get back, okay?"

"Don't break your promise. I'm doing this so we'll see it together."

He ran up the stairs and soon ran back down. We left the deck and sat down in the kitchen. He said, "You take it out."

I took the envelope and reached inside. Luckily, Mom folded it before reinserting it. There it was, folded in front of us. I said, "You open it."

He opened it and it said:

Congratulations! You have A Boy and A Girl!

We looked at each other and we both hollered. I finally cried. And not out of pity, but because I was genuinely happy. He and I both had tears of joy as he called Detroit. His dad answered and said, "Boy, I was just about to call you! Your mom just now told me the news. Another Benson generation. Praise The Lord!"

"Thanks Dad. We're very happy too. Is Mom around to pick up another extension?"

"Let me tell her to grab the phone in the kitchen."

"Wait Dad! Would you get on the intercom and ask everyone to grab a phone. I have something to tell all of you."

"Okay. Give me a minute."

After a couple of minutes, everyone had a phone. After pleasantries, Harold said, "I'm sure you've all heard that my beautiful Felicia is carrying a boy. What she waited until now to tell me is that my son has a twin sister. We're having twins! One of each!"

Everyone was ecstatic. Mom said, "Barbara told me you had twins. She said nobody believed her."

Mom was obviously crying again. I said, "Mom, now we need to pray twice as much."

She said, "Oh Felicia, yes we do. Are you okay with this? Has this news been difficult?"

"Yes, at first. But I'm better."

Melissa said, "I can't wait! Twin Bensons!"

A boy and a girl. Remarkable. Of course I selfishly wanted a girl, but since I was doing this for Harold, I wanted him to have his son. I think if I'd only had a girl, I would have felt bad for him and tried again for a boy. This way, everyone wins.

Friday morning started great. I woke up to find breakfast in front of me. Harold was sitting there with a smile on his face and a rose between his teeth. I smiled at him and then looked quickly at the clock and asked, "Are the boys up?"

"Yes, they're in the kitchen having breakfast and I'm taking them to school. Eat your breakfast and rest today. I'm staying home with you."

I sat up and felt the biggest kick in my side. I rubbed my side and got kicked again. I thought I was gonna throw up. I said, "Stop that little boy. I know that's you Harold."

Harold looked at me and said, "Excuse me?"

"I just got my first kick. I know it was Harold."

Harold came over to me and asked, "Where?"

"On my left side. I think when I sat up, I woke him."

"Can I feel it?"

"You can try, but they're still very small."

He put his hand on my side and waited. He said, "Babe, move again and wake him up."

I moved around and bam, he kicked Harold's hand. Harold jumped and said, "Oh My God! I can*not* believe that! And I beg to differ. I'm sure that was little Felicia."

We both laughed and he said, "That's our child. It's amazing."

He was awed and walked toward the door. He said, "I have to get the boys to school."

I thought I saw a tear in his eye.

When he returned, I had showered and was getting dressed. He came into my dressing room and watched me. He said, "I can't believe you're mine."

I turned to look at him and he said, "Stay right there."

He went into his closet and came back with his camera. He said, "It's just my luck that of the two boxes I brought over here, one had my camera."

"What are you going to do with that?"

"I assure you. These are for our eyes only."

I was clad only in my bra and panties. My hair was a mess and the fact that I hate taking pictures certainly needed to be addressed. He said, "Just continue dressing and pretend I'm not here."

"I don't think so. You probably don't know this about me, but I hate taking pictures."

"I just want to capture these precious moments Felicia. Please. I promise no one else will see them."

I looked at him and realized he just didn't get it. I've got to do something to change that. I said, "When I'm between seven and eight months we can hire a photographer and take some semi nudes. We can all be in them, okay?"

"That sounds so beautiful Babe. Yes, I look forward to that."

"So, take your camera and put it away."

"But I still want to do this. Please Felicia!"

I walked out and into my closet. I put on some sweats and a top. He asked, "Babe, are you really going to deny me?"

I turned to him and shouted, "Yes, Harold! Damn! I can't seem to *ever* do enough to please you!"

I grabbed my socks and went downstairs. My hair was still a mess and I was so upset that I cried as I opened a bottle of water. He came down about five minutes later. He poured himself some juice and said, "I...I don't know what to say. You're right as usual, and the truth is you please me beyond what I deserve or could have ever imagined. Please don't believe that. My selfishness, again, has me out of control."

I looked at him with tears streaming down my face. I said, "I don't know my life anymore. I'm carrying two babies and it scares me to death. Two more people looking to me for everything. I have a man that expects more than I have and it's frustrating and frightening too. My job is hanging on a string because I can't imagine putting the burden of two newborns on my middle aged mother, yet I would never put them in any other arms but hers. Because of that, I may not leave them until they go to college and I fear my career is being put to death as I speak."

I stopped talking because my grief had me overwhelmed. He said, "Babe..."

I put my hand up and said, "I don't want to hear you talk right now. As a matter of fact, I would like for you to grab your shit and go to your apartment for a few days. I don't want to see you or hear from you. Please."

I took my water and went upstairs. When I went into the bedroom, I saw his laptop and wallet. I placed them outside the door and closed it.

That afternoon I went to get my sons from school and we went to visit Aunt Carla. She was waiting for me when I got there and instructed the four boys to go out back and play. She and I went into her room and closed the door. I turned into her arms and cried. I said, "Carla, please get my dresses."

She got both dresses and laid them on her bed. I looked at both of them and tried on the second one. It fit beautifully. I twirled around and began laughing. Carla smiled and said, "I told you it would make you feel better. Put on the other one."

I looked at her and said, "That one scares me."

Carla said, "There are fifteen days before the wedding. If it doesn't fit today, at least you'll know now."

There was a tap on the door and Annette walked in. She looked at me in dress two and said, "Wow, you look great."

Carla said, "She was just about to try on the smaller one."

I looked at the dress and Annette came over to me and began helping me remove dress two. Carla stood in front of me and Annette held my hand while I slowly stepped into dress one. Once both feet were in securely, the two of them began pulling it up. Easily. I inserted my arms in the sleeves and looked at them. Carla zipped it up with no problem.

They both stepped back and smiled. I turned to look in Carla's full length mirror and stared at myself. I turned around and looked from side to side. It was still beautiful. *I* was still beautiful in it. Then I began to look down to see how much excess material I had. Still over two inches on both sides.

I looked up with tears still streaming down my face. They both came over and helped me out of it. I sat there in my undies and put my head down. I said, "I have to tell you something."

Carla and Annette looked at each other and sat on either side of me. Annette said, "Licia, I'm sure whatever it is, everything will work out fine. Do you really hate red wine, because red wine isn't so bad for a pregnant woman?"

"You know what. I will have just a little."

Annette went to get the wine. I asked Carla, "Do you think it'll still look good in fifteen days?"

"I would bet money on it. Especially if just your ass and hips expand. Girl, your ass comes straight from the Motherland! I'm not Gay, but *that* ass is beautiful."

"I looked at her and cracked up. Annette came back and Carla asked, "Nette, have you *ever* seen an ass like Licia's?"

Annette said, "That must be the secret to good coochie. Because every man that's had it has *not* been the same. And to answer your question, no I have never seen an ass like that. It's a thing of beauty."

"Now that we've established I have the biggest ass in New York State, I really need to talk about something."

We all laughed and picked up our wine. Annette brought mine in a shot glass. I picked it up and tasted it. It was awful. I said, "I can't do this Annette. I really wanted a little something, but it won't be that."

Carla handed me her glass and I took it. She and I are both white wine drinkers. She said, "What's the difference. A small taste is a small taste, no matter what it is."

I tasted it and my taste buds woke up. I took another small sip and handed it back to her. I said, "Yummy! That was so good! Okay, this has been my life over the last week."

I told them about Harold's and my promotions and my shower at work. I reminded them that I started classes. I explained to them that his family is wonderful, but they like Harold, are smothering the hell out of me. I have a wedding in two weeks and a weeklong honeymoon that I don't even want to go on. Not to mention I'm enduring a pregnancy that has almost taken me out of here.

Then I said, "And this is the icing on the cake. When I went to my ultrasound appointment, first I learned that my due date is March tenth. Then I was told that I was carrying a boy, and that he has a twin sister."

They both screamed. Loud. They were so happy. I thought about it a moment and realized that if either of them had twins, I'd feel the same way. Carla said, "Oh Licia. That's why you're so down. You wait. They'll bring you, and us, so much joy!"

Annette said, "Girl, I understand completely. If I was told I was carrying twins, I'd crawl off the table and whip somebody's ass! You didn't at least kick that bitch, Licia!?"

I looked at her and laughed my ass off. She is a fool! I know she was just trying to lighten the mood, and she did. They laughed with me and I got up and ran to the bathroom. Carla said, "Heffa, you better not pee on my floor. I just cleaned it!"

We eventually went downstairs and Carla fed all of the kids. Annette brought Tony when she came, so all five boys were sitting at the table enjoying their dinner. We went on the deck and I told them about my fight with Harold. Annette said, "Good. That's what he gets. They make me sick, always wanting everything their way. Selfish bastards, all of them!"

"I know I needed to do it, but now I feel awful."

Annette said, "There's plenty he can do. But most of all, he can think about what he's done. He'll be fine Licia."

Carla said, "I say you go over to his apartment tomorrow and love him up. He's already had his punishment."

They continued to disagree, and entertained me for the next hour.

That evening, the boys were with Todd and it seemed too quiet. He didn't call me, come by or even text me. Karen called me about ten thirty. She asked, "What the hell happened between you and my brother?"

"We just had a disagreement, but we'll be fine."

"You know he's here."

I sat up and asked, "He is?"

"Yep. And he's devastated. Said you put his ass out"

"I did not."

She cracked up and said, "One part of me thinks you should get on a plane and make it all better. But..."

I thought about that. Then I asked, "But what?"

"We let him have his way, because it was easy. It was a disservice to him, and now you. Stand your ground Felicia. You're really good for him."

"I'm growing weary of his selfishness and bratty behavior. I have two sons and two babies coming. I need his help, not his childlike antics."

"He admitted to Daddy he'd been relentless, and you told him there was no pleasing him. He wants to fix this, but he doesn't quite know how."

I paused and suddenly felt bad for him. I thanked Karen for calling. She said, "I hate to see you two at odds with one another. I hope you're not upset with me."

"No Karen. I love you for being concerned. I'll fix it, okay?"

She seemed better and we hung up.

The following morning I went to Harold's apartment. He was always so neat. But not that day. It wasn't just the boxes and wardrobes. Or the two glasses he had in the sink. It was clear he left here angry. Pillows and books were all over the room. His sofa was turned on its side. I went into his bedroom and it was better. Bed made up, and nothing out of place.

Then I went into his bathroom and all of my toiletries were neatly placed in a box, but many of his were thrown all over the place. There was broken glass and a lot of gooey stuff on the floor. I looked around and saw his tears. I had tears on my face as I cleaned his.

It took me four hours. I did it slowly so I wouldn't overexert myself. I packed most of his belongings and took them to my car. I cleaned his fridge out, and threw two bags of trash in the dumpster. I left the heaviest things.

I looked back and unexpectedly thought of my grandmother. She would say during trying times that God always gives us sugar with vinegar. I hoped during this difficult time for Harold, he recognized the love or *sugar* in what I did that day.

I actually considered going after Harold. More than once. But the more I learned from Karen and the rest of his family, the better I understood the workings of Harold Benson.

He was the only son amongst five sisters. They, along with their parents, as my mother would say, made a damn fool out of him. Because of his intellect and grace, and his loving and giving nature, it wasn't easily detected.

Not long ago he told me that because he's a *good guy*, he felt he should have his way. Maya Angelou said: If someone shows you who they are, believe them...*The first time.*

I went back home and relaxed on my deck. It was still early and I thought about him. I looked over at his chair, and missed him. I dosed off and the phone ringing woke me. I looked at the ID and it was Detroit. I started not to answer, but I did. Harold said, "Hi."

"You're in Detroit?"

"Yes. I called from the house phone because I knew you wouldn't ignore a call from my family."

"No I wouldn't. But I wouldn't ignore a call from you either. Since I asked you *not* to call me, I assume it must be important. So what is it?"

He was quiet, so I asked, "How is the family?"

"They're fine. I told them what I did and they want to put me out too."

He laughed sarcastically. I said, "I did not put you out. I asked you for a few days of solitude. By the way, I called Stephanie and cancelled the honeymoon. It'll be too difficult. I hope you're not too disappointed."

"You didn't cancel the wedding, did you?"

"No Harold, I didn't. Should I?"

He didn't answer me. I said, "*Harold*, I didn't hear your answer."

"Yes."

I hung up the phone. My throat went dry. I couldn't *believe* what he just said! I looked around the house and looked for…something. *Anything* to hang onto. The phone rang. It was him. I picked it up and yelled, "What!"

"What happened?"

"What do you mean what happened? Get off the damn phone so I can cancel the wedding. Then you'll have every damn thing you want."

"Felicia, what are you saying? Please don't do this."

"*I* am not doing anything except what you asked me to do."

"Why would I ask you to do that?"

"Harold. I asked if you wanted me to cancel the wedding, and you said yes."

"I said yes when you said my name. Didn't you say my name?"

"Yes I did, along with, *do you want me to cancel the wedding?*"

"I never heard that Felicia. Honest I didn't."

We were both quiet. He then said, "I shouldn't have called, huh?"

"No you *shouldn't* have called."

"Do you still love me Felicia?"

I closed my eyes. I said, "I'll always *love* you Harold. No matter *what* happens. But love isn't enough. We can't mistreat people because we know they *love* us. That's not fair. It's cruel. It's taking advantage of someone's heart. Like…a chipping away at a heart we only have one of. I want to love you *like* you need it and *how* you need it and when and where you need it. But if it kills me, or destroys me, what's the point? If my very soul implodes and the essence that is me withers away, who will raise our children? And who or what will *ever*.....love you like me? There's only *one me* Harold."

Silence. I asked if he was still there. Mom said, "Felicia, he left. He grabbed his stuff, said goodbye and walked out of the door."

Through tears I asked, "Did he hear anything I said?"

"We all heard it. Felicia, you're an amazing woman and exactly what my son needs. I hate to see you two suffering like this. And I *pray* that the two of you find a way to get through this. My kitchen phone has a short in it and malfunctions sometimes. That's why he didn't hear your question. But one thing is for sure. I'll never have to worry about those children. They have a mother that is one to be reckoned with."

"Am I still on speaker phone?"

"Yes, but it's just me."

"Is Dad okay?"

"He's fine. We realize we catered to Harold. More now than ever."

"Mom, I understand the love parents have for their children. But even when parents overdo some things, each of us is still responsible for growing up. I've never loved anyone more than I love Harold. I promise I'll take care of this and I'm looking forward to seeing you on Friday."

"I believe that Felicia. That spoke to my very soul, what you told Harold. When this has passed, he'll be better for it. I love you Child, and my babies. Kiss them for me."

"I love you too Mom, and don't worry. All is well."

It was after two o'clock. I clicked the remote and turned on the TV. I decided to cook something. I looked in the fridge and freezers, and decided on comfort food because I saw where Harold had taken out some ground turkey yesterday.

I threw together a meatloaf and cooked some rice. I found some frozen collards, already cooked. I thawed those and after another hour, the food was done.

I showered and put on some comfy silk pajamas. I waited. And napped. And waited.

About eight o'clock, the front door opened and he came in. I was looking through a magazine and didn't move until he was standing in front of me.

I set it on the coffee table and asked him how his flight was. He said it was fine and he asked what I'd cooked. I told him and he asked if I'd eaten yet. I said, "No, I was waiting for you. Are you hungry?"

"Yes, I'm hungry."

I got up and said, "Go and wash up and I'll fix your dinner."

"Felicia...."

"Go and wash up Harold."

He went upstairs and came back twenty minutes later. He was in sweats with no top on. His hair was still damp and he looked *very* sexy. I pretended not to notice. I set his food in front of him and gave him a glass of wine and a glass of spa water.

I sat across from him and we quietly ate our food. Eventually he said, "By the way, Mom sent you another body pillow. It's in the duffle bag in the bedroom. She wanted you to have two."

"I'll thank her tomorrow. I told Annette and Carla about the twins. They were ecstatic."

"I can only imagine. I would love to be a fly on the wall around the three of you. I bet I'd learn so much."

"Really, like what?"

"Like how to be your friend. You all never fight, do you?"

"No, we don't. However, we disagree a lot. But we never disregard the others' feelings or needs or especially the others' opinion."

He continued eating. He said, "This is delicious Babe. There's a lot of love in this meal. Like the way you cleaned my apartment."

I looked up and said, "Your things are still in the car. I thought I'd wait and let you and the boys carry them in."

He drank his water and sat back. He said, "I need to say some things to you, but I feel like you don't want to talk about it, or *hear me* talk."

He actually laughed when he said that. I laughed too and said, "We need resolution Harold."

He took my left hand and gently stroked my ring. He continued to look at my hand and said, "First of all, thank you for cleaning my apartment. I was ashamed that you saw it that way. I don't know if anyone can display love like you. I hope you didn't get hurt on that broken glass."

"No, I was careful."

"Secondly, I realized when I went home yesterday that my first order of business is to be your friend. Karen made me aware of that. By the way, she told me she called you. She said you told her you needed my help, not my childlike antics. That hit me like a ton of bricks Felicia. It was the first time that I was aware of, that you said you needed me. For anything!"

"You must know I need you Harold."

"And I need you too. I've never known anyone like you Felicia. I'm really sorry. And I promise to be more sensitive to your needs and what you're going through."

"What made you come home?"

"When you said I was destroying you. And if I destroyed you, who would love me like you?"

I shook my head and he said, "My dad left the room and my sisters and mom began to cry. Karen was the only one standing. She got my things and told me to take my ass home and fix this."

"I think you should move in tomorrow and we'll start working through this now. Are you okay with that?"

"Yes, I'd like that."

He removed our dishes and asked, "Could I stay with you tonight?"

My heart and body responded to his words. I said, "Of course Harold. This is your home."

I got up and together we cleaned the kitchen. He asked about the boys and I told him they were at Todd's. He brought me in his arms and held me for a long time. He said, "I've missed you so much."

He kissed me and I felt him harden. He put his head on my forehead and groaned. I released him and moved him away from the windows and deck and put him against the counter. I kissed him and then got in a squatting position. I began to taste him and moaned. I said, "Mmm you taste so good."

He groaned and reached for my hair and brought me closer. I took more of him and he begged me not to tease him. Finally, I slowly began to take all of him. He was beside himself and could do nothing but hold on to the counter and run his hand through my hair. He said, "Felicia, I'm not gonna last."

I increased my tempo and he growled and released himself. He held on to my hair like his life depended on it. I reached up and took his hand out of my hair. When I finally stood, or tried to, he laughed and helped me up. I said, "That isn't as easy anymore."

We turned off the lights and went upstairs. Make up sex is the best.

I was cleaning out his night stand when I ran across his condoms. I took them to him and asked, "Do you still need these?"

He laughed and said, "Throw them out Felicia."

"Actually, it raises the question about permanent birth control. Should I or should you?"

He looked puzzled and I asked, "Should I get my tubes tied, or should you get snipped?"

He looked horrified and said, "I dare not answer that. But would it help if I come totally clean and admit I'm scared to death to do that. Can we wait before making a permanent decision?"

"Okay Harold. But we will be doing something permanent."

He smacked my behind and we went back to work. It was hard to believe his whole life was in a few boxes.

We went to lunch and things seemed to be better. We talked a lot about things we'd missed over the last ten months. Like my dislike of taking pictures and bathing suits. And his dislike of dentists. I learned he was a virgin until he was seventeen and he learned that I need him to shave more often.

We decided to get the boys and lay out a plan for the next two weeks. We also agreed to go back to Geneva on the Lake for a few days after the wedding.

We looked at how many people would be in the house the weekend of the wedding. Eleven additional people. Five bedrooms. We decided to put the two married couples and their children in the boys' rooms. His parents in the guest room with the en-suite. The boys in the guest room on our floor and the remaining sisters in the basement. There was plenty of room down there. His cousins were staying at the hotel with the rest of the men.

Harold stayed home from work on Monday. He said it was important that we spent this quality time together. We spoke with Stephanie and she arranged for us to be in the bridal suite at Geneva on the Lake.

We looked at each other and asked if she'd ask Lauren if *our* room was available. Stephanie laughed and asked, "Oh, you have your *own* room?"

We laughed too and I said, "We've been there a few times and we've always stayed in the same room."

Monday evening we went furniture shopping again and got everything we didn't have. We decided to purchase televisions for two of the guest rooms and Todd Jr.'s room. Everything should be delivered by Thursday.

I found out I got a ninety five on my test last week. Due to my condition and the upcoming wedding, both of my teachers agreed to allow me to finish fifty percent of each class online. So I only had to go to one class this week and one class next week. That meant I didn't have to go back until next Wednesday. That helped me a lot.

Wednesday morning Mom came over and helped me get the house ready. Annette and Carla are coming over after work to help. She and I were in the kitchen when she said, "Jackie and I will be doing most of the cooking. I don't want you worried about that."

Daddy came in with two extra sets of glasses just like the ones we bought a few weeks ago. Mom said, "You're gonna have twenty people in here. You have to have enough glasses, silverware, dishes, etc."

Then Daddy said, "There's more. Jackie sent you more dishes and another set of silverware. She said you only had twelve of everything so she doubled all of it for you."

Mom commented on how nice the dining room looked. I had my grandmother's dishes in the china cabinet and Mom became a little teary eyed. She said, "Mom would use those dishes every Sunday. She treasured them because her mom gave them to her. When you were born, I was so happy I'd be able to pass them on."

"I really miss Grandma. She was something else."

I laughed and Mom asked me, "What do you know about Fannie?"

I looked at her puzzled, but I could tell there was a story behind those eyes. I said, "I don't know anything in particular Mom. What's to know?"

She laughed and said, "Your grandmother was a beautiful woman. The men loved her and she loved them too."

I cracked up. I said, "Really? I remember loving to comb her long hair. She was a looker."

Mom smiled and said, "Mom told me my father used to put it in a braid down her back. She was six months pregnant with me when he left and died in the war. I know I've told you several times, but you're the spitting image of her."

She went back to working with the silverware. I stopped removing the glasses and said, "Grandma gave both of us that hair. But what *aren't* you telling? I sense there's more."

She shook her head and laughed. She said, "Well, I asked her once after I was married why she dated so many men. She told me my dad never really brought out the woman in her. She was certain he loved her. But at night he would do his thing, roll off and go to sleep. She assumed it was supposed to be that way until Robert."

I stood there with my mouth opened. I was hearing a story about me. I wish I felt I could tell my mother. I asked, "So what happened after that?"

"I'd never seen her smile like that. After my dad died, she was forced to work. It was eight years before she let another man touch her. And Mr. Robert made her laugh. But, he was a ladies' man. He broke her heart."

Mom was remembering something. Then she said, "I must have been about thirteen when she started giving card parties. Men would come just to enjoy her good cooking and get a glimpse of her. She loved the attention, but she was partial to good looking men."

I dropped the glass in my hand and it shattered all over my ceramic tile floor. Mom panicked and sent me out of the kitchen. I went to the bathroom and put cold water on my face. I looked in the mirror and wondered if I was the new and improved Fannie Mae.

When I went back in the kitchen, Mom was still finding glass and made me stay away. I went upstairs and brought each of us a pair of slippers. When it was safe to go back in the kitchen, we took a break and Mom fixed us tuna fish sandwiches.

I looked at my mom and realized she's still a good looking woman herself. At forty nine, she still has her girlish figure. Her hair cascades down her back like Grandma's, and her skin is flawless. I began to wonder if she too, had issues like me and my grandmother.

I asked, "So Mom, did Grandma ever calm down?"

"Yep, she eventually met and married Mr. Palmer. He somehow stole her heart and they moved to Florida. Sadly, he died within four years of their marriage and she came back here and was never the same. She was still sassy and she still loved to cook, but she never looked at another man. She was gone about five years after him. I think she died of a broken heart."

"I remember Mr. Palmer."

I paused. But then I said, "You know Mom. I can identify with Grandma."

Mom looked up and asked, "How's that?"

"The truth is, Todd wasn't a very good lover. But I didn't know that until I met Harold."

"I'm not surprised. You two were so young. Young people have no business getting married."

Since I didn't shock her, I said, "I'm not proud of this, but I cheated on Harold once."

She looked at me and paused. I thought, *oh no, I went too far*. She got up and began rinsing our dishes and said, "That happens Felicia. Does he know?"

"No, I'm sure he doesn't."

"Good."

Then she said, "Your dad doesn't know about mine either."

She went into the bathroom and left me totally dazed. A minute later, I got a kick right in the ribs. I said, "Whichever one you is doing that, stop it right now."

Mom came out and asked who I was talking to. I said, "One of your grandchildren just kicked me in the ribs."

She came over and put both hands on my tummy. She said, "You're growing nicely Felicia. I hope I didn't shock you too much."

"Well, you did shock me. But I understand these things a lot better now. Do you care to share?"

She went back to work and I joined her. She said, "Your Dad cheated on me when you were about six. I found out and was beside myself. He swore he was innocent, but I knew it was true."

"How did you find out?"

"Your dad use to play the numbers and some guy called the house one day and told me to let him know that his number hit. So when he came home from work, I told him the good news and he said he would get his money after work the next day. I decided to surprise him and I went to get it. I didn't have a car then, so I walked the three blocks up Plymouth Avenue to the guys' house. When I told him who I was, he said, "Calvin's wife already picked up the money. She just left."

I inhaled and asked, "Mommy, what did you do?"

"I was shaking all the way home. When he got home I asked, "Did you get the money?"

He said, "Yep. I need to run a few errands, but I'll be back in about an hour and we can eat."

Before he left I asked him, "So who is she?"

He was smiling at first. He stopped smiling and asked, "What?"

"Who's the woman who picked up your money today?"

He reached for me and asked, "Barbara, what are you talking about?"

"I went to get your money and the guy told me your wife picked it up. I was gonna surprise you. I guess I was the one that got surprised."

"No Barbara, it's nothing like that. I wouldn't do that to you Baby."

He tried to kiss me and I told him to get the hell away from me. I wouldn't let him touch me for months. That's when I got the job at Rochester Products at night. I met a guy there named Daryl. He was nice and always tried to get me to go home with him at break time. I eventually learned to drive and got a car.

One night, I did go home with him and we saw each other for about six months or so. Calvin didn't like me away so much, so I quit the job and Daryl too. He was awful in bed!"

My mother was cracking up. I was leaning on the counter with my hands under my chin, shaking my head and learning a side of my mother I would never have believed existed.

After we put all the new dishes and silverware in the dishwasher, the last of the furniture was delivered. We went upstairs and Mom suggested we go ahead and make the beds. She asked me, "So why did you do it?"

"Well, it's rather embarrassing but I guess I'm a lot like Grandma. A good looking man turned my head."

She laughed and said, "I should've known. You're so much like her. And why is it that you and Harold have been fighting so much lately? Is it because of him?"

"No, that's over. It's because your girlfriend Jackie spoiled his ass, I mean, spoiled him so bad that he wants to control my life."

Mom's head went back and she cracked up. I said, "Sorry Mom. Anyhow, we fought a couple days after I told him about the twins. I asked him to go to his apartment but instead, he went to Detroit to cry on his mommy's shoulder."

Mom was leaning over laughing. She said, "Jackie had me in stiches too when she told me. I just can't see him as a spoiled brat."

We moved to the other guest room and started making the bed. She said, "I know you love him Felicia. But does he make you happy Baby?"

I smiled and said, "Yes Mom. He makes me very happy."

Annette and Carla arrived soon after Mom left, and we started in the basement. They cleaned the shower room and bathroom. They brought me a small tub of water and insisted I soak my feet. So I watched. They worked. Carla said, "You still look great Licia. Still no tummy to speak of."

"I have nine more days. But they've started kicking."

"Where are they kicking?"

"On my side or my ribs."

"That's good. They're still sideways."

She bent over and said to them, "Stay on your sides babies! Ha-ha."

When we left the basement, we fed the boys. Annette asked, "So how's Harold. Still licking his wounds?"

"He's been the perfect gentleman. We'll see how long it lasts."

While on the second floor I told them about my conversation with my mom. Carla said, "I could see my mom doing the same thing."

"I was floored when she told me that. But she did it to get back at Daddy. She said the guy wasn't even good in bed."

It had been a long day. After the girls left, I went online and did my assignment for the day. Harold was in the bedroom watching TV. He asked if I needed anything. I said, "No. I think I'll take a quick shower and crash."

When I went into the bathroom, I froze. There were candles around the tub and a bubble bath awaited me. I hated to bust his bubble, no pun intended, but I said, "Hun, I can't take baths until after the babies are born. This is so sweet Harold. So I insist you get in and enjoy it."

He got up and said, "Aw Babe, I didn't know."

"I forgot to tell you. My doctor told me at my last appointment."

So he undressed and sat back in the tub while I showered. When I got out, he was still in there with his eyes closed. I put on a nightgown and crawled into bed. Harold soon came in too. He put his arms around my tummy and kissed my neck. He inhaled and said, again, how wonderful I smelled. His hand went up to my breasts and he groaned and said, "Ummm, I just wanna eat them up."

I could feel his erection up against me. He released me and went under the covers and settled between my thighs. He said, "You don't have to move. Just stay there and enjoy it."

And I did. Both of his hands were massaging my breasts and I was in heaven. My orgasm was so intense that I held his head with both hands, begging him not to stop.

Harold crawled up and asked me if I was okay, because I was crying. I shook my head yes. I said, "I love you Honey. You make me feel so good."

"I love you more. And you make me feel even better."

I felt his erection and I said, "You're not totally happy yet, are you?"

"I know you're tired. I'll be fine."

I reached between us and began stroking him. He pulled my straps down and treated himself to my enlarged breasts. I soon stopped him and inserted him in my mouth. Then I sat up and said, "Sit on my chest."

"No Babe. I'm too heavy."

"Put your knees on either side of my head. I'll be fine. Come on."

So I put pillows against the headboard and I lay in an elevated position. He straddled my chest and held onto the headboard. I brought him closer and took him in my mouth and he loved it.

I urged him forward. I wanted all of him but he seemed hesitant. I urged him to move and finally he did. He groaned and moaned and finally was moving deeper and deeper. He became hesitant again because he knew he couldn't pull out when the time came. I had him locked in. He said, "Felicia, let go Babe."

I held on tighter and I sucked harder. He was very vocal and called my name repeatedly as he let it go. It was so intense that it appeared to overtake him. I reached up and gently pulled him toward me. He laid in my arms and finally began to relax. Now I knew what a blow job was like.

He was totally drained, but he got up and went into the bathroom. He brought me a washcloth and cleaned me up. I laughed and said, "You really think I'm a baby, don't you?"

"Are you all right Babe?"

"Yes. Are you?"

"You almost made *me* cry. What made you do that?"

"You do it all the time. I felt it was time for me to experience it. It wasn't bad, but I'm sure I just need to get used to it. Did you like it?"

"I loved it, but I hope you don't think I expect that, because I don't. But yeah Babe, it was great."

"We'll probably have more oral sex as I enlarge. We can still have intercourse, but it will become more difficult. So I think to keep you happy, I'll do more of that. Is that okay with you?"

"What I want is for you to do what comes naturally. I know I appear insatiable at times, but it's just because you're so damn sexy. Even now, as I look at that luscious chest, I want to do it all over again. So don't concern yourself with details."

Chapter Eighteen

By Friday, Harold's parents were here and Karen surprised us and came early with them. The weekend zoomed by and before we knew it, the whole clan was here.

There were people everywhere. They were touching me and listening to my stomach, and frankly it got on my nerves. By Tuesday, I'd had enough and safely escaped with Karen to Carla's house. She was working, but Earl was home and we went into their bedroom and pulled out the dresses.

I looked at both of them. One and then the other. Obviously, if dress one doesn't fit anymore, I'll have the bigger one altered. I rationalized that I was holding on to dress one for the wrong reasons. And my bump was obvious now.

I turned to Karen and said, "No need for me to try them on."

Annette tapped and came in. I said, "Don't bother to sit. I'm taking the first one back and getting the second one altered."

The salesclerk Helen was there. She immediately smiled when she saw me and asked how I was doing. I told her about the dresses and she said, "Let me get Taylor our seamstress. She's here today."

She came out and asked me to put the dress on, so I did. She also asked me to put the shoes on. They were tight. She asked me to turn around and she said, "This is such a beautiful dress. It looks like it was made just for you. I have a few suggestions."

She picked up a note pad and started sketching. She said, "This is the dress now. And this is what it'll look like altered. I'll slightly raise the waistline and relax the fabric around your tummy. It'll still be beautiful."

I liked it. I asked Karen and Annette what they thought. They both smiled and agreed it was great. I asked, "How soon could you do it?"

"If you leave it today, I'll have it ready for you tomorrow."

I asked Helen if she had the shoe in a larger size. She left us and came out with a box in her hand. She said, "This shoe is not exactly like yours, but very close. It's from our newest collection. Would you like to see it?"

"Yes, I would."

The shoe was prettier than the first one. I said, "I love them. Are they my size?"

"They're a half size larger. Try them while you have the dress on."

I put them on and they felt so much better. I looked at the girls and they said they loved them too. I asked, "Could I please buy this pair? I don't have time to order them."

She shook her head yes. I thanked her and turned to Taylor. I asked, "Will I see you tomorrow?"

"Yes. I'm here until noon tomorrow. If you could come around ten o'clock, I should be able to spend some time with you, okay?"

"I'll be here."

I turned around and Annette was gone. Karen said, "She got a call from work so she took it outside."

When we went out, the look on Annette's face told me she wasn't talking to anyone from work. She clicked the lock so we could get in the car. When she got in I asked, "Everything okay?"

"Yep. All is well."

When Annette dropped us off at Carla's to get my car, I unlocked the car and Karen got in. I went over to Annette and asked, "Who were you talking to?"

She said, "Benny wanted to get together again. I told him no."

Harold and I told the family we had to run an errand. It was Wednesday night and I had a test. Harold dropped me off at school and picked me up ninety minutes later. He asked, "So, how did you do?"

"I think I did well. Where did you go?"

He smiled and said, "I'm not telling you."

"Why?"

"Because it's a surprise. Not the kind that will piss you off though."

I looked at him and said, "Harold, I can't take any more surprises."

"It has to do with your wedding gift. Are you gonna make me tell you what it is?"

"I thought the house was my wedding gift."

"That's from my parents. Not me."

I looked out of the window and realized I had not gotten him a gift. What the hell was I thinking? I spent the rest of the night trying to come up with something.

The next morning I was still biting my nails, trying to figure out what to get him. The only thing I could think of was baseball. And the only person I could think to help me was Todd. What irony. I called him when Harold and Dad went to the store early that morning. He was working, but he answered. I said, "Hi."

"Hi, what's up?"

"I need a huge favor."

He laughed and said, "What else is new Licia?"

"Is there somewhere in Rochester to get authentic Yankee's stuff?"

"There's a place on Portland near Ridge Rd. It's a small shop that carries authentic sports memorabilia. But I can't guarantee they'll have any Yankee's stuff."

"Okay. Anywhere else?"

He laughed again and said, "I know a guy who has Derek Jeter's rookie card. It's autographed and worth about five hundred dollars. But he said the only way he'd sell it was if someone gave him a thousand for it."

"Ask him if he'll take seven fifty? If not, offer him a thousand."

"Damn Licia. It's like that! I shoulda been better to you, huh?"

"You should've been better anyhow!"

We both laughed and he said, "Okay, I'll call him."

"Todd, I need to know this morning, if possible. It's really important."

"You getting it for Harold?"

"Yes. The gift I got him won't get here until after the wedding, so I'm in a serious jam. Please let me know as soon as possible, okay?"

"Okay, I'll call you right back."

It was only seven forty-five and I really wanted to lay back down, but I didn't dare. So I got up and ran into the bathroom and turned on the shower. I was just about to jump in when my phone rang. I ran back and got it and it was Todd. I said, "Hello."

"Damn Licia, what the hell you doing?"

I laughed and said, "I'm pregnant Todd. So if I run, I'm all out of breath."

"Timmy said if you're serious, he'll gladly take seven fifty. You want it today?"

"Yes. It *is* authentic, right?"

"Yes. He has a certificate and everything. We took it to that shop on Portland, and the guy tried to buy it from him. It's the real deal."

I walked into the bathroom and turned off the shower. I asked, "How do I get you the money?"

"I have a break at noon. I'll meet you there and we can make the exchange. You free at noon?"

"Yes, thanks Todd. Can you text me the address?"

He said yes and we hung up. I hate telling lies, but I didn't want Todd thinking I was so stupid to forget something like that. But I guess I am.

After I dressed and went downstairs, Mom was in the kitchen as usual. I said, "Good Morning!"

"Good Morning Felicia, how are you feeling Baby?"

"Great Mom. How are you?"

"I'm wonderful. What would you like to eat this morning?"

"Just some fruit and spa water. And some juice please. Thank you."

The door leading to the garage opened and the men were back from the store. They both had bags of food. Dad loves Wegmans. Harold came over to me and kissed me and rubbed my tummy. He said, "Good morning Babe. You're glowing today."

"That's because I slept with you last night."

He kissed me again, but longer and sweeter. His Mom said, "Harold, not at the table. The food will spoil."

I hollered laughing. Mom asked, "You've never heard that before?"

"No, I haven't."

I laughed again. Harold and Dad went back to the garage to retrieve the rest of the groceries. Mom said, "Things seem a lot better. Are they?"

I smiled and said, "Yes, Ma'am. Much better. We're very happy."

She smiled and continued slicing fruit for me. She asked, "So what do you have to do today?"

"I have a final fitting in about an hour, and at noon I have to pick up Harold's gift."

I thought of something and excused myself. I went upstairs and called the boutique. I said, "Good morning Taylor. This is Felicia Wilson."

"Good Morning Felicia. Your dress is ready for you."

"That's great. Is it okay if I come out sooner than ten?"

"Sure. I'll be here. And bring your shoes."

I said okay, thanked her and hung up. I went back downstairs and asked Mom, "How would you like to come with me for my final fitting? This kitchen's not going anywhere, and I'll bring you right back."

"You know what. I'd love to go. And why don't we call Barbara and ask her to come with us?"

"That's a great idea."

I called Mom and she was getting dressed. I asked, "What are you up to this morning?"

"Nothing until later."

"I'm picking you up in about twenty minutes and you and Mom Benson are going with me for my final fitting. Okay?"

"I'd love to. I'll be ready when you get here."

It was funny watching the moms help me put my dress on. They were so worried I might fall, that they made it much more difficult. Taylor laughed. She came over and easily pulled it up and zipped it. I held onto the moms' shoulders as I put my shoes on. My mother said, "Those heels are a bit high, aren't they Felicia?"

"They're fine Mom. I'll be on Daddy's arm going down the aisle and Harold's the rest of the day and night. Besides, if they begin to bother me, Stephanie got me a beautiful pair of slides to put on."

I turned to look at the dress, and there was a collective sigh. I turned back to look at the moms and they were beaming. My mother said, "Felicia, it's beautiful."

Mom Benson said, "You're lovely. That dress was made for you."

Taylor came back with my headpiece and said, "I told her the same thing. Now hold your head down so I can see if I need to make any adjustments."

Once it was on, she said, "Take a look."

I turned toward the mirror and immediately looked at my tummy. And wow, did she nail it. I looked again at my midsection and I turned sideways. The bump was so subtle, it was barely noticeable.

I looked lower and the change was sexier. By raising the waist, the opening at the bottom showed more leg. I smiled and stood up straight and loved it. I turned to my moms and asked, "How do I look?"

They both said, "Stunning."

When we were back at the house, Mom was raving about the *errand* we had to run. It was still early, so I went upstairs and Harold was lying across the bed. He sat up and asked, "Where did you and Mom go?"

"I had my final fitting and she and my mother went with me. She's making a big deal of it right now, except she's not telling anyone where we went."

"She really loves you. She was ready to whip my ass over you!"

We both laughed and he said, "I love you so much. I can still remember seeing you in the hall at work and seeing your head go back as you laughed. You were so enchanting."

A chill went up my back. I couldn't believe he used that word.

I went into the bathroom and looked in the mirror. *Enchanting.* I came out and he was sitting on the edge of the bed. He said, "Come here Babe. You okay?"

I went and sat on his lap. I said, "I'm excited Harold. But I'm also conscious about not over doing it. Yet, at the same time I don't want to miss anything. I want every moment etched in my memory."

He smiled and held me tight. He asked, "So does your dress still fit?"

"Yes, with some altering."

"Good. What can I do for you today? I'm at your disposal until tomorrow evening when the real festivities begin."

"Nothing that I can think of. Why did you and Dad go to the store so early?"

"He had to be sure that big ass order was right. He is also having the cooks do the rehearsal dinner."

"I made Dad promise me he wouldn't do so much."

"No, he promised not to cook."

I laughed and said, "That's splitting hairs."

He smiled at me. I looked at the clock and it was almost eleven o'clock. I said, "I have to leave shortly to pick something up. When I get back, let's hide away in here and make love."

"I'd love to Mrs. Benson."

My transaction went very smooth. I really owed Todd. He's really a sweetheart, and truthfully will still do anything for me. I hid my dress in Mom Benson's closet and now I have to find somewhere to hide this card. I went to the mall and had it gift wrapped. I decided to put it with my dress and accessories. I also realized I had to pack for our getaway.

When I finally got home, the boys were there. I've been a terrible mother. Thank God Harold is a great dad. The entire Benson clan was in the kitchen. I asked Mom if I could see her for a minute.

She and I went into her room and I went into my purse and handed her the gift. I asked, "Would you please put this with my dress. It's Harold's wedding gift. We're exchanging our gifts privately."

"Of course Dear. Can I ask what it is?"

"It's Derek Jeter's rookie card."

"No. Are you serious?"

"Yes, do you think he'll like it?"

"He'll love it!"

"I want to show my sisters the dress. They're the ones who chose it."

"I'll get them."

Soon they were all in Mom's room. I said, "I want to really thank you all for helping me find my dress. I know Karen knows, but I chose the one you all voted on."

Tara said, "Oh wow. Can we see it?"

"Absolutely! But first I want to say this has been quite a journey for me, because that night I spent with you continues to stay in my heart. I remember so much about that night, especially Karen telling me not to get pregnant if I chose that dress."

They all laughed. I said, "Against all odds, I got into it this morning. It was very special having both of my mothers there to help me. And pardon my French Mom, but Carla said as long as you carry those babies in that big ass, you'll be fine!"

Everyone laughed again, even Mom.

Karen said, "That's what has Brother crazy as hell!"

I popped her on the arm and we all laughed again. I said, "The dress was altered this week, to custom fit it to my new body, but the changes are subtle. And thanks to Danielle, I got it way too big."

I unzipped the cover and removed it. Everyone loved it. Mom said, "Wait until you see her in it. She's breathtaking."

I also showed them the shoes and the headpiece. I said, "I want to thank you all again for that night. Who knows what I'd be wearing if not for you all. I love you my sisters."

They all hugged me and told me they loved me too. I realized how blessed I was that I would soon be a Benson too.

I went upstairs and Harold was in the same spot. I said, "If I hadn't seen you downstairs a minute ago, I would think you never moved."

"I'm being obedient. Come over here."

I went over to him and I sat on the side of the bed and kissed him. I said, "We can't do this. They're waiting for us."

"I know."

He got up and went toward the bathroom. I said, "Wait for me."

He looked at me and asked, "Wait for you?"

Are you going to….relieve yourself?"

"I was going to my closet…."

A smirk crossed his face and he asked, "Why, would you like me to?"

"I'd like to watch."

"And so you shall. Tonight. Okay?"

"I look forward to it."

Then he said, "I'll have another surprise for you."

He kissed me and his hardness made me want to stay at least fifteen more minutes.

We returned to our guests and Dad was in the kitchen. He was cooking those scrumptious crab cakes and he had two of his daughters next to him as he was cooking them in three pans. The man was awesome and his skills were something to behold.

Tammy asked, "Harold, what took you and Felicia so long? We thought you all had fallen asleep. Or something like that."

Dad cracked up and Tara asked, "Can't you two keep your hands off of each other?"

Harold said, "I told her to leave me alone, but she just can't resist me. So I had to…."

I said, "Hun, let's not tell tales. We were only talking."

Everyone laughed and said we must think they're stupid.

That evening, Harold and I were finally entering our bedroom about twelve thirty. We were both exhausted. Many of our friends came over, because no one was working tomorrow.

His family took all the kids to a Rochester Red Wings baseball game, our triple A team affiliated with the Minnesota Twins. When I crawled into bed, Harold said, "Don't go to sleep. I have something for you."

I looked up from under the covers and asked, "What?"

"You wanted to experience something, remember?"

"Oh yeah. I forgot. But, let's do it another time. I'm so tired and sleepy, I won't enjoy it. Okay?"

"We don't have another time. You must experience it before we're married."

I sat up and said, "Okay Mr. Benson, show me something."

"You won't just be an observer, you'll be a participant."

"Then it wouldn't be masturbation, would it?"

"You're not going to touch me, you will be touching yourself."

"No Harold. I just want to watch you, okay?"

"Okay. But promise me if you get turned on, you will. And if not, we'll do it together another time, okay?"

"I promise."

He asked me to remove my straps so he could see my breasts. I did as he asked and he sat in the middle of the bed, in front of me. He was naked and began to stroke himself. As if it was automatic, I put my hands under my breasts and began to lift them and play with my nipples.

He smiled and continued to watch me. He asked me to move the covers and open my legs. Again, I did as he asked and he also asked me to raise my knees. I raised them and he groaned.

He continued to look at me and he continued to stroke himself. He grew right before my eyes and I could feel myself getting wet. I watched him and again, as if it was automatic, I put my hand between my legs. I was so wet, I couldn't believe it.

Harold was really enjoying himself now, and never took his eyes off of me. I raised my left breast and inserted my nipple in my mouth.

He finally closed his eyes and groaned again. He increased his tempo, and kept his eyes closed. He suddenly stopped. Then I stopped. I asked, "Why did you stop?"

He said softly, "I want to be inside of you. My desire for you is preventing me from finishing."

I smiled and said, "Then come and get it Sweetie."

I opened my legs a little more. He groaned again and crawled over to me. Without any fanfare, he inserted himself and gently proceeded in and out of me. I asked, "What are you doing?"

"I'm afraid I'll hurt you or the babies."

"Harold, make love to me Sweetheart. You're not going to hurt me or the babies. Just keep your weight off of my tummy, okay?"

"Are you sure?"

"Yes. Lift my legs a little and you'll be fine."

He was still hesitant, but decided to put his head between my legs. He and I were both enjoying it. He finally turned me over and entered me from behind. Soon we were both at that place that has been ours since I kissed him on my doorstep.

Everyone was wasted. The bachelorette party was fabulous, at least what was left of it. The Benson sisters bought out the club, so it was just us.

We had food and an open bar. Top shelf only. I had pretend drinks. I got a lap dance from each of the three strippers, and Karen left with one of them.

He was really taken with her and they hit it off great. The other two strippers were busy getting tips and working *very* hard for them.

I couldn't believe how many of my old friends were there. And Lenora and Trina were there too. Finally Karen came back and we made our way to the limo. She had the entire limousine smelling like pot.

The rehearsal and dinner were great too. Dad asked Stephanie to locate a venue with a countryside setting that would allow his chefs in. Stephanie told me Dad was so easy to work with.

Until she told him, "Everything is all set Sir except I'm negotiating the costs, and I'm waiting...."

He said, "Young lady. I don't have time or patience for that. Accept their numbers and fax me the contract!"

I cracked up. She said, "It was like being scolded by my dad."

Annette and Carla stayed with me that night. The men were at the hotel.

Annette and Carla and me. All for one and one for all. Although we'd been down this road before, it was different this time. Once the house had finally quieted and the three of us were in my king sized bed, it was about three thirty in the morning and Carla asked, "So Licia, how do you feel?"

"On top of the world. I have mixed feelings about getting pregnant so soon now. I'm having a fairy tale wedding and I can't fully enjoy it. But on the other hand, I know I'll be glad I got it over with."

Annette said, "The good thing is you're not *so* pregnant that you can't still have fun. And speaking of having fun is Harold starting to reach your level of satisfaction?"

Carla asked, "Where the hell did that come from?"

I laughed and said, "Our sex life is great. We continue to do new things and I'm no longer shy about talking about it. Of course, we had to put the brakes on some things, but we're more creative now. It's been fun."

"And Bob?"

"You were right. After I shared with him I had it and liked it, we use it a lot. He loves it."

Annette chuckled and said, "I bet he almost fell out when he saw how huge it is!"

We all laughed and I said, "I concluded that although Sam was large, he was limited with that damn thing. And now that I've had that size, I'll always like it. But Sam the man, I can do without."

Annette said, "The size only matters when it's too small for that particular woman. Some women have only had small men and it suits them just fine. It's like the levels again. Once you've had a certain size, smaller might be a challenge."

Carla said, "Things are great in my house too. Earl is thrilled that he gets head at home now. I did what you said and it worked for us. Now he's home all the damn time!"

We all laughed and Annette said, "Tony and I have settled into a more relaxed and loving existence. We're also being more creative. Although he never admitted to cheating, neither have I. But we both admit that our love for each other and especially our son is worth the bumps that sometimes come during this journey."

I said, "And thank God Sam is gone and out of our lives."

Annette said, "Yeah, he's a lucky bastard. He was about eight seconds from me shooting his ass!"

Carla and I laughed and eventually, we all went to sleep.

At eight thirty the next morning, the stretch limo picked all twelve of us up and took us to the spa. That includes both mothers, five sisters, the granddaughters, and the three of us. We each received a massage, manicure and pedicure.

From there, we all went to the salon and got our hair done. Neither the spa nor salon was open for business until we left. I told Stephanie to pay whatever it cost.

I also surprised the men with massages and manicures. Stephanie informed them at the rehearsal dinner that the limo would pick them up at noon. There was light food and soft drinks at each stop, as well as wine and champagne. The photographer was also at each stop.

Once we were back at my house, we relaxed for a while. There would be two limos to take us to the church at four o'clock. Everything went according to plan.

While we were dressing before the wedding, I began handing out the garters to everyone. My mother presented me with a tiny pearl from her mom's pearl necklace. It hung on the thinnest gold chain and appeared to be suspended in air on my chest.

My pearl necklace is *old*.

My dress is *new*.

Harold's grandmother's bracelet is *borrowed*.

My garter is *blue*.

And tucked securely within my large bouquet is the tiny dress my daddy gave me. I just had to have it with me today.

While standing there, on my daddy's arm, I jokingly said, "Daddy, I don't plan to ever ask you to do this again."

He and I both laughed and he said, "Daughter, you were so young then. You've grown so much. I'm so proud of the woman you've become."

"Thanks Daddy. I love you too."

Todd and Mya were first. Then Marcus and Cheyenne. Perfect. Then Tammy and Steve. And Karen and Craig. Perfect. Annette and Carla turned to look at me. The love in their eyes said it all.

My sisters each stepped back and each kissed my cheek. Together, they stepped inside of the sanctuary. Cliff and Barry walked over to them and escorted my sisters down the aisle. Together. Both so beautiful, looking more like sisters instead of cousins.

Then the music changed. And little Harold kicked me. And his sister kicked him. Her name is Alysiya. And I took that as a sign they were ready to officially become Bensons. So Daddy and I began our journey, and I became the next Mrs. Benson.

Harold and I were whispering at the table and the glasses began to clink again. He and I kissed for the crowd again and Marcus came over and said, "Mommy, why do you keep kissing each other. That's nasty Mommy, and people can see you."

The entire wedding party laughed. He ran away to find Cheyenne. Harold said, "Lord have mercy, Felicia! That dress has every man in this room jealous of me! My college buddies almost lost their lunch Babe! Wow!"

I just smiled and asked for the tenth time, "You can't see the bump?"

"There's not a man in this room that sees a bump, except for that masterpiece in back."

When we went to cut the cake, Harold twirled me around. He was so proud of me. He said, "I wouldn't take ten billion dollars for her."

Everyone clapped and the men whistled. I said, "Harold, stop that!"

"You can't make me stop now!"

Everyone laughed and the party went late into the night. The food was exquisite and everyone wanted to know who catered it. When we gave our thanks, Harold announced that Benson's South of Detroit prepared the wonderful food.

He proudly introduced his dad as the proprietor and that he flew his chefs in for our special day. He said, "So for those interested, you will have to go to Detroit to enjoy this cuisine."

Finally we presented Stephanie with a beautiful tennis bracelet for her work above and beyond the call of duty.

The next morning, Harold and I said our goodbyes and we left the family in our home. They're leaving Tuesday morning. I told Harold that I thought we should at least stay until noon, but he wanted to start our honeymoon right away.

He even told our families that until we consummated our union, I wasn't Mrs. Benson yet. I couldn't believe he said that in front of my father. But my dad laughed right along with everyone else.

Barry said, "I'm surprised you didn't take care of that last night."

"Man, she was asleep before her head hit the pillow."

I said, "Barry, don't believe that. You know that has never stopped a man from getting what he wants. He was the one asleep!"

We all laughed again and as we were leaving, I saw Karen out of the corner of my eye. She saw me too. I had to say one more thing to her. I stood in front of her and caressed her face. My eyes were already welling up. I whispered in her ear, "I love you Sis."

She embraced me and started to cry too. I said quietly, "Miss Favorite, you were there for me every time I needed you. Thank you and remember. I'm always here for you. Always."

She whispered, "I love you too. So much Felicia. You're the only one who seems to accept me completely. Thank you too."

I looked into her eyes and kissed her on the side her face. I said, "I'm older than you by seven months, so you listen to me. Come back and spend a week with me. Just you and me, okay?"

"If you find a man for me to hang out with in this town of yours, you got a deal!"

I laughed and looked up and everyone was watching our exchange. Harold said, "Felicia, I can't wait much longer!"

We all laughed and soon we were on our way.

By seven o'clock that evening, we were both stuffed and being lazy. Lauren brought our dinner to us personally, and she promised us a weekend of special treats. We made love all day and now neither of us wanted to move. Harold asked, "Shall we exchange our gifts now?"

I sat up and said, "Yes let's do that. You go first."

He grabbed his briefcase and handed me an envelope. I looked at him and he said, "Open it Babe."

I opened it and it read:

> To my Bride and Joy, Felicia:
> This is to inform you that you and I are now the owners of the property at 7007 Carlton Dr., Detroit, MI. It will be our home away from home when we are in Detroit. Inside the sleeve of this card is a picture of the house. I pray our love endures until the end of time.
>
> Harold

I looked up and yelped. I said, "This is fabulous! We'll have our own place. Thank you Honey!"

I took out the picture and it was very nice. I reached over and kissed him and he said, "It's about three miles from Mom and Dad, but we'll have our privacy."

"My gift to you is nothing like this, but I think you'll like it."

I got it out of my suitcase and handed it to him. He looked at it and said, "I can't imagine what it is."

He tore the wrapping off and opened the box. He picked up the card and looked at it. He looked at the back and said, "There's no way this is real. Is it Felicia?"

I shook my head yes and his eyes got big. He said, "No way am I holding an authentic Jeter rookie card! Where did you find it?"

"I don't ask you those questions, do I?"

He got up and continued looking at it like it was a rare gem or something. He said, "I have to get it laminated, or whatever they do to cards to preserve them."

He turned to me and said, "Babe, you hit a home run! I love it! Thank you so much!"

The next day, he and I went for a walk along the lake. We held hands and talked about our future. We both agreed to name the twins Harold Calvin Benson and Alysiya Jacqueline Benson.

That night Harold was going through old mail forwarded from his old address. I was online looking at design ideas for the nursery. I could finally concentrate on my babies now. And eat what the hell I wanted to.

I asked Harold if he thought this particular layout would work for the nursery. He didn't answer me. I looked at him and he was looking at a piece of paper in his hand. I asked, "Harold, did you hear me?"

He got up and walked out of the door.

I picked up the paper and my blood stopped. I got up and ran after him. He was in the front of the inn, just standing there. I said, "Harold, you do realize this is a lie, don't you?"

He just stood there silently. I screamed, *"It's a lie Harold!"*

I finally convinced him to return to our room. He seemed to be in shock because he still had not uttered a word. I picked the paper up again and said, "We need to call the police and see if there are prints on this."

He still wouldn't say anything. I read it again. It read:

Harold:
If I were you, I'd get a paternity test done as soon as possible.

I was beside myself. I couldn't imagine who could be so cruel. I walked in front of Harold and said, "Look at me. Do you honestly believe that I would, *could* do that to you?"

He got up and poured a drink. He turned and said, "No."

I exhaled and went to him. I put my arms around him, but he wasn't responding to me. I said, "Harold, please. Say something!"

"I didn't think you'd do it again."

This time the blood *froze* in my veins. I stepped away from him and asked, "What the hell does *that* mean?"

"I knew about you and Sam, Felicia."

My entire muscular system shut down.

"I knew the day I *interrupted* the two of you that something was going on. I knew he lied about coming to bring you wine. I don't think either of you thought to look on the coffee table where two plates and two wine glasses were still waiting to be taken away. Not to mention the length of time it took you to open the door. Sam's friend Robert double crossed Sam. He became loyal to me because he's a junkie and needed the money."

He walked over to me. I had tears forming in my eyes. He raised my face to his and asked, "Are those babies mine?"

I couldn't look at him. I was now the silent one. He walked over to the mantle and said, "Listen. Sex is all you had with him. I know that. But I feared losing your heart to him."

He walked back over to me and embraced me. He brought my face to his and kissed my lips. He said very quietly, "Are they mine, Felicia?"

I was sick. I ran to the bathroom and threw up. When it passed, I walked out and said, "I admit that Sam and I had a brief fling."

"*Are. They. Mine?*"

"Yes Harold, of course they are. What kind of person do you think I am? Yes, I was curious. But it was just sex. The irony here is that you're the one who opened my legs and woke up my G-spot. I'm not blaming you for my behavior, but it is ironic. And yes, I wanted to experience it. I did and it's over. I was glad as hell to see him leave!"

I went into the bedroom and started packing my things. I couldn't bear the thought of a lifetime of guilt. He came behind me and stopped me. He asked, "If I was willing to accept it, why can't you?"

I just looked at him. He said, "I love you Felicia. I gave you more of me than I even knew I had. Don't you still love me?"

I continued to look at him and the babies started playing kickball. I sat down and rubbed my tummy. He got on his knees and reached for his children. He felt their movement and I turned my head as my heartache began to overwhelm me. He said, "I plan to spend the rest of my days with you. Don't you love me Felicia?"

No answer. He asked, "Do you want *him*?"

"I *never* wanted him. It was just sex. I told you that."

"But not for him. A little birdie told me he proposed to you."

I paused and felt nauseous again. I said, "I wasn't in love with him Harold."

I stood up. He stood too and said, "Maybe not."

He caressed my face and kissed me. I kissed him back and he put his arm around my waist and brought me close to him. His kiss became more passionate, and he brought me even closer, wanting me to feel his hardness. Then he said, "But I couldn't afford to risk it."

He lovingly played in my hair and kissed my neck. Then he moved to my ear and whispered, *"That's why I bought his fucking house!"*